*In Praise of Harmony*

FLOYD K. GRAVE AND MARGARET G. GRAVE

# In Praise of Harmony

## The Teachings of
## Abbé Georg Joseph Vogler

University of Nebraska Press: Lincoln and London

The paper in this book meets the minimum require-
ments of American National Standard for Information
Sciences – Permanence of Paper for Printed Library
Materials, ANSI Z39.48-1984.

Library of Congress Cataloging-in-Publication Data
Grave, Floyd K. (Floyd Kersey), 1945–
In praise of harmony.
Bibliography: p.
Includes index.
1. Vogler, Georg Joseph, 1749–1814.   I. Grave,
Margaret G., 1943–   .   II. Title.
ML410.V88G7   1988   780'.92'4   87-5926
ISBN 0-8032-2128-2 (alkaline paper)

# CONTENTS

Acknowledgments, vii

Introduction, 1

CHAPTER 1
The Science of Harmony:
Foundations for
an Enlightened System, 13

CHAPTER 2
Harmonic Analysis and
the Principle of Reduction, 50

CHAPTER 3
Progress and Restoration:
The Lessons of
Enlightened Criticism, 85

CHAPTER 4
Theory and Practice in
Music for the Church, 124

CHAPTER 5
Music and Drama, 178

CHAPTER 6
The Performer
and His Medium, 227

Epilogue, 267

Notes, 277

Bibliography, 311

Index, 331

❦

# Acknowledgments

T HE authors gratefully acknowledge the support of research grants from
the Rutgers University Research Council, the American Philosophical
Society (Grant No. 8379, Penrose Fund), the German Academic Exchange
Service (DAAD), and the University of Virginia.

Space does not permit proper acknowledgment of the invaluable assis-
tance rendered by librarians and archivists both in this country and abroad.
We nevertheless wish to express a debt of thanks to the following individuals
whose help proved vital to the accomplishment of our study: Dr. Robert
Münster and Dr. Liselotte Renner of the Bayerische Staatsbibliothek, Munich; Dr. Oswald Bill, Frau Pilz, and Fräulein Bröning, of the Hessische
Landes- und Hochschulbibliothek, Darmstadt; Ms. Anna Lena Holm and
Mr. Henrik K. Jörgensen of the Musikaliska Akademiens Bibliotek, Stockholm; and Dr. Schwarzmaier of the Generallandesarchiv, Karlsruhe. We are
likewise grateful for the courteous help extended by the staffs of the Bayerisches Hauptstaatsarchiv, Munich; the Hessisches Staatsarchiv, Darmstadt;
and the Österreichische Nationalbibliothek and Gesellschaft der Musikfreunde, Vienna.

Of the many archivists who responded to our letters of inquiry and
requests for information, the following are especially deserving of mention:
Dr. Rudolf Elvers and Hans Joachim Mey, Staatsbibliothek Preussischer
Kulturbesitz, Berlin-Dahlem; Dr. Marianne Rumpf, Universitätsbibliothek
der Freien Universität, Berlin-Dahlem; Ilse Otto, Universitäts-Bibliothek
der Humboldt-Universität, Berlin; Dr. Karl-Heinz Köhler, Deutsche Staats-

bibliothek, Berlin; Dr. Fischer, Universitätsbibliothek, Bonn; Dr. Heydrich, Hochschulbibliothekszentrum des Landes Nordrhein-Westfalen, Cologne; Christa Wolf, Hessisches Staatsarchiv, Darmstadt; Dr. Andernacht, Der Magistrat Stadtarchiv, Frankfurt am Main; Gisela Sledge, Stadt- und Universitätsbibliothek, Frankfurt am Main; Christel Benner, Universität Hamburg, Theatersammlung; Dr. Bernhard Stockmann, Staats- und Universitätsbibliothek, Hamburg; Dr. H. Mürmel, Karl-Marx Universität, Universitätsbibliothek, Leipzig; Dr. Hemmerle, Herr Liess, and Dr. Höppl, Bayerisches Hauptstaatsarchiv, Munich; Dr. Gertraut Haberkamp, RISM, Bayerische Staatsbibliothek, Munich; Dr. Hermann Köstler and Dr. Vogt, Bayerische Staatsbibliothek, Munich; Dr. Manfred Müller, Württembergische Landesbibliothek, Stuttgart; Erik Soder, Bischöfliches Ordinariat, Diözesan-Archiv, Würzburg; Dr. A. Tausendpfund, Staatsarchiv, Würzburg; G. Lehmann, Universitätsbibliothek, Würzburg; Eva-Brit Fanger, Det kongelige Bibliotek, Copenhagen; J. van Meurs, Universiteits-Bibliotheek, Amsterdam; Dr. H. ten Boom, Gemeentearchief, Rotterdam; and Sara Timby, Stanford University, Memorial Library of Music. Also meriting recognition in this regard are the staffs of the Hessische Landesbibliothek, Fulda; Universitätsbibliothek, Heidelberg; Bibliothèque nationale, Paris; Library of Congress, Washington, D.C.; and Yale University Music Library, New Haven.

Finally, it is a pleasure to record our indebtedness to special friends and colleagues: first, to Jan LaRue, Professor of Music, New York University, who bestowed generous quantities of moral support and pertinent counsel in scholarly and practical matters; to Elaine Brody, Professor of Music, New York University, who took a personal and lively interest in our work from the start, and who offered timely words of encouragement and advice at every stage along the way; to Roger Tarman of the Blanche and Irving Laurie Music Library, Rutgers University, whose patient attention to many bibliographical details helped ease the task of bringing our work to completion; and finally to Jean Bonin of Madison, Wisconsin, formerly Music Librarian at the University of Virginia. Endowed with limitless resources of energy, optimism, and good cheer, Jean shared in the inception of this project and gave unstintingly of her time and bibliographical expertise to assist our work in many ways and to help guide its direction.

❦

# Introduction

" **I**F only I could succeed in drawing a clear portrait of this rare psychological phenomenon in the arts, something worthy of the man himself and a lesson to students of music!"[1] Honoring the memory of his late mentor, these words of Carl Maria von Weber expressed a wish destined not to be fulfilled. For though Weber did manage to record impressions of Vogler in a published essay and a brief anecdote,[2] the effort did little to dispel the cloud of obscurity that had already begun to descend on the abbé and his accomplishments.

To this day Vogler stalks the annals of music history as an elusive yet fascinating figure. The guises in which he appears include the pious metaphysician of Browning's poem, the eccentric theorist of the Mannheim school, Mozart's villainous rival (despised by the younger musician no less for his courtly intrigues than for his outrageous pretensions as a performer), and the romantically inspired teacher of Weber and Meyerbeer. Among recent historians, Donald J. Grout calls him "one of the most bizarre characters in the history of music,"[3] and Paul Henry Lang declares that he possessed "one of the most original minds of the [eighteenth] century."[4]

The scattered sources on which much of our knowledge of the man depends—including his own writings, the testimony of contemporaries, and early biographical accounts—yield a vivid though fragmentary portrait whose complexity mirrors that of the age in which he lived.[5] Blessed with prodigious energy and an iron will, he strove for prominence as a composer, virtuoso performer, teacher, theorist, critic, scholar, scientific experimenter,

and innovative designer of church organs. In the process, he not only famil-
iarized himself with a broad range of current practices, but succeeded in
exploring new territories of theory and musical expression as well. An
inveterate traveler, he roamed as far as Russia, the British Isles, and North
Africa; plans were supposedly made for a journey to Peking, but they never
materialized.[6] As an advocate of artistic progress and improved educational
practices, he lectured widely, and his efforts as an authority on organ design
involved major projects for churches in northern and central Europe. He held
official posts at Mannheim, Munich, Stockholm, and Darmstadt, and in the
course of his career came into contact with such important figures as Hasse,
Padre Martini, Mozart, and Beethoven.

In the field of music theory and criticism, Vogler portrayed himself as a
champion of progress. His didactic pamphlets, handbooks, and treatises
attempted to spread knowledge of musical science in terms understandable to
the layman as well as the aspiring professional, and in so doing they addressed
issues of major importance in his day, including questions of fundamental-
bass theory, sacred music, fugue, music aesthetics, and the methodology of
analysis. The analytical technique of using Roman numerals to designate
scale degrees and their chord roots (an invention customarily ascribed to
Gottfried Weber) is traceable in Vogler's writings as early as 1776;[7] and his
published critiques, including several exploring the potentials of the Roman
numeral system, dealt with matters of melodic, rhythmic, and tonal organization in a vividly metaphorical detail which was virtually unique for its time.

As a composer, Vogler contributed large quantities of sacred vocal music
that embraced both Catholic and Protestant traditions. He wrote operas and
other stage music for theaters at Mannheim, Paris, Munich, Stockholm,
Vienna, and Darmstadt, and composed smaller quantities of symphonies,
concertos, and instrumental chamber music, as well as various secular works
for chorus and orchestra. Reflecting a diversity of regional and international
styles, these compositions vary in the nature and quality of their inspiration.
To be sure, Vogler's efforts included experiments that misfired, and there are
examples of conventional *Gebrauchsmusik* unlikely ever to enjoy long-term
popular success. But there is also much that is genuinely fresh, novel, and
ingenious (including, for example, an experiment in *Sprechstimme* in the
opera *Samori*),[8] and some of his works earned enduring public favor. Enthusiasm for his music to Skjöldebrand's *Hermann von Unna* was so great in
Copenhagen that prior to one performance several lives were reportedly lost

in a stampede for tickets.[9] Various works appeared on concert programs well into the nineteenth century (Vogler's music was praised by Robert Schumann as late as 1838),[10] and there are references to a custom at the court theater in Munich of incorporating a chorus of Furies from his *Castore e Polluce* into the damnation scene of Mozart's *Don Giovanni*.[11]

More spectacular, but also more ephemeral, were the abbé's exploits as a virtuoso keyboard performer. In this field, he abandoned traditional approaches in favor of a theatrical, experimental style that mimicked thunderstorms and imitated the textural and sonorous diversity of the modern orchestra. Cultivating the image of a flamboyant showman, he was condemned by detractors as a charlatan. Contemporary reviews nevertheless attest to his fame as a brilliant technician and improvisor of tone paintings on the organ.

Vogler's indomitable spirit, ambition, and devotion to his art are evident from the earliest phases of his career. The son of a musician and instrument-maker at the court of Würzburg, he is reported to have shown outstanding musical talent as a child. Pursuing musical interests actively during his years as a university student (he studied common and canon law at Würzburg and Bamberg), he played organ, composed sacred works including Masses and settings of the *Miserere,* and wrote a ballet piece, the *Schuster Ballet,* for a student performance at Würzburg. He was evidently endowed with a measure of political acumen as well: having obtained an introduction to the Elector Palatine Carl Theodor as early as 1767, he succeeded in obtaining the post of almoner to the Elector's court at Mannheim in 1770.[12]

The move to Mannheim marked the start of a decade of rapid progress in the young musician's development, rich in experiences that set the stage for major accomplishments in later years. He soon became active in teaching and composing as well as performing, and during his first year at Mannheim he composed a major theatrical piece, the *Singspiel Der Kaufmann von Smyrna,* for performance at the Electoral court.

Eager for opportunities to expand his musical knowledge, Vogler obtained his patron's sponsorship for a journey to Italy in 1773. Beginning in the spring of that year and lasting until autumn 1775, the Italian sojourn featured those decisive encounters which he emphasized in later autobiographical accounts: a meeting in Venice with the master of Italian opera Johann Adolph Hasse, a brief term of study with the Bolognese theorist and teacher Padre Martini, and a more extended period under the tutelage of Francesco Antonio

Vallotti of Padua. He also studied theology in Padua and received various honors while in Rome: Pope Pius VI named him a Knight of the Golden Spur, papal protonotary, and chamberlain, and the Arcadian Society granted him membership.

Inspired by his experiences in Italy, especially the months of study with Vallotti, Vogler embarked on a campaign of musical enlightenment upon returning to Mannheim, where he now held the titles of ecclesiastical councillor and second kapellmeister.[13] By 1776 he gained the Elector's support to establish a public music school, the *Mannheimer Tonschule,* and in that same year published two pedagogical works: *Tonwissenschaft und Tonsezkunst,*[14] concerned with the theory of harmony; and *Stimmbildungskunst,* a manual on training the voice. In the autumn of 1777, he confronted his younger rival, W. A. Mozart, who had come to Mannheim in search of employment, and whose professional frustrations (vividly recounted in a series of letters to his father) contrasted so sharply with Vogler's early success.[15]

Upon the removal of Carl Theodor's court to Munich in 1778, Vogler remained temporarily at Mannheim, working with his music school and undertaking further publications. These included the *Kuhrpfälzische Tonschule,* a two-volume compilation of didactic materials that included a reprinting of *Tonwissenschaft und Tonsezkunst,* and the *Betrachtungen der Mannheimer Tonschule* (1778–81), a serial whose essays, lectures, analyses, and students' compositions attested to the vitality and inventiveness of Vogler's pedagogical experiment.[16]

Incurably restless, he departed from Mannheim by the end of 1780 to take up residence in Paris and travel to London. These ventures yielded mixed results: initial controversy over his theoretical system, followed by grudging approbation from the Academy of Sciences in Paris and enthusiastic endorsement by Sir Joseph Banks and the Royal Society in London; performances and publication of instrumental compositions; and his persistent, though unsuccessful attempt to win acclaim with such theatrical works as the lost pastorale *Eglé,* the opera *Le Patriotisme* (performed at Versailles), and the two-act *La Karmesse, ou La Foire flamande.*[17]

During the 1780s, Vogler's pedagogical interests receded temporarily to the background as he assumed the role of traveling virtuoso performer on keyboard instruments, especially the organ. He gave concerts in both Paris and London, then proceeded to attract attention throughout Europe for performances of the spectacular tone paintings that became his trademark.

Successfully appealing to audiences' cravings for novelty and sensation (at Amsterdam, no fewer than 7,000 tickets were sold within two days for a single organ performance in 1785),[18] these concerts inspired widely divergent reactions from the press and the public.

Not abandoning the role of court musician altogether, Vogler succeeded Bernasconi as first kapellmeister at Munich in 1784. Though he remained at this post only a short time, the position did give him the opportunity to stage a major operatic work, *Castore e Polluce,* for the court theater.[19] In 1786, he obtained an appointment at the royal court of King Gustave III of Sweden. Evidently talented as a linguist, and socially adept despite his bluff manner and headstrong ways, he thrived at the Swedish court, where his circle of acquaintances included the kapellmeister Uttini, the opera composer Joseph Martin Kraus, the poet Johan Henrik Kellgren, who prepared the libretto for Vogler's lyric drama *Gustav Adolf och Ebba Brahe,* and A. F. Skjöldebrand, whose play *Hermann von Unna* was supplied by Vogler with choruses and ballet music. Resuming his pedagogical activities, Vogler established a music school, lectured, gave music lessons to the crown prince, and had several didactic works published in Swedish, including *Inledning til harmoniens kän-nedom, Organist-schola,* and *Clavér-schola* with its accompanying collection of keyboard studies, the *Pièces de clavecin.* Also active as a Catholic cleric, he assumed responsibilities as a representative of his church in this predomi-nantly Protestant land, a commitment which by no means hindered his interest and involvement in Protestant church music. His *Organist-schola,* for example, was addressed to the Protestant church organist, and was accom-panied by a compilation of ninety Swedish chorale harmonizations.

Enjoying the privilege of extensive travel, he was able to continue concertizing widely both in Sweden and abroad; during the time of his association with the Swedish court, his destinations included St. Petersburg, Amsterdam, London, Frankfurt, Kiel, and Copenhagen. In the course of these excursions, he presented himself not only as a performer but also as an authority on organ design. Building an experimental, transportable organ, the *Orchestrion,* as a point of departure, he devised a method of construction whose alleged virtues of efficiency, mechanical simplification, and cost re-duction enabled him to procure commissions for new and redesigned instru-ments while providing the basis for heated debate among critics and per-formers.

In 1792, the abbé's royal patron was assassinated at a masked ball (the event which inspired the libretto to Verdi's *Un ballo in maschera*), and it was shortly after this tragic occurrence that Vogler left his post to embark on the longest and most ambitious excursion of his career. Lasting more than a year, the adventure began with his departure by sea from Hamburg, with subsequent ports of call including Cádiz, Gibraltar, and North Africa. The central aim of the trip was to rediscover a lost musical tradition—the existing traces of an ancient musical practice on which Western customs were founded—and it provided Vogler with a stimulus for a major treatise on chorale accompaniment, the controversial *Choral-System* of 1800. The journey also permitted further pursuit of his keen interest in questions of national character and folk tradition, yielding a fresh supply of exotic themes that found their way into organ improvisations as well as published collections of keyboard pieces and chamber music.

Following the Mediterranean odyssey, Vogler returned to Stockholm in 1793 and retained an official position at the Swedish court until 1799.[20] This period was followed by brief residences in Copenhagen (1799–1800) and in Berlin (1800–1801), where he redesigned the St. Mary's organ and delivered a lecture on acoustics, subsequently published as *Data zur Akustik* (1801). In 1801 he settled temporarily in Prague. There, at Charles University, he offered a series of public lectures in 1801–2, and was granted the use of a hall in which he constructed a special acoustical wall to enhance the sound of his *Orchestrion*. It was in connection with the lectures that he published his definitive harmony treatise, *Handbuch zur Harmonielehre,* in 1802.

After travels in 1802 that took him to Schweidnitz and Breslau, Vogler appears to have arrived in Vienna by the end of the year. In 1803 his opera *Castore e Polluce* was revived in a benefit concert performance in which more than 200 orchestral musicians took part.[21] That same year he received a commission from Emanuel Schikaneder for the opera *Samori,* which premiered in May 1804 at the Theater an der Wien, where Beethoven's *Fidelio* was staged without success in November 1805. Vogler's name is linked with Beethoven's in various reports, including an account of a soirée in Joseph Sonnleithner's home, during which the two musicians competed, each improvising on a theme supplied by the other.[22] In addition to encounters with other leading figures, including Cherubini and Haydn, he made the acquaintance of two young artists who were to become his enthusiastic disciples: Carl Maria von Weber and the Austrian composer Johann Gänsbacher.

Vogler left Vienna for Munich in 1805, stopping along the way at Salzburg, where he redesigned the organ at St. Peter's. He resided in Munich for two years, striving to make himself visible and actively seeking an appointment at court. He acquired membership in the Academy of Sciences and pursued a variety of pedagogical and organ-related projects in addition to writing, composing, and performing. In a typically ambitious though unsuccessful petition for employment, the duties he proposed for himself included composition, performance, lecturing, writing, teaching, acoustical advice in the design of churches, theaters, and auditoriums, and jurisdiction over the building, repair, and renovation of organs.[23]

In 1807 he moved to Darmstadt, where the Grand Duke installed him as ecclesiastical privy councillor, a position he held for the remaining years of his life. Restless and active as ever, he concertized, composed major works, including a *Singspiel, Der Admiral,* and the widely admired *Requiem* in E-flat, and obtained further commissions to build and redesign church organs, most notably at Munich and Würzburg. His endeavors included work on a three-console, thirteen-manual organ, the *Triorganon,* never actually completed, which was to be played simultaneously by three performers; the formulation of a new theory of fugue; and the infamous publication of twelve revised Bach chorale harmonizations with analytical commentary by Carl Maria von Weber.

Though disappointed that his ideas failed to win the acceptance for which he had hoped, Vogler could nevertheless find solace in his later years through the loyalty and enthusiasm of an illustrious gathering of younger friends and pupils. In addition to Carl Maria von Weber and Gänsbacher, the group included Giacomo Meyerbeer, who came to Darmstadt as the abbé's pupil in April 1810, and Gottfried Weber, whose widely disseminated treatise borrowed Vogler's Roman-numeral analytical system and quoted liberally from his compositions. Though the group remained together for only a brief time, they formed lasting friendships and kept sporadically in touch with one another and with their mentor (to whom they referred as "Papa") long after their departure from Darmstadt.

Vogler, for his part, continued to pursue pet projects and new explorations, including a study of Hebraic scansion,[24] with unabated energy. As Gottfried Weber attested in a eulogy published in the *Allgemeine musikalische Zeitung* (May 1814), he had lived nearly 66 years [*sic*] without growing old.

Describing his final visit to the abbé, Weber reported finding him still full of youthful enthusiasm, eagerly analyzing his own compositions, and discoursing at length on matters of aesthetics and artistic technique.[25]

The subject of both acclaim and controversy during his lifetime, Vogler was by no means totally forgotten by posterity. His name appeared frequently in periodicals, often in connection with issues of church-music reform. Favorite compositions continued to enjoy performances, and his biography, initiated by Carl Maria von Weber, was eventually realized by another disciple, Joseph Fröhlich, whose account of Vogler's life attempted to defend the abbé's posthumous reputation.

But even during Vogler's lifetime it was clear that the greater part of his work was doomed to near oblivion. Lamenting this state of affairs in his 1810 essay on Vogler, von Weber blamed critics whose "misrepresentation . . . reduced Vogler, in the eyes of most music-lovers, to little more than a learned eccentric."[26] But clearly Vogler himself and the peculiar circumstances of his career must bear much of the blame for his fate. As Gottfried Weber complained, he chose to release only a small fraction of his compositions for publication.[27] His habit of wandering, combined with the bewildering diversity of his activities, prevented him from being clearly identified with any particular school, locale, or area of specialization; and some of his most important theoretical ideas were consigned to fragmentary essays, handbooks, or pamphlets that must have seemed enigmatic and obscure in the absence of an explanatory frame of reference.

Lacking the basis for a fair and informed appraisal, critics' judgments were all too frequently colored by observed eccentricities in the abbé's personality and his writings: the candid, sweeping pronouncements, for example, on the alleged faults of J. S. Bach and his North German champions; the blend of secular flamboyance and self-righteous piety that typified his manner and appearance; the pompous insistence on identifying his art with the discovery of incontrovertible truth; and the predilection for a superficially brilliant, sensational style of performance, notably in his programmatic organ improvisations. Though few contemporaries shared Mozart's devastating judgment of his technique and artistry, accusations of charlatanism surfaced early and persisted.

C. F. D. Schubart's remark on Vogler's slavish adherence to a theoretical system was symptomatic of a developing attitude,[28] as was the young Mozart's observation to his father that Vogler's harmony manual seemed more appropriate to the teaching of arithmetic than music.[29] Assessments such as that found in Lipowsky's 1811 lexicon, which dismissed Vogler's theories as pedantry, helped pave the way for posterity's misunderstanding.[30] Fétis, for example, roundly denounced Vogler's theory without knowledge of its substance,[31] and Otto Jahn's biography of Mozart pictured his subject's rival as a shallow man whose deficiency of creative genius had actually proved detrimental to the progress of true art.[32]

Such negative portrayals did not go unchallenged. In 1884, Ernst Pasqué published an appreciative account of Vogler's life and works.[33] Shortly thereafter, Karl Emil von Schafhäutl, a dedicated amateur, established himself as a worthy champion by producing a major study, *Abt Georg Joseph Vogler* (Augsburg, 1888), that answered Vogler's detractors and provided an opportunity to examine his accomplishments in a new light. With access to numerous scores, letters, and other pertinent documents, and equipped with at least a modest understanding of theoretical and stylistic issues, Schafhäutl put together a factual though sketchy account of the artist's life, a rudimentary explanation of some aspects of his harmonic system, and an enthusiastic description of some of the music he had encountered. His extensive list of Vogler's works, while useful in giving at least an approximate idea of the scope of the composer's output, left many questions of dating and authenticity unresolved.[34]

However limited as a biography or an appraisal of Vogler's music and his writings, Schafhäutl's book, reprinted in 1979, has retained its value as a foundation for further research into various aspects of Vogler's accomplishments. It is largely thanks to his initiative that at least fitful interest can be traced from the end of the nineteenth century to the present.

Early signs of a new, more sympathetic appreciation included two modestly sized German studies from the early years of the twentieth century: a monograph on Vogler's exploits as an organist by Emile Rupp,[35] and a dissertation on romantic tendencies in Vogler's music by James Simon.[36]

Larger in scale and more penetrating in detail was the work of the Austrian scholar Hertha Schweiger, who examined Vogler's activities as a performer and theorist of organ design. Her studies included a dissertation and an essay published in *Musical Quarterly* which provided English-speaking readers with important information on the abbé's life and works.[37]

Schweiger's publications were followed by two dissertations that helped clarify Vogler's accomplishments and historical significance. The first of these, by Helmut Kreitz (1957), provided much-needed correction of the rather muddled description of Vogler's theories found in Schafhäutl.[38] Yet it neglected important writings and provided only a superficial account of others. More recently, an American dissertation by David Britton contributed a concise overview of Vogler's contribution to the history of organ performance and design from an organist's point of view.[39]

Although these specialized studies have added to our knowledge of Vogler, each concentrates on a particular aspect of his contribution—whether musical style (Simon), the organ (Rupp, Schweiger, Britton), or harmonic theory (Kreitz)—at the expense of a comprehensive view of their interaction. Especially notable is the lack of any extensive inquiry into the relationship between Vogler's theories and the musical practices represented in his compositions.

Addressing this aspect of his achievement, the present study has been guided by a conviction that Vogler's manifold activities—as theorist, critic, composer, and performer—can shed light on one another, and that studying them side by side can improve our understanding of the man and his significance.

The first step has been to examine Vogler's attitudes, ideals, and limitations as reflected in the theoretical and critical writings with which he was occupied for most of his career, including essays, handbooks, treatises, pamphlets, and encyclopedia articles. In these miscellaneous publications, generally either misunderstood or ignored in the existing literature on music theory and criticism, Vogler attempted to convey his insights into the nature of musical organization. He claimed that, in addition to furnishing a unified picture of the music of his day, his theory of harmony guided his own practices as a composer. And as proof of the extent to which his works reflected his teachings, he published analyses in which his own model compositions were subjected to theoretical scrutiny.

To what extent can correspondences be found between Vogler's musical idiom and the theoretical foundations on which it rested? Did he obey his own rules? Can we determine particular ways in which he was either inspired or inhibited by his precepts? Such questions are important, not only to the study of Vogler, but to our understanding of the historical changes and developments of which he was a part. For despite his eccentricities and the controversies they provoked, he was fully engaged in the mainstream of European musical activity for most of his career, and the unusually broad range of his experiences enabled him to command a nearly all-embracing view of contemporary practices. Thus, to the extent that this view is reflected in his writings and compositions, Vogler is well qualified to furnish us with a reflection of the musical aspirations, limitations, and accomplishments of his day.

In attempting to appraise the significance of Vogler's teachings, this study begins with an examination of his theory of harmony, an inquiry into the concepts of musical analysis that he derived from his theoretical principles, and an overview of his approaches to music criticism and aesthetics. This survey of fundamental issues provides the backdrop for an exploration of the three areas in which his efforts as a practical musician were most heavily concentrated: compositions for the theater, sacred music, and organ design and performance.

It is hoped that by clarifying some of the connections between Vogler's writings and his music, this endeavor will not only promote further understanding of the abbé and his contributions, but will also shed light on pertinent aspects of the age in which he lived: the nature of its evolving musical styles and changing attitudes, and the frame of reference in which music of the time was created, taught, and appreciated.

## CHAPTER I

# The Science of Harmony:
# Foundations
# for an Enlightened System

U PON return to Mannheim in 1775 following his sojourn of study and travel in Italy, the young Abbé Vogler set about to establish a music school for amateurs and aspiring professional musicians. Intimately associated with this enterprise was the formulation of a theory of harmony on which the school's teachings were to be based, and the essential ingredients of the new "system," as Vogler described it, were set forth in a handbook called *Tonwissenschaft und Tonsezkunst* (The Science of Harmony and the Art of Composition). Published in 1776, this eighty-six-page summary furnished a basis for much elaboration and development in later writings.

Like the texts of numerous German contemporaries, including Johann Friedrich Daube, Georg Andreas Sorge, Friedrich Wilhelm Marpurg, Johann Philipp Kirnberger, and Heinrich Christoph Koch, Vogler's handbook reflected fundamental changes that made traditional pedagogical methods seem at least partially obsolete in the latter half of the eighteenth century. The venerable discipline of counterpoint, codified in Johann Joseph Fux's *Gradus ad Parnassum* of 1725,[1] was still invaluable as a key to the craft of voice leading and as a link with the *stile antico;* and the study of thoroughbass, which explained harmonic textures in terms of intervallic relationships above the bass line, continued to furnish a viable basis for the teaching of composition. Yet neither approach was especially well suited to explaining newer musical styles in which rhythmically flexible homophony and clearly punctuated phrases had supplanted such outmoded traits as motoric rhythm, polyphonic elaboration, and melodically continuous bass lines. Moreover, the traditional methods did not adequately address the needs of dilettantes, whose increasingly prominent role in central-European music-making was stimulating a demand for easier, quicker routes to rudimentary knowledge of musical grammar.

These factors help explain the growing enthusiasm in the later eighteenth century for a relatively new and immensely important theoretical concept, the fundamental bass. As set forth in Jean-Philippe Rameau's *Traité de l'harmonie* (1722)[2] and elaborated in subsequent treatises over the next several decades, fundamental-bass theory promised to facilitate the study of composition by reducing vertical sonorities to a triadic basis and by prescribing a relatively simple, all-encompassing set of rules for dissonance treatment and chord succession. Although Rameau's proposals at first encountered resistance, they gradually gained a foothold among theorists in Germany as well as France. Jean le Rond d'Alembert's 1752 summary of Rameau's theory, the *Elémens de musique, théorique et pratique, suivant les principes de M. Rameau* (translated by Marpurg in 1757 as *Systematische Einleitung in die musikalische Setzkunst nach den Lehrsätzen des Herrn Rameau*), helped quicken the process of dissemination, and by the time Vogler came of age as a theorist in the 1770s, the fashionably enlightened concept of the fundamental bass was familiar enough to German readers to be widely accepted as common currency.

The circumstances surrounding Vogler's own introduction to fundamental-bass theory and the rationalist principles on which it was based remain unclear. Few documents have come to light regarding his early education, his musical training, or the influences under which his opinions and predilections were formed. Quite possibly, his commitment to rationalism, and the attendant preference for mathematical demonstrations and chains of deductions, found early encouragement from his instructors at the Jesuit school in Würzburg, where he was likely to have gained exposure to the teachings of Leibniz, Christian Wolff, and the ideals of the German *Aufklärung*. It is also possible that his early studies led to encounters with such rationally oriented writings as those of Leonhard Euler and Lorenz Mizler as well as Daube, Sorge, and Marpurg, though Vogler's writings make no mention of such influences.[3]

In any event, it is clear that his rationalist outlook was well formed by the time of his journey to Italy in 1773. Traveling to Bologna to study with Padre Martini (1706–84), one of the most learned musicians of his time and internationally famous as a teacher, Vogler soon discovered that this master's brand of pedagogy could scarcely offer the kind of enlightenment he sought. "We have no system other than that of Fux," Martini is reported to have confessed, and according to Vogler's own account, it took no more than a brief confrontation with this approach—which he perceived as theoretically groundless and contradictory—to convince him of the need for an alternative.[4]

Following the episode with Martini, Vogler turned to Francesco Antonio Vallotti (1697–1780), *maestro di cappella* at the basilica of San Antonio in Padua, who was destined to become his true mentor and source of the insights for which he had undertaken his search. Renowned as a composer of church music and widely respected for his knowledge of the sacred polyphonic tradition, Vallotti published the first book of a major treatise, *Della scienza teorica, e pratica della moderna musica,* in 1779. The rest of his work (Books 2–4) was left in Padre Martini's care after Vallotti's death and remained unpublished until 1950.[5]

As represented by the 1950 edition, Vallotti's treatise is a traditionally learned compendium of musical knowledge, replete with references to the ancients as well as to recent masters, including Rameau and Tartini. In accordance with the age-old dichotomy between the theoretical and the practical, Book 1 is devoted largely to mathematical operations: divisions of the monochord, and the demonstration of relationships involving the arithmetic, geometric, and harmonic proportions. While Book 2 elaborates the rudiments.of modern music, Book 3 applies the proposals of Book 1 to the explanation of chords and their inversions, the fundamental bass, and the concept of dissonance treatment. Book 4 is devoted to a discussion of the church modes.

In its reliance on Cartesian rationalism and the demonstration of correspondences between mathematical and musical relationships, Vallotti's theory bears comparison with that of Rameau (with whom he nevertheless took issue) as well as that of his Paduan associate, Giuseppe Tartini (1692–1770), from whom he appears to have borrowed the idea of deriving dissonances from the geometric progression.[6] But his treatise is most directly indebted to the teachings of an obscure yet historically important predecessor, the former Paduan *maestro di cappella* Francesco Antonio Calegari (1656–1742). According to Vallotti's account, Calegari (whose own theoretical writings were never published) proposed a concept of chord inversion and fundamental bass contemporaneously with Rameau and independently of any knowledge

of the Frenchman's writings.[7] Calegari's notion of the fundamental bass
(which he called *basso fondamentale*) was linked to a theory of dissonance that
contrasted sharply to that of Rameau. Calegari proposed that notes of the
scale within the octave could be divided into the three consonant tones of a
triad (1, 3, and 5) and four dissonances (2, 4, 6, and 7); but since the numbers
2, 4, and 6 can represent consonant chord tones by inversion, the dissonant
intervals in question must be derived from outside the octave, where they are
properly designated as 9, 11, and 13, and where they remain unaffected by
processes of chord inversion within the octave.[8]

Calegari's principles, which evidently made no claim to any mathematical or acoustical foundation, permitted construction of triads on each degree
of the scale, and allowed each to be adorned with any of the four available
dissonances. These aspects of Calegari's theory were assimilated by Vallotti
and integrated within his own rationally conceived design. Declaring that the
entire system of modern composition could be reduced to the harmonic
proportion 1:1/3:1/5,[9] Vallotti constructed a method that accounted for
available musical resources, including intervals, scales, triads, and dissonances, while managing to sidestep such notoriously problematical concepts
as the *double emploi* and dissonance by supposition that had caused Rameau
and his followers such difficulty.[10]

Vallotti's system was a revelation to Vogler. In the course of several
months' study at Padua, he endeavored to conquer this mathematically
inspired theory and reconcile its principles with his own convictions regarding the nature of musical organization. Following Vallotti's lead, he drew the
conclusion that musical knowledge was indeed founded on the natural resonance of the sounding string. When a string was caused to vibrate, it produced not only the octave of the fundamental and the double octave (1:2, 1:4)
but a fifth (1:3) and major third (1:5) as well. A three-fold harmonious unity
emerged, and in this manifold sonority lay the controlling source of all
musical diversity. Thus the basis of musical understanding was fundamentally simple. It rested on irrefutable scientific foundations, and its principles
were readily accessible to anyone with an unprejudiced mind, a sharp ear, and
an elementary knowledge of arithmetic.

Adopting Vallotti's teachings as a foundation, Vogler reassembled his
mentor's precepts to suit his own didactic purposes, and he drastically simplified the older theorist's reasoning.[11] Although he characterized the result
as an authentically rational, mathematically based system, Volger's method

involved a marked avoidance of theoretical detail. In this respect it presented a striking contrast not only with the writings of Rameau and Vallotti, but even with the less complex approaches propounded by Marpurg and Kirnberger. It was central to Vogler's purposes to show that the science of musical organization, far from being arcane, was universally accessible. This conviction furnished a guiding principle for his pedagogical endeavors.

### THE SYSTEM

In *Tonwissenschaft und Tonsezkunst,* the essential features of Vogler's approach are clearly established. Division of a sounding string into two, three, and five parts provides a point of departure. Thus having established the fundamental consonances, he proceeds to fashion a chain of deductions, organizing his proposals and observations in a way that progresses from the simple to the complex, from unity to diversity. The intended result is to have all materials of the tonal spectrum fall into a self-evident, hierarchic pattern. Every phenomenon is assigned its proper place in the hierarchy, ultimately proceeding from—and reducible to—the relationships residing in the three-fold unity inherent in the major triad.

For more than two decades, *Tonwissenschaft und Tonsezkunst* served as his point of reference for various writings—including analytical essays in *Betrachtungen der Mannheimer Tonschule* (1778–81), articles for the *Deutsche Encyclopädie* (begun in 1778), and the Swedish harmony manual *Inledning til harmoniens kännedom* (1794)—that relied on its premises and amplified its deductions. The 1802 *Handbuch zur Harmonielehre* was put together as a supplement to the theorist's public lectures at Charles University in Prague. The *Handbuch* drew extensively on *Inledning til harmoniens kännedom* and other previous writings for its content and organization. Although it covers much the same ground as *Tonwissenschaft und Tonsezkunst,* there are significant changes in order and in manner of presentation.

The earlier volume, addressing the heterogeneous readership of the Mannheim music school, proposed a simple dichotomy between theoretical foundation and practical application: *Tonwissenschaft,* the science of music, subsumed the explanation of tonal resources, including the triad, the scale, and the consonant and dissonant intervals; while *Tonsezkunst,* the art of composition, explained how these materials were organized and put to use. It dealt with the preparation and resolution of dissonance, the function of cadences and chord succession, rules for part writing, the concept of tonality, and modulation.

The *Handbuch,* by contrast, addresses a more sophisticated reader. The amateur is not excluded, and Vogler strives just as eagerly as before to persuade his reader of the essential simplicity of his system. Yet now the method is more tightly constructed. The less rigorous dichotomy yields to a continuous chain of reasoning that spans the gamut of compositional resources and encompasses both theoretical principle and musical practice. The new approach in no way repudiates the earlier one. The two volumes, engendered by different circumstances, represent alternative ways in which the ingredients of the system may be put together. In the belief that the two manuals can shed light on each other, the discussion that follows takes both into account. Their points of intersection and divergence help clarify underlying consistencies in Vogler's thinking as he pursues his concept of an enlightened, rationally ordered theory of harmony.

### INITIAL PREMISES; THE *TONMAASS*

In both *Tonwissenschaft* and the *Handbuch,* Vogler begins his exposition with acoustical observations and corresponding mathematical operations performed on a measured string. It is typical of his irreverence toward theoretical traditions that he chose to discard the time-honored monochord, replacing it with a multi-string instrument that he called the *Tonmaass.* This device contained a total of eight strings stretched parallel across a frame, each tuned to the same pitch (great F, one and one-half octaves below middle C).[12] Fixed bridges, placed on the rectangular body of the instrument beneath each string, marked their division into 9, 10, 11, 12, 13, 14, 15, and 16 parts respectively. The resulting divisions yielded all relationships necessary to the tonal language encompassed by the system.

But why abandon the monochord? Could a single string, equipped with a movable bridge, not serve equally well to demonstrate the necessary proportions and intervals? Vogler scorns the traditional instrument for reasons having to do not only with its sonorous limitations but also with alleged inadequacies of the operations customarily performed on it. He explains that, following the example of the Greeks, theorists are accustomed to calculating arithmetically on the monochord. Accordingly, the octave is reckoned as 1:2, the fifth as 2:3, the fourth as 3:4, and the major third as 4:5. As one divides the string, the identity of the lower tone keeps changing. It appears first as the entire string length, then half the length, then a third, and so on. There is no fixed point of reference from which different intervals can be specified, compared, and appraised with respect to their relative harmonic importance. On the monochord, for example, it would appear that the fourth is more important than the third, since it precedes the third in the arithmetic series. The instrument furnishes no basis for drawing any other conclusion.

The *Tonmaass,* by contrast, presents a single fundamental tone, great F, from which all harmonic relationships arise. When the eight unstopped strings are struck simultaneously, the sound of a triad is heard, since the harmonic divisions of third and fifth occur naturally as overtones. When these harmonic proportions are marked off and sounded on the different strings, the harmonic derivation of each tone from the fundamental becomes readily apparent. Whereas the proportions on the monochord are figured arithmetically (1, 2, 3, 4, 5, etc.), the acoustical law of nature is harmonic (1, $1/2$, $1/3$, $1/4$, $1/5$). And it is precisely this natural, harmonic order that the *Tonmaass* is designed to make accessible simultaneously to the hand, the eye, and the ear (see Example 1).[13]

Example 1

Generation of consonances from a
fundamental (F) on the *Tonmaass.*

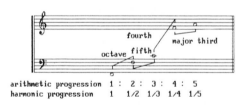

By virtue of this lesson in harmonic proportions, to which the *Tonmaass* is so well suited, the true status of the fifth and the third as primary consonances is clearly demonstrated, and the subordinate position of the fourth is affirmed, for now it appears not as a primary consonance, but merely as the inversion of the fifth.

In the *Handbuch,* Vogler devotes an entire introductory essay to the demonstration of harmonic relationships on his *Tonmaass* before continuing with the exposition of his system. He gives an account of the instrument's utility in deriving and comparing the different scales, the consonant intervals, and the sevenths. In *Tonwissenschaft und Tonsezkunst,* by contrast, he proceeds immediately from derivation of the consonant intervals to the second step in his chain of reasoning: the construction of the scale, and the establishment of the scale as a point of reference for all deductions that follow.

THE SCALE

An important novelty of Vogler's system is the fact that it employs not one basic scale but two: a "natural" scale and its "artificial" relative. On the *Tonmaass,* which extends the division of the string to sixteen parts, an eight-tone series can be located within the octave bounded by the eighth and sixteenth partials. Identifying this as the "natural scale" produced by the trumpet and horn, Vogler represents the series as shown in Example 2.[14]

Example 2

The natural scale.

Vogler is no more tempted than any other theorist of his day to rely solely on this fact of nature as an explanation for scalar organization. Nevertheless he finds it useful, for it furnishes proof that such an ordering of tones can be traced more-or-less directly to natural origins. As it stands, however, this natural scale is unusable in tonal music. The fourth degree is too high, the natural sixth and seventh too low. Another method is necessary, and in putting it together, Vogler follows a procedure essentially similar to those found in the writings of Tartini and Rameau:[15] he measures his fundamental triad on F, adds a second triad a fifth above, on C, and then a third triad on G. When collapsed within the range of an octave, the tones of these chords produce a diatonic major scale on C (see Example 3).

It had been a source of embarrassment to Vogler's predecessors, most notably Rameau, that a scale produced in this fashion seemed to be based on a dominant rather than a tonic.[16] If the note F is our fundamental point of

Example 3
Construction of the artificial scale.

reference—the ultimate source from which all else emerges—then how can we justify this scale in which F is merely a lower fifth and not the tonic itself?

Vogler's solution involves his "natural scale" and the concept of a chain of deductions. The procedure he follows, simple enough in substance, is central to the nature of his system. He does not try to claim that the diatonic scale is based directly on a natural foundation. Instead, he derives it logically from the preceding links in his chain of reasoning, i.e., the triad and the natural scale. The natural scale provides a model for the artificial, and the intervals of fifth and third (whatever the actual pitches involved) provide the natural material from which it can be built: a designated tonic triad, a triad a fifth above tonic, and a triad a fifth below. Nothing in this line of reasoning prevents him from choosing C rather than F as his central reference point for this operation and for subsequent deductions. Indeed, it was the anticipation of this step that informed the theorist's very first move: the tuning of his *Tonmaass* not to the note C (which would have led to an artificial scale on G) but to the lower fifth of C.[17]

Vogler's next step is to construct a minor scale. In accordance with the pattern of deductions already established, this scale requires no direct, natural basis. In *Tonwissenschaft,* he obtains it simply by measuring a major third, then locating this third below the first, fifth, and second scale degrees of the diatonic major scale. This yields the necessary tones A-flat, E-flat, and B-flat.[18] In the *Handbuch,* he offers an alternative approach by designating the note A as tonic, then following a procedure comparable to that used in deriving the artificial major scale: to the tones of an A-minor triad, he adds those of the minor triads occurring a fifth above, on E, and a fifth below, on D, thereby creating a diatonic minor scale on A.[19] Finally, as described in *Tonwissenschaft und Tonsezkunst,* he forms a complete chromatic scale by combining the seven tones of his major scale, the three additional tones of the minor, and two further tones: a half step below the fifth degree (comparable in size to the interval between B and C), and a major third above the sixth degree. With this last procedure, he has supplied himself with the tonal materials needed to proceed with the construction of his system.

CHORD FUNCTIONS AND CADENCES

In *Tonwissenschaft und Tonsezkunst,* Vogler progressed from the presentation of scales to the consideration of intervals: first the consonant spans and their inversions, then dissonances, and finally those intervals involving an inflected scale degree, including the augmented fifth and the diminished third. In so doing, he followed his principle of going from simple to complex; but by the time he conceived the *Handbuch,* he had evidently sensed the need for a more compelling logic in the ordering of his materials. In *Tonwissenschaft,* he had selected the artificial scale as a point of reference. Following a line of reasoning to be examined in detail below, he had attempted to show how the various diatonic and chromatically inflected intervals could be derived from his basic materials of chord and scale. But where do intervals such as the diminished seventh, the augmented fifth, and the diminished third actually come from? How, in other words, do the inflected scale degrees on which these intervals are based arise? In the *Handbuch,* we learn that the inflected intervals originate in certain chord progressions whose origins, in turn, lie in the scale and its three constituent triads. To make the order of his presentation conform to this more cogent line of thought, Vogler now proceeds from the scales to the question of chord succession.

Having created his artificial scale from a conflation of three triads whose roots occupy the first, fourth, and fifth scale degrees, the theorist has no hesitation in building triads on all the other degrees as well.[20] By analogy with the three primary chords, these additional triads are to be understood as fundamental, regardless of the size of their fifth. Unlike Rameau and his followers, Vogler does not shirk from regarding a triad whose fifth is diminished, such as B–D–F in C major, as a legitimate triad. He suggests that such a chord need not stand on its own acoustically. Instead, it acquires its fundamental status from the key in which it originates. Chords on all degrees of the scale, in other words, are understood as sovereign representatives of their key. This is the path of reasoning that leads Vogler to invent the system for representing chords that has since become standard: each degree of the scale is assigned a Roman numeral, which designates its function as a chord root within a key.[21]

Although any chord in a scale may stand on its own as a representative of its key, the origins of the artificial scale suggest to Vogler a hierarchy of importance among the available chords. Operations on the *Tonmaass* have shown that the fifth is the first, most perfect, and hence most decisive interval to arise after the octave. It was this interval that gave rise to the formation of a scale from three primary triads (I, IV, and V). These observations lead to the conclusions that the most decisive progressions in a key are those in which the chord roots are a fifth removed from tonic (up or down), and that the most important progression of all is from V to I. Because of its elemental nature and acoustical simplicity, this V–I progression gives the impression of final-ity, or closure. It is therefore *schlussfallmässig,* or cadential. Vogler decides that, in addition to the fifth relationship, it is the acoustical perfection of the penultimate chord that gives the progression its cadential quality (the fact, in other words, that the V chord is endowed with a major third). For this reason, the third of the V chord must be raised in minor in order for it to yield a satisfying cadence.

The reverse of the V–I cadence, I–V, lacks the inherent finality of its relative, and is used as an intermediary close within a composition. The progression IV–I, less strong and decisive than V–I or I–V, is in a sense retrogressive (*rückgängig*). Potentially ambiguous, since it is indistinguishable from the half cadence I–V when heard out of context, it is theoretically unusable in minor, for neither of its members possesses the mandatory *schlussfallmässig* major third that Vogler declares to be necessary in any prop-erly decisive cadence.[22]

Having set forth the cadences involving the primary triads, Vogler proposes that the basic types give rise to others. First of all, the progression VII–I in major is cadential, for not only does it feature the crucial, cadential third of the V chord (the seventh scale degree), but the chord in its entirety is contained within a V chord with added seventh.[23] This cadence is available in minor as well, since the seventh scale degree has already been raised to accommodate the cadential V–I progression.

The theorist's next step is to recall that in the natural scale the fourth degree was too high—so high, in fact, that the distance between fourth and fifth degrees approximated the half step between the cadential seventh degree and tonic. Because of this, our ears are naturally attuned to the possibility of a cadential, raised fourth degree in the major scale, analogous in function to the seventh. In a major key, then, the progression of raised IV to V yields closure on the fifth scale degree just as VII–I produces a cadence on tonic. If the raised fourth yields a legitimate cadence in major, we should be able to use it in minor as well. Here Vogler finds a new and different chord quality, that of the diminished third (e.g., D♯–F–A in A minor), which becomes an augmented sixth by inversion. Now, by analogy with the relationship between the VII chord and a V chord with added seventh (e.g., B–D–F, which is contained within the chord G–B–D–F), the II chord in minor with raised fourth and added seventh may be added to the ranks of cadential harmonies (the chord B–D♯–F–A embodies the cadential D♯–F–A). The cadential II with added seventh in major (D–F♯–A–C) is a hypothetical possibility, but Vogler excludes it from his repertory of cadences, since it implies not merely a cadence on the fifth (II⁷–V),[24] but an actual modulation to the key of the fifth (i.e., V⁷/V to V). All in all, Vogler's reasoning yields a total of ten cadences, which may be arrayed as follows (see Example 4).

By drawing on the phenomena of the natural scale, the artificial scale, and the V–I progression, Vogler has assembled a useful and diverse repertory of chord successions involving his primary triads and their close relatives (i.e., the VII chord and the altered II). He has laid a firm foundation for a grammar of chord succession and, moreover, has offered plausible explanations for two characteristic scale inflections: the raised fourth, and the raised

Example 4
The ten cadences.

V – I    I – V    IV – I    VII – I    ♯IV – V

V – I    I – V    ♯VII – I    ♯IV – V    II – V

seventh degree in minor. He is now ready to proceed with a full tabulation of available intervals, and to account for each within the hierarchic order of his system.

### INTERVALS: THE SEVENTHS

By examining the major triad and the various cadential chords derived from the major and minor scales, we find that Vogler has accumulated a total of five primary intervals: major third, minor third, diminished third, perfect fifth, and diminished fifth. To this tally may be added the augmented fifth, which arises when the III chord in minor employs the raised seventh degree (e.g., C–E–G♯ in A minor). Inversion of these six intervals yields six more, for a total of twelve.[25]

The list of intervals may be completed by the addition of the sevenths and their inversions. Up to this point, Vogler's line of reasoning has not required the use of any intervals outside the triad (with the exception of the altered II[7] in minor and the notion of a V[7] that was invoked to explain the cadential VII). But for further deductions, the seventh proves indispensable, and the reasoning he applies to intervals of this category counts among the most original and provocative aspects of his teachings. He distinguishes three main types of seventh (major, minor, and diminished), and these, combined with their inversions and added to the twelve intervals already accounted for, yield a count of eighteen intervals in all. Within the category of the sevenths, however, he finds no fewer than seven kinds whose differences in origin and functional significance may be specified.

Basic to Vogler's approach to the sevenths is the rejection of Rameau's teachings, in which the derivation of tonal materials is restricted to the division of a sounding string into no more than six parts,[26] in favor of Vallotti's, whereby one may divide the string further without hesitation.[27] The first six partials have produced a perfect triad. Addition of the seventh partial to this harmony yields a new sound, one which sustains the listener's attention with a mildly restless quality that demands resolution. Neither consonant nor sharply dissonant, this is the *Unterhaltungssiebente,* or "tension-sustaining seventh," that Vogler will call on for his dominant seventh.[28] To understand how he uses this resource of the natural seventh, we need to examine the intervallic relationships obtained within the artificial scale, which he has set forth as follows:[29]

| C | D | E | F | G | A | B |
|---|---|---|---|---|---|---|
| 1/24 | 1/27 | 1/30 | 1/32 | 1/36 | 1/40 | 1/45 |

| | E♭ | | | A♭ | B♭ | |
|---|---|---|---|---|---|---|
| | 5/144 | | | 5/192 | 5/216 | |

He points out that the natural seventh (1/4:1/7) is smaller than any diatonic seventh that appears in his scale, but that the seventh between G and F (1/9:1/16) approximates this interval closely enough to serve as a practical substitute. This moderately dissonant seventh that will adorn the V triad may be freely sounded, Vogler declares. Moreover, under certain conditions it may resolve upward as well as down (see Example 5, taken from the illustration of modulations in the *Handbuch:* on beat 2, the consonant E-flat becomes a seventh, and on beat 3 it rises chromatically to become the leading tone of another dominant seventh as the modulation takes place).[30] Its nature having thus been determined, the dominant seventh will serve as a yardstick for the measuring and appraisal of the other sevenths.

Example 5
The upward-resolving seventh.

The diminished seventh, for example, built on the raised seventh scale degree in minor (e.g., G♯–F), is smaller than the dominant seventh, hence less dissonant; therefore it too may be freely sounded and resolved up or down. The seventh on the seventh degree in major (e.g., B–A) is the same size as that of the dominant seventh G to F (1/45:1/80, or 1/9:1/16), and thus it requires no preparation (though it is not permitted upward resolution). Matters become more complex with the minor seventh built on the second degree of the minor scale. In *Tonwissenschaft,* Vogler notes that, while the chord B–D–F–A as a cadential VII in C major is ostensibly the same as the non-cadential II chord with seventh in A minor (which requires preparation), there is a significant difference. In the former, the tones B–D–F are the same as the third, fifth, and seventh above the dominant G. In the latter, by contrast, the theoretical distance between the inner notes D–F is actually that found between the tones F and A-flat in the artificial scale cited above.

In the *Handbuch,* Vogler finds a more persuasive explanation for the difference between these two chords, for here the minor scale is formed from minor triads on A, D, and E. Using the new measurements that result, he can demonstrate the difference of a syntonic comma (80:81) between the note A as the third above F (its origin in the major scale) and the same note calculated as the fifth above D in the A-minor scale. The interval of the seventh from B to A in the A-minor scale is thus higher, and therefore more dissonant, than the interval B–A in C major. Unlike the smaller sevenths, it requires preparation as a consonance in addition to downward resolution.

Difficulty arises once again with the seventh above II in major, for as we have seen, the distance between D and C is the same as that between B and A. Yet Vogler is convinced that the non-cadential II[7] is more dissonant than the cadential VII[7], and that for this reason it requires preparation as a consonance. His explanation is that the symmetry of thirds in the II[7] chord (two minor thirds separated by a major third) is comparable to that of the highly dissonant tonic seventh chord (C–E–G–B), which exhibits two major thirds separated by a minor third.

With the seventh above the third and sixth degrees of the major scale, Vogler has a more secure footing. Here he can show convincingly that in the artificial scale, the distance between A and G, and between E and D, is greater than the smaller minor sevenths considered above. These more dissonant sevenths therefore require preparation as well as resolution.

The last of the sevenths to be considered is the most dissonant of all: the major seventh ($1/8:1/15$) found between C and B in the major scale. Without question it requires the same strict treatment—consonant preparation and downward resolution—demanded of the larger, non-cadential minor sevenths.

Through his exploration of the sevenths, Vogler has attempted to show that within his artificial major and minor scales, distinctions can be drawn not only between diminished and minor, or minor and major, but between different sizes of minor seventh as well. We find that he is able to prove with at least partial success that the more remote, non-cadential sevenths are by nature more dissonant—hence different in quality and function—than the closer, cadential sevenths. A hierarchic pattern results, enabling one to progress naturally through the available chords of a key, moving always from greater to lesser degrees of dissonance. In the major scale, the path leads from the harsh major sevenths ($I^7$, $IV^7$) through the larger minor sevenths ($III^7$, $VI^7$), to the less dissonant $II^7$, and finally to the cadential $VII^7$ or $V^7$.[31]

### DISSONANCE AND THE SYSTEM OF REDUCTION

Following Vallotti's example, Vogler has progressed from the consonances of the triad to the realm of dissonances by reaching to the seventh partial of the sounding string. He now continues to follow his Paduan mentor in pursuing a comprehensive theory of dissonance. Unlike Rameau, who attempted to derive all dissonances from the seventh, Vallotti adopted a method that involved reaching beyond the octave to the ninth, eleventh, and thirteenth.[32] Vallotti's reasoning may be interpreted as follows.

Among the seven tones of the scale, we have found a total of three (i.e., root, third, and fifth of a triad) that are consonant with one another. Division of the string into seven parts yields an additional, dissonant element that may be added to the triad if properly accounted for by preparation and resolution. This leaves three further tones, each of which likewise produces dissonance when sounded against the triad. The tones in question, lying a second, fourth, and sixth above our triad root, may either clash simultaneously with notes of the triad, or they displace triad tones whose appearance is delayed. In either event their effect is manifestly dissonant, and in order for them to be intelligible grammatically they must be prepared as consonances, held as the harmony changes, and resolved downward to the new consonant chord tones. Vogler, in comparing such dissonances with the sevenths, draws a distinction comparable to Kirnberger's dichotomy between essential and non-essential dissonances: whereas a seventh is essentially part of a dissonant *chord,* which resolves only when the harmony moves to a new root, the ninth, eleventh, and thirteenth function as dissonant elements above a persisting root. In Example 6 (taken from Vogler's *Handbuch*),[33] the tones F, A, C, and E are all prepared as consonances (measure 1). In measure 2, all four are held over to sound as dissonances against the triad G–B–D. One by one the suspended tones resolve downward by step, until finally the seventh resolves when the harmony changes at measure 3.

In addition to the seventh, then, there appear to be three more disso-nances. But immediately one confronts a paradox. The law of inversion

Example 6
Dissonances and their resolution.

dictates that the sixth is the inversion of the third, the fourth the inversion of the fifth. A configuration such as that seen in Example 7a must therefore be called a consonant triad in second inversion. A similar problem arises with the interval of the second, as in Example 7b. The second is surely a dissonant interval, but which is the dissonant note? According to the law of inversion, this interval is an inverted seventh. Hence the second above the bass in our example cannot be one of the three additional dissonances we are trying to specify, but simply one we have already accounted for: the seventh (A–G), which appears here in the bass by inversion.

Example 7
Consonant and dissonant
configurations: (a) inverted
consonant triad; (b) triad with
inverted seventh; (c) prepared
dissonances (eleventh and
thirteenth), resolved above the
chord root G.

Thwarted by the law of inversion in the attempt to identify these suspension-type dissonances as sixth, fourth, and second, the theorist must look elsewhere for an explanation. Vallotti's solution was to employ further divisions of the string: just as he divided the string in seven parts to obtain the seventh, he acquired three new intervals (ninth, eleventh, and thirteenth), by dividing his string into nine, eleven, and thirteen parts respectively. Like the sevenths, each may be understood as a genuine, original dissonance above a chord root. Applying this theory to Example 6, we can now reason that the note C above the bass G is only apparently a fourth. Prepared as a consonance in measure 1, it sounds as a dissonant eleventh in measure 2, where it resolves downward to a tenth (or third). Likewise, the apparent sixth and second in this example are in fact the thirteenth and ninth, suitably prepared and resolved. In accordance with their origin as consonances in the preceding chord, these notes are dissonant with the chord root G; and since the dissonances in question come from outside the octave, they are unaffected by the law of inversion. According to Vallotti's theory, the dissonant status of the eleventh and thirteenth prevails whether or not they clash with sounding chord tones (e.g., the notes B and D in Example 6).[34] The configuration seen in Example 7c, measure 2, is therefore not a consonant ♮ but a root-position triad with two dissonant notes (eleventh and thirteenth) suspending the delayed consonances, B and D.

When Vogler incorporates this notion of dissonance into his system, he finds that his own chain of deductions offers further validation for Vallotti's explanation. For in Vogler's system we are in familiar territory with these distant intervals. They have already been sounded on the *Tonmaass,* where the smaller aliquot parts (ninth through sixteenth partials) were enlisted in the generation of the natural scale. Just as the natural scale presents tones which approximate those of its practical equivalent (the artificial scale), so the ninth, eleventh, and thirteenth have their practical equivalents of second, fourth, and sixth within the octave.

The origins of the three suspension dissonances have now been accounted for, but we have yet to learn how to distinguish such dissonances from the consonances in a given sonority. How, for instance, can the root for a configuration such as A–C–E–G be determined unequivocally (see Example 8)?

Vogler's solution to this central quandary is to declare that "this precept is unavoidable, . . . namely: that all possible chords may be related to the simplest figuring of 3 and 5; that the tone to which these notes relate must be designated as the root; and that from this [tone], all consonances and dissonances are reckoned, and are subject to the same rule, whether they lie above or below."[35]

This rule of *Tonwissenschaft* is modified as follows in the *Handbuch,* where the theorist defines it as the "system of reduction . . . by which one resolves all vertical sonorities (*Gestalten*) to a single and simple triad, and can rest assured that for any harmony that occurs, no matter how complicated it appears, a root with third and fifth may be discovered, and that the third and fifth form a root-position chord."[36]

What is Vogler's meaning? By asserting that any chord may be reduced to the thoroughbass figures 3 and 5, he tells us that a grammatically correct combination of tones may be separated into consonant notes of a triad (i.e., a nominally consonant third and fifth above a chord root) and one or more dissonances (such as the notes C and E in Example 7c) which either accompany or replace tones of this fundamental triad. In clarifying this theory in the *Handbuch,* he confirms the conclusion implied by the formulation of his rule: namely, that the behavior of the dissonance is the decisive factor in determining the functional root of the harmony. If the chord in question is grammatically correct, then the dissonances will be suitably prepared and (or) resolved. The consonant chord tones will therefore be those whose behavior is not thus restricted. The harmony in Example 7a would be interpreted as a C-major chord in second inversion if each of its tones were freely sounded and therefore comprehensible only as consonances. In the context of Example 7c, however, the apparent sixth and fourth above the bass are treated as dissonances (i.e., thirteenth and eleventh), and the essential triad must therefore be G–B–D. Likewise, the chord A–C–E–G appears to be an A-minor triad with an added seventh if we examine it out of context (Example 8a). But the grammatical significance of this chord is altogether different as it appears

Example 8
(a & b). Grammatical
reinterpretation of triad with added
seventh (A–C–E–G) as major triad
(C–E–G) with dissonant thirteenth
in the bass.

Fundamental bass

in Example 8b. Here G is freely sounded, and A is treated as a dissonance. The essential triad is therefore C–E–G, and A is a dissonant thirteenth, which happens to appear in the bass.[37]

Applied in this manner, the rule of reduction provides the means for encompassing dissonance within the system and for unequivocally identifying the scale-tone root by which a given sonority—consonant or dissonant— is controlled.

THE CONCEPT OF TONSETZKUNST

In the early manual, the enunciation of Vogler's reduction theory completes the main substance of *Tonwissenschaft*. With the aid of the *Tonmaass,* the available consonances, scales, intervals, and dissonances have been derived and classified. In accordance with the dichotomy proposed, we must now set the *Tonmaass* aside and rely on the established premises of *Tonwissenschaft* in advancing to the realm of practical application.

The second part of the book, concerned with "the art of musical composition," begins with matters that would later be partially subsumed in the earlier chapters of the *Handbuch*. The dissonances are examined, and we learn about the circumstances under which they may be prepared and resolved. For example, each of the dissonances may be prepared not only by a consonance but also by a less remote dissonance. Thus the ninth may be prepared by a seventh, the eleventh by a seventh or ninth, and a thirteenth by a seventh, ninth, or eleventh (see Example 6, where the note E, sounded as a thirteenth in measure 2, is prepared as a seventh in the second half of measure 1).

Concerning the resolution of dissonances, Vogler proposes that a dissonant note (e.g., the note D in Example 9a) need not resolve directly, but may be held in abeyance while a consonant note (G) intervenes. Moreover, a dissonant note sounded in one voice (e.g., the note F in Example 9b) may migrate to another before it resolves.

From lessons in dissonance treatment, the 1776 manual proceeds to matters of cadence and chord progression. We learn that the cadential root movement by fifth furnishes a natural model for all chord succession. While this succession is strongest and most desirable, movement by other intervals is not excluded. Root movement by second, however, is subject to an important injunction: one should avoid placing two chords of the same type in succession (e.g., E minor, D minor; C major, D major). The sole exception

Example 9
(a) Dissonant ninth (D) resolved
downward to C in measure 2; (b)
dissonant seventh (F) resolved
downward in bass to E in
measure 2.

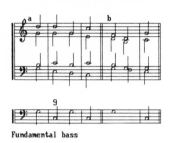

Fundamental bass

to this rule is the traditionally problematic succession IV–V in major, arbitrarily permitted by Vogler if the V chord is followed by a cadence.

The monotony of parallel octaves and perfect fifths is forbidden on the grounds that their acoustical simplicity affords too little variety of sound. The latter may occur without detriment, however, in a heavily scored orchestral fabric (between viola and bass, for instance). Thirds, being acoustically more diverse, may appear in succession if they are of different types (i.e., major followed by minor, or vice versa). Vogler scoffs at the traditional prejudice against hidden fifths and octaves, showing that they are not only harmless but virtually unavoidable in modern practice.

Following the discussion of rules for the craft of part writing, Vogler concludes *Tonwissenschaft und Tonsezkunst* with the study of modulation. He begins by declaring that the composer must not modulate to a key more than one accidental removed from tonic. The available keys therefore include the fifth above and below tonic, the relative minor, and the keys of its fifth above and below. If one steps outside this circle of close relationships, tonal unity is lost. It then cannot be said that the piece in question is in a particular key, but merely that it begins and ends in that key.

The question of modulation takes on a different complexion for the church organist, however, who has to extemporize transitional modulations between pieces of music in distantly related keys. Suggesting that the performer may use enharmonic equivalents as an efficient means of tonal connection, the author proceeds to show how one can move neatly and quickly from any one of the twenty-four possible keys to any other. Specifically, he proves that, from a given tonal center, it is possible to modulate to eleven different major keys and an equal number of minor keys. Since the same twenty-two keys are available from a minor center as well as a major, this number may be doubled to yield forty-four possible modulations.

This lesson in tonal connection, ostensibly intended as an aid to the church organist, was likely inspired by Vogler's own experience as a master of improvisation. As represented in *Tonwissenschaft und Tonsezkunst,* it may be understood as a theoretical tour de force, an ultimate demonstration of the thorough interrelatedness of the system. In any event, Vogler pursued this aspect of his system avidly. In the third volume of *Betrachtungen* (1780–81), he includes an extended essay entitled "Summe der Harmonik," accompanied by a stout fascicle of music examples, in which he executes and describes forty-four modulations from each of the twelve tones in the chromatic scale: a total of 528 modulations in all.[38]

### MULTIPLE FUNCTION CHORDS: THE CONCEPT OF *MEHRDEUTIGKEIT*

In the *Handbuch,* the discussion of modulation is preceded by a chapter on *Mehrdeutigkeit* (multiple function), the phenomenon of tonal pivots by which the immediate connection of chord functions in one key to those in another may be effected. The previous deductions set forth in the *Handbuch* have amply prepared the reader for this study of multiple functions. A repertory of ten cadence types has been demonstrated, and the grammatical significance of each tone and chord within a key has been considered. We have also seen that the meaning of a harmony or its constituent tones is not fixed: a change of context may enforce a corresponding change in grammatical meaning. For example, the chord B–D–F–A has one meaning as a cadential VII[7] in C major, but quite another as a non-cadential II[7] in A minor. Pursuing this line of thought, Vogler has taken exception to Rameau's notion of the cadential leading tone, the *note sensible.* We have not one leading tone but nine, he asserts, and he clarifies this point with a remarkable illustration (Example 10).[39]

The pitch in question here is G-sharp, which leads to the note A in each of nine harmonizations. Measures 2 and 3 present this G-sharp in the context of V–I progressions in major and minor; measure 4 introduces it as a member of

Example 10
The nine leading tones.

Fundamental bass:

the altered, cadential II⁷ in minor; in measure 5 it forms the fifth of an augmented triad, the altered III in minor. Especially noteworthy is the progression in measure 6, where Vogler identifies his chord on beat 2 not only as the altered III in A minor, but also, by virtue of the added *Unterhaltungssie-bente,* as an altered dominant of F. Measures 7 and 8 display the G-sharp as root of the VII chord in major and minor; the progression in measure 9, apparently identical to that of measure 7, is understood in accordance with Vogler's Roman-numeral analysis as the ♯IV–V progression in D major. The final bar gives us the ♯IV–V in D minor. In each instance, the G-sharp may be construed as a "leading tone," yet each time it occurs its grammatical meaning and expressive effect are different.

The idea that a single tone or chord may have multiple functions now becomes the focus of a systematic survey as Vogler considers the different chord types and examines the diverse meanings they can acquire in different contexts.

To clarify his presentation, he isolates two types of *Mehrdeutigkeit:* one category in which chords that are spelled differently have the same function, and another in which chords may be spelled the same way yet have different functions. Together, these two groups encompass his entire spectrum of possibilities for modulatory pivot chords.

Concerning the second, fundamentally simpler, category, it is shown that a chord of C major may represent as many as six different functions: I in C, III in A minor, IV in G, V in F (major and minor), VI in E minor, and VII in D minor. Any given minor chord proves comparably versatile, and a diminished triad may be either a VII or ♯IV in major, or a II in minor.

Beyond this realm of elementary pivots lies the real essence of *Mehr-deutigkeit:* the category in which enharmonic equivalents (e.g., G-sharp and A-flat) yield opportunities for connection between distantly related keys. Chords in this group originate with the alterations applied to cadential harmony in minor keys: the raised seventh scale degree, the raised fourth degree, the cadential II, and the augmented III.

Within this category of multiple functions, attention focuses initially on the cadential VII[7] in minor. The raised seventh scale degree has given rise to a diminished seventh. On the keyboard, the inversion of this interval is an augmented second, which is equivalent to a minor third. The chord may therefore be spelled in four different ways by virtue of the respelling of each of its minor thirds as the augmented second between a designated root and its seventh. This VII[7] chord can thus claim allegiance interchangeably to four different minor keys (see Example 11).[40]

Example 11
Enharmonic spellings of the
diminished-seventh chord.

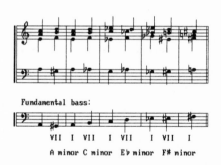

The vocabulary of enharmonic links is further enriched by the chords of the raised fourth in minor. In A minor, for instance, the IV chord with a raised fourth scale degree and added seventh would be spelled D♯–F–A–C. By replacing the D-sharp with its enharmonic equivalent, E-flat, we obtain a V[7] chord in B-flat (Example 12a). The cadential II with added seventh is likewise ambivalent, for if we examine this chord as it appears in A minor (B–D♯–F–A), we find that it proves equivalent in sound to the chord F–A–C♭–E♭, the cadential II[7] in E-flat minor (Example 12b).

Vogler completes his repertory of enharmonic pivots with the aug-

Example 12
Enharmonic respelling of (a) the ♯
IV⁷ in minor; (b) the cadential II⁷ in
minor.

A minor: ♯IV – V     B♭: V – I     A minor: II – V     E♭ minor: II – V

mented triad in minor—the III chord with raised seventh scale degree (e.g.,
C–E–G♯ in A minor). Like the VII⁷ in minor, this chord divides the octave
into equidistant intervals: the augmented fifth between the outer tones in-
verts to a diminished fourth, which is enharmonically equivalent to a major
third. Therefore, by respelling major thirds as diminished fourths, one can
assign the same chord interchangeably to three different minor keys (Example 13).[41]

Example 13
Enharmonic spellings of the
augmented triad.

A minor: III     F minor: III     C♯ minor: III

The concept of multiple-function harmonies having thus been introduced, the reader of the *Handbuch* now advances to the application of these
chords in moving from one key to another.

MODULATION

As had been demonstrated in the earlier, exhaustive *Betrachtungen* essay
"Summe der Harmonik" (from which the examples in *Handbuch* are largely
drawn), the essential elements of a modulation are the point of origin, the

destination, and the vehicle by which the two are connected. The problem of achieving the connection efficiently and convincingly is fully encompassed by the study of *Mehrdeutigkeit*. By virtue of this resource, firmly grounded in nature, one may modulate from any given key to any other without resorting to *Zwischenharmonie,* i.e., mediating chords that belong neither to the key of origin nor to the key of destination.[42]

Connections between closely related keys cause no difficulty. The move from D-flat major to E-flat minor, for example, is accomplished by the effortless progression to VII$^7$ in the new key (Example 14a).[43] More remote relationships call for use of the enharmonic equivalents. To progress from D-flat major to D minor, for instance, one may move from the initial tonic chord to the not-too-distant diminished seventh, G–Bb–Db–Fb (VII$^7$ in A-flat minor), which enharmonically spelled may become VII$^7$ of D minor (C#–E–G–Bb; see Example 14b). In similar fashion, one-step modulations may take advantage of the ambiguous chord of the raised fourth. For example, Vogler shows a connection from C-sharp major to A major in which the chords E–G#–B–D and Fb–Ab–Cb–D are interchangeable (Example 14c). Here the procedure may be interpreted as follows: from the tonic chord in D-flat major (the enharmonic equivalent of C-sharp major), it is but a short step to the chord of the raised fourth with added minor seventh in the key of A-flat major (D–Fb–Ab–Cb). Since this chord is the enharmonic equivalent

Example 14
Modulatory connections without
*Zwischenharmonie:* (a) D-flat major to
E-flat minor; (B) D-flat major to D
minor; (c) C-sharp major to A
major. (Chords in brackets added to
clarify enharmonic equivalents.)

of V⁷ in A (E–G♯–B–D), this single pivot has led us directly to our goal, the tonic chord in A major.

The demonstration of such direct connections between keys is important to Vogler's defense of his system and its capacities. He has determined that a single, cadential chord may represent a key; and he has also shown that his cadential harmonies bear the potential for *Mehrdeutigkeit*. Combined and put to work as in the examples witnessed above, these two propositions suffice to illustrate the diversity and coherence of the tonal language.

It is clear, however, that directness and economy need not be the only aims of a modulation. The practical art of changing keys (for the church organist, for example, or the opera composer) may involve elements of surprise, deception, or calculated digression from the expected path toward a modulatory goal. The progression may be bold or devious, but the pattern should nonetheless be grammatically logical and smoothly executed. There may be several steps, and each should follow convincingly from the last. The intermediate harmonies should be cadential, so that a sense of expectation is generated, and the rules for treatment of the different sevenths must be respected (a dominant seventh may be freely sounded, for instance, and may under certain conditions resolve upward).

Among the modulations illustrated in the *Betrachtungen* essay and in the *Handbuch,* some furnish the listener with readily perceptible clues to the direction of the harmony. In demonstrating a move from C major to G minor, Vogler immediately leads the E-natural in the soprano down to E-flat, thereby enabling the listener to anticipate a turn to the minor realm (Example 15a).[44] Comparable guideposts are found in more distant territory as well. The move from C major to B-flat minor involves gliding from the initial tonic to an intermediate zone of F minor (the parallel minor of a closely related key), which is then transformed to become a cadential harmony in the key of destination (V⁷ of B-flat minor; Example 15b).

Other examples—especially those that use the principle of *Mehrdeutig-keit*—prove more radical in exploring the potentials of chromatic harmony and the powers of cadential expectation. Typically, the departure from tonic to an intermediate cadential harmony leads the listener to expect a particular goal; but this destination is averted as the cadential chord is magically transformed to its enharmonic equivalent. The bewildered listener is thereby spirited to an unexpected, foreign terrain. The logic of the whole is perceived only in retrospect. Example 15c leads from V in C major to the cadential VII⁷ in D minor. Reinterpreted enharmonically (C♯–E–G–B♭ = G–B♭–D♭–F♭), this chord lands us suddenly in the distant key of A-flat minor. Even more devious is the path Vogler clears to lead from C minor to D major (Example 15d). The second beat progresses to the dominant of a closely related key (A-flat), which functions enharmonically as the chord of the raised fourth (♯IV⁷) in the key of G minor (E♭–G–B♭–D♭ = C♯–E♭–G–B♭). But now, instead of proceeding to the expected dominant of G minor, we slide, enharmonically and chromatically, to the dominant of its fifth, D minor. Finally, this dominant (A major) resolves not to the anticipated minor, but to D major instead.

Example 15
Modulatory paths between remotely
related keys: (a) C major to G
minor; (b) C major to B-flat minor;
(c) C major to A-flat minor; (d) C
minor to D major.

The chromatic progressions featured in these examples typically involve movement from cadential harmony in one key to cadential harmony in another. Successive keys are alluded to by harmonies that represent them without recourse to an intermediate tonic chord. A succession of cadential harmonies, bridging the gap between two keys, generates the sense of expectation that gives logic, continuity, and diversity to the progression. By exploiting this potential, Vogler has opened a virtually limitless realm of harmonic possibility.

## TEMPERAMENT

In identifying the resource of enharmonic equivalents and the manifold possibilities of modulation, Vogler has assumed a tempered scale that can accommodate all twenty-four major and minor keys. The exact nature of such a temperament he leaves unexamined in *Tonwissenschaft und Tonsezkunst,* but in the *Handbuch* he caps the exposition of his system by raising the issue and describing his own preferred concept of unequal temperament.

After introducing the question of temperament, he discredits mathematically calculated approaches such as those proposed by Marpurg and Kirnberger.[45] Logarithmic numbers can be appreciated only by the eye, not the ear, he declares; and the equalization of half steps within the octave results in a meaningless tonal neutrality. Adjustments must be made if the entire tonal spectrum is to be available on a keyboard instrument, but the compromise must not obliterate the individuality of different keys.

What does Vogler mean by the individuality of the keys, and how can it be preserved in a system of temperament? The artificial scale, as we have seen, is constructed from natural materials: the pure fifths C to G, G to D, and F to C; and the pure thirds C to E, G to B, and F to A. The minor scale introduces additional pure thirds (E-flat to G, A-flat to C, and B-flat to D), and the chromatic spectrum is completed by two additional half steps (C to D-flat, and F to G-flat). The twelve-tone scale thus assembled reveals the contrast between large and small half steps that Vogler has already exploited in distinguishing different sizes of minor seventh. The potential of this scale for making such distinctions was seen by the theorist as a resource bestowed by nature upon his system. This same resource yields a natural contrast in sound between one key and another when different tones are chosen as tonic.

However, the purely intoned intervals of the artificial scale will not only engender a difference in harmonic quality between chord functions in one key and the same functions in another; they will also cause such distortions in more remote keys as to render them useless.

Vogler's solution is to devise a compromise that favors those keys with fewer accidentals, while nevertheless making all keys available. This system has the result of preserving what Vogler regards as their natural character. His presentation of the procedure for procuring this "characteristic temperament" may be summarized as follows:[46]

1. Within the boundaries of the C octave, G is tuned as low as the ear will tolerate.

2. F, the fifth below the upper C, is correspondingly tuned as high as possible, so that a comparably narrow fifth results.

3. Within the smaller-than-perfect fifth from F to C, the major third A is tuned as high as possible; E is then tuned to make a comparably high third above C.

4. D is tuned to A to produce an interval that approximates the narrow fifths already obtained.

5. B is tuned to produce a comparably sized fifth with E, but at the same time a wide enough third with G.

The tones of the C-major scale having thus been adjusted, Vogler now proceeds with the remaining five notes. It is here that the quality of characteristic temperament arises. First, the F-sharp must be tuned high, so that the major third D–F♯ is comparable to the previously adjusted thirds, but not so high as would be necessary to make a perfect fourth with B. (In other words, the fourth F♯–B must be wide, just as the previously adjusted fifths are narrow.) The same procedure is then applied to C-sharp (high relative to the major third A below; low relative to the fourth F-sharp above), G-sharp, then D-sharp. Finally, B-flat is tuned as a high major third above F-sharp, and a wide fourth above F.

The net result of this procedure is a tempered chromatic scale in which the major thirds between white keys on the keyboard (e.g., C–E, F–A, and G–B) are wide and bright, as are the major thirds between white keys and black (A–C♯, D–F♯, E–G♯, and B–D♯). The major thirds between black keys and white, by contrast, are narrow and dark (e.g. D♭–F, E♭–G, and A♭–C). A corresponding contrast therefore emerges between the sharp and flat keys.

As explained in Vogler's early article "Ausdruck" for the *Deutsche Encyclopädie* (1779), major keys become more intense, penetrating, and make more of an impact as they ascend by fifth (G, D, A, E); but as they descend by fifth (F, B♭, E♭, A♭) their force diminishes, and they become duller and darker. The specific nature of individual keys is then considered in detail: "C is . . . perhaps the most appropriate key for a painting, for pure water arias, for pure subjects. G is already livelier, but surely not boisterous. [Representation of] naive subjects, especially of innocent pastoral pleasures, can be expressed more simply in this key than in the others. D ignites fire in the heart. Now the entire body is animated, the spirit soars to heroic deeds, is incited to bold, joyful, even rather exuberant songs of praise. Even the god of thunder has claims to this key. A is sharper yet: but since its compass does not [allow it to dominate] the middle [strings] of the violin, that is, as D dominates the middle strings D and A, it cannot serve as well as D to represent the boisterous. It depicts more successfully the fire of an amorous and thus tender passion than of an impetuous [passion]. E can depict fire best of all insofar as it catches the eye through the intensity of its most piercing flames. F serves for a dead calm; B-flat for dusk; E-flat for night; A-flat for Plutonian realms."[47]

In an essay of 1812 concerning an organ at the Neumünster in Würzburg, he supplemented these descriptions.[48] C was now described as majestic, full of gravity, splendid, and having little charm. G was seen as somewhat livelier, a favorite for pastorals and bright landscapes. D was much stronger, even noisy, a lively key suitable for pomp, bustle, sounds of war, and the like. A and E were both termed very penetrating, although A, while bright and luminous, was not as much so as E, whose sharp third, almost an A-flat, was very striking. B, F-sharp, and C-sharp were much stronger yet because of their high thirds, though they rarely occurred as a main key. On the flat side, F was perceived as calm, used in Gluck's *Orpheus* and Vogler's *Castore e Polluce* chiefly in association with the quiet joy of the happy shades in Elysium. B-flat was likewise seen as calm and pleasant, some of its special tenderness borrowed perhaps from E-flat, a key associated with depictions of night. A-flat was seen as blacker yet and almost more tender.

### THOROUGHBASS

With the discussion of characteristic temperament, Vogler brings to a close the exposition of his system in the *Handbuch*. The chain of deductions is complete, all elements having been accounted for. He is reluctant to conclude, however, without appending a final essay on a subject that had long been a preoccupation of his: the teaching and practice of thoroughbass. His intention in offering this appendix is both to put the antiquated tradition in its proper place—as a pupil's exercise—and to sound its death-knell as a convention of musical practice.

From Vogler's vantage point, the study of thoroughbass is not only devoid of any scientific basis, but it actually presupposes a complete knowledge of harmonic principles. Thus its proper place would indeed seem to be at the end of a course of theoretical study. Asserting that the traditional practice has outlived its usefulness, Vogler observes that in modern music the realization of figured basses has been made excessively difficult by fast tempos and complexity in harmony and part writing. As the organist scrambles to find his proper notes, he detracts from the music instead of contributing to its strength. How much more effective is a fully realized accompaniment, such as the one the author himself provided for his *Deutsche Kirchenmusik!*[49]

The theorist acknowledges that, however obsolescent the craft may be, competency in thoroughbass is still a requisite part of the modern musician's equipment. Allowing a single exercise of sixteen measures to suffice as an illustration of infractions and the steps necessary to avoid them, he offers four general rules: first, when a tone is common to successive chords, it should be held in the same voice; second, if a note sounded in one chord is to become a dissonance in the next, it must be held over in the same voice; third, each voice in the texture (but especially the two outermost voices) should form a coherent melodic line in and of itself; and finally, the performer should be wary of the basic part-writing violations, including cross-relations and parallel octaves and fifths as well as omitted or excessively doubled chord tones.[50] The other examples of thoroughbass technique which he supplies consist of model realizations of ascending and descending scales: major, minor, and chromatic.[51]

### CONCLUSION: THE HIERARCHY OF TONAL ORGANIZATION

Rejecting thoroughbass as a foundation, Vogler has chosen a method allegedly based on scientific principles. The natural resonance of a sounding string proves to him that the essence of modern harmony resides in the threefold unity of the major triad, represented by the proportions $1:1/3:1/5$. Through a chain of reasoning that develops from this principle of harmonic generation, he derives his natural and artificial scales, ten cadences, seven sevenths, eighteen intervals, twenty-four keys, and forty-four modulations from a given tonal center. The resources of the system are thus arrayed in a logical, hierarchic order, enabling one to reduce the greatest complexity in musical practice to the simplest triadic configuration.

In assembling his system, Vogler does not claim that either he or his Paduan mentor had actually discovered the scientific foundations upon which it rested. Indeed, he credits Rameau with the most important discovery of all: that the source of harmony is traceable to the mathematical and acoustical unity of the sounding string.[52] He regards this discovery as an all-important landmark in the advancement of musical knowledge; and in using Rameau's principle of harmonic generation, his theory bears close resemblance to those of the French master and his followers. Yet there is a difference that sets Vogler's method apart: it lies in the particular nature of the chain of deductions he adopts in attempting to fashion a connection between theoretical principle and practice.

In clarifying his own stance by comparison with those of his predecessors and contemporaries, Vogler calls attention to basic flaws in the French approach that doom it to failure as a practical guide to musical understanding. He observes, for example, that Rameau's system is unable to acknowledge the full legitimacy of a minor triad with added seventh built on the second scale degree ($II^7$ in major). Since the French theorist insisted that only a major triad could be fundamental, he invented the anomalous *sixte ajoutée,* by which the chord F–A–C–D would claim F rather than D as its root. The note D is thus understood as an added dissonance. But wherein lies its dissonant quality? Not only in customary practice, but in Rameau's own examples, this added sixth enjoys all the privileges of a sovereign consonance, requiring neither preparation nor resolution. This single example, Vogler tells us, suffices to reveal the weakness that undermines the French master's system.[53]

Kirnberger's concept of the fundamental bass can be comparably faulted, Vogler suggests, in its failure to accept a chord built on a diminished fifth. According to Vogler's theory, the VII chord with added seventh in C major (B–D–F–A) is understood as a fundamental triad with a cadential minor seventh that may be freely sounded in accordance with the theory of sevenths. But Kirnberger's theory requires that the chord be interpreted as an incomplete dominant ninth (G–B–D–F–A) whose root is missing. Here the older theorist contradicts himself, Vogler claims, for if A is indeed a ninth, then it must be suitably prepared as a consonance in accordance with Kirnberger's own rules. And yet Kirnberger has no hesitation in allowing this note to be freely sounded as a minor seventh.[54]

The essence of Vogler's criticism is that, by adhering to their fundamental bass as sole point of reference, Rameau and Kirnberger are obliged to sacrifice a basic musical consideration—the context of the part writing—as a factor that may determine the function of a chord. According to their theories, each vertical sonority must provide its own acoustical justification, quite apart from its place in the linear flow of the voice leading. In Example 16a, the note C quite obviously appears as a consonance at *x,* sounds as a dissonance at *y,* and resolves downward by step at *z.* But according to Rameau, the C in question must be interpreted as a consonant note, i.e., the fifth of the fundamental triad F–A–C. The freely sounded D is then labeled as

Example 16
(a) The dissonant note C, prepared
at *x*, sounded at *y*, resolved at *z*; (b)
the note A as a freely sounded
seventh above B.

a dissonance, the infamous *sixte ajoutée*. In Example 16b, the note A is manifestly a cadential seventh above the root B. Yet according to Kirnberger, the legitimate root of this chord is the implied dominant, G. The A would therefore have to be labeled, unacceptably, as a freely sounded ninth.

How has Vogler's system saved him from such alleged pitfalls? By proposing his own brand of deduction, each principle forming a basis for the next, he has enabled his system to use the scale, rather than the more fundamental principle of harmonic generation, as a point of reference in building chords. Whereas other fundamental-bass theorists must look for a hypothetically perfect triad as the root of any vertical sonority, Vogler's method permits him to build a nominally consonant triad on any degree of the scale, including the acoustically groundless raised fourth and seventh degrees.

With the system thus liberated from the tyranny of the perfect triad, determination of the root of the chord and the function of its tones becomes a simple matter. The nominally consonant members of the triad are those which are freely sounded, whereas the dissonances (whether non-cadential seventh, ninth, eleventh, or thirteenth) are those which are duly prepared and resolved as such.

Vogler would perhaps have said that, in their challenge to the thoroughbass tradition, Rameau and his followers had gone too far. The laws of harmonic generation and inversion had banished the confusion inherent in reckoning harmony from the bass line, yet in doing so they caused a breach between theoretical basis and the manifestly musical considerations of context and voice leading. For the thoroughbass theorists, the matter of context had been of utmost importance. It was the vital element by which the pupil could gain access to a workable understanding of musical grammar,[55] and it was precisely this element that Vogler would attempt to incorporate, with remarkable results, into his system.

Vogler's opposition to thoroughbass methods resides not in their emphasis on voice leading, but rather in their insistence on looking to the bass line, rather than the chord roots, as the foundation for their rules. By mastering thoroughbass, as Vogler himself attempted to do in his student years, the pupil can gain a glimmer of insight into the role of voice leading in the grammar of harmony—the interplay of consonance and dissonance that animates the underlying harmonic order—but he learns nothing of the rational foundations on which that order rests.

Vogler's solution is to combine the principal advantages of fundamental-bass and thoroughbass approaches in his own system of reduction. As in a rigorous fundamental-bass system, the root of the chord is the foundation of the harmony, regardless of which note lies in the bass. But Vogler's notion of what constitutes the root of a chord is quite different from Rameau's: it is a scale degree, pure and simple, regardless of the quality of its third or fifth, and its location is determined by the context of the voice leading in accordance with the system of reduction.

The stable basis of Vogler's system, then, is not the perfect triad on one hand, nor the bass line on the other, but the tonal center represented by a scale. For Vogler, any given sonority may be explained in terms of its relationship to a scale-degree root within a key. By virtue of this proposal, he succeeds in drawing a direct line from the elaborated surface of a musical texture to a tonal center, represented by a scale and the triads built upon any of its degrees. More remote relationships are then perceived as embellishments or elaborations of these secondary centers.

If we search for the essence of this dual process of elaboration and reduction, we find that it lies in the structural significance of the fifth, the first tone to proceed from the sounding string after the octave, and the constructive element from which the artificial scale is assembled. As Vogler pursues the ramifications of his theory he discovers that it assigns special importance to this cadential, key-defining interval, and that the fifth plays a primary role in governing the equilibrium that must prevail between unity and diversity. According to his notion of the tonal realm, diversity has to do with building new relationships from an established foundation; unity has to do with preserving the sense of hierarchic order by which diversity must be harnessed. A cadential progression (such as V–I or I–V) promotes tonal unity. But as Vogler suggests in an essay in *Betrachtungen,* the structural formula may be embellished with intervening harmonies. A cadential progression such as F–C in F major or A–E in A minor may be modified to embrace an interpolated root, for example F–D–C, or A–F–E. In either instance, "an embellishing harmony is inserted at the very place where the decisive cadential [chord] should have stood," and the cadential function of the underlying fifth progression is retained.[56]

The principle applies on higher levels of the structural hierarchy as well: "Between C and C, with which I wish to begin and end, an intermediate element must be introduced in order for something to be expressed: as long as we hear only C, nothing has been determined. This intermediate harmony must indeed be the most closely related, either F or G."[57] The unified scheme may be adorned by an intervening modulation, just as a cadential progression may be elaborated by an intervening harmony. "[One composer], for instance, begins his piece in C, then goes to G, according to the strictest rules of tonal succession. But this is so dull—so commonplace. Then comes another, who also heeds the rules but knows how to insert such unexpected digressions, slipping away quite unnoticed into D minor before establishing G."[58] In the instance the theorist describes, a hypothetical modulation to II serves to embellish the structurally predominant move from tonic to V.

Through interpretations such as these, Vogler finds that he is able to derive all musical diversity from the unity of a single sounding string, and to formulate a concept of tonality based on the fifth relationship and the diatonic scale. As we shall see in the next chapter, this interval of the fifth eventually acquires an almost magical property as the essential unity-in-diversity of musical expression. Retaining its identity as a relationship between tonalities, keys within a movement, chords, or tones, it imposes itself as the fundamental organizing force that resides ultimately in the sounding string and its resonating third partial.

It was only gradually, however, that Vogler realized such consequences of his theory. In *Tonwissenschaft und Tonsezkunst,* the implications of the newly assembled system remained largely unexamined. Yet the author had much confidence in the efficacy of his method, having reduced the materials of composition to a finite, hierarchically structured repertory of resources, each with naturally ordained functions but with unlimited potentials. He saw his system as a bold and necessary reform at a time when modern musical practice had left existing pedagogical methods far behind. Mannheim of the 1770s was witnessing an ascent to new heights of technique and expression in operatic, symphonic, and sacred music. To gain dominion over territories being explored, the amateur, the critic, and the aspiring composer must abandon antiquated methods and follow the light of reason. This was the unshakable conviction that guided the theorist as he set about to present his system and explore its consequences.

## CHAPTER 2

# Harmonic Analysis
# and the Principle of
# Reduction

THE eighteenth-century rationalists, including Rameau, Vallotti, and their followers, had various traits in common in reducing the study of harmony to natural principles. Through numerical demonstrations and observations involving a sounding string, they obtained a perfect triad and proposed the concept of the fundamental bass. Though formulations of the idea differed from one theorist to another, most agreed on the essential purpose of their fundamental-bass systems: to bestow order on the study of harmony and voice leading by reducing a given musical fabric to a logically ordered succession of triadic chord roots. The teaching of musical grammar, previously a tedious and complicated task, was rendered simple with the new approach. Instead of a multiplicity of empirical and sometimes contradictory rules, this rational method offered a single principle—the natural, perfect triad and the relationships it embodied—as the foundation of harmonic organization.

Naturally, theories based on such a premise bore implications beyond the reduction of vertical sonorities to their roots. The sounding body, or the string on which mathematical operations are performed, constitutes a point of origin from which deductions are drawn to obtain the elements of harmony. The delimiting octave, the structurally preeminent fifth, and the third necessary to complete the triad are understood as primal materials. However the theorist may proceed from here, a single source has been identified, an all-embracing unity from which musical diversity arises, and to which all diversity may ultimately be traced.

In other words, a hierarchic tonal order is assumed. Within its framework, a designated tonic (representing the natural, perfect triad) reigns supreme. Far-reaching tonal excursions are subsumed by relationships closer to the tonic, and these, in turn, are subsumed by the tonic itself.

Such rationally inspired concepts of tonal unity were common property among eighteenth-century theorists, but they generally occupied little space in their treatises, whose main purpose, by and large, was to clarify the grammar of consonance and dissonance, chord structure, and voice leading. Vogler himself, in his handbook of 1776, offered little more than the standard criteria for tonal unity and the routine admonitions against stepping beyond its bounds.

Yet Vogler's formal treatises represented only a fraction of his theoretical output. As a whole, his efforts were dominated not by expositions of principle but by projects in analysis and criticism that attempted to put theoretical principles to practical use. In these experimental writings, uninhibited by the constraints of a formal treatise, the theorist took up the challenge of proving a basic assertion: that musical elaboration, no matter how far reaching or complex, could be encompassed within the hierarchic order of his system and reduced to its fundamental principles. The ultimate justification of his system lay in its efficacy as a basis for analysis; and in the course of his analytical inquiries, hierarchic order and tonal coherence emerged as issues of central importance.

The idea of using harmonic analysis as a pedagogical tool was by no means Vogler's invention. Rameau had supplied fundamental basses to samples of Lully's music as well as his own;[1] Kirnberger incorporated his harmonic analysis of a fugue in the first volume of *Die Kunst des reinen Satzes in der Musik* (1771); and Kirnberger's pupil, J. A. P. Schulz, included two analyses from Bach's *Well-Tempered Clavier* in *Die wahren Grundsätze zum Gebrauch der Harmonie* (1773).[2] Vogler nevertheless stands out as a major and hitherto unrecognized pioneer in this field. The very scope of his explorations, spanning the three volumes of *Betrachtungen* and more than half a dozen publications from his later years, was unprecedented. But more significant than the sheer volume and variety of his analyses was their penetrating substance. Not content with the labeling of chord roots and dissonances, he advanced into virtually uncharted territory by attempting to explain the structural and expressive significance of tonal hierarchies, harmonic elaborations, and the tensional relationship of unity and diversity that he discerned in the musical idioms of his day.

To appreciate this aspect of Vogler's teachings, it should be noted that few writers of the time so actively combined the career of theorist and teacher with that of composer and practical musician. Professing to have little use for speculation as an end in itself, he aimed to place matters of application foremost in his teachings. Though Mozart scorned *Tonwissenschaft und Tonsezkunst* as a book more appropriate for learning arithmetic than music,[3] calculations actually occupy far fewer pages in his writings than in those of most rationally inclined contemporaries and predecessors. He had absolute faith in his theoretical principles, and his rationalism was as uncomplicated as it was ardent. Its purpose was not to display erudition but to promote understanding and reform in musical practice: to bestow enlightenment on the amateur, guide the fledgling composer toward mastery of his art, and render the ideal of a musical order in tune with natural law universally accessible. These were aims that could be only partially accomplished by treatises and composition manuals. More on the order of a celebration than a lesson in harmony, the essence of Vogler's message was such that it could sooner be imparted in song than through the admonitions of a textbook. Indeed, his compositional output includes major works whose inspiration stems directly from the theorist's mission in communicating his vision of a harmonious tonal universe.

Such a composition is his *Trichordium und Trias Harmonica,* a festive setting of a poem by August Gottlieb Meissner, "Lob der Harmonie," (In Praise of Harmony) for four vocal soloists, chorus, and orchestra.[4] In a preface to the published score, the composer describes aspects of his intentions with characteristic humor, naiveté, and earnestness of purpose. He borrows a special theme for his basic material, a melody by Jean-Jacques Rousseau (*Comme le jour me dure*) which uses only three different pitches,[5] and thereby furnishes himself with the vehicle for a musical message and a program (see Example 1).

Though he admires the melody's simplicity, Vogler suggests that Rousseau erred by implying that such a tune could exist independently of harmony.[6] Drawing an analogy first invoked in *Betrachtungen,* he proposes that the ear perceives a melody the way the eye perceives a burning coal spun around in the dark on a tether. Just as the spectator sees a perfect circle, so the listener comprehends a complete harmony.[7] All tones of this harmony need not be present (the image of a half moon implies the form of a circle) in order for the essential truth of this comparison to hold: that any melody may be understood as a constituent part of a harmonious whole.

Example 1
Rousseau's three-note melody, as
borrowed by Vogler for *Trichordium
und Trias Harmonica* and set to
Meissner's text.

But contrary to Vogler's assertion, Rousseau had insisted on the supremacy of melody. In this respect Vogler viewed him as a philosophical opponent; and to prove him wrong, he forged an alliance between the Frenchman's melody and the natural harmony from which it must have sprung. With the addition of Meissner's text, a metaphorical triad of melodist, harmonist, and poet materializes, the efforts of each contributing to the union proclaimed by the title: "Trichordium" and "Trias Harmonica."

At the outset two horns intone the theme, the three-note melody in the first horn accompanied by the simple purity of root, third, fifth, and octave in the second. Soprano and alto soloists now take up the theme, moving in parallel thirds and sixths; and when tenor and bass enter for the word "Harmonie," fully formed chords become manifest simultaneously in word and song.

Subsequent stanzas unfold in the manner of variations on a theme. Each retains the three-note melody intact; only in a minor-mode verse does the third note appear as the minor scale degree rather than the major. Otherwise, diversity arises solely through the accompanying parts, which progress from the elemental harmonic outline of the opening to a complex intertwining of contrapuntal, chromatically inflected lines. The spectrum of colors expands from the initial monochrome to a kaleidoscopic array of orchestral color, and the range of dynamics spans the gamut from whispered echo to thunderous declamation. Increasing variety in rhythm likewise comes into play, enhancing the impression of an immense diversity incorporated within the design.

In its role as the source of this edifice, Rousseau's three-note melody serves not only as a melodic agent, but also as the emblem of a harmonic foundation. The notes involved, comprising the first three degrees of a scale, suggest the relationship of tonic harmony and fifth, and in accordance with Vogler's theory, this relationship of two primary chords embodies the essence of tonal organization. It acts as the generative force from which elaborations proceed as a composition runs its course. In this particular work, the elaborations become increasingly varied from one stanza to the next. The piece thus embodies a process of growth from a simple kernel to a grandiose display of musical variety. By virtue of this plan, *Trichordium* exemplifies a musical hierarchy. And the demonstration of connection between unity and diversity is rendered all the more distinct by the fact that both the melody and the harmonic foundation it implies persist in the foreground throughout.

A work like *Trichordium* reflects the composer's perception of an eternally valid order on which his system is based. At its heart lie the elementary materials inherent in a sounding string, the triad and fifth relationship: they give rise to harmony and the phenomenon of a coherent musical process unfolding in time. The utter simplicity of this order accounts for the potential strength of tonal organization, its ability to exert control over diverse elaborations, and its capacity to affect the sensibilities of a sympathetic listener. As represented in *Trichordium,* musical diversity is virtually limitless, and its powers of expression derive from the connection to an overriding unity which prevails in accordance with natural law.

In the attempt to explain musical organization in terms of tonal unity and diversity, Vogler's preferred method involved the analysis of exemplary compositions. The early *Betrachtungen der Mannheimer Tonschule* (1778–81) provided a vehicle for some ambitions and extensive explorations in this domain.[8]

### ANALYSES IN THE *BETRACHTUNGEN DER MANNHEIMER TONSCHULE*

Encompassing a wide variety of styles and genres, the works selected for discussion included no fewer than forty compositions, many with multiple movements. Most were published in their entirety in accompanying fascicles of music, entitled *Gegenstände der Betrachtungen*. This repertory of pieces furnished material for commentaries that extended to matters of taste, expression, and style; but the explanation of harmonic organization was the author's chief concern, and some kind of harmonic analysis, whether of chord roots or larger patterns, appears in virtually all the discussions. In several instances, most prominently in the first volume, analysis entails a comprehensive account of materials and interrelationships, including the reduction of entire movements to their constituent chord roots and key areas. Among these studies is one which attempts to explain every note of a piece in terms of its contribution to the diversified unity of the whole.

The piece in question, the *andantino* second movement from one of the theorist's own accompanied sonatas,[9] is designed as a theme with three variations. Cast in a symmetrical binary form, the G-major theme divides into two eight-measure periods, each of which comprises a pair of four-measure phrases. The economy of the plan is such that the second phrase of the second period duplicates that of the first. The parts may therefore be labeled

$$\|\!: \quad A \quad B \quad :\|\!: \quad C \quad B \quad :\|\ .$$

Each of the variations retains the phrase division and the basic harmonic plan of the theme, and this element of consistency suggests to the author the possibility of reducing the entire composition to a single diagram. Occupying a large sheet, folded several times and bound within the fascicle, the diagram is divided into ten columns representing ten different measures (i.e., the content of the four-measure phrases A, B, and C, minus the first two measures of B, which duplicate those of A). In each column, vertically arrayed boxes show the content of each measure of the theme and the corresponding measures of the variations (the diagram for variation 2, in the minor mode, occupies the reverse side of the sheet). Inside each box, letter names, figured-bass symbols, and various abbreviations serve to explain the function of each pitch involved. At the bottom of each column, in large type, Vogler displays the roots of the chords—the harmonic foundation on which the elaborations are based. With evident pride in the ingenuity of his scheme, he observes that the essential difference between diagram and notated score lies in the fact that the latter merely conveys the notes, whereas the former specifies their function as well. By way of illustration, the example below

Example 2
Vogler's theme and variations,
measures 1–4, with his analysis of
measure 1.

Part I: first measure

|  |  |  |  |  | PT |  | PTs |  |  |
|---|---|---|---|---|---|---|---|---|---|
| violin: | *d* | *g* | *b* | *a* | *g* | *f♯* | *e* | *d* |  |
|  | 5 | 8 | 3 |  | 8 |  |  | 5 |  |
| keyboard   RH: | *g* |  |  | *a* | *b* |  | *b* |  |  |
|  | − |  |  | − | − |  | − |  |  |
|  | 8 |  |  | PT | 3 |  | 3 |  |  |
| LH: | 5 |  |  |  |  |  | 6 |  |  |
|  | 3 |  |  |  |  |  | 3 |  |  |
|  | *g* |  |  |  |  |  | *b* |  |  |
| chord roots: | G |  |  |  |  |  |  |  |  |

shows the theme, measures 1–4, and the analysis for the first measure as represented in the diagram.

It can be seen at a glance how the theorist takes pains to represent the content of his piece: the register for every pitch is specified, each bass note is supplied with the appropriate figured-bass symbol, and the numbers adorning letter names in the upper parts identify chord tones of the underlying triad. The additional abbreviations identify dissonances, which (apart from the disregarded turn embellishment) include merely three passing tones in the violin part and one in the keyboard. As it accounts for these various details, the diagram reduces the harmonic structure of the movement to the series of chord roots displayed at the base of each column. On this level, the usefulness of the diagram ends, since it offers no means of explaining relationships among the designated chord roots. Analysis of higher structural levels is thus relegated to the explanatory text, where the author begins by summarizing the phrase structure and constituent chords as follows (letter names designate chord roots, while vertical strokes represent the bar lines).

First part

G | A  D | G  C♯ | D |
G | A  D | G  D  | G |

Second part

D G | D  G | D  G | D |
  G | A  D | G  D | G |

Aligning the analysis of chord roots and phrases in this manner facilitates comparison of these four structural units and their punctuating cadences. Vogler points out that three types of close are involved: the decisive cadence from fifth degree to first that ends both main parts (D–G), the less decisive succession from first to fifth (G–D) that concludes the third phrase, and the ambiguous cadence at the end of the first phrase, C♯–D, which could be interpreted either as seventh degree to tonic in D or raised fourth to fifth in G.

Commenting on this last-mentioned cadence, Vogler indicates that, given the context in which it occurs, a decisive close in the key of the fifth (i.e., chord roots A–D instead of C♯–D) would be out of place. Since the process of change in key that the stronger progression suggests requires more room than this four-measure span allows, the gentler, less decisive cadence C♯–D makes a better choice. In effect, the triad on C-sharp functions as a leading-tone chord. Lightly tonicizing the fifth scale degree, it designates the fifth as an intermediate goal. Yet at the same time it retains its identity as the triad of the raised fourth degree.

With regard to relationships in the second part, the theorist observes that its first half (phrase C) consists wholly of fluctuation between tonic and fifth, the latter harmony temporarily enjoying the stronger metrical position. In effect, these two most closely related chords remain poised in equilibrium, yielding a pattern that is finally broken by the half cadence G–D, and the recurrence of the B phrase with which the theme ends.

From the description offered, the reader gains a sense of the diversified unity that characterizes the theme. The first half involves departure from tonic to fifth and return; the second half starts by wavering between tonic and fifth, and the closing phrase of the second half duplicates that of the first. Harmonic resources are used sparingly, and the hierarchic order is clear: tonic prevails over its fifth, which comes to the fore by way of a fleeting tonicization in measure 4 and the fluctuating harmonies of the second half; the C-sharp chord adorns the dominant, and the only other chord in question is the A-minor triad of measures 2, 6, and 14, which stands between tonic and fifth in each instance.

Since the pattern of chord roots and phrasing heard in the theme repeats in each of the variations (except for alterations of detail when the key shifts to minor), Vogler's explanation combines with his diagram to yield a comprehensive view of the whole. All notes are explained as part of a hierarchic design, and the analysis thus succeeds in linking the smallest details with the large-scale harmonic framework. Dissonances, arpeggiations, and inversions are interpreted as elaborations of the chord roots, and the chord roots themselves are embraced within a unified plan that controls the theme and each variation.

The analysis of Vogler's theme and variations neatly illustrates the principle of reduction as expounded in *Betrachtungen*. But because of its small dimensions, structural simplicity, and elementary vocabulary of harmony and embellishment, such a piece scarcely challenges the system's potential for explaining musical organization. In discussing longer, more complex works, the theorist does not attempt to provide comprehensive chord analyses or reductive diagrams. Nevertheless, he does adhere to the idea of multi-level reduction, and whatever he sacrifices in thoroughness he redeems with the incisiveness and penetration of his analysis on one structural level or another.

On the lowest level of the hierarchy portrayed, surface elaborations call for application of the reduction-system and the analysis of embellishments above a sustained chord root. Formulas involving the cadential $\frac{6}{4}$, for example, though absent from the miniature theme and variations movement, are virtually ubiquitous among larger model works. In those instances in which the $\frac{6}{4}$ is prepared by the preceding chord, Vogler is able to analyze this configuration not as a second-inversion tonic chord but rather the adorning of a dominant root with suspensions, the eleventh and thirteenth. Calling attention to such a pattern in discussing a D-minor symphony by the young Mannheimer Peter Winter, he explains that the chord outlined in the latter

Example 3
Peter Winter, Symphony in D
minor, third movement, measures
82–87 (wind parts omitted).

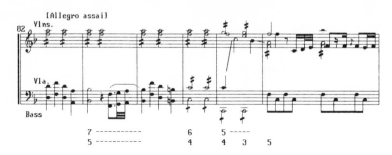

part of the third measure in Example 3 (the triad B–D–F adorned with the seventh, A), progresses to the sonority C–F–A in which the F and A must be understood as a dissonant eleventh and thirteenth, respectively, the latter prepared by a lesser dissonance (the preceding A as seventh), and resolved down by step to G in the measure that follows.[10]

He goes on to observe that if the $^6_4$ in question were interpreted as a tonic triad in second inversion, the preceding A would have been transformed from a dissonant seventh into a consonance instead of being properly resolved. Thus, according to Vogler's method, the single chord root C must span the fourth and fifth measures of the quoted excerpt; and the effect of the $^6_4$ is to withhold consonant tones of a dominant chord, C–E–G.

The ability of this approach to accommodate flexibility and expansion may be seen in the analysis of a passage from the allegro of Vogler's overture to Shakespeare's *Hamlet*.[11]

Starting at measure 66, a series of soaring scale lines in the first violin adorns the approach to the cadence in measure 71. Heard in isolation from the surrounding context, the span from measure 64 to the third beat of measure 70 resounds continuously with the chord and scale of B-flat, so that B-flat would appear to be the controlling chord root. A broader view of the passage, however, suggests that these bars all constitute an elongated, cadential $^6_4$, dramatized and embellished, but otherwise not unlike the example cited from the third movement of Winter's symphony. Indeed, the diagram offered in the text clearly implies such an interpretation.

In a succinct commentary on this passage, the author suggests that, while the dissonant B-flat of measure 62 appears to become a consonance without

Example 4
Vogler, Overture to *Hamlet*,
measures 61–71 (wind parts
omitted).

## Example 5
### *Betrachtungen* analysis of the
### Overture to *Hamlet*, measures
### 61–70.

| | 61 | 62 | 63 | 64–67 | 68 | 69 | 70 |
|---|---|---|---|---|---|---|---|
| | | 6 | 6 | 13 | 13  12  6  5 | 6 | 6   [5] |
| | 3b | 6 | 5 | 7b  11 | 11  10  4  3 | 4 | 4   3 |
| bass line: | G | D | Eb | E | F | F | F |
| | | | 7 | | | | |
| | | | 3b | | | | |
| chord roots: | G | Bb | C | E | F | F   [Bb]  F | Bb | Bb   F |

resolving, it may be observed that "after prolonged delay" ("nach langem Zaudern"), it does eventually resolve downward in evident obedience to the rule (measure 68). By this interpretation, the B-flat and the D (by association) function as dissonant eleventh and thirteenth, suspended over the sustained chord root F.

By helping to identify an essential source of tension in this passage—the drawn-out suspensions above the dominant chord root—this analysis demonstrates the potential of Vogler's system for explaining harmonic embellishment and elaboration. But the analysis betrays limitations of the method as well, for according to the analytical diagram, the spell of the dissonant ♮ is broken by the second beat of measure 68, where the eleventh and thirteenth resolve. Therefore, on beat 3 (in the absence of any preparatory suspension) the dissonant ♮ becomes a consonant ♮, and in the following measure, the root is designated as B-flat, not F. Surely the sense of a cadential ♮ persists (as the description of the passage implies), but the system requires that such dissonances be prepared. Once the dissonant notes have been resolved, the theorist has no choice but to analyze the ♮ as a second-inversion tonic triad!

Beyond the question of chord-root and dissonance analysis, reductive procedures found elsewhere in *Betrachtungen* follow a course basically similar to that witnessed in the theme and variations. But within the small dimensions of that initial example, relationships among chords involved nothing more elaborate than a passing tonicization of the fifth scale degree before reaffirmation of tonic. With more extended pieces, the system faces steeper challenges in the attempt to explain connections between patterns of harmonic elaboration and the overall unity of a composition.

Addressing this issue in various contexts, Vogler emphasizes his premise that an underlying framework of departure and return must feature the closest relationships to the main center: those that lie a fifth above or below.[12] If other key centers are incorporated, they must be accounted for as subordinate members. Under certain circumstances a subordinate key may impose itself as an intruder, in which case modulation becomes an act of usurpation: according to basic principles of the system, every tone, by virtue of its resonating partials, bears the potential to function as a tonic, subjugating other tones in its vicinity as it forms its own circle of relationships. When this happens in the course of a passage, the prevailing, higher-level tonic is temporarily canceled or displaced.[13]

In the *Hamlet* overture, the elaborately prepared cadence in B-flat was a major structural goal: the arrival in the key of the fifth after departure from tonic. But movement from tonic to fifth did not take place directly. Following the initial phrases in tonic, a modulatory passage touched briefly on G minor. Describing this turn to a subordinate key at measure 60, the author writes: "Since one assumes that B-flat must follow as the tonic, the progression achieves a splendid turn, [when] the cadential dominant of G minor, with a major third, perfect fifth, and seventh, appears in place of the anticipated tonic." A tonal inflection (*Nebenentwischung*) transpires as the G-minor chord appears in measure 61, but this tonicized scale degree "immediately relinquishes the field to its rightful possessor, B-flat."[14]

In the foregoing passage, allusion is made to a favorite Vogler metaphor, the struggle for territory.[15] Such a contest must be decisive, if only momentarily; otherwise tonal confusion results. And it is for this reason, incidentally, that Vogler forbids the immediate succession of two major or minor triads a step apart (for example, the major triads F and G). Neither is subordinate to the other, both merit equal claim to the status of tonic, and a tonal deadlock ensues. Only if the context clarifies their subordination to a third tone (C, for example) can the juxtaposition be condoned.[16] In the passage in question from the *Hamlet* overture, G minor (understood in retrospect as the sixth degree of B-flat) interferes at measure 61. Acquiring its own dominant and a metrically strong position, it displaces B-flat for an instant before that key is affirmed as the structurally preeminent center.

Such tonal contests normally engage only closely related keys. In accordance with the dictates of *Tonsezkunst,* a sense of tonal unity is lost once the boundary between close and remote relations is overstepped. The available tones that may temporarily claim territory as tonics are limited to the scale degrees that bear a perfect fifth (i.e., all but the seventh degree in major and the second in minor). Modulation is thus equated with the tonicization of scale steps. Indeed, even though the overriding center is temporarily supplanted, the new tonic must keep its identity as a scale degree. In effect, a tonally unified composition contains no modulation at all (in the sense of decisive removal from the realm of tonic), since a perceptible relationship to an all-embracing key center must always be retained.[17]

Elaborating this concept in the third volume of *Betrachtungen,* Vogler takes pains to distinguish between the terms *Übergang,* which applies to movement among closely related keys, and *Ausweichung,* which has to do with the connection among remote centers. *Ausweichung,* he asserts, is principally a concern of the church organist, who must devise connecting links between pieces in different keys.[18] (Curiously, Vogler does not maintain this terminological distinction elsewhere. He generally prefers the term *Ausweichung* for all instances in which one tonic replaces another, regardless of how long the span in question.)[19]

Do Vogler's assertions mean that remote centers are to be excluded altogether? Although the injunction does apply with few exceptions to music found in the *Betrachtungen,* the theorist acknowledges the possible acceptability of tonal digressions.[20] In the slow movement of Winter's symphony, an instance of apparent digression occurs in the course of transition from tonic (F major) to the key of the fifth.[21] Within this relatively compact binary form of sixty-four measures, the first part comprises three periods, the second of which involves tonal change. After analyzing the chord roots of this mediating period as follows,

$$
\begin{array}{ccccccccc}
 & & & & 7 & & & & \\
 & & & & 3\natural & & & 3\natural & [3\natural] \\
F & | & F & | & C & | & C & | & G & | & C & | & D & | & D & | & G
\end{array}
$$

he declares that "one must not regard the major third F-sharp above D and the tonicized chord of G major as an aberration, as if this modulation contradicted the unity of the tonic F; for this momentary digression is sufficiently justified by the resolution of the [dissonant note] F as the seventh of the chord

G, [which functions as] the fifth of the tonic C."[22] The tonicized G major, in other words, is justified as a dominant of the dominant in the period that follows, where the key of the fifth, C, asserts structural predominance.

A comparable circumstance arises in the first movement of an accompanied sonata by another pupil, Wilhelm Freiherr von Kerpen.[23] The passage in question, a figural transition phrase within the first part, reaffirms the dominant key, C major. In its course, the composer extends a D-major chord for an entire measure through arpeggio and scalar activity, then extends a G-major chord with similar figuration in the measure that follows. This bold and fiery progression, the author observes, hovers on the borderline of aberration ("am Rande der Ausschweifung"). However, since both the D- and G-major chords are supplied with their dominant sevenths, the entire pattern may be interpreted as part of a unified scheme: F is the tonic, he explains; C is its fifth, and G is the fifth of C. Within this scheme, D, with its seventh, appears momentarily as the fifth of G.

In a notable instance, the theorist himself decisively oversteps the border of normal procedure in a passage that constitutes a true digression. This occurs in a *Rondo alla polacca* that forms the final movement of a miniature concerto for keyboard, the second in a set of six such works discussed in the second volume of the *Betrachtungen*. Following an extended episode, the opening phrase of the refrain is announced. But after coming to a half cadence on F, the fifth of the tonic B-flat, the anticipated refrain dissolves into a sequentially developed thematic motive accompanied by a rising chromatic scale in the bass.

Vogler declines to comment in detail on the dozen measures of chromatic extravagance that follow the half cadence (see Example 6). Leading the way to a cadenza, this passage constitutes a kind of parenthesis in the course of the movement. The analysis provided for these measures employs symbols for bass line and figured bass only. By omitting mention of any chord roots, Vogler suggests that the harmony involves a purely linear elaboration, with no harmony of structural importance occurring between the two dominant chord roots that frame the chromatic scale.[24]

Although this digression is especially extravagant, the justification for its occurrence is typical: within the unified structure that prevails, it constitutes a mere embellishment. A natural order, embodied within the system and reflected in a work conceived according to its principles, designates a single tonic as a central unifying force, whence a virtually limitless array of elaborations may proceed.

# Example 6
## (a) Vogler, Concerto No. 2 in B-flat, second movement, measures 73–89;
## (b) Vogler's analysis.

| | 73 | 74 | 75 | 76 | 77 | 78 | 79 | 80 | 81 | 82 | 83 | 84 | 85 | 86 | 87 | 88 | 89 |
|---|---|---|---|---|---|---|---|---|---|---|---|---|---|---|---|---|---|
| | | | | | | 7 | 7 | | | | | | | | | | |
| | | 6 | 7♭ | 7♭ | 6♭ | 5♯ | 5[♯] | 6 | 7 | 7 | 6 | | | | 6 | | 6 |
| | 7 | 4 | 5 | 5 | 4 | 3♯ | 3[♯] | 4[♯] | 3[♯] | 3[♯] | 4 | 7 | 7 | 3 | 4 | 7 | 4 |
| bass line: | F♯ | G | A♭ | A | B♭ | B | B♯ | C♯ | D | D♯ | E | F | F♯ | G | F | E | F |

preparation for
the cadenza

As Vogler explores the consequences of his system through the analyses in *Betrachtungen,* his original dichotomy between *Tonwissenschaft* and *Tonsezkunst* becomes obsolete. As set forth in the 1776 manual, this separation of the science of harmony from the art of composition perpetuated a customary distinction between theoretical speculation and prescriptions for practice. In the *Betrachtungen,* Vogler finds instead that musical analysis, pursued according to the idea of a structural hierarchy, supplants prescription as a vehicle for musical enlightenment. In this respect the Mannheim serial foreshadows the structure of the later, more definitive *Harmonielehre,* which proposes a single chain of deductions reaching from fundamental principle to the furthest regions of musical diversity.

To some extent, however, the constraints of *Tonsezkunst* persist in *Betrachtungen,* as witnessed in the rather limited approach to the concept of a hierarchy of structure and embellishment found in the analyses. The cadential $^6_4$, for example, required preparation of the dissonances if they were to be interpreted as such, and the rule prohibiting remote relationships (including even the change of mode from major to minor or the reverse) appeared to exclude practices well on their way toward common usage by the 1780s.

In the *Handbuch zur Harmonielehre,* by contrast, restrictions evident in *Tonwissenschaft und Tonsezkunst* are substantially loosened. The domain of surface embellishment has been expanded, and injunctions regarding tonal unity are overshadowed by an emphasis on the possibilities for executing modulations among all the keys. In effect, the structure of the *Handbuch* bespeaks a change of outlook traceable to *Betrachtungen* and other earlier writings. But the altered emphasis reflects other circumstances as well, most notably the acknowledged advances in contemporary compositional practices. Vogler, by no means a reactionary, has taken advantage of increased harmonic resources in his own compositions, and in the spate of analysis projects that marks his later years, he clearly accepts these advancements as a challenge. Exploring the potentials of his system afresh, he now finds that his methods permit growth and expansion as he applies them to music which uses a more highly evolved language than that witnessed in *Betrachtungen.*

### LATER EXPERIMENTS

The later experiments in analysis achieved their most original and provocative results in a little-known publication of 1806 entitled *Zwei und dreisig*

*Präludien . . . nebst einer Zergliederung in ästhetischer, rhetorischer und harmo-*
*nischer Rücksicht.* A product of the author's ongoing quest for edifying connections between theory and practice, this endeavor featured a group of
modernized reworkings from an early collection, the *112 petits préludes pour*
*l'orgue ou fortepiano,* first published in 1776. In the commentary accompanying the music, Vogler suggests that these pieces may be regarded as models of
counterpoint and harmonic practice. Their small dimensions (lengths of
individual preludes range from 25 to 88 measures) enable the forms to be
"more easily grasped and perceived; the pupil of composition can [thus] all
the more easily abstract rules of procedure for his future compositional
technique."[25]

Application of the system to these works involves procedures comparable to those followed in *Betrachtungen.* Once again, the theorist relies on
spontaneous, isolated insights more than detailed or comprehensive analysis.
The commentaries thus amount to a puzzle-like array of observations, a
composite lesson in which the principle of harmonic reduction figures prominently. As in the earlier writings, analysis on lower hierarchic levels begins
with the reduction-system and the basic issue of distinguishing consonance
from dissonance. Essentially, the same rules apply, but in dealing with the
more complex language of the preludes, Vogler finds himself obliged to
penetrate the significance of his rules more deeply and to interpret them with
greater flexibility.

In *Betrachtungen,* he had demonstrated that a cadential $\frac{6}{4}$ could be analyzed
under certain conditions as a pair of suspensions above a prolonged dominant
root. This analysis could be justified if the sixth and fourth had been present,
either as consonant notes or lesser dissonances, in the preceding sonority.
Otherwise, the rule of reduction would dictate that the $\frac{6}{4}$ be analyzed as a tonic
triad in second inversion. The later publication shows a more flexible application of this principle. In Example 7, from Vogler's Prelude No. 15 in F, a
progression appears in measure 32 that might be analyzed as I$\frac{6}{4}$–V[7] in accordance with the Roman numerals that Vogler now assigns to his chord roots.
Such an interpretation seems required, in fact, by the reduction-system as
applied in *Betrachtungen:* both the F and the A above the C are sounded freely;
moreover, the A is not resolved in the manner normally required of a
dissonant thirteenth, i.e., downward by step to a consonant tone of a triad.

But Vogler's analysis indicates that the F and A are to be understood as
the dissonant eleventh and thirteenth. This is because the immediately pre-

Example 7
Vogler, Prelude No. 15 in F,
measures 31–33.

ceding chord, the ♯IV at the end of measure 31, must proceed to a V in accordance with the rules of cadential progression. The B-natural constitutes a leading tone to the dominant, and when this leading-tone root proceeds to the fifth scale degree, thereby completing the cadence, the sixth and fourth above must be comprehended as dissonances.[26] By this interpretation, which involves the logic of cadential progression in addition to the requirements of voice leading, all of measure 32 and the first three beats of measure 33 may be analyzed as the elaboration of a single dominant root.

The importance of context, a crucial factor in the analysis of the foregoing example, is underscored by Vogler's interpretation of the phrase quoted below from the Prelude No. 8 in D minor (see Example 8).

According to the analysis that he provides, the arpeggiation of the tonic triad in measure 1 justifies the label of tonic harmony for beats 1 and 2. In the second measure, the B-flat suspends the root of the V chord, and in measure 3, both the F and the D function as suspensions, suitably prepared and resolved. The harmony of the entire bar is therefore that of the V triad. But in

Example 8
Prelude No. 8 in D minor, measures
1–4.

measure 4, the issue of relationship between consonance and dissonance proves more complex: the theorist observes that, in the middle of this measure, the open-fifth sonority A–E might plausibly be heard as an independent chord: a V triad with missing third. Yet such an analysis would ignore the larger issue of voice leading, for the note F at the end of this measure must be understood as the proper, stepwise resolution of the dissonant G, tied over from the preceding measure. This means that the intervening E behaves not as a chord tone but as an embellishment that delays the inevitable resolution. Thus the A in the bass is an arpeggiation of tonic harmony and not a chord root in its own right.[27]

In another instance, the reader's attention is called to an embellishing sonority that would be identified as a four-part chord if detached from its context. As shown in Example 9, from Vogler's Prelude No. 14 in E minor, the independent paths of the voices in measure 17 produce the sound of a diminished triad with diminished seventh.

Example 9
Prelude No. 14 in E minor,
measures 16–18.

Since every acceptable chord must have a scale-degree function, and since the only function assignable to the sonority in question is that of the VII[7] in minor, then any legitimate occurrence of the chord must be understandable as part of a VII[7]–I progression (or a deceptive variant) in one minor key or another. Here, in the absence of such a cadential formula, the tones producing this apparent chord must be heard as melodic embellishments above a sustained chord root (the dominant F-sharp) in the bass.[28]

As in *Betrachtungen,* the principle of reduction applied here provides a way to distinguish between structural roots and the embellishment by which chords might be prolonged. But in *Präludien* the complexities of surface elaboration reach beyond those encountered earlier, and the importance of context is correspondingly increased. Even less than in *Betrachtungen,* in other words, is fundamental-bass analysis merely a matter of pinning labels on vertical sonorities in a musical fabric. The labels obtained by reduction must have functional significance, and as witnessed in the examples cited above, Vogler now avails himself of a method that facilitated their interpretation: in place of the letter names employed in the *Betrachtungen* analyses, he now uses his Roman numerals to designate scale degree roots.

The Roman numerals were an improvement over letter names in several respects. To begin with, they provided a convenient shorthand, enabling the theorist to design compact diagrams and saving the trouble of spelling out chord names and relationships repeatedly in the course of an analytical discussion. Moreover, the Roman numerals helped direct attention to a hierarchy of tonal functions rather than to individual chords in isolation. But there was a more compelling reason for switching from letter names to Roman numerals: they allowed the analyst to specify scale-degree roots without committing himself to actual changes of key in the analysis of a passage. This would prove to be a matter of decisive importance in the process of harmonic reduction on higher levels of structure.

As we learn from the analyses and commentaries in *Betrachtungen,* modulation is a matter of degree and context. From the start Vogler's purpose was not to label chords and keys arbitrarily, nor to proclaim rigid criteria for distinguishing functions of one key from those of another. On the contrary, he favored a broadly defined concept of tonal unity. In the third volume of *Betrachtungen* he had gone so far as to suggest that, in a unified composition, no matter how complex harmonically, there were no modulations. A single tonic prevailed from beginning to end, temporary excursions (*Übergänge*) notwithstanding. In his later writings, even more than in *Betrachtungen,* Vogler seemed determined to explain the unity and coherence of a complex structure in terms that were both hierarchic and open ended. To accomplish this aim he needed tools which, if applied to the analysis of an entire composition, would show that the tonal design could be grasped as a whole, not as an accumulation of discrete and disconnected parts. As revealed in the late analytical projects, Roman numeral symbols offered the means he required.

Vogler's experiments in supplying entire compositions with Roman numerals include three noteworthy attempts that appeared in published form: two of the thirty-two preludes (Nos. 8 and 10), and the contemporaneous *Davids Buss-Psalm,* a sacred vocal piece in chorale style supplied with a commentary and printed in 1807 as the first of the author's two late didactic endeavors published in Munich under the rubric "Utile dulci: Voglers belehrende musikalische Herausgaben." In both these early examples of the technique, the symbols appear not beneath the staff but in the body of an accompanying commentary. Here the reader finds several layers of analytical symbols: letters (designating bass line and chord roots), Arabic numbers (identifying voice leading, dissonances, and inversions), and on the lowest level of the analytical scheme, the Roman numerals themselves. (For *Buss-Psalm,* Vogler gives letter names for the roots of chords only, not the bass.) As can be seen in Example 10, which quotes an excerpt from the *Buss-Psalm* (measures 31–39, with the accompanying analyses), identifications of key or points of modulation are conspicuously absent.[29]

In his commentary on this remarkable work,[30] which features the continual reharmonization of recurring segments of a cantus firmus, the author implies that the key of A minor should be understood as the reigning tonic throughout. This means that the progressions represented by the Roman numerals involve a variety of borrowed functions, parenthetical departures from tonic, secondary-dominant relationships, and temporary tonicizations.

In the first of the three phrases shown above, one chord root in measure 32 (F) pivots to become the dominant of B-flat major, and another scale-degree root (D) is temporarily tonicized in measure 33. The analysis, in the absence of any sign for change of key, suggests that these inflections are taking place without significant departure from tonic. The second phrase begins and ends with scale-degree functions in A minor without making any reference to the tonic chord itself. Instead, two tonicized scale degrees are featured, G and C, and their functions are curiously interlocked: the chord on F-sharp in measure 34 acts as VII of G major, but also as ♯IV of C major; the root G, however, occupies the strongest metrical position in measure 35, thereby declining to subordinate itself as the dominant of C major, even though C clearly represents the center about which the fifth relationships of measure 35 revolve. With the aid of his Roman-numeral symbols, Vogler succeeds in analyzing such ambiguities with a precision and economy hitherto unavailable.

In Vogler's *Präludien* analyses, relationships between adjacent chords are generally less intricate. The structural hierarchies are deeper, however, and the theorist finds it necessary to supplement the Roman numerals with commentary on the relationship between details and larger aspects of organi-

Example 10
(a) Vogler, *Davids Buss-Psalm,*
measures 31–39 (text omitted); (b)
Vogler's Roman-numeral analysis.

|  | 31 |  |  |  | 32 |  |  |  | 33 |  |  |  | 34 |  |  |
|---|---|---|---|---|---|---|---|---|---|---|---|---|---|---|---|
|  |  |  |  |  |  |  |  |  |  | 7 |  |  |  |  | 7 |
| chord roots: | - | 3♮ | 3♮ | 5 | 5 | 5 | 5 | 7♭ | 3♮ | 3♯ | 5 | 5 |  | 7 | 3♯ |
|  | - | A | D | G | C | F | B♭ | C♯ | D | - | E | F | F | - | F♯ | D |
| functional |  |  |  |  |  |  |  |  |  |  |  |  |  |  |  |
| analysis: | - | I | IV | ♮VII | III | VI | I | ♯VII | I |  | V | VI |  | VII | V |
|  |  |  |  |  | V |  |  |  |  |  |  |  |  | ♯IV |  |

| 35 |  |  |  | 36 |  |  | 37 |  |  | 38 |  |  |  | 39 |  |  |
|---|---|---|---|---|---|---|---|---|---|---|---|---|---|---|---|---|
|  |  |  |  |  |  |  |  |  |  |  |  |  |  |  | 7 |  |
|  |  |  |  |  |  |  |  |  |  |  |  |  |  |  | 5♮ |  |
| 9 | 5 | 5 | 5 | 7 | 7 | 3♯ |  | 3♮ | 3♮ | 3♭ | 7♭ | 5 | 3♮ | 5 | 3♮ | 3♯ | 3♮ |
| G | C | F | C | D | B | E | - | A | D | G | C | F | D | B♭ | A | E | A |
| I | IV | IV | I | II | VII | V |  | I | IV | II | V | I | VI | IV | I | V | I |
|  | I |  |  |  | II |  |  |  |  |  |  |  |  |  |  |  |

zation. Concerning his analysis of the D-minor prelude, he explains measures 1–29 (see Example 11)[31] as follows: "The first two phrases, each four measures long, present the main subject. The two-measure unit beginning in measure 9 leads to F major, the two-measure unit beginning in measure 11 leads to A minor. From measure 13 to the third quarter note of measure 20, C major is the prevailing key, from measure 21 to measure 29, A minor [prevails], and at the same time closes the first part in this metrical, precisely tailored work."[32]

By means of this commentary, combined with the analysis of chord roots, Vogler manages to distinguish several layers of tonal organization

Example 11
Vogler's analysis of Prelude No. 8,
measures 1–29 (figures for bass line
omitted).

```
                1        2          3            4        5       6          7
bass line:      D  -     C# -  D    A  -  -      D  A  D  D  C#    D  -  -     E  -  C#
                         9  8       13 12 7      11 -  10          13 12 -     11 10
                         3# -       11 -  10#    9  -  8           11 10 -     9  8#
chord roots:    D  Bb    A  -  D    A  -  -               D  -  -  D  C#    D  -  -     C# -  -
tonal function: I  VI    V          I    V                I               #VII  I            #VII


                8        9        10      11      12       13     14          15
bass line:      D  E  F  D  -     C  -    F  -    E  -     C  B   C  -  A     G  -  -
                11 - 10  5        11 10            11 10#  7      11 10 5♮    11 10# 7
                9  - 8                                     3♮
chord roots:    D  -  -  D  Bb    C  -    F  D    E  -     C  G   C  -  F#    G  -  -
tonal function: I        VI  IV   V   I   IV  V   I        V  I   #IV         V


                16       17      18        19        20       21        22
bass line:      G  -  -  C  B    C  -  A   G  -  -   G  E  D  C  -  G#   A  -  D
                9  8  3# 7       11 10 5♮  11 10# 7  9  8  7♮ 13 12          5♮
                         3♮
chord roots:    C  -  G  C  G    C  -      F#        G  -  -  C  -  G#   A  -  B
tonal function: I        V  I    I         #IV       V        I   #VII   I         II


                23       24         25       26       27        28        29
bass line:      E  -  -  F  Eb  D   D  -     C  -     A  -  D    E  -  -   A
                7                   5        13 12    11 10 5♮             
                9♮ 8  3# 7b         7                            9♮ 8  3#
                                    3♮
chord roots:    A  -  E  F  -   Bb  Bb  G#   A  -  G# A  -  B    A  -  E   A
tonal function: I        V  VI  V   I        #VII  I  #VII  I    II        V  I
```

without recourse to any rigid conception of modulation. He indicates that the progress of the piece after an initial, tonally stable phrase-pair involves two periods: the first centered on C major, the next on A minor. A distinction is drawn between the main, structurally important goals and the mere allusion (*einlenken*) to the keys of F major and A minor in measures 9–12. In addition, tonicizations occur which are deemed too insignificant structurally to merit comment: within the span on C, two ♯IV–V progressions momentarily tonicize the G (measures 14–15, 18–19), and in the A-minor period, the VI chord in measure 24 acquires a seventh to become the dominant of B-flat major.

As Vogler had demonstrated in earlier writings, the basis for such a hierarchic analysis is readily found in the precepts of the system: the chord of the sharp fourth, whose root acts as a leading tone to the fifth degree, functions as a VII of V, thereby opening a path to the possibility of secondary dominants and tonicizations of scale degrees. But the above excerpt includes a tonicized degree foreign to the prevailing scale (B-flat in the context of A minor). This chord of the flat second degree, which Vogler cites in another context, is explained as a convention sanctioned by custom.[33] But his Roman-numeral analysis indicates that it can nevertheless be rationally comprehended as an instance of borrowing: in the traditional cadential formula, this so-called Neapolitan sixth constitutes a IV chord borrowed from the key of the sixth degree:

|  |  | 5 |  |
| --- | --- | --- | --- |
|  | 6♭ | 3♯ | 3 |
| bass line: | D | E | A |
| chord roots: | B♭ |  |  |
|  | IV of F | V | I |

Thus, in addition to secondary dominants and tonicized scale degrees, the system now incorporates the possibility of embellishing a progression in one key with functions borrowed from another. As Vogler suggests in a remarkable digression within the commentaries, virtually any succession of roots may occur within a tonal vocabulary thus extended. By way of illustration, he offers a pair of model phrases (the second of these is depicted in

Example 12) in which harmonic antipodes, i.e., triads a tritone apart, are logically juxtaposed.[34]

In this analysis, the dominant chord F is adorned with its own dominant, C. Since this secondary dominant follows the VI chord (G-flat), the antipodal relationship is suitably enveloped in a tonally unified progression.

Example 12
Vogler's analysis for an example of
harmonic "antipodes" within the key
of B-flat minor.

|  |  |  | 5♮ |  |  |  |  |  | 5 |  |
|---|---|---|---|---|---|---|---|---|---|---|
|  | 3♭ | 5 | 3♮ | 3♮ | 7♭ | 3♭ | 5♭ | 3♭ | 3♮ | 3♭ |
| chord roots: | B♭ | G♭ | C | F | A | B♭ | C | B♭ | F | B♭ |
| tonal functions: | I | VI | V | V | VII | I | II | I | V | I |

Thus, according to Vogler's Roman-numeral analyses a key may incorporate multiple levels, any tonicizations within a phrase or section being understood as embellishments of an overriding tonic. This approach sheds light on proposals advanced earlier in *Betrachtungen* regarding the issues of tonal unity and digression: when analyzed in accordance with the teachings of *Präludien,* momentary inflections such as those cited (in the second movement of the Winter symphony, for example, or the von Kerpen sonata) would simply be understood as subordinate relationships within the prevailing key.

But what about higher levels of structure? Notwithstanding his allowances for inflection or parenthetical excursion, Vogler adheres to a rather strict criterion for tonal unity in *Betrachtungen:* only the closely related keys are permitted, and among them, those closest to tonic must receive greatest emphasis. The line is clearly drawn between *Übergang* and *Ausweichung,* leaving little room for expansion of the tonal spectrum.

While Vogler still subscribes to his principle of tonal unity in *Präludien,* the preference for closely related keys no longer denotes an arbitrary outer limit. Applied now to pieces that include excursions to remote areas between an initial departure from tonic and an eventual return, the rule serves as a means of distinguishing between close relationships that confirm an overriding tonal unity and more remote centers that struggle against its force. In this capacity, it aids the theorist in specifying the tensions created by remote centers that temporarily hold sway over closer relatives of tonic.

A striking instance of such a remote relationship occurs in Vogler's Prelude No. 3 in C minor. He cites this piece specially as an exemplary miniature, declaring that the lessons it teaches can be applied to music conceived on a larger scale. Within its mere thirty-eight measures, several remote centers are touched, including C major (Vogler now fully endorses the change of mode as a legitimate extension of a tonal center) and the antipodal relationship, G-flat major, momentarily suggested at the midpoint of the design. Concerning the approach to this latter region, which emerges following an initial elaboration confined to close relationships, the theorist writes as follows (see Example 13): "From measures 17 to 31 the modulation steadily advances [and] allows no retrogressive movement; tension is maintained constantly, every event is new. The chord of D-flat major in measure 17 indeed appears intent on announcing itself as the subordinate sixth of the preceding F minor, but takes the liberty at once of reigning as tonic. It turns in measure 18 to G-flat [major] as the cadential fifth."[35]

Example 13
Prelude No. 3 in C minor, measures
16–18.

Logically approached as a scale degree (VI) of the subdominant key, the chord of D-flat threatens the tonal stability by proclaiming itself as a tonic. Then an apex of tension is reached in measure 18, where the note C-flat transforms the arpeggiated D-flat chord into a dominant, thereby implying the move (never actually realized) to G-flat major. Tonal unity is challenged, yet ultimately preserved intact, as a remote center temporarily wields its force in the unfolding of the composition.

Not all the remote goals explored in *Präludien* have to do with struggles for territory among relatives of tonicized scale degrees. In the commentary on the D-minor prelude (No. 8), the reader's attention is called to an eight-measure span (measures 57–64) in which E-flat major emerges as a temporary tonic. Appearing toward the close of this eighty-eight-measure piece, the segment in question forms a kind of plateau between the chromatically inflected, developmental sequences of the preceding passage and the declamatory epilogue that follows. To justify the remote area and explain its significance, Vogler begins by asserting that the logic of the whole presents no difficulties, since "all the keys that occur here are related to the tonic D [minor], and in their key signatures are no further removed than by a single accidental (for only through combination and juxtaposition do keys on either end of the spectrum [of closely related keys] appear remote from one another)."

As for the move to E-flat, he continues as follows: "Since even a key removed by two accidentals, E-flat major, to which we are accustomed in the following progression:

$$
\begin{array}{cccc}
 & 6 & 5 & 3 \\
6\flat & 4 & 3\sharp & \\
G & A & - & D
\end{array}
$$

exercises rights of sovereignty merely by prolongation (*Verweilen*), and clings to the tonic so intimately, in so neighborly a manner, we need only survey the given analysis to be convinced" of the overall logic.[36]

By stating that the piece includes no modulation to a key further removed than one accidental from tonic, Vogler indicates that the eight-measure passage on E-flat need not be called a modulation at all. Instead, the excursion is to be identified as an instance of the conventional flat-second relationship, prolonged to the point where it temporarily functions as a tonic. In contrast to the dramatic struggle of the C-minor prelude, this remote center serves as a kind of mediation, a moment of suspended animation between the preceding climax of developmental activity and the clamorous reaffirmation of tonic with which the piece closes. As in that other instance, the theorist is able not only to account for the appearance of a remote key, but to identify as well its function as part of the logical and rhetorical order of his design.

In the lessons of *Präludien* cited above, Vogler pursues one of his central aims by striving to explain contemporary practices from the standpoint of his system. As witnessed throughout his analytical writings, the attempt gives rise to a flexibly conceived theory of structural levels. The foundation of these is represented by the rational bases of harmony: the sounding string, the all-important interval of the fifth, and the perfect triad. The scale steps of a tonic key, tonicization of these degrees, and various secondary and remote relationships all occupy intermediate levels, while functional chord roots and the interaction of unity and diversity symbolized by the Roman numerals lie closer to the surface. Finally, surface elaborations involve the embellishing dissonances with which triadic functions may be adorned.

By applying his scheme of harmonic reduction, tentatively in *Betrachtungen* and then more boldly in *Präludien,* the theorist came close to his cherished goal of tracing a binding connection between theory and practice. One step remained: the reduction of a composition not merely to a tonally unified design based on a tonic key and its close relatives, but all the way to the *Urstoff* (primal materials) of the sounding string and the elemental relationships it represented. Such a reduction is implicit in discussions of pieces in *Betrachtungen* whose essential tonal scheme Vogler describes as a pattern of tonic, departure to the fifth, and return. Given the conceptual link his teachings suggest between scale-degree root and key area, the reader can easily surmise a connection between this archetypal tonal framework and the form of a cadential progression. Once this connection is established, the process of reduction is virtually complete, for he has shown that the materials of the cadence—triad and fifth relationship—arise directly from relationships in a sounding string. In the writings examined thus far, he has been content with merely alluding to such an ultimate reduction without specifying how it might be accomplished. That final step he saves for a later study, the *System für den Fugenbau,* written in 1811 but not published until around 1817, several years after his death.

In this last major project of his career as a theorist, Vogler intended to formulate a set of rules for fugal procedure in accordance with the principles of his system. Taking up the theme of fugue broached earlier in *Betrachtungen,*[37] he conceives fugal writing as the harmonically unified, homogeneous elaboration of a thematic kernel, and he proposes that a strictly conceived fugue may stand as a classic model of musical organization. The essence of such a work, the seed from which the design in its entirety must grow, resides in the subject and in the special procedure he prescribes for the relationship between subject and answer: these two complementary elements must form a tonally symmetrical pair, the subject modulating from tonic to fifth, the answer responding by moving from fifth back to tonic.[38]

Once established, subject and answer form the basis for an exposition in which the voices enter, each in its turn, until all parts are sounding. The result is a contrapuntal-harmonic network consisting of subject, answer, and the subordinate counterpoints accumulated in the course of the exposition. This multi-voice complex, called the *enucleatio fugae,* constitutes the material of fugal elaboration. With a model *enucleatio fugae* in hand, the theorist delineates two main objectives: (a) creation of an entire model fugue that illustrates continuous elaboration of the basic material, and (b) analysis of the *enucleatio* itself by tracing it to its source in the simplest mathematical relationships residing in a sounding string. In pursuit of this second goal, he finds himself further extending his inquiry into the principle of reduction.

As shown in Example 14, Vogler isolates the *enucleatio* for the subject and answer of his model fugue and supplies both with a set of Roman numerals to indicate chord roots. This compositional unit he identifies with the idea of *Gesangverbindung* (a uniting of melodic lines), in which each melody enjoys limited sovereignty, just as each heavenly body in a solar system turns on its own axis. The central organizing force, without which the study of fugue would be merely a groundless, empirical exercise, is the overriding unity of the harmony, the source from which melodic diversity arises and to which it may ultimately be traced.[39]

The unity to which Vogler refers is embodied in the harmonically symmetrical correspondence of subject and answer. The Roman-numeral analysis calls attention to this symmetry by revealing that each half of subject and answer forms a harmonic unit: the chord functions in the first three measures of the subject represent the tonic key; the corresponding measures of the answer represent the key of the fifth. Likewise, the second three measures of the subject represent the key of the fifth; the second half of the answer, the tonic. The pivot in this scheme is the *Gränzscheidung,* or borderline, where modulation takes place in subject and answer. At this point the tonal center moves down a fourth in the subject, from tonic to dominant, and rises a fourth in the answer, from dominant to tonic.

Vogler suggests that such a pattern is reducible to a pair of cadences. Applying this notion to the model fugue in question, he explains that "since in any fugue two key centers appear both in subject and answer, . . . the

Example 14
The *enucleatio fugae* of Vogler's
model fugue.

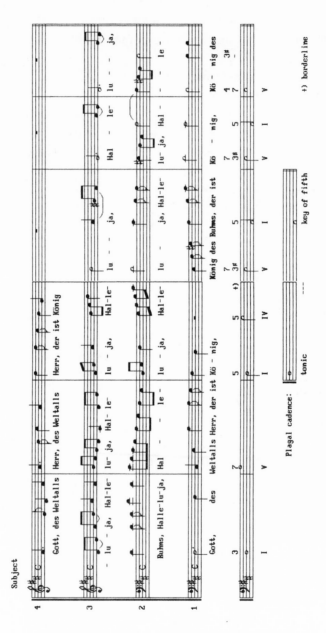

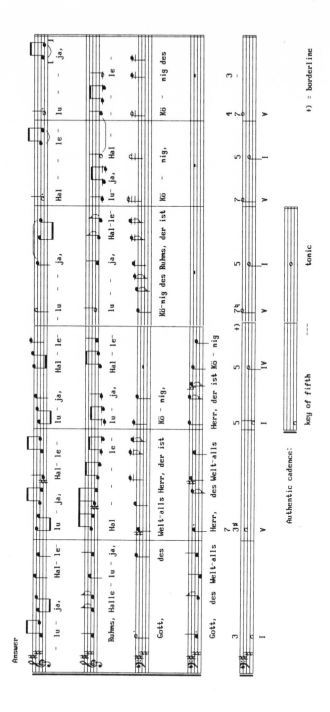

analyst is not deceived by the embellishing chord roots, but rather immediately perceives the main tonal centers, and thus it becomes clear that the tonic chord D in the first half of the third measure forms a plagal cadence with the [tonic chord] A in the second half of the fourth measure of the subject; correspondingly, an authentic cadence is produced in the answer by the tonic chord A in the first half of the third measure and the tonic chord D in the second half of the fourth measure."[40] Here the distinction is clearly drawn between structural chord roots, D and A, and embellishing harmonies (e.g., the fourth of D, the fifth of A) that flesh out the harmonic skeleton. In accordance with the theorist's proposal, the entire pattern is thus reducible to the plagal and authentic cadences. But why does the plagal precede the authentic? It is not that the plagal takes precedence over the authentic, he suggests, but rather that the plagal is less conclusive. It is appropriate that the plagal cadence be embodied in the subject, for this initial statement, which must give rise to an answer, should be relatively tensional. Correspondingly, the answer should yield satisfaction and express relative stability.

In effect, the harmonic structure of the subject may be reduced to two chord roots, functioning as IV–I from the standpoint of the fifth, which constitutes the harmonic goal of the subject. Correspondingly, the answer represents a V–I relationship from the standpoint of tonic, the goal of the answer. By virtue of this analytical device, Vogler succeeds in drawing a functional connection between tonal framework and cadential progression. In the process of departure, the fifth steps forward as tonic, hence the relationship IV–I; this fifth is in turn subordinated to tonic as the decisive return is accomplished, now symbolized by the cadence V–I.

Pursuing the idea of reduction still further, Vogler draws on mathematical operations (resembling those employed by his Paduan predecessors Vallotti and Tartini)[41] in order to derive his hypothetical pair of cadences from a single, irreducibly simple numerical series. The essence of his procedure is to relate the difference between his two cadences to the difference between the arithmetic and harmonic proportions. Between the numbers 12 and 6, taken as outer terms, he finds 9 to be the arithmetic mean (half the sum of the outer terms, i.e., 18 divided by 2), while 8 is the harmonic mean: double the product of the outer terms (144) divided by their sum (18). Now if each of the numbers representing the arithmetic progression 12:9:6 is supplied with a numerator of 1, the resulting series of fractions ($\frac{1}{6}$:$\frac{1}{9}$:$\frac{1}{12}$) constitutes a harmonic proportion. (Compare the string lengths 12, 8, 6 [Vogler's harmonic proportion in whole numbers] with the proportion ½:⅓:¼ [i.e., ⅙:⅑:¹/₁₂ with denominators reduced to smallest terms], understood as divisions of a single string whose entire length is 24.) In this sense, the series 12:8:6 is shown to be equivalent to ⅙:⅑:¹/₁₂, and thus both the harmonic and arithmetic proportions are related to the same three numbers: 6, 9, and 12. Division of each of the numbers by 3 reduces the relationship to its simplest numerical representation: 2, 3, 4.[42]

Example 15
Vogler's reduction of his fugue
subject and answer.

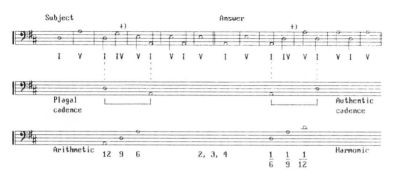

+) = borderline

The path to reduction is thus finally cleared. From the melodic diversity of subject, answer, and attendant counterpoints, a series of chord roots may be extracted (see Example 15). The pattern formed by these roots then reduces to a pair of cadences, plagal and authentic, and these two cadences may be represented in terms of the arithmetic and harmonic proportions. By the operations noted above, the two number series (12, 9, 6 and ⅙, ⅑, ¹/₁₂) can be consolidated in the numbers 2, 3, 4. Significantly, this may be understood as the simplest series from which the relationships of root, fifth, and octave— all residing in a single resonating string—may be obtained.

By tracing a path of reduction from an elaborated surface, represented by the *enucleatio,* to elemental harmonic and numerical relationships, the late fugue treatise revealed one way in which the gap between musical practice and theoretical principle could be bridged. To this extent, *Fugenbau* stands as a confirmation of Vogler's lifelong crusade and a fitting culmination to his experiments in harmonic analysis.

In the course of these endeavors, the principle of the fundamental bass formed the starting point in a search for harmonic order in contemporary musical practice. The quest, involving the discovery of connections between the deductions of Vogler's system and structural hierarchies evident in the music he analyzed, led to observations about tonal organization rarely encountered in formal treatises of the time. As revealed by these analyses, Vogler managed to depict a dynamic order in which the reign of a single tonic must prevail, even while being challenged by other tones exercising their naturally ordained potential to function as tonics themselves.

Unique in terms of the results he achieved, Vogler's notion of harmonic reduction did not represent a radical departure from theoretical norms of his time. His basic materials are readily traceable to the teachings of his rationalist predecessors, including Rameau as well as Vallotti, and though his device of Roman-numeral analysis does stand out as a novel invention, the fact of this innovation is less significant than the boldness of the attempt to pursue musical applications of his theories. In so doing, he developed the means to describe not only the logic and clarity he observed in the musical language of his day, but also its potential for achieving drama, tension, novelty, and astonishment through the masterful use of available harmonic materials.

## CHAPTER 3

# Progress and Restoration:
# The Lessons
# of Enlightened Criticism

T HE principles of Vogler's system, allegedly simple enough to be grasped with a minimum of instruction, were intended to supply a foundation for all aspects of musical pedagogy. In the teaching of rudiments, they served as an initial point of reference: the intervals, chords, and scales studied by the beginner were the very elements of natural order on which the theorist's chain of deductions was based. As the pupil progressed, the application of theoretical principles advanced correspondingly. The singer learned proper intonation, while the student accompanist learned the harmonic foundations of his craft. At higher levels of instruction, the study of exemplary pieces—such as those in the *Betrachtungen der Mannheimer Tonschule*—revealed further insights into connections between musical theory and practice. Through analysis, the student of the system learned to distinguish consonance from dissonance, to identify the chordal foundation of a musical fabric, and finally, to trace all harmonic elaborations to the primal materials (*Urstoff*) of sounding string, tonic triad, and scale.

But the theorist's plan was not limited to the teaching of harmony. It extended to a wide range of matters relating to musical practice, including the resources of musical expression and the criteria for distinguishing good taste from bad. In these latter respects, his ambitions were similar to those of prominent critics from an earlier generation, notably Johann Mattheson and Johann Adolf Scheibe, as well as contemporaries such as Johann Adam Hiller. His approach differed from those of other writers, however, in the nature of his rationalist point of view and its consequences. Vogler treated criticism as an extension of the procedures he applied to harmonic analysis, and his method involved a similar kind of instruction by example. In contrast to the generalizations of his predecessors and rival critics, whose efforts he disparaged, he aimed to address specifics, using exemplary works to relate aspects of musical design and expression to natural principles. This became a guiding purpose behind his analytical publications, beginning with the *Betrachtungen* and its accompanying musical supplements.

## THE *BETRACHTUNGEN DER MANNHEIMER TONSCHULE*

The format of the Mannheim serial, incorporating music as well as text, recalls precedents from earlier in the century. These include Telemann's pioneering *Getreuer Musikmeister* (1728), a periodical consisting almost entirely of music, and Hiller's *Wöchentliche Nachrichten* (1766–70), an immediate precursor that regularly included music in its weekly issues. In taking up the idea, Vogler declared his intention to combine the attributes of a periodical devoted to the publishing of music (such as Telemann's) with those of a pedagogical manual. The practical and theoretical were to be intertwined, affording the reader both musical enjoyment and edification. As wide a territory as possible would be covered within the projected volumes; and among his miscellaneous readership, all temperaments and levels of advancement would be addressed through a variety of music for church, theater, and chamber or concert hall.

Beyond the general aim to be comprehensive and satisfy as many divergent tastes as possible, the issues of *Betrachtungen* betray no apparent order or organizational scheme. The author adhered only loosely to his original plan of monthly issues, the contents of the musical supplements were not always coordinated with the text of a particular fascicle, and some items announced on title pages never made their way into the publication. Some of the music appears in a kind of reduced score, clearly intended more for study than performance, whereas other pieces, such as the six miniature concertos for keyboard, add bulk to the supplements with their complete sets of orchestral parts. With works in different idioms and genres juxtaposed, and the commentaries interspersed with essays on theory, aesthetics, and matters of style, the whole evinces a quality of randomness that may have been at least partially intentional, as if this patchwork quality represented the diversity of the art itself, upon which the rational system must impose order.

At the start of the first issue, Vogler eases into his task by charming the reader with a vocal rondo. In this most popular of genres, the characteristic simplicity of design and materials guarantees accessibility even to the untrained ear. The rondo usually conveys an idyllic mood, he observes, and it generally calls for regular phrasing and uncomplicated harmony. While its refrain typically balances an antecedent phrase closing on the dominant with a consequent statement cadencing on tonic, the intermediate sections afford opportunities for diversity in key and mood. Because nuance and gentle sentiment are characteristic of this idiom, Vogler continues, the recent usurping of heroic arias by *galant* rondos on the operatic stage is inappropriate: the narrow range of expression appropriate to the rondo is far more suitable to the concert hall than to the theater.[1]

Against the backdrop of this introduction, the theorist presents his own example of the type: a modest yet intensely felt piece, featuring a three-stanza text in which tender yearnings, *galant* exclamations, and declarations of faithful love give the composer ample opportunity to illustrate musical characteristics typical of the genre:

> Sì mio ben sarò fedele,
> Non temer sarò costante,
> E saprà quest'alma amante
> Per te vivere, per te morir.
>
> Prima il mar vedrà senza onde,
> Senza arene, o senza sponde,
> Che s'estingua nel mio seno
> Un sì nobile pensier.
>
> Resta in pace e pensa, o cara,
> Che mi struggo ai lumi tuoi,
> E che sola, oh Dio! tu puoi
> Farmi dolce ogni morir.

In setting these lines, Vogler chose the meter and tempo of a minuet, designing a voice part in which expressive leaps and cadential embellishments enhance a predominantly smooth, conjunct melody. To support the voice, he uses an orchestra of flutes and horns in pairs, and an independent bassoon part in addition to strings and *continuo*. For the refrain, he deploys these forces with the ingenuity typical of his style, assembling a fabric whose patterns are simple yet vividly colored by interaction and exchange. Then, offsetting this diversity of texture and embellishment, he applies a leaner, more intimate sound to the two subsidiary stanzas, omitting the winds and providing an introspective turn from major to minor.

Such matters of style are largely left for the reader to observe and appreciate: the explanatory text concentrates mainly on the analysis of harmonic structure, including cadences and periodization in addition to a nearly complete account of dissonances, chord roots, and key relationships. Yet there is more to the analysis than merely an account of the harmonic resources employed. As Vogler explains his setting of the text, line by line, he takes pains to draw specific connections between the expression suggested by the words and the harmonic materials employed.

For example, chromatic inflections applied to the line "Resta in pace e pensa, o cara," serve to represent the "expression of a sensitive heart" ("dienen zum Ausdrucke eines empfindsamen Herzens"). The exclamation "oh Dio!" is underscored by the tension of a diminished seventh chord, appropriately enhanced by the upward leap of a diminished seventh in the vocal line; and in the phrase "farmi dolce ogni morir" (measures 55–59), harmonically restless dominant sevenths underscore repetitions of the word "dolce" (see Example 1).

The author observes that at the end of this last-mentioned phrase, the juxtaposition of two major triads a step apart (E and F) lends special emphasis to the word "morir." In accordance with Vogler's theory, the succession represents a clash of tonal allegiance, since either chord can claim priority as a tonic. But in the context of the phrase in question, the listener understands the progression as an allowable V–VI deceptive cadence in minor. Acceptable from this standpoint, it presumably retains something of the harmonic tension inherent in the forbidden succession it resembles. In a situation like this, the theorist declares, the mathematical principles of harmonic organization confirm on paper the expressive effect perceived by the ear.[2]

This notable experiment in criticism reveals features that prove typical of Vogler's approach throughout the *Betrachtungen*. Addressing his reader from a position of experience in contemporary styles and fashions, he offers his model as an example of good taste and authentic expression. That the piece is exemplary in terms of structure and proportion is tacitly assumed. It is not the author's purpose to dwell on matters of custom and convention, nor to

Example 1
Vogler's Rondo, *Sì mio ben*,
measures 43–61.

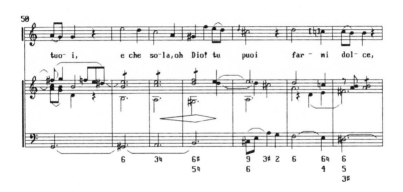

supply prescriptions for structural stereotypes common to the readers' every-day musical experiences. Instead, his critique centers on connections between compositional technique and expression, and for each of the details he cites, he attempts to show that the rational laws of harmony can explain how the musical setting has given expressive voice to sentiments suggested by the words.

In pursuing the quest for rational understanding, Vogler acknowledges that, while the ingredients of an existing composition can be ascertained and explained, his system cannot prescribe aesthetic perfection. Standards and predilections in Italy are different from those that prevail in Germany, France, or England, and the materials and effects appropriate to the theater are different from those suitable to the church. The knowledgeable listener gains an understanding of these matters through experience, which must guide him as he proceeds to analyze each of the parts and comprehend their relationship to the whole.[3]

The critic's method, then, is to start with an exemplary work, acquaint the reader with its merits as an example of its type, and then examine the individual instance of expression which can be linked to a fundamental principle. According to the tenets on which this approach is based, musical expression is not empirical. A tangible connection exists between the composer's resources and the available realm of expressive effects; and even though his choices cannot be prescribed by rules, they must conform to natural principles. This assertion, critically important to the message of the *Betrachtungen,* is elaborated near the end of the final volume, which offers an extended lecture on the subject of fundamental materials and their application in practice.

Vogler's plan in this valedictory lesson, entitled "Harmonie zwischen den Grundsäzen, ihrer Anwendung und der Wirkung der Musik" (Concord between Principles, Their Application and the Effect of Music) is to cover the territory of his system—the tonal universe as he perceives it—in fifteen propositions.[4] For each statement of principle (*Grundsaz*) he cites the relevant demonstration on his *Tonmaass,* records observations on its practical application (*Anwendung*), and then points out the consequences or potential effects of the applications proposed (*Wirkung*). He begins with the principle of identity embodied in the unison: it applies to the conventions of doubling in an orchestra, and such doublings may be used to underscore the impact of an initial thematic statement that will be subjected to elaboration and development. Having established this pattern of explanation, he proceeds through the materials of octave, fifth, and third, the diatonic scale, derivation of the minor third, the minor scale, and the different sevenths. He then completes the study by examining more complex principles involving the altered tones in minor, the dissonances of ninth, eleventh, and thirteenth, inversion, the chromatic scale, and last of all, the principle of multiple function (*Mehrdeutigkeit*).

This procedure offers Vogler a vantage point for a sweeping overview of available musical resources. Concerning the phenomenon of the fifth, for example, he observes that this interval is essential to the formation of a cadence, and that the phenomenon of the cadential fifth relationship is basic to chord succession, part writing, and the concept of fugal subject and answer. And since the last of the principles discussed, multiple function, accounts for the phenomenon of modulation through enharmonic equivalents, its applications embrace virtually the entire universe of tonal relationships.

In the course of this inquiry into the connection between theory and practice, issues of expressive effect figure prominently. We learn that the derivation of the chromatic scale is linked to the identification of the syntonic comma, which in turn leads to the concept of temperament; and the applications of unequal temperament lead to the affective differences among the various keys. Comparably tangible links between principle and expression involve the fundamental contrast between the natural major third and the artificially derived minor third of the minor triad. Because of its natural foundations, a major key sounds stronger and brighter than a minor key. The former is therefore more suitable to operatic music, while the latter finds its proper place in the church. In a musical illustration provided, an archetypal phrase in operatic style (in which the lively pulsation of the bass enhances the natural buoyancy of major harmony) stands in contrast to a passage in which sustained tones and a prevailing legato amplify the inherently somber and passive quality of the minor key (see Example 2). Significantly, neither model is supplied with a text. The implied contrast between secular and sacred is conveyed solely by the tones and their interrelationships.[5]

Further examples illustrate the contrasting effects associated with certain chromatic alterations. Because of their characteristic use of altered scale degrees, the minor keys are rich in harmonies that evoke gloom and sorrow; and the cadential chords of the augmented fifth and diminished third, both

Example 2
Major vs. minor: Vogler's model
phrases illustrating contrast between
(a) operatic and (b) sacred style.

indigenous to minor, suggest deepest lamentation. A model phrase, with the text "et amara valde" provides an appropriate illustration (see Example 3).[6]

On the second beat, retention of the G-sharp from the V chord gives rise to an augmented fifth as the root changes from E to C. On beat 4, the setting of the last syllable of "amara" is endowed with pungency in accordance with the rules of cadential progression: since this IV chord progresses to a cadence on V, its root has been raised by analogy with the standard ♯IV–V cadence in major. Transferred to the minor mode, which features the lowered sixth scale degree, this inflection yields the affectively charged chord of the diminished third. Stressing the importance of understanding such connections, the theorist proposes that natural inclinations and a sensitive ear can lead a gifted

Example 3
Vogler's model phrase exploiting
expressive inflections of a minor key.

composer for only part of the way. In effect, innate genius is insufficient: the unerring artist is one who comprehends the relationship between principles and the effects he strives to create.[7]

By elaborating such ideas about the link between theoretical principle and expression, Vogler betrays his allegiance to a rational aesthetic deeply entrenched in much critical writing of the time. Echoing the French aesthetician Charles Batteux and his central European followers, Vogler observes that, just as words constitute the expression of thoughts, so music constitutes the expression of passions.[8] Not unlike earlier generations of neo-Classical and rationalist critics, he tends toward the description of musical phenomena in terms of their specific expressive content. And in keeping with this approach, he continually implies that a text, program, or some other extramusical frame of reference is necessary to the realization of expressive potentials in music. Upholding the time-honored practice of calling music an imitative art, he extols its power to enthrall the listener through the images it conjures and the passions it excites.

According to Vogler's view, musical expression must be intelligible, engaging not only the senses but also the mind. A composition lacking expressive significance (a ballroom dance, for example) may have its purpose, but it merely tickles the ear. By contrast, when music paints a picture or powerfully represents the passions, the hearer is enthralled, and can experience that which is being expressed or depicted.[9]

As expounded in *Betrachtungen,* Vogler's concept of musical expression appears to hinge on tangibility—on the ability to specify what is being expressed. As seen in his discussion of the vocal rondo, passions suggested by the text clarify the meaning communicated by particular musical devices. Inevitably, such an approach gives preference to vocal music, or to music associated with an extra-musical purpose. Such works play a dominant role in the *Betrachtungen* as they do generally in Vogler's output as a composer, and the distinction he draws between the merely sensual appeal of a minuet and the unlimited eloquence of music that bears a specific message underscores his bias.

As might be expected from a composer and critic of this persuasion, Vogler betrays a somewhat condescending attitude toward abstract instrumental music. Most, though not all, of the instrumental pieces included in *Betrachtungen* seem intended to address the senses more than the heart or mind, and the author often appears to be at a loss to explain their significance.

It was a nearly universal complaint among critics of the time that expression remained undefined in a purely instrumental language, and Vogler's writings reflect the prevailing frustration. When found in a piece of instrumental music, phenomena such as a deceptive cadence or a modulation from major to minor convey only vague or ambiguous suggestions of expressive content. But when applied to specific expressive purposes, as in the theorist's exemplary rondo, they acquire tangible significance.

Aesthetic commitments notwithstanding, Vogler seems reluctant to ignore instrumental music altogether, to deny its expressive value, or to deprive it of any higher purpose than mere entertainment. Music for instruments alone need not be devoid of content, even though its substance must somehow be conveyed without reference to an extra-musical message. In accordance with his rationalist, mimetic doctrine, he suggests that the instrumental composer does not imitate a model in nature. Instead, he uses the language of imitative music in the construction of freely invented, coherent forms. If its statements are fluid and orderly in design, an instrumental piece may succeed in satisfying the listener, even though its message must be communicated in terms that cannot be translated. In this vein, he draws the analogy between the instrumental composer and a painter who depicts an imaginary landscape—an image that may indeed correspond to a model in nature, but that nevertheless does not imitate nature directly.[10]

This line of reasoning gives the critic a foothold in the territory of instrumental music. It liberates him from the restrictions of a rigidly conceived doctrine of imitation, and it gives him a basis for describing the significance of a serious and elaborate instrumental composition. But how can the design of an abstract composition be justified? How can a spontaneous unfolding of contrasting themes and harmonies be explained? The standard forms of Vogler's exemplary chamber works—whether binary, sonata, rondo, or theme and variations—he accepts as matters of custom and convention. These are tried and true formulas that merit preservation and exploitation because of their limitless capacity for nuance and variation in detail. They afford the opportunity for achieving a balance of unity and diversity, and in one way or another they involve a course of musical events that conforms to the rules of rhetoric.

It is fitting that, given his rationalist predilections, Vogler should call upon the doctrines of rhetoric and insist that they pertain to music.[11] Like his neo-classical predecessors, he subscribes to a belief in the concept of binding laws that link all the fine arts and enable them to be understood in terms of a single set of principles. In *Betrachtungen,* his references to musical rhetoric reflect an adherence to traditional precepts, yet his employment of the idea is novel in its freedom and flexibility. Applied as a convenient tool for dealing with instrumental music, it supplies him with a set of firm but scarcely specific or restrictive requirements: these include a clear initial statement, an ordering of materials that serves to clarify the relationship of parts to one another and to the whole, and a scheme of departure and return that involves the building of intensity to an apex, followed by a tightly knit summary, or epilogue.[12]

Though such a scheme offers a basic frame of reference, applicable to a wide variety of instrumental forms, its ingredients are too generalized to permit any kind of detailed application to a given work under discussion. Consequently, the critiques of instrumental pieces must center on those aspects of organization that can be specified in the absence of any other source of explainable meaning. This generally means harmonic analysis: the accounting for pitch relationships on different levels of structure in accordance with theoretical principles. But in *Betrachtungen,* Vogler proposes yet another angle: analysis of specific thematic processes by which the composer achieves a desirable balance, not unlike that of an oration, between unity and diversity.

The question of thematic elaboration and development stands out prominently in Vogler's critiques of abstract instrumental composition. As discussed in *Betrachtungen,* the issue involves differentiating between two types of process: *Fortführung* and *Ausführung.* The first describes instances in which a continuation is fashioned in accordance with the shape of the foregoing material: an idea appears that has not been stated before, yet it bears a tangible, unified relationship to that which has preceded. It is different, but it must sound as if it evolved from a previously stated idea. *Ausführung,* by contrast, applies to the actual recurrence of an idea. But instead of mere repetition (*Wiederholung*) or transposition (*Versezung*), it involves some kind of alteration or transformation.[13] Illustrating this distinction with the aid of a model phrase (see Example 4), Vogler shows that the unison triadic statement of measure 1 undergoes *Fortführung* in measures 2–4. The material is then treated to *Ausführung* in the final four measures, where the initial unison idea provides the basis for a pattern of imitative entries.[14]

Applied to instrumental pieces in *Betrachtungen,* Vogler's notion of the-

Example 4
Vogler's model for thematic
development: Statement (measure 1),
*Fortführung* (measures 2–4),
*Ausführung* (measures 5–8).

matic development helps account for sources of tension between unity and diversity in the unfolding of a conventional design. The finale of Winter's D-minor symphony he interprets as a binary design whose second part presents not merely the transposed recurrence of material from the first, but also new material based on the foregoing. We find that the second part begins with a theme whose texture, profile, and general quality of movement recall a secondary theme from the first part; and this *Fortführung* flows into a transitional passage where motivic fragmentation and dialogue use material derived from the opening subject and closing theme of the first part.[15]

Vogler seldom ventures to say just how the listener is affected by thematic processes such as those seen in the Winter symphony. Like the harmonic analyses, discussions of development mainly address the mind, and the reader is left to infer that reason plays an essential role in the appreciation of an abstract, instrumental composition; for only through an awareness of the relationships involved—the purely musical drama of an unexpected *Ausführung,* for example, or the logic of a particular harmonic inflection—can the listener comprehend whatever significance the piece has to offer.

The theorist's cautious stance toward instrumental music is reflected in the discussion of his six keyboard concertos.[16] Intended for the amateur's entertainment, these pieces were designed to be easier than most concertos, yet more difficult than a typical sonata. In the spirit of the *Betrachtungen,* they encompass a wide span of styles and shapes, as well as technical challenges for the performer. Of the six, only two could be described as standard, three-movement models. One of the concertos features an opening slow movement, while another sports a descriptive title, *L'agnello perduto e ritrovato.* As the composer explains, he has scored the works and had them engraved in a manner that allows for three different kinds of rendition: as solo sonatas (the tutti parts having been realized on the keyboard staff), as accompanied sonatas, or as actual concertos, employing the *ad libitum* string and wind parts included in the musical supplements.

Before analyzing specific pieces from the set, Vogler contemplates the distinctive qualities of the genre and offers speculations on its origins. The melodious utterances of primeval man, he proposes, led to the phenomenon of choral singing in later epochs. Then, closer to modern times, the practice of featuring the contrast between a soloist and a concerted group furnished a vocal model that would eventually be imitated by instruments; and thus the modern concerto arose. While he calls attention to the inherent virtue of the genre—the delineation of a primary voice against the background ensemble—he laments its misuse in the acrobatic, fulsomely embellished style of contemporary practitioners. Addressing the need for reform, the model concertos illustrate an approach that emphasizes sentiment rather than showmanship while placing soloist and accompaniment in a balanced relationship.

The discussion of the pieces begins with generalization on overall design, then proceeds by relating the first movement of a concerto to that of a typical sonata. The correspondence he describes calls to mind the procedures Mozart used to transform an existing sonata into a concerto.[17] The principal parts are comparable, he observes, but the repeats are deleted and ritornellos are added to punctuate the main sections. Drawing a comparison with the background of a painting, he cautions against allowing these portions to overshadow the solo.

Basic elements of structure having thus been explained, the discussion of the second concerto concentrates on the analysis of harmony and periodization. The sole mention of expressive or pictorial significance concerns a brief introductory phrase in the first movement—characterized by sustained tones, a gradually rising line, and a long, continuous crescendo—which is compared with the image of dark mists arising from the underworld.

By contrast, the programmatic third concerto, *L'agnello perduto e ritrovato,* offers a pair of movements (opening allegro and rondo) in which tones are to some extent endowed with utterable meaning. In the first movement, aspects of melodic line, harmony, and rhythm join forces to create what is described as a picture of unadorned nature, a pastoral character, and an air of tender sadness. The rondo, which features the imitation of a shepherd's horn, depicts contrasting sentiments of hope and despair, then closes with an expression of rejoicing as the stray sheep is found.

Not much is made of this program in the explanatory text, which dispenses with the matter in little more than a short paragraph. In style and design, this concerto resembles the others. Like them, it borrows conventions of theme, phrasing, rhythm, and texture from operatic music, and quite apart from its special depictive aspect, one senses that it too may stand on its merits as an abstract composition.

The potential significance that Vogler grants to abstract instrumental music, however untranslatable its language, is clarified in his discussion of the single large-scale sample found in the *Betrachtungen,* the D-minor symphony by Peter Winter mentioned above. The critique, which takes up each of the three movements in turn, betrays features typical of Vogler's analyses of instrumental music: emphasis falls on the logic of the tonal scheme and on details of harmony, theme, texture, and orchestration. Although the reader is left to surmise that the young symphonist's technical mastery is the chief virtue to be appreciated, the critic nevertheless does offer hints of a more specific point of view.

Describing the nature and characteristic function of a symphony in general terms, he cites its use as the prelude to a dramatic production. It need not make reference to the drama that follows, but it must stir the spectator and prepare him by lowering his resistance to the force of those passions that will be represented on the stage. Displaying fire and splendor, it must enthrall the listener by virtue of the force of its harmonious organization.[18] Evidently, such a work is meant to stimulate the listener's fantasy and to strike a deeper chord of response than would a playful minuet, for instance, or any piece of music designed for a more superficial kind of entertainment.

With regard to the opening movement of Winter's piece, Vogler cites a special problem resulting from a discrepancy between basic ingredients the composer has chosen and the norms of the genre. Whereas the mandatory brilliance and pomp of a symphony normally call for the major mode and duple meter, Winter has selected a minor key and triple time. According to the system, the minor keys lack vigor, for the softness of the artificial minor triads on tonic, fourth, and fifth scale degrees determines their essential character. And the three-beat measure, likewise contradictory in this context, tends to drag as a result of the inherent contrast between long downbeat and short upbeat. In effect, the critic suggests, these are obstacles that the composer has overcome. Thus the work betrays a peculiar intensity that comes from cutting against the grain of convention and winning mastery over the given materials.

Having explained this circumstance, Vogler proceeds phrase by phrase through the opening movement, citing instances in which the composer succeeds in affecting the listener. In the process of transition from tonic minor to relative major, the combined effects of detached arpeggiation in the bass, scalar figuration in the first violin, and animated rustling in the inner parts excite the imagination (see Example 5). As the passage unfolds, the unexpected turn toward G minor (measure 32) causes astonishment—redoubled by the sudden shift from G major as a temporary tonic to a dominant of the dominant that announces the turn to the secondary key, F major.[19]

Here the artist's purpose is not merely to entertain but to move the listener, an aim his symphony must accomplish by the stunning impact of its content: the theatrical gestures, now fiery, now beguiling; the brilliant orchestral colors and vivid contrasts; and perhaps most important of all, the inspired control of harmony, by which the composer astounds the listener while achieving a logically coherent design.

Proudly displaying this symphony in the pages of the serial, Vogler draws a connection between Winter's achievement and the distinctively progressive quality of music at Mannheim. Of course, he takes pains to associate this phenomenon with the fruits of theoretical knowledge. From his

Example 5
Winter, Symphony in D minor, first
movement, measures 27–38 (wind
parts omitted).

rationalist point of view, it would seem inevitable that the dissemination of musical science should give rise to improvement in the practice of the art, and that confusion and prejudice should wither under the scrutiny of an enlightened system.

As we have seen, Vogler does not claim to have initiated the enlightenment of which he speaks. According to his account, the great strides in theory and practice were initiated in the early eighteenth century. Prior to that time, progress had been imperceptibly slow, and music, pursued in ignorance of the principles on which natural harmony is based, was consequently primitive. True, the art of the older masters (most notably Palestrina) was endowed with a timeless sublimity in tune with natural order, but music of greater complexity and wider expressive range demanded a degree of theoretical control unavailable before the time of Rameau. Through the epoch-making achievements of the French theorist and his successors, theoretical enlightenment had prepared the way for new advances.[20]

But ignorance persisted among conservatives, most notably the North Germans, who insisted on clinging to old-fashioned ways. From Vogler's perspective, whereby scientific knowledge was the *sine qua non* of progress, they were destined to pursue a wayward, benighted path. Unenlightened, critics were unable to recognize good taste, composers created artificial, disorganized music, and theorists and teachers spread confusion, succeeding only in placing obstacles in the way of the hapless pupil.

Vogler's attitude, perhaps symptomatic of an antipathy between north and south, surfaces frequently in *Betrachtungen*. On the defensive from the start, the theorist alludes darkly to unjust criticism of his system. A hostile Berlin reviewer is mentioned in the fourth fascicle. In the final issue of the first volume, the critique in question is reprinted, and three of Vogler's pupils are called on to supply explanatory essays in response to objections that have been raised.

The fourth issue of *Betrachtungen* came to grips with a Hamburg critic who had condemned Ignaz Holzbauer's German opera, *Günther von Schwarzburg*, premiered in 1777. Taking the older Mannheim composer to task for his alleged mistreatment of the German language, the North German critic upheld the art of Handel and Telemann as models for German composers. The reply, penned by an anonymous amateur, defends Holzbauer, Vogler, and the progressive style of the Mannheimers. Citing the previous year's performance of Handel's *Messiah,* which evoked yawns from all members of the audience, he points out the fallacy of calling on the alleged authority of the older German masters to judge a modern composition.[21]

The evils of prejudice and conservatism, it would appear, were responsible for the disparity portrayed in *Betrachtungen* between artistic progress at Mannheim and backwardness in the north. And the northern attitude, reflected in the scathing critique of Vogler's system by the Berlin critic, was being perpetuated in the writings of the northern theorists. Foremost among these was the Bach disciple Johann Philipp Kirnberger. The last book of his magisterial *Die Kunst des reinen Satzes in der Musik* had appeared in 1779, and in the third volume of *Betrachtungen,* Vogler takes the opportunity to denounce the treatise in an extensive review.[22] Calling attention to Kirnberger's veneration of Bach's art as a pedagogical model, he decries the author's distinction between free and strict styles. A true science of music permits no exceptions. Since its precepts are based on natural principles, they apply universally. Kirnberger's reliance on the practices of Bach evidently had caused him to become mired in contradictions. The implication is that Bach's idiom, however inspired, was eccentric, contorted, and artificial, and therefore hopelessly inappropriate as a guide for the student of composition.[23]

Pursuing his argument, Vogler cites a pair of Bach chorales that Kirnberger had presented as models of strict style in the second part of his treatise.[24] Pointing out Bach's errors, he reinforces his argument by offering his own, improved harmonizations. He observes that in Bach's setting of *Das alte Jahr vergangen ist,* the B-flats and C-sharps in the opening phrase have the effect of obliterating the very Dorian mode of which the chorale was supposed to be an illustration (see Example 6a). No less problematical is the treatment of dissonance: the abrasive C-natural in the tenor (measure 1, beat 1), the discordant double passing tones in the upper voices (measure 1, beat 2), and the accented, unprepared D that intrudes in the penultimate chord.[25]

Proceeding to revise the phrase in question, Vogler attempts to preserve the essential framework of Bach's harmony and voice leading, while purging the original of its errors (see Example 6b). Apparently reasoning that the need for an accidental arises only at the cadence, where the V chord must be major to signal a decisive close, he abolishes all inflections but the last C-sharp. Concerning the treatment of dissonances, he applies the rule that quarter notes and eighth notes should be explainable either as members of a consonant harmony or as dissonances correctly prepared and resolved. Although the revision does not relieve Bach's harmonization of all improper passing tones, it does cure the phrase of the more obvious alleged asperities. Moreover, the accompanying voices now flow more smoothly, they balance one another in degree of movement, and the felicitous effect of imitation between bass and tenor is allowed to stand out in relief.

With Bach's music as their guide, no wonder the northerners remained muddled and ineffectual in their compositions! A song by Kirnberger, reviewed in the second volume of *Betrachtungen,* betrays the affliction. The Berliner's use of the minor mode proves inappropriate to the heroic manner of the text, dissonances are treated improperly, and melody as well as inner

Example 6
(a) J. S. Bach's harmonization of *Das
alte Jahr vergangen ist* (measures
1–2) with Vogler's fundamental-bass
analysis; (b) Vogler's revision.

voices tend toward monotony and disorganization. Eccentricities of harmony and rhythm prevent the listener from making any sense of the whole.
In his setting of the second stanza, the composer changes his temporary tonic,
C major, to a dominant in the fourth measure, thereby tonicizing the subdominant—a retrogressive inflection that properly belongs to the conclusion
of a musical discourse, not its beginning (see Example 7). Here, in effect, the
inflection represents a return before departure has taken place.[26]

  Sharply contrasted to Vogler's assessments of North German contemporaries and predecessors are his observations on the Italians, among whom he
finds practices truly worthy of emulation. Though he does credit his own
countrymen with a penchant for rich harmony and inventiveness, he senses
that they have much to learn from the Italian gift for natural, unadorned

Example 7
J. P. Kirnberger, *Lied nach dem*
*Frieden,* measures 9–16.

song, so different from the German tendency toward turgid and artificial expression. In Italy, earlier masters had possessed a unique gift for authenticity and simplicity of expression. These traits, combined with an innate feeling for design and proportion, had enabled them to develop a style on which subsequent generations of composers could build.

This genuine, spontaneous art of sentiment and natural proportion finds expression in an aria by Galuppi, offered as a model in the first volume of *Betrachtungen*. The song, "Se cerca, se dice," taken from Galuppi's thirty-year-old setting of Metastasio's *Olimpiade,* exemplifies the naiveté and accessibility of the composer's language. It illustrates his gift for characterization, the flexibility and poignancy of his contrasts, and the remarkable diversity he achieves with the simplest of means. Yet along with these positive traits, the piece reveals weaknesses which are perhaps attributable to an epoch when ears and minds were imperfectly attuned to natural correspondences between harmony and expression. In setting the words "ah nò sì gran duolo non darle per me," the composer introduces an expressively appropriate inflection, turning from major to minor with good effect. But in the phrase that follows, the reversion to the major mode contradicts the sorrowful expression that should prevail (see Example 8). Vogler concedes that the passage is musically inspired, with its arpeggiated melody in the cello set off against the tremolo of the upper strings and the reinforcing winds. But

Example 8
Galuppi, Aria "Se cerca, se dice,"
measures 23–29.

the composer has nevertheless erred, evidently having substituted elegance in these measures for the pathos demanded by his text.[27]

Vogler's general fondness for Italian music notwithstanding, his critique of a recent setting by Anfossi of this same aria betrays severe misgivings about contemporary theatrical practices.[28] It would seem that, although the range of available resources has expanded, sensitivity, nuance, and the feeling for natural depiction of sentiment have been pushed aside. Virtuosity has become an end in itself, and tendencies toward excess have gone unchecked by any heed to the enduring values of simplicity. Vogler's commitment to innovation is thus tempered by a yearning for the restoration of lost virtues that came naturally in former times. Tempted and perplexed by a wealth of available materials, the modern composer must make the conscious effort to regain what has been lost, and to seek renewal by assimilating the lessons preserved in naturally inspired masterworks of the past.

This attitude of enlightened nostalgia claims a prominent place in Vogler's message. Not unlike his older French contemporary Rousseau, he calls for a return to the wellsprings of pure, natural, and simple expression. Yet he advocates progress as well, as if by combining technical advancement with comprehension of a lost natural innocence, his countrymen would find themselves on the proper path toward improvement in musical expression.

Pursuing this issue, he turns to a universally known masterpiece of an earlier generation, the *Stabat Mater* of Pergolesi, and proposes to use the work as an object lesson. By examining its strengths and weaknesses, then subjecting each of its movements to revision, he intends to demonstrate the capacity of his system to promote enlightenment by uniting the virtues of an old style with the new.[29]

Distributed over the course of the three volumes, Vogler's study of the *Stabat Mater* stands out as the most ambitious project in the *Betrachtungen* and the most rigorous test of his principles. With the aid of the system, the hidden merits of Pergolesi's work must be brought to light and its faults corrected: the violations of harmonic order, the awkward, asymmetrical phrasing, and the dryness and monotony of textures and rhythm that mar the original work and demand improvement.

Vogler's procedure of revision (*Verbesserung*) furnishes an incomparably useful tool for criticism. The method involves placement of original and revision on facing pages of the musical supplements so that the two may be compared as the reader studies the text. Numbers and letters placed on the score facilitate reference to specific instances of "error" and "improvement," and the resulting accumulation of details yields a coherent picture of the whole. The system, previously limited to specifying errors or felicities in a given work, now gains a new purpose, for in highlighting the contrast between original and revision, it provides a measure of the stylistic distances traversed in the half century between Pergolesi's time and Mannheim of the late 1770s.

To achieve the aim of his *Verbesserung,* Vogler's procedure requires transformation of the work's substance while leaving the outlines of the original movements recognizably intact. With the exception of the two fugal movements ("Fac ut ardeat" and the final "Amen"), both of which are thoroughly rewritten, the burden of revision falls on the bass, the instrumental accompaniments, and the ritornellos. Only rarely does Vogler change the profile of Pergolesi's vocal lines, and in just one instance (the setting of the verse "Sancta mater") is the original tonal scheme overhauled.

Concentrating on bass line and scoring, Vogler scorns the thin, polarized textures that predominate in the original work. In their place he designs textures in which the bass loses some of its melodic significance but gains in rhythmic stability and harmonic emphasis. The viola part likewise takes on a different personality, casting off its subordinate role in the original work, where it often merely doubled the bass, and acquiring rhythmic flexibility, eloquence, and expressive impact.

The first three measures of Example 9a, from Pergolesi's original "Quae moerebat," show a stepwise descending bass, doubled at the octave by viola. The texture of the phrase as a whole is spare and uniform, and except for the vocal melisma in measure 46, rhythmic variety is minimal. The revision, shown in Example 9b, combines a stabilized bass line with enrichment of the upper string parts and increased rhythmic diversity. Commenting on his improvement of the harmony, Vogler observes that in measure 43 of the original movement, a B-flat occurs against the C-minor harmony of the upper parts. Occupying half a measure, the note lasts too long to be sanctioned as a passing tone; and since it lacks preparation as a suspended consonance, it constitutes an unjustifiable dissonant seventh.[30] To correct the problem, he simply abolishes the stepwise descent and replaces it with an oscillating bass whose tones conform to the prevailing harmony.

Here, according to Vogler, knowledge of the science of harmony has enabled him to identify an error in the original. Correcting the fault by redesigning the bass line, he then uses his new bass as the foundation for a rhythmically differentiated, firmly punctuated phrase that encompasses diversity in dynamics, texture, and movement. In the process, the vocal line remains virtually untouched. The natural simplicity of its utterance is enhanced by the new accompaniment. The virtues of old and new styles are thus brought together in harmony, the weaknesses of the original are precisely identified, and the differences between original phrase and revision serve to dramatize the advantages of the modern idiom. Drawing strength from a rectified harmonic foundation, the phrase acquires a capacity for richness and variety unthinkable from the standpoint of the original piece and its language. The materials of harmonic unity have been fortified, structural articulation has been clarified, and a widened spectrum of possibilities for diversity has consequently become available.

In his discussions of the revised *Stabat Mater,* Vogler says little about the practical utility of the modernized work. Is the revision suitable for performance, or is it intended primarily for study purposes? Vogler frequently alludes to the need for compromise, and one senses that he felt the revision to be something of an anomaly. He had a sound reason for retaining much of the original vocal material intact, for it provided a necessary point of contact between the two versions. But in so doing, he often found himself emphasiz-

Example 9
(a) Pergolesi's *Stabat Mater*, "Quae
moerebat," measures 43–48; (b)
Vogler's revision.

ing the contrast between Pergolesi's approach and his own, rather than bridging the stylistic gap and achieving a convincing, performable work.

However imperfect stylistically, the revision stands on its merits as a lesson in artistic progress. Potential strengths are realized in accordance with advancements in the language of musical expression. Within the improved

idiom thus attained, tonal unity prevails in the unfolding of a design characterized by diversity in texture, rhythm, and dynamics. Each segment of the
design bears a clearly defined purpose in relation to the whole; the articulation
of the parts is appropriate to their function; and the structural units of a stable,
hierarchic framework stand in balanced relationship to one another.

Though the promises of such a style remain unfulfilled in the works of
the modern Italian dramatists, Vogler does cite two composers of the time,
Hasse and Jommelli, whose accomplishments come within close proximity
of his ideal. Hasse, whom Vogler regards as an outstanding genius of the age,
is admirably melodious and concise. Placing the singer in the foreground,
with little competition from the accompaniment, he has created lasting
models of lyric invention. The equally great Jommelli, by contrast, is noted
for his elaborate orchestral textures, which he applies with superlative dramatic effect. Characterized by instrumental richness, harmonic density, novelty, and detail, his art commands an unlimited domain of expression, and its
appreciation requires the sophistication of a connoisseur. His widely imitated
extravagance (with predictably deplorable results) has caused noisy endings
to become mandatory, and owing to his influence, a true *cantabile* has become
a rarity. The composer himself, Vogler maintains, envied Hasse's restraint.[31]

Vogler concludes that these two great artists exhibit complementary
strengths: simplicity in Hasse, expressive capacity in Jommelli. If a better
understanding of taste and musical science had been available to their age,
they might have approached the greatest heights of artistic accomplishment.
But as matters stand, the arrival of a master who might combine theoretical
understanding with Hasse's melodic genius and Jommelli's powers of expression remains the hope of a future generation.

### PROGRESS AND DECLINE

From his vantage point as commentator in the *Betrachtungen,* Vogler succeeded in pointing to a line of progress from the innocent age of Pergolesi and
Galuppi to the brilliance and variety—not to mention confusion and excess—
that characterized Italian operatic music of the 1770s. By the time the last
issue of *Betrachtungen* reached its readers in the spring of 1781, Vogler had
already taken leave of Mannheim and begun his sojourn in Paris and London,
thereby abandoning his inquiries into musical analysis and initiating a time of
varied endeavors as traveler, music director, performer, and composer. When

he returned to projects in criticism—first in the early 1790s, then with greater intensity in the first decade of the nineteenth century—he approached the task from an altered point of view. In the course of the 1780s, he had witnessed developments that the author of the *Betrachtungen* critiques could scarcely have anticipated, and he was consequently obliged to take a fresh look at questions of musical progress and style.

In the early years of the new century, Vogler recorded his impressions in an essay whose title includes the question, "Has music advanced or declined in the past 30 years?" ("Hat die Musik seit 30 Jahren gewonnen oder ver-lohren?") Appearing in 1808 within the second of his "Utile dulci" publications, the essay accompanied a revised version of the composer's German Mass, the *Deutsche Kirchenmusik* of 1777.[32] The need for a preface to his critique of the revision served as a pretext for the essay, which takes up the theme of musical progress that had figured so prominently in the *Betrach-tungen*.

He cautions that the question at hand promises no easy solution. One must distinguish between progress in theory and advancements in practical music, and for the latter, between performance and the various branches of composition: music for church, theater, and concert hall or chamber. In the domain of theory, he asserts that no other methods have appeared that stand comparison with his own, and he deplores the persistent tendency among theorists to derive their rules from the arbitrary practices of composers (rather than from the eternally valid laws of nature). But if he felt embittered by his contemporaries' reluctance to adopt his method in preference to others, he does not dwell on the matter here, nor does he allow this problem to interfere with the issue foremost in his mind as a critic: the remarkable advances that had taken place since the 1770s.

Performers, he finds, have become increasingly proficient, and their more highly developed skills have been a source of encouragement to composers. No longer inhibited as he works in the isolation of his atelier, the artist rests assured that players can be found who will do justice to his music. Yet there is evidently a negative side to this very advancement in technique, for improvement in execution has coincided with the decline to aesthetically meaningless excesses on the part of composers as well as performers. If virtuosity and exhibitionism had threatened to debase the art thirty years earlier, as suggested in the pages of the *Betrachtungen,* the threat was even greater now: more than ever the critic senses the need for restoration through return to the virtues of truth and simplicity of expression.

In the realm of sacred music, the need for reform has proved especially compelling. The customs of the theater have invaded the church to such an extent that one can speak only of decline. Reaffirming an allegiance confessed in earlier publications, Vogler now declares that no modern church music can compare with the choruses of Handel.[33] This opinion represents something of an about-face from the pages of the *Betrachtungen,* where Handel had been paired with Bach as a model of North German conservatism. But the Handelian revival had intervened, sweeping from England to the Continent in the course of the 1780s, and Vogler himself had joined the converts.[34] His antipathy toward the music of Bach remained, but the Handelian fugues and choruses won his wholehearted endorsement, and he now judged them worthy of emulation as superlative models of contrapuntal technique and expression.[35]

The field of sacred music, then, has witnessed decline. But music in the theater and concert hall has progressed immeasurably, outdistancing the predictions made in *Betrachtungen.* Doubtless more rapidly than he had anticipated, the Germans have overtaken the Italians, and there remains no need to look to the south for a worthy successor to Jommelli or Hasse. The greatest masters of the late eighteenth century have appeared on home ground, introducing hitherto unavailable resources of dramatic and instrumental expression. Standing foremost among them are the names of an older contemporary, Joseph Haydn, and a former rival, W. A. Mozart.

Vogler had come to recognize the towering stature not only of Haydn, but also of W. A. Mozart, and he honored both artists in a publication entitled *Verbesserung der Forkel'schen Veränderungen über das Englische Volkslied "God Save the King"* (Frankfurt am Main, 1793). In this critique of an opponent's error-ridden efforts, it is no longer the Italians' or Mannheimers' competency that he cites by way of contrast, but rather the inimitable inspirations of the two Viennese masters.[36] Reaffirming this positive assessment, Vogler's 1808 essay awards the music of Haydn and Mozart a prominent place in the portrayal of modern advancement, notably in the fields of opera, oratorio, and instrumental music.[37] In these genres unprecedented heights have been attained. But newly acquired resources must be used with discretion, lest the virtues of simplicity, restraint, and solidity of structure be obscured amid the excessive noise and virtuosity that threatens to engulf theater and concert hall as well as the church.

Thus introduced by Vogler's essay, the revised German Mass constitutes an exemplary combination of old and new. The original conception of the 1770s provides a respectable if somewhat antiquated foundation (its merits as a model of sacred style are discussed in Chapter 4), and the newly added instrumental parts demonstrate a wealth of materials available to the modern, early nineteenth-century composer. Incorporating organ, trombones, trumpets, and timpani in addition to a full complement of woodwinds and strings, the orchestra is substantially larger than those seen in works from the *Betrachtungen,* and it offers the theorist a chance to expound on the question of contemporary orchestration.

The size and flexibility of this ensemble permits division into choirs: strings, reed instruments (including flute), brass (horn, trumpet, and trombone), and timpani. In this early description of a modern orchestra and its capacities, he suggests that his instrumental divisions may be understood as organic units whose functions are interdependent and complementary. Balancing one another, these choirs furnish a virtually infinite variety of timbres. More important than the diversity of colors, however, is the interdependence of the parts. The revised Mass could not achieve its aim if any of the ingredients were missing—all must be engaged, or else none—and the tightness of the fabric in which they interlock stands as a measure of the unity of the whole.[38]

In its division of the orchestra into subgroups, its varied colors, and its generally rapid changes in sonority, the orchestrated Mass resembles the later symphonies of Haydn (which Vogler singles out in his discussion of recent advancements in composition) and the Viennese piano concertos of Mozart. Though no direct connection with the Viennese masters is actually drawn in the critique of the Mass, Vogler does offer an addendum that pays homage to Mozart specifically and betrays the author's indebtedness to his example.

The addendum in question features a curiosity: an eighteen-measure ballet-pantomine piece written as early as 1768, during the composer's student days at Würzburg, and prepared for a student performance there at the university. Taking up this *Schuster Ballet* forty years later, he now revises it as a stylistic lesson comparable in principle to the earlier *Stabat Mater* project. In a brief introduction to the critique, he calls attention to two outstanding traits: first, the employment of two pairs of horns (Vogler believes his to be the first instance of this practice); and second, an uncanny resemblance between his opening phrase and the theme with which Mozart began the second movement of his late Piano Concerto in D, K. 537 (see Example 10).[39] In general, the style of this early effort resembles that of the unpretentious chamber works printed in the *Betrachtungen* supplements. Marked by a *galant* naiveté and a simple, homophonic texture, the piece uses wind instruments to highlight the melody, add weight to the bass, or punctuate the phrases. The chief idiosyncrasy, apart from the prominent use of four horns, is the inequality of the phrasing: 3 + 4 in the first part, 4 + 2 + 5 in the second. Disparaging this asymmetry now as old-fashioned and aesthetically askew— a kind of *Kakorhythmik*—he offers a revision in which a stable, eight-measure period in the first half balances a comparably structured second part. And within this regularized design, he infuses the material with the energy and diversity of modern orchestral practice.

As witnessed in Example 10, which compares the opening phrase of the original *Schuster Ballet* with that of the revision, the similarity in scoring between the latter version and that of the Mozart concerto is striking: the previously monotonous, motivically repetitive melodic line, carried by the strings with wind reinforcement, becomes something not unlike a Mozartean dialogue between strings and winds. The texture is further enriched by the independence and flexibility of the four horns, which display a more vivid, dynamic presence than in the original dance.

No less remarkable than the interaction of upper wind and string parts is the revision of the bass line. In the passage quoted above, the stepwise eighth-note lines of measures 3 and 4 add melodic interest and rhythmic continuity to the connection between the end of one phrase and the beginning of the next. Apparently, the tendency toward a rhythmically and harmonically simplified bass that typified the revised *Stabat Mater* had lost its novelty and freshness by the time of the *Schuster Ballet* revision: clarity and order having long since been won, the composer now strives for animation and diversity, enabling the bass to contribute rhythmic and textural interest in addition to harmonic support and structural punctuation.

As seen in this excerpt from the revised *Schuster Ballet,* the amplified orchestral resources of late eighteenth-century music (most prominently that of Haydn and Mozart) have made a deep impression. Vogler's notion of progress is influenced accordingly, and he attempts to incorporate something of the new technique in his lessons and models. But in so doing he confronts a

Example 10
(a) Vogler's *Schuster Ballet* (original
version), measures 1–3; (b) 1808
revision, measures 1–4.

challenge to the views on aesthetics outlined in *Betrachtungen,* where instrumental music stood uncomfortably in the shadow of vocal expression. Although Vogler did not disqualify instrumental works from higher purposes, the notion of abstract significance—of musical meaning not associated with an extra-musical frame of reference—was pondered more as a possibility than as an acknowledged aspect of contemporary practice. But circumstances had changed since the 1770s, and late eighteenth-century developments had revealed to Vogler a compelling force not previously suspected. Accordingly, in two major projects of his later years, the *Zwei und dreisig Präludien* of 1806 and the posthumously published *System für den Fugenbau,* he explores more extensively than in earlier writings the idea of purely musical significance, and he attempts to relate the phenomenon to his theories.[40]

### MOTIVIC DEVELOPMENT AND RHETORICAL DESIGN

In these late critical studies, the field of inquiry has narrowed to questions of contrapuntal organization. The rigors of the so-called strict style, not very heavily emphasized in the pages of the amateur-oriented *Betrachtungen,* come to the fore now, as Vogler describes with great relish an approach to composition in which every note counts as an integral part of a unified thematic fabric. Some of the music discussed in these publications betrays a neo-Baroque quality: resemblances to the keyboard music of Bach can be heard in several of the preludes, and *Fugenbau* openly declares an affinity to the style and spirit of the Handelian chorus. More pointed than any dependence on Baroque models, however, is the correspondence between these pieces and the style of a late eighteenth-century development section: motivic fragments are reiterated sequentially, set off against one another, and tossed about from one part of the texture to another in a manner that calls to mind a Haydn string quartet or a Mozart concerto.

In *System für den Fugenbau,* the more systematic and detailed of the two publications, the object of discussion is the master's reworking of a choral fugue composed by a pupil, the young Meyerbeer. The text consists of the line "Gott, des Weltalls Herr, der ist König des Ruhms," followed by the Handelian exclamation "Halleluja!" These words help determine the shape of the subject, and they suggest an appropriate character for the composition as a whole; in these respects they lend an extra-musical dimension to the composition. But the text does not determine the course of events as the fugal elaborations unfold, and it is the significance residing in this very process— the disposition and relationship of parts within the whole—that Vogler concentrates on explaining.

Though the analytical techniques employed are more refined than those seen in *Betrachtungen,* the approach is similar in principle. The theorist uses the teachings of his system to identify main sections, key areas, periodization, and the chord roots that comprise the phrases.[41] He discusses overall shape and compositional procedure by calling on his notion of musical rhetoric, and he uses his concepts of statement (*Vortrag*), transposition (*Versezung*), elaborative continuation (*Fortführung*), and motivic development (*Ausführung*) to account for various aspects of unity and diversity. In a work of this type there are no extraneous elements: all voice parts are thematic, and all derive from the subject and its counterpoints. Given this circumstance, it proves essential that the issue of thematic elaboration should occupy a major portion of the discussion.

In *Betrachtungen,* Vogler had distinguished between *Fortführung* and *Ausführung* as two basic kinds of continuation from an initial thematic statement: the former involving generation of new ideas from the preceding, the latter designating processes of fragmentation and sequential elaboration of previously stated material. While these options sufficed in the 1770s, the theorist chose to expand his categorization in later writings by including a third process that he called *Durchführung*. The new term, eventually destined to become a standard word for thematic development, furnished a means to distinguish between such customary, utilitarian devices as sequence and fragmentation, and the daring or unexpected manipulation of musical ideas. The author grants that there may be only a fine line of distinction between these processes, and clearly there is a good deal of overlap between categories in the extensive list of examples he cites. Nevertheless bent on applying the new term to his analysis, he shows that in the passage quoted below (Example 11), the soprano line presents an *Ausführung* of the fugal answer, measures 5 and 6 (see Chapter 2, Example 14, which shows Vogler's representation of subject, answer, and attendant counterpoints). But *Durchführung* takes place as well, for material from one of the original counterpoints (measure 6, tenor line) has been taken out of its original context, doubled in alto and tenor, and treated in sequence against the two-measure fragment of the answer in the soprano part.[42]

The discussion of development in *Fugenbau* serves a purpose comparable to the analyses of chord roots elsewhere: it provides a means of accounting for all the notes, and it explains fundamental sources of organization and coherence. Just as the chord roots represent the elaboration of a fundamental harmonic unity, so the melodic processes in the different voice parts are understood as the unfolding of an initial thematic kernel to which everything

Example 11
Vogler's model fugue, measures
31–33.

in the piece may ultimately be related. In *Fugenbau,* however, such technical analysis merely provides a prelude to the discussion of musical significance that he discerns in the musical organization.

According to Vogler's approach, the work in question embodies a network of interacting processes that affect the ear, the heart, and the mind. This interaction can be comprehended in terms of three complementary vantage points: the rhetorical, logical, and aesthetic. Though he does not define the three aspects in detail, the terms play a prominent role in his account of musical purposes and effects. Thus the plan of a fugal subject and answer reveals a rhetorical aspect: the initial modulation gives rise to discussion, and the answer responds with a tonally coherent reply. At the same time, the plan is logical, for the answer follows the subject as its consequence; and the coherence of the scheme has the ability to move the hearer persuasively, so that it possesses an inherent aesthetic quality as well.[43]

We learn that in a given composition, ingredients may be interpreted from these different perspectives. Each facet may be isolated for purposes of criticism. Each reveals a unique truth, and in a harmoniously constructed work the three join together to explain the meaning conveyed by the whole. Considered in terms of rhetoric, a composition follows an orderly course of events that somehow corresponds to the form of an oration. Regarded logically, it comprises patterns that stand in the relationship of cause and effect, or whose relationship may be understood as a consequence of natural law (the ingredients of a suitably placed cadential formula, for example). Finally, in terms of aesthetics, the materials involved in the rhetorically and logically organized plan will enhance one another (the start of a rhetorical epilogue, for example, will coincide with a return to tonic, or a melodic highpoint, or a full-bodied, *forte* exclamation) so that the listener's emotions are affected persuasively. Like three graces, rhetoric, logic, and aesthetics join hands in the creation of an exemplary work of art.[44] The critic's task is to explain musical expression as well as order in terms of these three aspects and their interaction.

Vogler places his discussion of musical meaning at the end of the treatise, where it rests on the foundation of the foregoing commentary. The author's plan is to go through the fugue once more, this time examining its course of events in terms of his rhetorical, logical, and aesthetic points of view. At measure 111, not far beyond the midpoint of this 199-measure piece, the soprano and bass lines embark on a pattern of imitation in stretto, the organ introduces a prolonged pedal point, and thus "the fugue seems to be pressing toward conclusion." From the rhetorician's point of view, the passage appears to proclaim that "all confutations have been set aside," and that "now the truth triumphs resoundingly." The logical argument appears to have been resolved, and the aesthetic requirements of conclusion seem satisfied. "But no! The *suspensio* enters," taking the form of a close stretto that engages all parts, and "from measure 122 on, a general tension develops." Here, various ingredients are united to give logical coherence and aesthetic impact to a rhetorical device (*suspensio*), by which the expected progress of the oration is interrupted; and in the coordination of elements thus engaged lies the source of the meaning conveyed by the music.[45]

With the aid of this critical method, musical elements are shown to communicate meaning by virtue of their interaction.[46] The commentaries on the earlier *Zwei und dreisig Präludien* (1806) cover similar ground. The individual pieces are much shorter, but all are comparably serious in intent and rigorous in technique. Nearly all of them involve the elaboration and development of a single thematic idea, most involve the working out of contrapuntal textures, and one (No. 8) is actually designated "fuga d'imitazione" (i.e., a quasi-fugal elaboration of a subject). Like the exemplary work featured in the fugue treatise, these pieces constitute models of a strict style that excludes any material not derived from an opening subject or thematic idea.

In the theorist's treatment of the preludes, much attention is paid to the sources of unity and structural organization. References to thematic processes are ubiquitous. The new term *Durchführung* appears, and several experiments in periodization are undertaken, possibly prompted by the discussions of period structure in Heinrich Koch's *Versuch einer Anleitung zur Composition* (1782–93). In one such attempt (Prelude No. 16), seven periods are identified by Roman numerals as an aid to the analysis of tonal articulation and thematic content. In another instance (Prelude No. 25), phrases are marked with Arabic numbers to reveal a pattern that might be described as an acceleration in the rhythm of the phrasing from four-measure to two-measure units.

The plan proposed for interpreting these resources foreshadows the scheme of the fugue treatise: three vantage points are mentioned, including rhetorical, aesthetic, and a third (roughly comparable to the logical aspect of *Fugenbau*) which Vogler designates here as "harmonic." No attempt is made to define the terms rigorously, but the reader may infer from the analyses that "harmony" in this context has to do with the logic of chord succession and tonal unity, "rhetoric" with issues of structure, processes of elaboration, and timing, and "aesthetics" with relative degrees of emphasis and the balanced coordination of musical elements.[47] As in the later study, the author suggests that the music is endowed with weighty yet abstract significance, and he indicates that a major goal of his analysis is to explain the nature of the musical content he perceives.

The main emphasis falls on the principle of musical rhetoric. By and large, the rhetorical designs examined involve a declarative statement, an extended elaboration involving departure from tonic toward relatively remote tonal regions, and an *epiphonema,* or epilogue, in which the theme reappears intact and the tonic key is reaffirmed decisively. In addition to the basic factor of tonal movement, elements contributing to this characteristic scheme include dynamics, the rhythm of the phrasing, and the manipulation of thematic ingredients. Typically, these materials cooperate to bring about a particular kind of intensification that leads to a point of climax before the epilogue. In the extended critique of Prelude No. 8, Vogler calls attention to a pattern of fragmentation in the phrasing, from four- to two- to one-measure units, and shows how this plan is coordinated with a goal-directed harmonic process that reaches culmination just before the establishment of the flat-second scale degree as a temporary tonal center.[48]

Except for the detailed, eleven-page discussion of the eighth prelude, musical analysis in *Präludien* bears no comparison in thoroughness to that of the fugue treatise. Yet in some respects, the freely sketched commentaries of the earlier study penetrate further than *Fugenbau* into the realm of criticism. In *Präludien*, where each design is understood to be unique and none follows a prescribed or stereotyped procedure, Vogler resorts to a vocabulary of metaphor and personification in order to explain novel effects and patterns. Certain processes acquire a personality and a will of their own, enabling his interpretation of musical meaning to assume a relatively concrete shape.

The commentary to Prelude No. 22 calls attention to the final three measures of a middle section—the highpoint of a twenty-three-measure discourse that has involved the change from major tonic to parallel minor, and that now requires a transition back to major before the start of the epilogue (see Example 12). The preceding phrases have featured a one-measure kernel comprising antecedent and consequent members (*Vordersatz* and *Nachsatz*, as indicated in the opening thematic statement). The climactic passage in question dissects this main subject, offering three statements of the antecedent followed by three of the consequent (measures 21–23). Thus "the antecedent of the theme imposes itself three times in succession, without yielding to the consequent, which for its part appears to avenge itself in the second half of the 22nd and in the 23rd measure by likewise commanding the field exclusively three times in succession."[49]

Here the tension between antecedent and consequent gestures provides

Example 12
Vogler, Prelude No. 22 in G,
measures 1–2; 21–23.

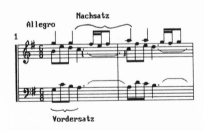

the basis for elaboration and intensification in the unfolding of the design. At the moment of greatest intensity, the two particles are pulled apart. The unit of phrasing is compressed, from whole measure to half measure, and the antecedent temporarily overcomes the consequent in a rising sequential passage. The consequent, refusing to be silenced any longer, responds by insisting on three statements of its own. The author's description of this passage reaches beyond the identification of chords, structural functions, and thematic derivations: by personifying the purely musical interactions in the measures described, it captures a specific aspect of their meaning.

Different kinds of tension and different sources of significance may come to the fore elsewhere in a rhetorical plan. In Prelude No. 3, the epilogue yields a conclusion of extraordinary intensity (see Example 13). Before it begins, the main theme reappears in the major mode *anspruchslos* (unassumingly) at measure 30. Then it returns, "consoled," to the minor (measures 31–32). At this point the discourse becomes more animated, and the music presses forward with ever-increasing urgency toward an energetic close. In measures 33 and 34, a stretto-like *Ausführung* of a thematic fragment gives the impression of exhausting the rhetorical argument. The final four measures "close with commotion," deeming themselves unable to carry the discourse further.[50]

As in the excerpt cited from Prelude No. 22, the personification of

Example 13
Prelude No. 3 in C minor, measures
30–38.

relationships within a rhetorical design enables Vogler to interpret musical processes without drawing on anything outside the music itself. The former instance involved a struggle between antecedent and consequent units; the second, an almost violent exclamation, an outcry whose emphatic syncopations and dissonances nearly threaten to burst the design asunder on the threshold of conclusion. As these passages convey their musical truths, their significance has nothing to do with scene-painting, dramatic representation, or pantomine. The musical language represented here has surmounted older limitations of abstract composition and entered a realm of musical expression that speaks to the heart as it engages the intellect. In response, the critic undertakes his search for a method by which its meanings can be interpreted in accordance with the teachings of his system.

To judge from his own disclaimers, Vogler did not pretend to accomplish more than a tentative pedagogical sketch in either *Präludien* or *Fugenbau*. Nevertheless these projects, along with the theorist's earlier endeavors, constitute a landmark in critical analysis. Thirty years previously, he had set out to demonstrate the efficacy of his system, a goal that required model analyses of existing compositions. From the start he had asserted that all details of a composition must relate to fundamental principles, but that a theoretical system could not arbitrarily dictate formulas for musical design and expression. This circumstance helped define the purpose of an enlightened criticism: it must evaluate existing musical practices in terms of theoretical truths, and offer guidance by revealing pertinent connections between appropriate materials and the theoretical foundations on which they rested.

Between the time of *Betrachtungen* and the later analytical experiments, musical styles underwent change, and Vogler's procedures of criticism changed accordingly. Keeping abreast of his times as a composer, teacher, and critic, he strove to come to terms with innovations and incorporate them into his teachings. Because his efforts involved placing contemporary practices in a historical perspective, they furnish a stylistic portrait of the age. According to its outlines, the ingredients of a modern idiom had been established in the music of Pergolesi and his Italian contemporaries, and from that time on, progress was marked by expansion in technical means and enrichment of the capacities for musical expression. As composers' vocabularies expanded, resources that served to convey imagery and expression in vocal or depictive music were successfully incorporated into abstract instrumental composition. Meanwhile, the notion of progress itself grew more complex, the celebration of advancement vying with an increasing sense of nostalgia for a lost nobility and simplicity of former times. Ties with the past were strengthened as the theorist joined his contemporaries in looking with ever-greater absorption to the music of an earlier day for guidance and inspiration. The ideal of advancement toward a foreseeable goal of perfection thus changed to a quest for unlimited vistas, extending into the past as well as the future.

## CHAPTER 4

# Theory and Practice in
# Music for the Church

F ROM the time of his earliest musical accomplishments to the end of his
life, Vogler was engaged almost continuously as a composer, performer,
teacher, or critic of church music. A cleric who had gained entry to Carl
Theodor's court as a member of the sacred establishment, he cultivated sacred
music as his natural milieu, the territory on which he could speak with
greatest authority. He was already experienced in this realm by the time of his
arrival at Mannheim; and the journey to Italy soon thereafter enabled him to
learn from two prominent masters of church music, Martini and Vallotti, and
to familiarize himself with traditional customs and styles of Italian sacred
music. While serving at the Elector's Catholic court, he gained proficiency
with the highly elaborate, orchestrally enriched settings for which Mannheim was famous,[1] as well as with simpler modes of sacred expression. In
later phases of his career his explorations extended further, eventually encompassing Protestant traditions as well as Catholic.

As a critic and composer, Vogler pursued a course whose changing
directions reflected major quandaries and cross-currents of the eighteenth
century, notably those involving the clash of traditional values with such
emerging reform movements as the Palestrina revival and the beginnings of
Cecilianism. In response to the prevailing diversity in thought and practice,
he sought to define appropriate criteria for sacred music in terms of persisting
customs and changing requirements. His efforts led to proposals that sometimes proved contradictory but nevertheless dealt directly and imaginatively
with issues at hand.

The questions he addressed in his theoretical writings and in practical compositions centered on the suitable choice of materials in setting sacred texts. In light of the widespread use of virtuosic, theatrical elements in sacred music (a tendency that extended to the wholesale incorporation of operatic arias supplied with sacred texts), this was a major concern among both Protestant and Catholic critics;[2] and though opinions were divided on the particular form sacred music should take, there was considerable agreement on matters of stylistic and aesthetic orientation. Enlightened thinking of the time emphasized instilling a devotional attitude, or *Andacht,* in the worshipper, and this was a goal to which the noise, confusion, and exhibitionism of modern, secularly oriented fashions seemed detrimental.

The belief that something was amiss, that foreign elements threatened the ideal purity of sacred expression, was reflected in the papal bull known as *Annus qui* issued by Pope Benedict XIV in the year of Vogler's birth, 1749. In it, the pope firmly opposed theatrical ingredients of all kinds—including particular instruments that evoked the spirit of the theater, such as trumpets, timpani, and horns—and in their place advocated an approach that would move the "souls of the faithful . . . to the contemplation of spiritual things."[3]

Prior to this document, and for decades to come, the protest against secular contamination was voiced in many quarters. Typically it was linked with another aspect of enlightened thinking, an ideal of simplicity that touched all areas of worship, from the order of the service to the music. Critics of sacred music who subscribed to this ideal spoke of applying it to all genres, including larger, concerted works as well as harmonized plainsong, chorales, and hymns. Their reformist attitude required that textural complexity, and vocal and instrumental virtuosity, be avoided. Late in the eighteenth century the promotion of simplicity came to include Palestrina and the *a cappella* ideal, while reform movements gathered momentum and critics reached into the past in search of suitable models.

As can be surmised from *Annus qui* and other writings of the time, comprehensibility of text stood beside simplicity as a guiding principle. If sacred music was to inspire devotional thought it must be readily understood. The text must be neither distorted by musical virtuosity nor overwhelmed by an orchestral accompaniment. Use of the vernacular became an important part of the quest for comprehensibility, especially among Catholics, and it was a vital aspect of reforms such as those undertaken by Joseph II.[4]

Elaborating these topics in writings that spanned more than three decades, from the 1778 *Kuhrpfälzische Tonschule* with its basic statements of principle to the late *System für den Fugenbau* (1811), Vogler pondered the fragility of sacred music and its vulnerability to corruption. Early on he acknowledged that sensual, profane music appealed most directly to the appetites of audiences, and that the opera composer was consequently destined to win greater fame than the church musician.[5] The challenge facing the latter was to abstain from luxurious theatrical style without lapsing into dryness or monotony,[6] primarily through the cultivation of an ideally pure, vocally inspired art of expression.

The vocal ideal, variants of which are found with increasing frequency among late eighteenth-century writers on church music, was one that Vogler modified repeatedly yet nevertheless attempted to sustain in most subsequent writings. Explaining the basis for his view in an early essay on his C-major *Miserere,* he conjured an image reminiscent of Rousseau's musings on primeval music by describing human song as the earliest form of musical expression, awakened by sounds of nature.[7] He linked this notion of primeval song with worship, and characterized unaccompanied vocal music as the "oldest, purest, and most sublime" form of music that "emanates from the soul, . . . [bearing] eternal awesome truths that lift the heart to the Creator."[8]

Cherishing the pristine quality of pure vocal music and its capacity for timeless endurance, Vogler sensed that this was one kind of musical utterance that could permit no embellishment. In an essay in *Betrachtungen,* "Thätige Geschmaks-Bildung für die Beurtheiler der Tonstücken," he speaks of the "noble simplicity of unadorned nature"—the quality that made the Medici Venus a universally appreciated masterpiece and that typified such works as the *Miserere* settings by Allegri and Baj, Palestrina's *Improperium,*[9] Pitoni's sixteen-voice *Dixit Dominus* for four choruses, the 50 Psalms of Marcello's *Estro poetico-armonico,* and certain sacred vocal compositions by Vallotti.[10] As was the case with Herder, Reichardt, and other reformers,[11] Vogler's reference to models of vocal purity betrays a bias in favor of the Italians—the same leaning that marks his early writings on opera and secular vocal music, doubtless nurtured by the impressions of his Italian sojourn.

Vogler's discussions of his vocal ideal suggest that the concept of "noble simplicity" must be qualified when applied to modern, practical composition. To achieve the powerful effects of which it was capable, sacred music called for more than an attitude of artless devotion on the part of the composer: it required an understanding of the sophisticated *stile antico* as well. A characteristic reference to the subject in an essay of 1782 associates sacred music with majestic style, tied notes, numerous dissonances, and the avoidance of perfect cadences within units shorter than eight to ten measures.[12] Waxing eloquent in *Betrachtungen,* Vogler identifies sacred music with "a solemn manner, splendid movement, artful texture, sustained notes, and ideas of awe-inspiring magnificence for the competing essential parts."[13] In more specific terms, he cites the importance of an artful weaving of inner voices, a solid bass line, and a sustaining of the open vowels of important words.[14] Elsewhere he stresses the desirability of rounded, independent contours in the individual voices by drawing his favorite analogy with a planetary system: just as each planet rotates about its own axis, each voice enjoys limited independence within the harmonious order of the overall design.[15]

Along with its allegiance to the *stile antico,* Vogler's sacred ideal embraced the technique of fugal polyphony. He proposed that fugal writing be understood as the exclusive property of the church, capable of powerful expression when combined with a sacred text,[16] and he applauded the effectiveness of the great choral fugues of Handel.[17] To be sure, his concept of appropriate fugal style was restrictive (while admiring Handel's fugues for their clarity, simplicity, and power, he condemns what he perceived as excessive density and artifice in those of Bach),[18] but he clearly parted company on this issue with such leading reformers as Doles, Hiller, and Reichardt, who disparaged fugal writing altogether because of its complexity and its interference with clear delivery of text.

Also liberal by comparison with more zealous advocates of reform was Vogler's attitude toward the use of instruments. Declining to forego altogether the benefits of modern orchestral color as a resource for church music, he argued that instruments can support and elevate the voices, and if properly used can endow a sacred composition with deepened significance.[19] In the 1807 orchestrated version of his *Deutsche Kirchenmusik* (to be examined below), he supplied a practical model for their acceptable use in accompanying a chorus.

But Vogler did object to what he felt was a pervasive misuse of orchestral accompaniments, and in this sense he believed that papal bans against instruments in the church were justified.[20] In particular, he deplored certain secular or theatrical modes of expression that seemed inappropriate for sacred texts: a *Miserere* adorned with sprightly leaping figures in the strings, or a *Kyrie* whose pleas of pious supplication are overpowered by thunderbolts from trumpet and timpani that shake the very foundations of the church.[21] Ever vigilant in decrying such abuses, he addressed the issue pointedly in the 1808 essay that asked "Has music advanced or declined in the past 30 years?" Sacred music has been overwhelmed by the style of the opera house, he declares. The rigors of vocal fugue and counterpoint have been supplanted by light-minded song and noisy orchestration. Melodic invention has come to rely too heavily on ornamentation and harmonic effect, while choral writing has become excessively dependent on instrumental accompaniments. As modern orchestras drown out the singers, deafen the audiences, and render the words unintelligible, genuine sacred expression slides toward the abysses of Janissary music.[22]

As the foregoing passages from Vogler's writings suggest, it is difficult to categorize his views on sacred music in any simple way. On one hand, he envisaged a pure, unaccompanied vocal music characterized by clarity and simplicity. On the other hand, he evidently preferred not to let his commitment to such an ideal dampen his enthusiasm for the diversity, novelty, and textural richness that he deemed essential to the expressive potential of modern music, sacred as well as secular. Inclined to endorse an amalgamation of stylistic possibilities while nevertheless frowning on theatrical extravagance, the theorist himself saw the mixture of restraint and expressive freedom he advocated as a worthy subject of clarification through analysis and demonstration. In the volumes of the *Betrachtungen* he included no fewer than three enlightening examples from among his own works—compositions that represented divergent yet acceptable practices within the realm of sacred non-orchestral vocal music.

### CRITIQUES OF EXEMPLARY SACRED WORKS: THE VOCAL IDIOM

The works in question include a twenty-two-measure Latin motet, *Ecce panis angelorum;* a six-movement *Miserere* in C major, for choir with *basso continuo;* and the *Deutsche Kirchenmusik,* a nine-movement setting of the vernacular *Singmesse* text accompanied by organ. As with most other analyses in the *Betrachtungen,* the content of these critiques serves to illuminate the theorist's harmonic system, including questions of harmonic progression, voice leading, and dissonance treatment. But the issue of appropriate sacred style is also addressed, and the reader is offered guidance in the evaluation of expressive, depictive, and rhetorical devices as they pertain to these model settings of sacred Latin and vernacular texts.

The first of the analyses appears early in the initial volume of the serial (1778) and concerns the motet *Ecce panis angelorum,* a piece supposedly first performed on Corpus Christi of the preceding year.[23] Lamenting a general decline in part-writing skills and a corresponding tendency to conceal poor craftsmanship with the veneer of orchestral accompaniment, Vogler suggests that in this modest vocal piece, conceived in a harmonically enriched, homophonic idiom, his deployment of vocal resources yields results no less effective than those of a richly scored work for chorus and orchestra.

Proceeding to a technical description of the piece, he calls attention to the simple yet shrewdly designed interaction of voice parts within each of the neatly detached phrases. This trait is exemplified in the opening measures (see Example 1a), where he shows that each part has a distinct and independent profile, and where the embellishing figures in the alto yield diversity and spontaneous movement against the backdrop of half notes in soprano, tenor, and bass.

As Vogler's commentary suggests, his setting amplifies the text without overstepping the limitations appropriate to sacred music. For an expressive climax on the words "non mittendus canibus" (see Example 1b)—where the dynamic level changes suddenly from *piano* to *fortissimo,* the melodic lines become animated and disjunct, and the previously homophonic texture is enriched by a pattern of close imitation in the soprano and bass—he explains that the stately progression by fifths represents true church style: it is expressive, and the minor chords convey an appropriately sorrowful quality. Then he shows how the conclusion of this phrase leads to an instance of vivid imagery and stunning contrast: the logically approached yet unexpected D-major chord in measure 16 is followed by the likewise unanticipated descent in the tenor from F-sharp to F-natural, and now, as the placid and guileless opening phrase returns in rondo-like fashion, the juxtaposition of the bestial and the godly is accomplished with superb effect.[24]

The effort to achieve unity and expressive impact economically also extends to the special manipulation of text for symbolic, structural, or rhetorical purposes. Vogler explains that, for the third phrase, he has united the prevailing tonic harmony of the first phrase and the dominant orientation

Example 1

*Ecce panis angelorum,* (a) measures 1–4;
(b) measures 13–18.

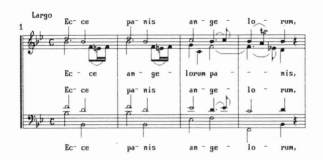

of the second by designing an alternation of tonic and dominant. Here, the recurrence of the initial word "ecce" enhances the sense of structural unification. Sung by the alto (whose F, the note common to both chords, is sustained for more than four measures), it then appears in the bass, whose punctuating octave leap in quarter notes clearly recalls the initial half-note leap on "ecce" in the opening phrase.

At the very end of the piece, the word "ecce" is summoned again, this time to replace the conventional "amen" and thereby enhance the unity of the setting while at the same time intensifying its rhetoric. Vogler claims that this final "pious cry" exerts a piercing effect on the listener, and the accompanying crescendo-diminuendo effect, a favorite rhetorical device of his for the end of a piece or section, proves "capable of moving the heart of the sensitive listener with intense magical power" if executed with precision by the singers.[25]

The discussion of Vogler's second exemplary Latin composition, a *Miserere* for voices and *basso continuo,* is withheld until the last volume of the *Betrachtungen,*[26] although the work appears to have been written before *Ecce panis angelorum.* (According to an extant dated autograph, it originated no later than March 9, 1776.)[27] The composer himself seemingly thought well of this early effort.[28] The published score, engraved by Bossler and included in the *Gegenstände* (July–August 1780), bears a dedication to the pope, and its elegant title page awards prominent space to the abbé's long list of honorary titles.

The analysis that Vogler supplies echoes that of *Ecce panis angelorum* in its emphasis on vocal craftsmanship, appropriateness of text setting, restraint, and consistency. But now the work being addressed is far larger and more complex. All but one of its movements are considerably longer (their lengths range from 32 to 111 measures), and its broader spectrum of stylistic and expressive contrasts leads to a more intensive inquiry into basic issues of sacred tradition and innovation.

To begin with, the question of key is more complex. Despite the theorist's general preference for the minor in sacred music, only two of the six movements are set in minor keys. The tonal center of the work is C major, a choice that Vogler is obliged to defend on the grounds of tonal logic, convention, and the requirements of the text. Asserting that "a serious, steady, solemn performance can convey supplication even in the lively major mode,"[29] he explains that the text of the closing fugal movement (beginning with "Gloria patri et filio") requires the key of C major (which elsewhere he associates specifically with splendor).[30] And in accordance with the principle of tonal unity, the key of the final movement must be that of the work as a whole.

As might be expected of a solemn, late eighteenth-century *Miserere* dedicated to the pope himself, the work pays homage to strict style—most notably in the closing fugue, but also quite conspicuously in the third movement ("Docebo iniquos"). Taking the form of a free fugue (*fuga d'imi-tazione*), the movement has the *alla breve* meter that Vogler identified with strict style,[31] and it makes prominent use of such *stile antico* conventions as imitative texture, syncopations, and legato, conjunct vocal lines (see Example 2).

Example 2
"Docebo iniquos" from *Miserere,*
measures 23–30.

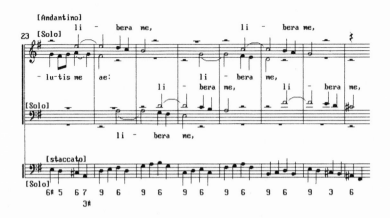

The imitation seen in Example 2 is merely one of many kinds of texture that lend diversity to the work despite its generally restrictive vocal idiom. Between the extremes of homorhythmic declamation and strict fugue are numerous gradations, including paired imitation, motivic imitation in four parts, dialogue-like fragmentation, counterpoint with two, three, and four independent lines, and instances of alternation between full ensemble and groups of soloists. Calling attention to a striking textural arrangement in the fourth movement, Vogler reports that "the fine manner of singing by the soprano solo voice on the word 'contribulatus' resembles that splendid [style of] performance transmitted through tradition in Rome, and the effect is enhanced even more as the choral singers gradually join in and utter the touching word as the solo voices sustain it plaintively"[32] (see Example 3).

As revealed by the *Miserere* excerpts quoted here, Vogler has not re-stricted himself to a pure vocal texture. In fact, he readily condoned the support of a figured bass as a means of keeping performers in tune and

Example 3
"Sacrificium" from *Miserere,*
measures 6–12.

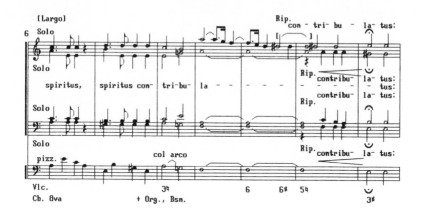

together in an otherwise unaccompanied fabric; nor did he exclude the possibility of orchestral participation, as witnessed in his optional orchestral parts.[33] For this special, model work, the *continuo* reaches well beyond a merely utilitarian function to become a real textural resource and thus a means of enriching an otherwise austere, homogeneous sound. Four instrumental parts are specified: organ, cello, bassoon, and contrabass. Typically, they form an independent line with a distinctive contour that variously involves a walking bass, broken chords, scalar passages, or other more elaborate motivic configurations. In one remarkable passage in the second movement, the *continuo* divides into an accompanying counterpoint of four separate parts for a span of sixteen measures: the bassoon dwells on tied pitches in the tenor register, the cello negotiates wide arpeggiations in eighth notes, the contrabass marks the beat with a pizzicato broken-chord pattern, and the organ supports the one-change-per-bar harmonic rhythm with its sustained chord roots and improvised realization (see Example 4).

Ingenuity of the kind witnessed in this example, typical in reflecting the composer's aim to extract textural diversity from limited resources, is further exemplified in his efforts to create moments of vivid text expression. Given to describing expression as the soul of music,[34] he distinguishes between its two aspects in his article "Ausdruck" for the *Deutsche Encyclopädie:* the expression of human passions (to stir the emotions and cultivate the spirit)

Example 4
"Auditui meo" from *Miserere,*
measures 26–29.

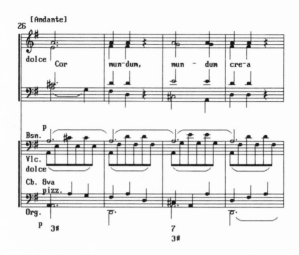

and the depiction of natural phenomena (to persuade the senses).[35] The second movement illustrates the former, affective approach in its use of two contrasting, recurrent bass figures: a vigorous, sharply detached scalar motion and a wave-like legato arpeggiation. Vogler calls attention to a passage that juxtaposes both patterns, the restless and the placid, in a manner especially appropriate to the text[36] (see Example 5). Whereas the plea "and take not Thy Holy Spirit from me" gains impact from the staccato articulation, the tonally unstable, inflected harmonies, and the relatively fast harmonic rhythm (measures 51–54), the change to a more graceful legato figure, with its blissfully quiescent harmony and mollified recitation, serves to enhance the words "restore unto me the joy of Thy salvation" (measures 55–58).

In the fourth movement the other, depictive style of expression is featured in a passage where the image of the contrite heart ("cor contritum") is vividly enhanced by loud heartbeats from the *continuo*[37] (see Example 6). Denounced by other writers as unsuitably theatrical, such pictorialism in sacred music clearly escaped Vogler's censure.

While the *Miserere,* like *Ecce panis angelorum,* exemplifies the composer's attempt to adorn his Latin text settings with expressive devices, it also shows a determination to keep the vocal parts simple, to avoid distracting theatrics, and to concentrate on clear, emphatic delivery. This centrally important issue

Example 5
"Auditui meo" from *Miserere,* (a)
measures 51–54; (b) measures 55–58.

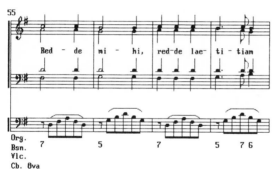

of austerity and clarity in text setting arises even more prominently in the third and longest of Vogler's model sacred works, the nine-movement *Deutsche Kirchenmusik* of 1777.

The *Deutsche Kirchenmusik* is a setting of the German *Singmesse,* which freely interprets the Latin Mass text. A manifestation of the eighteenth-century German vernacular movement, it reflects a timely concern with comprehensibility of text and music in the church. According to Vogler, the initial stimulus came from the author of the text himself, Johann Franz Seraph von Kohlbrenner, who sought to promote vernacular singing in Bavarian churches.[38] The text had made its original appearance in Kohlbrenner's German hymnal, *Der heilige Gesang zum Gottesdienste in der römisch-katho-*

Example 6
"Sacrificium" from *Miserere,*
measures 13–16.

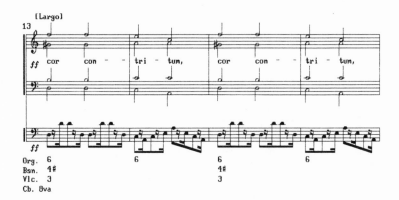

*lischen Kirche,* published at Landshut in 1777, with melodies and organ accompaniments contributed by Norbert Hauner. It was then revised for Vogler's setting, possibly by Vogler himself.[39]

Introducing the work in *Betrachtungen* with suitable pomp and ceremony, Vogler extols the enlightened ideal of accessibility. He praises Carl Theodor for guiding his obstinate fellow citizens toward the discovery of German taste; and he rejoices that church music will soon resound in the vernacular, addressing the emotions more directly than would be possible in any foreign language. He praises the text as being "comprehensible to the common folk [yet] not too humble for the learned," and asserts with rational conviction that tones remain silent unless the listener can comprehend their meaning, expressive import, and imagery.[40] (However fervently expressed here, Vogler's enthusiasm for the vernacular movement was limited: apart from the *Deutsche Kirchenmusik,* he adhered to the traditional Latin for nearly all his sacred works but his chorales and chorale-like compositions. For practical reasons, he refused to translate the tempo and expression markings for this work into German,[41] and in the *Musikalische Korrespondenz* of 1790 he scorned the latter 1770s at Mannheim as the "time of the revolution of Germanness, in which a German Society was founded, in which we were all infected with a bigotry toward German, in which we feared it a sin to use a naturalized foreign word, wanting to substitute *Nasenkrautstaubschachtel* for *tabatière.*")[42]

Originally published for voices and organ, the *Deutsche Kirchenmusik* is cited in the second volume of *Betrachtungen* as a worthy example of a setting without orchestral accompaniment. Seemingly, it constitutes another example of Vogler's sacred vocal ideal, but here the composer's zeal was specifically linked to pragmatic considerations. As he explains, the omission of orchestra had a purely practical aspect, since the work was meant to be usable in poorer villages where resources were inevitably limited. On comparably pragmatic grounds, he included a fully realized organ part designed to compensate for the deficiency in thoroughbass skills among parish organists into whose hands the work would fall.[43] As with the *Miserere,* orchestral reinforcement was condoned. Vogler supplied optional string and wind parts for the first performance at Heidelberg in 1778, as indicated on the title page of his edition for chorus and organ;[44] and in the advertisement printed on the verso he announced the availability of manuscript copies of the string parts, the wind parts (not individually specified), and the score.[45]

Vogler begins his description of the music by observing that, despite some resemblance to Lied style, the diversity and richness of the middle parts prohibit any comparison with mere street songs. To make the music and text comprehensible to the devout listener, he avoided long spun-out melodies, except in the texturally more continuous second movement, and restricted himself to a limited spectrum of keys throughout.[46] Characterizing all but the first two movements as *liedermäsig* [*sic*],[47] he calls attention to his use of stanzaic patterns of musical repetition in the manner of a strophic song. He cites three examples of this approach—the *Credo,* Offertory, and *Sanctus*—and indicates that in such movements, for which the text bears a single or primary message, recurrent musical ideas could be set to new texts without detriment to expression. These parts of the work he distinguishes from the vernacular *Kyrie* and *Gloria,* whose words seemed to require more flexibility of rhythm, harmony, and line.

Though Vogler does not dwell on the Lied-like quality that he associates with the latter movements of his German Mass, it can be seen that to some extent these movements share traits which he identifies with the Lied: relatively short phrases, simple harmonic scheme, structural repetition, and in some instances strophic design. Yet the movements by no means conform to a uniform style. As revealed by the excerpts quoted in Example 7,[48] Vogler's notion of *liedermäsig* encompassed a wide range of possibilities. The first excerpt, from the opening of the *Credo,* betrays the naive, folk-like manner to which the theorist alludes in his essay. Although the phrasing is not strictly regular, the materials of rhythm, texture, and melody are quite simple—so plain, in fact, that Vogler came to repudiate this movement in his *Deutsche Kirchenmusik* essay of 1808, where he suggests that its quaint, outmoded materials lacked the strength to endure without the benefit of orchestral reinforcement.[49]

In contrast to this naive, ingenuous passage from the *Credo,* the opening measures of the Gradual possess an almost Mozartian sophistication of line, texture, and harmony. Indeed, the initial phrase, with its gracefully arched profile, smooth voice leading, and well-coordinated climax of rhythmic, harmonic, and melodic intensity in measure 3 ("höchsten"), could well have provided a model for the remarkably similar second-movement theme of Mozart's A-major piano concerto, K. 414, of 1782. (Mozart may have heard the work at Mannheim. It is also possible that both Vogler and Mozart were inspired by an earlier source, the second movement of J. C. Bach's overture to *La calamità de' cuori* [1763].)[50]

Curiously, one of the movements that Vogler identifies as Lied-like he also describes as the sole example of strict church style in the work: no. 7, "Nach der Wandlung."[51] While the plan of phrase repetition in this move-ment suggests the domain of the Lied, aspects of melody, texture, and rhythm suggest the *stile antico.* As shown in Example 8, these traits include a stepwise, legato melody, suspensions, and patterns of imitation among the voice parts. In contrast to the distinctly popular idiom of the *Credo,* which according to the composer's admission proved perishable, he declares that this seventh movement will still be as valid in 100 years as it was when first performed.

## THE NON-ORCHESTRAL SACRED REPERTORY

To what extent do the foregoing samples of non-orchestral sacred vocal music form a coherent group? It is clear from this selection of works that Vogler has declined to adopt a monolithic stand on the issue of sacred propriety. It is also evident that the pieces in question have to do with markedly different aims and approaches. Nevertheless, the models do bear resemblances that point toward a certain stylistic ideal, and their common features can be specified partially in terms of what they omit (most notably the virtuosic display and elaborate ornamentation associated with theater

Example 7
*Deutsche Kirchenmusik,* (a) *Credo,*
measures 1–6; (b) Gradual, measures
1–4; (c) Mozart's Piano Concerto in
A Major, K. 414, second movement,
measures 1–4.

Example 8
"Nach der Wandlung" from *Deutsche
Kirchenmusik,* measures 9–13.

music), and partially in terms of their references to traits customarily linked with sacred music: austerity, dignity, and the time-honored conventions of the *stile antico*.

As a defining characteristic of this idiom, melodic simplicity is paramount. Wide leaps, complex motivic elaboration, and embellishment are generally eschewed in favor of conjunct lines and a clearly articulated, mainly syllabic text setting. To these qualities may be added those that Vogler describes as Lied-like in his discussion of the vernacular Mass, including short phrases, simplicity of harmonic design, and melodic repetition. As if to compensate for the uniformity to which this approach might all too easily lead, the models betray a remarkable amount of textural variety, a modest degree of contrapuntal independence, and an occasional tendency to exploit rich harmonic possibilities when justified on grounds of text expression.

In sum, it is safe to conclude that the models served to uphold some distinction between sacred and secular, and that the theorist viewed their churchly nature as something more than the fact that they featured pure unaccompanied chorus or chorus with *basso continuo*. The nature of the distinction, and the stylistic possibilities and constraints it implied, are further clarified by traits seen in other surviving works that can be attributed to Vogler. These compositions—their virtues, limitations, and special means of expressive strength—can also shed light on the portrayal of a sacred vocal ideal as sketched in the discussions of the models.

Works belonging to this repertory, which excludes chorales, plainsong harmonizations, and related pieces, are mostly based on Latin texts drawn from the Mass and Office. Documentary evidence suggests that the majority originated after 1800, and that they reflect the ground swell of interest in unaccompanied sacred music apparent toward the close of the eighteenth century.[52] They generally prove comparable in style to the models, and most are cast in major keys—a fact which suggests that Vogler's justification of the major for his *Miserere* was more the endorsement of a standard practice than the defense of an exception. In keeping with the syllabic, even-paced rendering of text that Vogler preferred for this idiom, rhythmic diversity is limited. Cross-rhythms and syncopated accents are generally avoided, though allusions to the *stile antico* sometimes result in suspension figures and rhythmically independent voice leading.

A striking instance of such an allusion occurs in Vogler's *Ave maris stella* (see Example 9), published in *Zwölf Kirchen Hÿmnen für dreÿ, vier und acht Vocal-Stimmen*.[53]

Example 9

*Ave maris stella,* measures 1–10.

The composer designates the opening and closing sections *a capella* [*sic*], a term he defines in the *Encyclopädie* as singing "in that manner and in the same tempo as the papal choir." By this, he means performance in a "lively and uniform tempo," except in sorrowful pieces; use of the *alla breve* meter; and a compositional procedure whereby each voice has the same text and melody, as well as its own decisive entry.[54] In this instance, Vogler confirms the designation by using the appropriate time signature and imitative entries. As in the *Miserere* and the *Deutsche Kirchenmusik,* however, *stile antico* elements are juxtaposed with others clearly belonging to a modern idiom. These include reliance on the symmetries of structural repetition, the use of tonally directed chord progressions involving secondary dominants, and the emphasis on a regular, rhythmically accentuated pulse.

In addition to showing Vogler's use of *a cappella* conventions, the example quoted above is typical of his unaccompanied church music in the relative austerity of rhythm and melodic line and in the overall quality of gravity. Likewise typical is the large-scale strategy for which it sets the stage: a scheme involving the gradual accumulation of energy and intensity toward a rhetorical climax. The very placidness of the opening provides the point of departure for a long-range increase in intensity—a potential alluded to though not fully realized in the model works. In executing such a design, Vogler typically draws on the resources of texture, rhythm, and dynamics: fragmentation, dialogue, and antiphonal effects (most notably in the several pieces involving double choir), combined with long crescendos, intensification of rhythmic activity, and the juxtaposition of dynamic contrasts.

The passage quoted in Example 10, from the *Salve Regina* of 1809, exemplifies Vogler's concept of rhetorical climax. Although the extended melismas seen here are relatively uncommon in this repertory, the effect is characteristic in principle. The florid setting of the word "salve" forms the highpoint in an extended pattern of increasing animation, both rhythmic and textural, that lends the piece an overriding sense of goal-directed movement.

The central challenge, implied in the theorist's discussions of his models and emphasized throughout his sacred vocal repertory, was to achieve a vivid, sharply etched musical design within the technical and aesthetic constraints of the genre. In addition to the creation of a suitably emphatic climax, as seen in the melismas on "salve" in the foregoing example, this involved realizing the pictorial and expressive potentials of a given text. As Vogler observed repeatedly in his discussions of text setting, both sacred and secular, the issue of text expression was paramount. The inclination toward pictorialism, an essential trait of his musical personality, was something that must be accommodated, however restrictive the medium in question.

That special expressive and pictorial effects were not inconsistent with Vogler's vocal ideal is revealed by his model works in *Betrachtungen,* and their acceptance is readily confirmed by the repertory. Characteristically, these works show resourcefulness and ingenuity in promoting the direct communication of a message to the listener's sensibility. Pictorialisms of the type witnessed in the *Miserere,* with its representation of heartbeats, sometimes occur in even more vivid, striking forms. In a passage from an *Alma Redemptoris Mater* setting for four voice parts, the composer uses a rapidly ascending, portamento-like figure to enliven the word "surgere" (see Exam-

Example 10
*Salve Regina,* measures 137–49.

ple 11). Such acrobatics are evidently accepted as a means of eloquent text expression despite their resemblance to the language of the opera house.

However striking the indulgence in such pictorialisms, the affective treatment of a word or passage is more typical of Vogler's approach—for example, the use of chromatic inflections on words such as "lacrimarum," "miserere," or "passionis" to underscore the expression of sorrow and an-

Example 11
*Alma Redemptoris Mater,* measures
25–30 (soprano only).

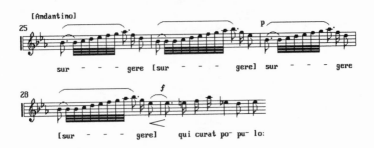

guish; or the application of various expressive techniques (typically involving aspects of rhythm, harmony, and dynamics) to convey the sense of an entire passage or section.

In the absence of great diversity in timbre, the resource of dynamics (including contrasts, echo effects, and broadly extended crescendos and diminuendos) stands out as an indispensable agent of depiction and expression. But as witnessed in *Ecce panis* and the accompanying essay, the special manipulation or rearrangement of words in a text furnished an additional means of accomplishing a particular expressive effect. Vogler's penchant for this technique sometimes led to far more pronounced distortions than any seen in the models. In a climactic passage from his *Ave Regina coelorum* in F major, different lines of text are not only sung simultaneously, but the original syntax is distorted. As declaimed in the soprano part, the original lines

> Gaude Virgo gloriosa,
> Super omnes speciosa:
> Vale, o valde decora,
> Et pro nobis Christum exora.

are fragmented, rearranged, and subject to word repetition as follows:

> Christum exora
> Christum Christum exora
> Christum exora exora exora
> Gloriosa
> Speciosa
> Ave Ave.

It might be argued that such an effect contradicts the theorist's ideals by complicating the relationship between music and text. Certainly this setting goes against contemporary doctrines of comprehensibility. But as Vogler's writings suggest, he would perhaps counter objections on the grounds of text expression and the aim of projecting key words as forcefully as the given limitations allow.

Text distortions, melismas, and other special effects notwithstanding, the unaccompanied repertory as a whole confirms Vogler's commitment to the sacred vocal ideal expressed in his writings. That this relatively austere, though sometimes unconventional style did not preclude other approaches is evident from his many sacred pieces that feature elaborate orchestral accompaniment in addition to vocal soloists and chorus.

### ORCHESTRALLY ACCOMPANIED SACRED MUSIC

The vast majority of known works with orchestral accompaniment are settings of Latin texts. Among these, many are Masses and unattached Mass movements, while the remaining Latin works include settings of the *Magnificat, Te Deum, Miserere,* and Vespers psalms, as well as numerous smaller motets. Though this body of works includes compositions from various phases of Vogler's career—among them such well-known repertory pieces as the *Missa pastoritia* in E (1775, revised in 1804), *Missa solennis* [*sic*] in D minor (1784), and *Requiem* in E-flat (1809)—most compositions in the group were written in the years 1775–77 and intended for performance at the Mannheim court. Following the removal of the Elector's court to Munich and the redirection of Vogler's attention to other interests, sacred works with orchestral accompaniment were destined to appear only sporadically.[55]

Do the surviving pieces of this type betray Vogler's own cherished ideals? From the standpoint of his early teachings, sacred compositions with orchestra were difficult to justify, especially those that featured a vocal soloist, thereby incorporating wholesale the musical fabric of opera. But more to the point than the existence of an orchestral accompaniment were the questions of how the instruments were used and whether they amplified or detracted from the sacred message of the text. After all, for two of the sacred vocal models, the *Miserere* and *Deutsche Kirchenmusik,* the composer himself supplied optional orchestral parts.

Vogler's writings include only one major project that confronts the issue directly in his own music: his essay on the revised *Deutsche Kirchenmusik* of 1807. The revision, which incorporates the original vocal parts nearly intact (except for changes in the order of movements), was designed in part to furnish a lesson in modern orchestration, but it also served to address the specific question of how an orchestra may be used to amplify the choral rendition of a sacred text. Acknowledging that the original work was conceived in a somewhat dry, now outmoded style, Vogler describes his act of reviving and modernizing through a newly created orchestration as something of a tour de force: a uniting of two different entities, one vocal, one instrumental, composed at an interval of thirty years.[56] Unlike the transformation of a sonata into a concerto (as described in *Betrachtungen*), or the extensive structural overhauling of Pergolesi's *Stabat Mater,* this task was accomplished without adding ritornellos or otherwise tampering with the original design.

Explaining his procedures in making this revision, the theorist observes that a distinction can be drawn between an accompaniment that merely lends harmonic and textural reinforcement (*Ausfüllung*) to existing material, and the genuine participation (*Beitritt*) of an independent instrumental ensemble. While the former term describes the simple, utilitarian accompaniment supplied for the original work in 1777, the latter clearly applies to the 1807 revision.[57]

Calling the added instrumental parts a separate "choir" (as opposed to the existing vocal choir), Vogler proceeds to describe the instrumentation specifically as a group of four complementary choirs (*Neben-Chöre*): the strings (two violins, viola, cello, and bass), reed instruments (pairs of flutes, oboes, clarinets, and bassoons), brass (two trumpets, two horns, three trombones), and timpani.[58] Each group is described as a sonorous unit, capable of working with the others in a variety of combinations. An organ part (more elaborate than the original one) is also provided, and Vogler explains that it may be used either with, or in place of, the orchestral ensemble.

Given the premises of the revision—retention of both the original vocal parts and the original structural framework—the instrumental parts inevitably follow the voices rather closely. Much of the instrumental activity amounts to doubling, but there is also much variety. The instrumental timbre and alignment change frequently, as Vogler uses his added resources to provide extra color, textural support, and rhythmic animation. There is also considerable new material, usually involving fragmentary motives and counter-melodies, string figuration, or sustained color.

Vogler's commentary on his use of the instruments is neither comprehensive nor systematic, but his descriptions do furnish clues to how choices of particular instruments and combinations were made. He shows that in the more serene movements, a light, economical instrumentation spares the listener's sensibilities while providing a foil for the appropriately timed unleashing of the thunderous full ensemble. With respect to movements 6, 7, and 9, he explains that contrasting colors highlight the delineation of large-scale patterns of repetition and variation. Specific instances cited from the last movement involve the sustained color of the clarinets in the second strophe (against eighth-note figuration in first violins, doubled at the octave above and below by flute and bassoon), and a combination of clarinets and oboes throughout the third strophe (as the strings engage in "frenzied movement").[59]

In addition to emphasizing structural punctuations and bestowing a distinctive color on a section or passage, the instrumentation serves to enhance, clarify, and support the thematic content of the different movements. With reference to a passage from the second part of the *Agnus Dei,* Vogler explains that he has sought to reinforce the soprano and alto lines by having them doubled, respectively, by first and second flutes an octave above, and by first and second clarinets an octave below; and in the *Credo,* whose original substance he now finds outmoded, he cites instances in which the modern orchestration has shored up weaknesses in the original work. These include figuration in the strings to enliven the third strophe, and passages in which solo oboe and clarinet serve either to enrich the vocal texture with a new motive, or to lend continuity at a cadence by introducing a motive that overlaps the voices.[60]

Elsewhere, the use of timbral contrasts lends a source of tension and animation. Discussing the *Gloria,* Vogler mentions a passage in which different colors are juxtaposed to create a "fiery friction" of instruments in the course of a motivic dialogue. As he explains, the rapid alternation of instruments enlivens the passage so forcefully that it acts as a substitute for other kinds of rhythmic activity.[61]

Although the symbolic or pictorial use of instruments is not emphasized, either in the work itself or in the commentary, such resources are not excluded. With reference to the *Kyrie,* for example, the theorist explains that he has associated the flutes with childlike supplication, the combination of oboes and horn with lachrymose expression, and trumpets and timpani with the majesty of God.

The premise on which the revised *Deutsche Kirchenmusik* is based—dependence on the structure of a pre-existing, unaccompanied model—causes it to stand apart from other orchestrally accompanied works in terms of the relationship between voices and instruments. Not only are ritornellos and various kinds of dialogue texture unavailable, but also the otherwise common fabric of an instrumentally accompanied vocal solo.

Yet despite its limitations, the *Deutsche Kirchenmusik* and the accompanying essay prove useful as a backdrop for examining the orchestrally accompanied repertory at large. The revision was, among other things, a reaffirmation of Vogler's insistence on the notion of a distinctive sacred idiom. The procedures he applies are concerned with articulating, projecting, and coloristically enhancing the setting of a sacred text, and the issues raised are at least theoretically relevant to other sacred works composed for similar forces. To be sure, his output includes compositions in a frankly operatic, soloistic idiom that has little to do with any sacred ideal proposed in his writings. But many of the extant works do offer grounds for comparison with the revised German Mass setting—grounds on which the significance of the work as a model of sacred propriety can be clarified and appraised.

To begin with, it is clear from the *Deutsche Kirchenmusik* that Vogler condones the use of instruments for more than mere reinforcement of vocal lines. The selection of particular colors for certain lines of text, the "fiery friction" of juxtaposed instruments and groups, and the rhythmically animated accompanying parts (especially in movements 4, 6, and 9)—these features point to the use of instruments in a special kind of partnership with the voices. While Vogler restricts them to supporting the vocal parts rather than competing, he portrays them as active participants in a musical design, complementing the voices, compensating for their limitations, and contributing both structural delineation and rhythmic momentum.

Comparably supportive roles for the orchestra are evident throughout the repertory. A typical circumstance involves settings such as that seen in Example 12, in which orchestral activity balances the rhythmic and melodic uniformity of the choral parts. In the quoted passage, from the Offertory "Christus natus est nobis" in the *Missa pastoritia,*[62] sixteenth-note arpeggia-

Example 12
Offertory from *Missa pastoritia,*
measures 39–41.

tions in the solo flute and clarinet lend rhythmic propulsion and coloristic enhancement to the relatively homogeneous, predominantly quarter-note texture of the voices.

Not unlike the passages of animated string figuration in *Deutsche Kirchenmusik,* this kind of texture readily applies to settings in which a more vocally active, polyphonic style would be impractical or inappropriate. On occasion, the instruments attain even greater prominence relative to the voices. In *System für den Fugenbau,* Vogler acknowledges the possibility of an actual reversal of roles in which the voices are more accompanimental than independent and the instruments carry a thematic line. An example he cites occurs in the *Credo* from his Mass in D minor (*Missa solennis*) of 1784.[63] In this movement, as illustrated in Example 13,[64] the declamatory choral writing is consistently more uniform rhythmically, melodically, and texturally than that seen above in the *Missa pastoritia.* Thematic interest is sustained either by a lyrical melodic line in the first violins, as shown in the example, or (in the

Example 13
*Credo* from *Missa solennis,* measures
1–7.

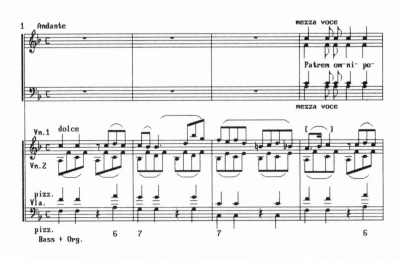

"Et incarnatus") by recurring melodic figures in muted first violins and solo bassoon.

A different kind of partnership between voices and instruments is seen in a work such as the second movement of *Serenissimae puerperae sacrum* (1804). In setting this text, the psalm "Laudate pueri," Vogler mainly adheres to an austere rendition of the psalm tone in unison or octaves, permitting little departure from the tonic key of E-flat. Compensating for this uniformity, he calls on the resources of orchestral texture and figured accompaniment for variety, contrast, and structural delineation. As in *Deutsche Kirchenmusik,* the instrumental ensemble divides into choirs (strings, woodwinds, brass), which are variously juxtaposed and blended to provide contrast between verses or larger sections. Accompanimental patterns generally change from one verse to the next, and sometimes at the midpoint of a verse as well. Contrasting orchestral sonorities and textures help punctuate the structural divisions, and connecting instrumental passages between verses feature poignant contrasts in color. In the passage quoted in Example 14,[65] reaching from the end of the second verse to the beginning of the third, an arpeggiated string figuration yields to a blended choir of winds (horn, flute, oboes, and clarinet), smoothly overlapped by the bassoons, and finally contrabassoon, before the voices reenter to the sound of the wind choir with which the instrumental passage had begun.

Vogler's penchant for vivid and memorable instrumental effects is further exemplified in the somber exchange of low clarinet and horn in the opening measures of the late *Requiem* in E-flat (Example 15).[66] In addition to creating a coloristically appropriate backdrop for the entry of the voices, the unique sonority impresses upon the listener an essential thematic motive to be exploited in the course of the movement.

The passages quoted below from *Serenissimae puerperae sacrum* and the *Requiem* are clearly different from the *Deutsche Kirchenmusik* in that they involve the concentration of orchestral effects within passages for instruments alone—the very texture unavailable in the model work. They nevertheless bear comparison with the orchestrated Mass in terms of aspiration and technique, notably in the judicious selection of blended and contrasted colors that enhance expression or clarify articulation. To this extent they may be understood as partial reflections of the ideal sacred style that the revised Mass was intended to represent.

More problematical are the instances of soloistic and even virtuosic writing for instruments. Instrumental virtuosity would have been scarcely feasible in a work like the *Deutsche Kirchenmusik,* and in Vogler's discussions of sacred music the question of elaborate solo parts is left largely unexamined. Yet the use of embellishing solo instruments is featured prominently in many of his settings of sacred texts. Especially typical in his church music from the 1760s and in surviving pieces from the Mannheim years (but by no means abandoned thereafter) are textures such as that seen in Example 16, from a

Example 14
"Laudate pueri" from *Serenissimae*
*puerperae sacrum,* measures 36–46.

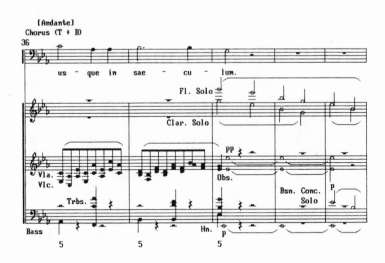

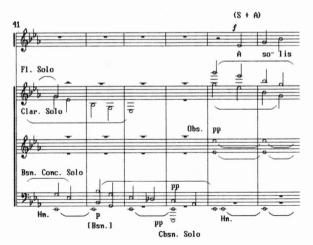

C-major *Magnificat.* Quoted from the "Suscepit Israel,"[67] this lightly scored, harmonically simple passage belongs to the Italianate, *galant* idiom of the 1770s, complete with turn figures, syncopes, appoggiaturas, decorative melismas, and dialogues between voice and instruments.

In other instances, comparable to that cited in Example 17, the entire

Example 15
*Kyrie* from *Requiem* in E-flat major,
measures 1–6.

Example 16
"Suscepit Israel" from *Magnificat* in
C major, measures 19–24.

Example 17
*Magnificat* from *Vesperae de Paschate,*
measures 38–43.

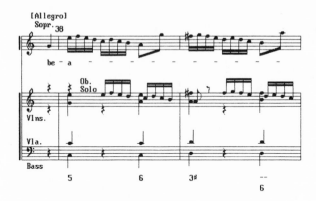

vocal and instrumental fabric seems all too closely related to the musical profanity of the theater. The passage in question comes from the *Magnificat* movement of *Vesperae de Paschate* (1805). After beginning with a gracefully ornamented ritornello, the piece proceeds with unembellished solo and choral statements. It then blossoms into an elaborate dialogue between solo soprano and oboe, which in turn leads to the extended *passaggio* on the words "beatam omnes generationes," quoted in part in the example, where the oboe imitates the voice.[68]

At times the solo instrumental writing proves even more remote from the sober realm of sacred purity. In the *Gloria* of the 1784 *Missa solennis,* passages such as the one shown in Example 18 display an extravagance of wind colors that derives from the virtuosic idiom of the concerto. Following a brilliant opening tutti phrase and an initial flourish by solo flute, the oboe and bassoon join the flute's lead in the manner of a *sinfonia concertante.* Here, it would seem, the competitive, exhibitionistic style of the theater has sup-

Example 18
*Gloria* from *Missa solennis,* measures
7–12.

planted the elevated cooperation of voices and instruments that Vogler endeavored to promote in his writings on sacred music.

Where, then, do the boundaries between sacred and secular lie? Vogler piously deplored the tendency of sacred music to acquire traits of secular style. But as we have seen, his declarations were not free of contradiction, and in some respects, techniques witnessed in the sacred repertory underline the conflicts evident in his statements as a critic. Side by side with works that adhere to an ideal of sacred purity and restraint, whether for voices alone or with orchestral accompaniment, are compositions that either transcend his restrictions or else ignore them in favor of a style in which solo voices and instruments adorn sacred texts with the raiment of the theater.

### CRITICAL ASSESSMENTS

The issue of sacred propriety raised by such works surfaced prominently in early nineteenth-century German criticism, and Vogler's compositions (though not his writings on the subject) were implicated in the debate. Gottfried Weber, writing in the mid 1820s in the journal *Cäcilia,* confronted the question of distinguishing between sacred and secular style.[69] Attempting to define the nature of true church music, he takes issue with aestheticians who have set forth arbitrary rules, and opposes those who would separate sacred from secular on the basis of proscribed techniques and modes of expression. He condemns strictures that would place artificial limits on harmonic procedure and vocabulary, or give preference to one kind of texture over another (such as fugal texture over unaccompanied chant). He also disparages the notion that sacred expression be restricted to the manifestly pious and edifying, or to the imitation of a sixteenth-century style. Instead, he simply advocates religious feeling as a guide, leaving the composer free to decide whatever means he judges appropriate to achieve a desired aim.

In this context the abbé's name is invoked: Weber regards Vogler, along with Mozart and Joseph Haydn, as an artist whose music exemplifies such an independent path, and he singles out the *Gloria* from Vogler's 1784 *Missa solennis* as a sacred work that he specially admires for its instrumental brilliance.[70] Elaborating this view, he declares his refusal to join other critics in condemning rapid passages, unprepared dissonances, or astounding instrumental effects in compositions that succeed, on their own terms, in sustaining a fervently religious quality.

However, Weber does object to self-indulgent contrivances that detract from the requisite mood of sacred dignity. As an example he cites the "Et incarnatus" from Vogler's *Missa pastoritia,* where the composer employs a *Kuhreihen* for horn, whose lilting, §️ melody outlines the natural triad. He adorns this pastoral allusion with the expected echo effects, but as he attempts to capture those echoes in the choral parts he creates a travesty of the text. The device of having the words "et incarnatus est" echoed by "natus est" thus elicits the author's wry verdict "How clever!" ("Wie schlau!").[71]

Reactions on the part of other contemporaries were largely confined to fragmentary observations on the relatively small number of Vogler's sacred works known through publication or performance.[72] Various listeners raised objections that echoed Vogler's own complaints in his criticisms of contemporary practices: one writer leveled the charge of frivolity against a certain *Requiem* chorus, while another claimed that the noisy trumpets and timpani in a fugal "Pleni sunt coeli" obscured the design.[73]

According to other judgments, Vogler was capable of striking a successful balance between sacred dignity and secular splendor. The *Missa pastoritia* was admired not only for its melodic richness and contrapuntal mastery, but also for the freshness of its harmony and the superb effects achieved through the composer's genius for combining instrumental sonorities.[74] Published reactions to the *Missa solennis* were no less enthusiastic. The brilliant and diverse instrumentation was among its most admired features, and one critic was moved to declare that the work never overstepped the appropriate boundaries of true sacred style.[75]

Highest praise was reserved for the *Requiem* in E-flat, which the composer purportedly had intended as a *Requiem* for himself. (As reported by Carl Maria von Weber, Vogler forgot its original purpose when he heard of Haydn's death and attempted, though unsuccessfully, to have it performed first at the deceased composer's funeral in Vienna, then at a memorial service for Haydn in Frankfurt.) Weber heard the *Requiem* and wrote in 1810 that it "includes all that art and artifice can achieve, treated with such genius, taste and skill that the listener is less aware of them than of the feelings which they arouse."[76] To most others, the work first became accessible after its publication in 1822 from a source in Vogler's *Nachlass.* It was then that Rochlitz came to know it, and in his review of the orchestral and keyboard editions, judged it to be Vogler's most splendid work.[77]

Even more warmly appreciative was Joseph Fröhlich, who reviewed these same editions of the *Requiem* in the first year of *Cäcilia* (1824). Finding the musical language both natural and rigorous, its emphasis on simple choral writing conforming "to the spirit of the ancient Catholic rite," he spoke of Vogler's aim "to unite the refined spirit of antiquity with the mystical, lofty [ideals] of the modern age; to bring together the noble simplicity and utmost accessibility of the former with the grandeur, opulence, power, and intensity of the latter." The result was an "ingenious blending" of styles in the vocal writing that reached from Palestrina to Pergolesi to the present.[78]

As implied by the early nineteenth-century commentators, Vogler's orchestrally accompanied sacred works embodied a certain stylistic tension. They displayed the self-consciously imposed restraints on which the theorist insisted in his writings on sacred style. Yet they also incorporated, and certainly profited from, the fruits of progress as cultivated in secular vocal and instrumental music. Artistic advancement, it would seem, was inevitable for music that employed the contemporary language, whether sacred or secular. Within this repertory, then, which included the church music for which Vogler was best known, the ideal of a truly timeless, sacred style was unobtainable in any strict sense.

But even though distinctions between sacred and secular are less sharply drawn than Vogler's writings would lead us to expect, some differences are nonetheless maintained. Unlike traditional operatic style, text settings are predominantly syllabic, the melodic profiles less embellished, less rhythmically animated, and more conjunct. Offsetting these inhibiting factors is a marked emphasis on contrast and novelty in sonority, dynamics, and harmony. The net result, not infrequently, is a felicitous relationship among elements in which clarity of text delivery takes precedence over virtuosity, restraint is accomplished without monotony or uniformity, and stunning effects are achieved without excessive recourse to theatrical conventions.

### HARMONIZATION OF MODAL SACRED MELODIES

More problematical than orchestrally accompanied sacred music, and less susceptible to easy compromise, was the issue of harmonized chorale and plainsong. The topic attracted special attention on the part of eighteenth- and early nineteenth-century critics, whose discussions concerned the organist's manner of embellishing a sacred melody (i.e., a chorale melody being sung by a congregation) and the related question of modal purity. Should an old, modal melody undergo distortion in keeping with the premises of modern, tonal harmonization? If not, how should the purity of the melody, and indeed the harmonization, be conserved?

Approaches by eighteenth-century organists to chorale and hymn accompaniment differed widely, ranging from austere, homorhythmic settings with unadorned melody to richly ornamented renditions with imitative textures. Typically, eighteenth-century chorale collections furnished a melody and figured bass only, leaving the realization of inner voices to the performer. While some sources included notated embellishments, it appears that most were designed merely to provide a foundation for elaboration by the organist. As writers of the time suggested, a homorhythmic accompaniment could be transformed by the performer, depending on his stylistic orientation and improvisatory skills.

Inevitably, organists' propensity for improvised embellishment led to excesses, which in turn called for denunciation by such prominent critics as Scheibe, Adlung, and Türk. In a representative complaint, Adlung despaired of organists whose elaborate variations and diminutions only confused the congregation and interfered with their devotional thoughts. He also frowned on printed melodies that were excessively burdened with ornaments.[79] These remarks and others like them betray the existence of practices that sanctioned both the embellishment of traditional hymns and the use of expressive, chromatically inflected harmonizations. Such customs offended advocates of austerity and comprehensibility, and they also had the effect of obscuring or neutralizing the modal character of the old melodies.

Despite the fact that the modes had fallen into disuse (Catholic plainsong had lost its primacy to modern, concerted styles, and new, tonal repertories had largely supplanted the modal hymns, both Catholic and Protestant), the question of modal purity was a focal point for theoretical discussion throughout the eighteenth century and beyond. Johann Gottfried Walther raised the issue in his *Musikalisches Lexikon* (1732).[80] Later in the century, Kirnberger made a point of observing that much music in both Protestant and Catholic repertories had modal origins. He discussed the structure of the modes, recommended avoiding the use of accidentals in a modal melody, and proposed appropriate choices of cadences in harmonizing such a melody.[81] Later still, Justin Heinrich Knecht advocated retaining the spirit of the church modes in modern harmonizations, and likewise provided tables of suitable cadences.[82]

Indications of Vogler's interest in church modes can be discerned as early as the *Kuhrpfälzische Tonschule* (1778), where he observes that the development of plainsong would offer the basis for a fascinating book.[83] However, his writings include only sporadic discussion of modes until the end of the century and the publication of his Swedish *Organist-schola* (1798–99).[84] The Swedish manual provided descriptions of the modes, guidelines for the correct harmonization of modal melodies, and explanatory critiques of Vogler's own harmonizations contained in the accompanying *Choral-bok,* which consisted of ninety chorales based on the Protestant *Swenska Psalm bok* (Stockholm, 1701).

Material from *Organist-schola* was soon incorporated in a major, definitive treatise, the *Choral-System* of 1800, comprising a volume of text and a companion volume of music.[85] In this most ambitious of all his inquiries into sacred music, Vogler shows much the same didactic, reformist zeal that typifies his other writings. Extolling traditional modal melody as a universal sacred legacy, indispensable to the divine service, he denounces existing practices and proposes a rationalistically contrived solution to the persisting dilemma of modal purity versus tonal logic in the harmonization of chorales.

According to a suggestion by Gottfried Weber, Vogler may have been motivated to write this treatise at least in part by his long-standing antipathy to the Bach tradition and the North German master's champions.[86] Vogler himself described his effort as an act of vindication against those who called his organ concerts a desecration of the instrument and who denounced him, a Catholic, as unqualified to play Protestant chorales.[87] According to Caspar Anton von Mastiaux's *Ueber Choral- und Kirchen-Gesänge,* Vogler had promised that before the beginning of the nineteenth century he would show that the greatest harmonist among the Protestants (i.e., J. S. Bach himself) did not know what a true chorale was.[88] Vogler did indeed use his *Choral-System* as a sounding-board for railing against the corrupt practices he aimed to reform. Bach stands out as the most conspicuous target, and in this respect the treatise renews Vogler's combat with the Bach legacy begun in the pages of the *Betrachtungen.*[89] C. H. Graun and Kirnberger come under attack as well, in addition to all organists who betray deficient knowledge and skill in the domain of chorale accompaniment. On occasion, the vehemence of Vogler's rhetoric even extends beyond the field of sacred expression to encompass the entire realm of eighteenth-century music.[90]

Despite the fact that the treatise deals mainly with chorales, the issue at

hand is the sacred modal tradition in general. The rules proposed are therefore as valid for plainsong as for chorale, and they rest on what the theorist
claims to be a solid theoretical and historical foundation. The argument he
presents divides into four main parts:

I. "Historical Revision of Musical Theory." A synopsis of Vogler's harmonic
system, included in order to clarify the underlying differences between modern
harmony and ancient melody, and to provide the reader with a basis for better
understanding the errors in harmonization to be uncovered and corrected.

II. "Historical Deduction Concerning Ancient Psalmody." The heart of the
system, with formulation of rules and guidelines for organists on how to treat both
melody and harmony in accompanying chorales, and with preparatory material
containing Vogler's deductions on the origins, development, and dissemination of the
church modes.

III. "Improvement and Revision of Faulty Treatments of the Six Greek Modes."
A discussion of seven faulty chorale harmonizations (five of them by Bach, two from
Swedish chorale books) followed by Vogler's revisions.

IV. "Rigorous Examination of Four-Voice Chorale Accompaniments and Choruses." Commentary on selected harmonizations from Vogler's collection of ninety
chorale harmonizations (mentioned above in connection with *Organist-schola*).

Occupying the heart of *Choral-System* is the author's historical deduction
of Part 2, in which he recounts the results of a remarkable odyssey. On the
night of March 15–16, 1792, Gustave III of Sweden was assassinated. Vogler,
who had evidently been planning an extended journey, now proceeded to put
his plan into action.[91] He traveled by sea to Gibraltar, Cádiz, Tangier, and
(possibly) further into the Mediterranean on an excursion that lasted to the
latter part of 1793. Equipped with a clavichord to help record the music he
heard, he became acquainted with regional folk songs and succeeded in
detecting what he thought to be the remnants of ancient chant.

Though the extent of his journey remains a mystery (did he actually
reach Greece, Carthage, and the Adriatic on this trip?), a fragmentary record
of his adventures and ports of call survives. During his stay in Gibraltar, he
practiced his clerical profession by delivering numerous sermons.[92] From a
letter of Bernhard Anselm Weber we learn that in Cádiz Vogler was mistaken
for a spy, detained, then eventually rescued by a Swedish consul who was able
to vouch for him.[93] Later, in Tangier, the ruler of Morocco placed at his
disposal a servant and escort who sang, played instruments (a guitar and a

two-string violin), and taught the traveler countless melodies during the course of his stay.[94] Two of the melodies he learned (*Romance africaine* and *Air barbaresque*) were later incorporated in *Polymelos* and *Pièces de clavecin;*[95] a third, *Terrassenlied der Afrikaner* (Terrace Song of the Africans), he performed in organ concerts. He also had the good fortune to enjoy the assistance of a Jewish cook who spoke Arabic, Spanish, Danish, Swedish, and English.[96]

As for the fruits of these explorations and the "historical deduction" to which they led, Vogler wisely assured the reader that his purposes were limited to reporting what he had learned in his travels to the Mediterranean and Africa: he did not aim to write a history of music or song, nor did he consult libraries.[97] Rather, he pursued a theory about the migration of modal formulas in ancient times, and the essence of his procedure was to combine his perceptions of ancient Hebrew and Greek music (as his early nineteenth-century critics observed, these were based partially on historical misinformation and fantasy) with insights gained from his collected samples of Mediterranean sacred music and folk song.

Speculating on the results of his quest, Vogler attaches great significance to connections he evidently discerned between ancient Greek music and practices he witnessed—and took part in—at a church on the "Armenian Islands," whose worshippers he classed among the Uniat Greeks.[98] Specifically, he claims that the music performed there expressed a "Mixophrygian" mode, which he believed to have been the oldest of the Greek scales. The mode in question, a seven-note series from B to a, he describes as being composed of two conjunct tetrachords: B c d e / e f g a. Taking his hypothesis a step further, he suggests that this Greek scale may have originated among the Hebrews, and possibly with King David himself. He reasons that David's ten-string instrument (he called it decachordon rather than *kinnor*) could have produced a ten-note series equivalent to the above-mentioned Greek scale with an added conjunct tetrachord: B c d e / e f g a / a b c' d'.[99]

After tracing his connection from ancient music to current practices in a Mediterranean church, Vogler turns to Morocco, where he witnessed schoolboys chanting a text from the Koran. The primitive melody he reports having heard there was equivalent to the solfège syllables mi–fa–mi–re, mi–fa–re–mi, and this pattern he classifies as belonging either to Phrygian or to his Mixophrygian. Again he sees a link with ancient Greece, proposing that the melody must have migrated from Athens to Morocco at a time when Carthage was a flourishing state.[100]

Concerning the relationship between such melodies and the system of church modes, Vogler cites the traditional grouping of modes in pairs according to range (i.e., authentic and plagal) as the basis for speculating as follows: the Phrygian came about as a fifth-related offspring of the ancient mode on B. The Aeolian and its fifth-related offspring, the Dorian, came next—made possible by the addition of the note A to the Greek scale system (an accomplishment he erroneously ascribes to Pythagoras). With the addition of the G below the A (Guido is credited with this milestone) came the Mixolydian and its corresponding relative, the Ionian. Finally, in order to incorporate the Lydian within this strangely anachronistic scheme, he invokes the major scale on C—that product of triadic tonality, created from a three-fold *trias harmonica* (i.e., triads on C, G, and F, as set forth in his theory of harmony)—to which the Lydian stands in the corresponding fifth relationship.[101]

What has Vogler accomplished in pursuing the tortuous path mapped out thus far? By tying together the proposed tuning of the ancient *kinnor,* the Greek mode on B, present-day singing of the Armenians and Moroccans, and the system of church modes, he portrays an authentic, timeless tradition—an enduring, natural wellspring that unites different peoples and reaches across the centuries. This panoramic sketch of a melodic commonwealth gives him the foundation he needs for the bold proposal that follows: whereas the ancient modal traditions have been preserved among primitive and non-European folk, the encounter with a sophisticated, evolving Western culture has led to their destruction.

Pondering the reason for this state of affairs, he points to the negligible influence of either the organ or musical notation outside the Western tradition and concludes that, paradoxically, it is the fact of oral transmission that has guaranteed a measure of purity in the music in its passage from one generation to the next. The development of Western practices (in which musical instruments and notation played crucially important roles) had the effect of virtually obliterating the ancient songs through melodic excrescences, tonal harmonization, instrumental accompaniment, theatrical brilliance, and the like.[102] In the relatively primitive cultures he encountered, the lack of instruments helped prevent such corruption, and the presence of many aural witnesses, as in a church, tended to inhibit the practice of alteration.[103]

These observations lead the theorist to his crucial indictment: customary Western notions of harmonization are based on false premises. The modern tonal system has not somehow absorbed or replaced the priceless modal heritage, but has merely denied its enduring existence. To apply the conventional rules of harmony to a chorale or plainchant accompaniment is to contradict the modal character rather than enhance its strength. What is needed, Vogler claims, is a new method of harmonization by which the modal design of the melody—rather than allegiance to a given key—is the decisive factor in determining cadence and chord choice.

The ultimate purpose of Vogler's historical deduction, then, has been to furnish the keystone for his argument in proposing a new, modally oriented method of harmonizing chorales. He begins by asserting that the modal purity of the melody itself must be upheld by having it remain free of chromatic alteration or ornamentation. As for the accompanying harmony, the theorist's unavoidable frame of reference is the modern grammar of chords and cadences expounded in his harmony manuals. However, he explains, a distinction must be drawn between two different approaches: tonal and modal ("die Musikalische und die Choral-Behandlung").[104] According to the former, all aspects of harmonization and chord choice are related directly to the given key. Though this is the normal orientation for contemporary tonal practice, Vogler asserts that in the harmonization of modal chorales, it must yield to the latter method, in which modal considerations outweigh those of key or tonal unity.

Elaborating his notion of an appropriate *Choral-Behandlung,* Vogler proceeds to assemble three sets of guidelines for the suitable treatment of modal chorales. Though not unrelated in principle to other theorists' recommendations, Vogler's scheme proves ingenious in its special use of materials derived from his theory of harmony: the principle of *Schlussfallmässigkeit,* the analysis of chord functions using Roman numerals, and the concept of a hierarchy in harmonic organization.

First, in keeping with the fifth relationship suggested by the division of the modes into plagal and authentic ranges, he decrees that the final note of each phrase must represent either the root or fifth of the underlying chord, not the third. (Without examining the arbitrary nature of this rule, which says nothing about the degrees of a given mode on which cadences are likely to fall, Vogler stubbornly insists on its importance. Certainly by imposing limits on harmonic choice at cadences, it does provide a means by which a modal melody can exert direct control over the harmonization.)

Next, he proposes various restrictions on harmonic content and dissonance. His aim is to avoid certain materials and devices typical of theater music, including embellished ("boisterous") cadences, arbitrary modulations, successions of "decisive major harmonies," and, to be sure, the tonally decisive dominant seventh. In place of these proscribed sources of diversity, he advocates ties, suspensions, and suspension chains ("Verkettungen von Uebelklängen"); and to inspire the worshipper to devotion, he recommends the relative serenity of the minor.

Finally, he outlines rules for specifying the available cadential patterns within a given mode. Adopting the premise that a cadence must involve a major triad, either as final or penultimate chord, he distinguishes between authentic (V–I) and plagal—a category which subsumes all other cadential formulas (see description below). If needed to form either an authentic or plagal cadence, certain accidentals may be employed. Since their purpose will be essentially limited to transforming a minor chord into major, the sanctioned accidentals can only be those that raise, rather than lower, an uninflected pitch; and since the melody must remain pure, they can only take place in the accompaniment. Vogler further explains that his authentic and plagal cadences have nothing to do with the range of the melody and can be used for plagal as well as authentic modes: what was said for Dorian applies also to Hypodorian, and so forth.[105]

As a consequence of the rules for forming cadences, the choice of cadence types within a given mode is carefully circumscribed. As shown in Example 19, Vogler summarizes the essential correspondence between cadence type and mode as follows:

*Authentic cadences* (V–I) - Dorian, Lydian, Aeolian, Ionian: both Ionian and Lydian possess the necessary major, cadential V chord; although the Dorian and Aeolian require sharps, the accidentals are condoned, presumably because neither destroys the distinguishing characteristic of the mode (raised sixth in Dorian, lowered sixth in Aeolian).

*Plagal cadences* - Ionian: two kinds are available, IV–I and IV–VII–I; Mixolydian: IV–I; Phrygian: lacking the possibility of a true authentic or plagal cadence, the Phrygian employs an "apparent plagal" which uses the same cadential E-major chord as that identified as V in Aeolian, and which Vogler likens to an Aeolian "reversed authentic" (A–E; I–V) if the A-minor chord precedes; Aeolian: plagal cadence (D–A), which resembles a reversed authentic in Dorian (D–A; I–V) just as the Phrygian A–E resembles a reversed authentic in Aeolian.

As he qualifies and elucidates this set of possibilities, Vogler observes that

Example 19
Cadences for the church modes.

the first of his Mixolydian cadences cannot properly be used in strict style, since the melody would end on the third of the underlying chord. He explains that the authentic cadence is inappropriate in Mixolydian because it would require introducing an F-sharp, which is incompatible with a chorale melody, but that the G-sharp may be used in Aeolian since there is no true plagal cadence available as in Mixolydian. In other words, the F-sharp, whether in the melody itself or merely in the accompaniment, contradicts the defining characteristic of the mode (i.e., the lowered seventh scale degree).

The theorist further clarifies his rules by noting the kinds of errors often committed in the harmonization of modal chorales. These include both distortion of the melody (by diminutions, appoggiaturas, trills, and chromatic passages between verses), and violations of harmonic purity (by inappropriate major harmony, dominant sevenths, remote modulations, cadences with the third of the chord in the melody, and chromatic alteration of the melody to accommodate improper cadences).

Significantly, Vogler allows certain practices sometimes forbidden by authors of eighteenth-century thoroughbass manuals in their rules for accompaniment: he permits dissonances, where some harmonists allow only triads; he condones inversions as well as the root-position chords to which other methods are limited; and whereas some purists insist on a strict, homorhythmic alignment of the accompaniment with the melody, Vogler endorses the cautious but deliberate use of passing tones, or *Zwischenklänge*. Dissonances by suspension are justified as a desirable source of harmonic cohesion and continuity, and $\frac{6}{4}$ chords, though considered by Vogler less felicitous than root-position harmony, are nevertheless accepted as a useful resource for avoiding parallel motion and rounding out the bass line. With regard to the *Zwischenklänge* (in *Harmonielehre*, p. 11, Vogler describes these as dissonances that occur between two harmonic tones; in *Choral-System,* he uses the term to mean either harmonic or nonharmonic tones that fall between the beats), he observes that they can be used to circumvent problems in voice leading, but that they must be restricted to inner voices. The melody admits none because the chorale must remain pure, and the bass must avoid them as well because the unmeasured performance that Vogler advocates requires synchronization of bass and melody: the small notes, destroying the inherent solemnity of the lowest part, would sound wholly inappropriate when amplified by a penetrating organ pedal.[106]

As Vogler suggests, his admonitions furnish a general guide for practice. They were not intended as a Procrustean bed, and the theorist himself shies away from consistently strict application: departures from the rules, often justified empirically on grounds of taste, are not infrequent in the ninety harmonizations published with the treatise. Furthermore, he points out that various accidentals in the melodies have found their way into the music through custom, and that by declining to purge them he has merely chosen to recognize habits that have accrued over the centuries.[107]

Rules for harmonizing modal chorales having been established, Vogler devotes Part III of the treatise to demonstrating the practical application of his theory. As in his earlier didactic writings, the preferred method is one of *Verbesserung:* he takes a sampling of existing harmonizations, points out their faults, then offers revised, more stylistically appropriate versions. Selecting seven chorales, two in Phrygian and one for each of the other five authentic modes, he singles out J. S. Bach as a principal culprit.

The most extended critique concerns two settings by Bach of the Phrygian chorale, *O Haupt voll Blut und Wunden,*[108] both of which prove to be heavily laden with errors. The initial chord of the first setting (a V$\frac{4}{2}$) strikes him as objectionable in the extreme: if the seventh in the bass voice were to be sounded on the thunderous 32′ pedal of the organ, he writes, it would shatter the eardrums, bewilder the mind, and convulse the nervous system.[109] The issue of modal purity stands out prominently in Vogler's commentary. He points out not only that Bach features all twelve chromatic tones in both settings, but that his choice of cadences effectively destroys any sense of mode. In the first of the two settings, the penultimate cadence falls on a G-major chord (harmonizing the B in the melody), while the final cadence is on C (with E in the melody), thereby subjugating the final of the mode, E, to a usurping C major. To thus wipe away the Phrygian mode "as with a sponge," the author declares, is something one would not expect from a composer who has been called by some the greatest harmonist of the age.[110]

Vogler details further objections with the help of an extended table which specifies twelve categories of infraction (including matters of chord choice, dissonance treatment, voice leading, and the use of accidentals) and lists instances from the two settings. Faults cited in the passage quoted as Example 20a (measures 7–10 of the first setting) include the choice of a modally inappropriate, inflected chord with diminished seventh (measure 7, beat 2); the failure to resolve the seventh of that chord, the B-flat in the bass; the violation of the chorale melody's purity with a passing tone (measure 9); an inappropriate cadence on G in measure 10, with the third, B, in the melody; and a choice of harmonies immediately preceding this cadence (dominant chords on A, then D) that seem more appropriate to "luxurious theater style" than to the chorale.[111]

Vogler's own harmonization addresses the problems he perceives in Bach's versions, and the result is a setting that bears little resemblance to either. As witnessed in Example 20b, which quotes from measures 7–10 of the revision, the melody is restored to an unadorned state, dominant sevenths are abolished, and the accompaniment is purged of unnecessary inflections. The thoroughly revised bass line is harmonically stable, and the choice of cadences on A and E conforms to the mode.[112] Diversity is not altogether lacking, however. The inner voices are enlivened with passing tones (including an F-sharp in the tenor in measure 8, logically justifiable on grounds of voice leading), and the last beat of measure 7 is enriched by a modally acceptable diminished seventh: its only inflection, G-sharp, anticipates the approaching cadence on A.

Proceeding from the excoriation of Bach and the demonstration of how harmonizations could be judged according to his system, Vogler turns in Part IV to the analysis of his own chorales. Though he treats only a small number of settings in detail, his commentaries focus sharply on central issues: modal purity, cadential formulas, chord choice, passing tones, and dissonances.

Example 20
(a) J. S. Bach, *O Haupt woll Blut und Wunden,* setting no. 1, measures 7–10; (b) Vogler's setting, measures 7–10.

Occasionally he selects passages for alternative harmonization, thereby evidently to improve on his own work or at least to illustrate other feasible solutions. Many of the chorales do indeed betray liberties, but a fair number are strict enough to demonstrate the system in reasonably pure form. Among them is a setting of the famous melody *Aus tiefer Not,* no. 99 in the *Swenska Psalm bok* (see Example 21).

In describing a related harmonization of this chorale in the first volume of *Organist-schola,* one whose cadences correspond to those in the *Choral-System* version, Vogler analyzes the cadential chords as follows, with letters signifying chord roots and Roman numerals denoting function:[113]

| 3♯ | 3♯ | 3 | 3 | 3♯ |
|----|----|----|----|----|
| E | E | A | G | E |
| V | V | I | V | V |

By furnishing this analysis, the theorist proposes that the first two chords may be understood as V of Aeolian, the third as I of Aeolian, the fourth as V of Ionian, and the last as V of Aeolian. The Roman numerals come from

Example 21
*Aus tiefer Not* from *Choral-System.*

Vogler's system of tonal harmony, and their use here promotes the theorist's aim of uniting tonal harmony and modal melody in a way that allows the former to enhance the latter without diluting its effect. Involving a curious mixture of modal and tonal terminology, the analyses do not signify either key centers or modulations, nor do they designate any change of mode. They simply represent the grammatically appropriate plagal and authentic cadences as dictated by the given, modally pure melody, whose modal design furnishes the requisite source of unity for the chorale as a whole.

Closer examination of this chorale from the standpoint of the system's precepts shows how these particular cadences were chosen. As required, the final note of each phrase forms either the fifth or octave of the cadential chord. Each cadence, then, offers no more than two choices. At the end of the first phrase, a cadence on B would necessitate accidentals (F-sharp and D-sharp) that would abolish any sense of modal purity. A cadence on E is thus the sole possibility, and the inflection in the alto (G to G-sharp) is necessary in order to form a *schlussfallmässig* plagal cadence. For each subsequent phrase, the melodic close forms the octave of the chosen chord, and satisfactory plagal or authentic cadences are accomplished. As Vogler has taken pains to clarify, the anomalous Phrygian mode allows no authentic cadence on its final, and as witnessed in this harmonization, the plagal harmony with which the first, second and final phrases close is borrowed from Aeolian.

In accordance with the restrictive harmonic language of the system, this setting uses no chromatic inflections except in cadential formulas, where they supply the requisite major triads. Through the simplicity of the harmony and the avoidance of dominant sevenths, Vogler has avoided the secular elements he finds offensive in chorale harmonizations. By the same token, he takes nearly every opportunity to use the ties and suspension dissonances that he deems essential to sacred style. In the bass line, root-position chords are predominant, although first inversions occur frequently and $\frac{6}{4}$ chords are not excluded (see measure 1, beat 4; measure 3, beat 4).

By thus engaging the principles of his system, Vogler creates a suitably austere, modally oriented harmonization. Treating his rhythmic texture with comparable restraint, he maintains a quarter-note pulse in all but the last measure. There, he introduces eighths in the alto and tenor, presumably to compensate for the arrested movement of the melody. That such a harmonization pales by comparison with the affective intensity typical of many Bach chorales (or for that matter some of Vogler's own) is clearly irrelevant: adherence to an essentially impersonal, timeless ideal is the theorist's main object here. His intention is merely to underline rather than supplement the expressive content of the original melody and its text. The elements of novelty, originality, and inventiveness reside in the creation of the system and its use as a tool for criticism, and not in the creation of unique, individualistic settings of traditional melodies.

Though it never enjoyed wide circulation, the *Choral-System* was nonetheless something of a landmark in its field, and its message did not escape the notice of important contemporaries, several of whom offered critical assessments of the theory and its application. Ernst Ludwig Gerber, in his lexicon of 1812–14, expressed highest praise for the system, judging it to be filled with great and significant truths.[114] Gerber, who was himself an organist and an advocate of simplicity in the art of chorale accompaniment, had elsewhere applauded Vogler's exercise of restraint in his chorale book (i.e., the ninety settings that accompanied his text), and had attributed this quality to the composer's wisdom as an artist.[115]

J. H. Knecht's assessment was likewise respectful, if somewhat more reserved. Reviewing *Choral-System* in an early issue of the *Allgemeine musikalische Zeitung,* he proposed that it merited the attention of all organists and theorists: first, "because it has as its author a man of profound powers of observation, comprehensive knowledge, and abundant experience"; second, because it concerned a subject as important as chorale, an area generally regarded as insignificant.[116] But while praising the instructive value of the system, Knecht by no means wholly endorsed it as a practical method to be followed. In his own, earlier treatise on chorale accompaniment,[117] Knecht had also advocated the specialized harmonic treatment of modal melodies, but his rules were less strict and he acknowledged the potential validity of a variety of different approaches. Moreover, as an experienced, pragmatic church organist, he was prompted to challenge the strictness of the abbé's approach on practical grounds: the difficulty of weaning a congregation from their familiar, chromatically altered melodies (Vogler had alluded to this problem in *Choral-System,* and Knecht acknowledged this allusion); and the limited capacity of the average churchgoer for true comprehension and appreciation of the ancient modes, which tended to seem dry and remote.

Gottfried Weber, less enthusiastic than Knecht, questioned the theoretical foundations of Vogler's *Choral-System.*[118] Generally disdainful of other theorists' precepts, Weber complained that rules in use for harmonizing modal melodies were largely based on arbitrary assumptions—a circumstance that accounted for the absence of any unified, coherent system. Finding no valid basis for the abbé's rule that a verse may never end with the third in the melody, nor for his banning of the dominant seventh chord, he declared that neither Vogler's rules nor anyone else's possessed a "valid, rational, satisfactory" foundation.

As might be expected, Vogler's *Choral-System* was destined to gather only a limited following as a guide for the church musician. By furnishing rules for the harmonization of traditional sacred melodies, the treatise did address an important practical concern. But even though Vogler developed a unique approach in formulating his rules, his results were not so strikingly different or efficacious as to allow his system to exert an especially strong or widely felt impact.[119]

The treatise is nevertheless important as a historical document. Reaching well beyond such mundane issues as keeping a congregation in tune, it was both original and uniquely ambitious in its attempt to combine historical speculation with what virtually amounts to an early ethnomusicological perspective in the search for a viable, fresh approach to the harmonization of modal chorales. It thereby furnishes a vivid reflection of contemporary interests, both in Protestant and Catholic circles, in the preservation and revival of sacred traditions.

By proposing certain solutions to the question of modal purity, Vogler did not necessarily mean to exclude less restrictive approaches. Among the ninety harmonizations in *Choral-System* there are examples of such liberties as dominant sevenths, accidentals in mid-phrase, and cadences in which the final note forms the third of the harmonizing chord. In other words, even in works that purportedly reflect his system, the composer did not let issues of purity and austerity thwart his fondness for harmonic richness and diversity.

A liberal attitude toward his own principles is evident throughout Vogler's repertory of Protestant chorales and related compositions for Catholic use. This fairly extensive body of works encompasses not only the ninety chorales accompanying *Organist-schola* and *Choral-System,* but also the manuscript collections *14 Choräle,*[120] *13 Kirchengesänge,*[121] *[12 Cantiques],*[122] and an assortment of harmonizations in other manuscript sources, several published posthumously. Most pieces in this category have vernacular texts (Swedish, German, French), although there are comparable settings that involve Latin plainsong. Texturally, all are essentially homorhythmic. Most of them are fully realized in four parts and suitable for performance by voices, organ, or both.

Among these works, many of which appear to have been composed, assembled, and published later than the treatise and its ninety chorales, departures from *Choral-System* principles are not hard to find. In the *14 Choräle* the modal settings include chromatic enrichments that Vogler forbids, such as secondary dominants and diminished sevenths within the body of a phrase. Other violations in this collection include use of the dominant seventh (occasionally it appears as the closing chord of a phrase), and inappropriate cadential formulas, such as V or V[7] to I in the Mixolydian or—even less acceptable theoretically—in the Phrygian mode. Remarkably, the last note of a phrase is not infrequently harmonized as the third of a chord.

The somewhat free-wheeling approach typically found in Vogler's own chorale collections suggests that the time may not have been ripe for the kind of doctrinaire austerity advocated in *Choral-System.* Zealous reform movements such as that led by Sailer and the Regensburg school were to get underway in earnest somewhat later. A subsequent approach by Mettenleiter proved far more restrictive by forbidding accidentals altogether. While *Choral-System* foreshadows this trend, Vogler clearly cannot be described as a single-minded exponent of austerity on the basis of his own compositions.

The ambiguous attitude—in part reformist yet at the same time musically opulent and experimental—is reflected in his orchestrally accompanied pieces that involve quotations of Gregorian melody. These include certain settings based on psalm tones (e.g., the "Laudate pueri" movement of *Serenissimae puerperae sacrum* [1804], in which an unembellished rendering of the psalm tone is set against a coloristically diverse accompaniment featuring rhythmically animated arpeggiations in the strings). Comparable ambiguities are evident in several pieces of accompanied plainsong (*Pater noster, Praefatio di S. S. Trinitate,* and *Praefatio de Beata Maria Virgine*), each of which may well have originated after Vogler's formulation of his system.[123] Intended for delivery by a priest, they involve a single line of chant whose texturally simple organ accompaniment is filled with harmonic extravagances of the kind deplored in *Choral-System.* The settings also feature striking, meticulously marked dynamics—involving crescendos and diminuendos as well as sharply contrasting dynamic levels—that were a trademark of Vogler's secular styles as well as his orchestrally accompanied and unaccompanied sacred music.

As exemplified by such pieces as these, anything resembling close adherence to the system is rare, apart from the volume of chorale harmonizations that accompanied the treatise. To Vogler the musician, the question of modal purity was easily overshadowed by other artistic concerns. But the prescriptions of *Choral-System* also came into conflict with certain of Vogler's theoretical principles and their application, a problem that arises in the abbé's own later writings.

One of the documents in question is an analytical essay accompanying the *Davids Buss-Psalm* (1807), a setting of Moses Mendelssohn's translation of the Fiftieth Psalm (Fifty-first in the Authorized Version) which Vogler published as one of the two items in his short-lived "Utile dulci" series.[124] This chorale-style piece employs a modal *cantus firmus* previously used by Vogler in a funeral ode. But unlike the theorist's model chorales in *Choral-System,* modal properties here are obscured rather than enhanced by the harmonization: while remarkably austere rhythmically as well as texturally (uniform half-note movement prevails throughout all voice parts), the work displays an astonishing variety of chords in what amounts to a veritable showcase of harmonic possibilities.

Given the vernacular text, the rhythmically undifferentiated, syllabic idiom, and the use of a modal *cantus firmus,* this piece would seem to bear comparison with the harmonizations of *Choral-System*. But evidence of those rules is negligible, for here Vogler proceeds from an altogether different premise: as his analysis confirms, his aim is to create a model of harmonic diversity rather than a lesson in sacred purity. The three segments of the original melody recur many times as the 127-measure piece unfolds, each time with a different harmonization.[125] Heedless of the restrictions of *Choral-System*, this tour de force of harmonic variation uses dominant sevenths, secondary dominants, and a diversity of other chords that involve noncadential accidentals (see Example 22).[126] Also discarded are the rules forbidding melodic accidentals and cadences with the third in the melody.

Even further removed from the ideals of *Choral-System*, though once again directed toward the problem of J. S. Bach and his reputation as a master of chorale harmonization, is the late collaboration of Vogler with his famous pupil: the *Zwölf Choräle von Sebastian Bach, umgearbeitet von Vogler, zergliedert von Carl Maria von Weber* (Leipzig, [1810]). As in *Choral-System*, Bach's harmonizations are offered along with Vogler's revisions, and the

Example 22
*Davids Buss-Psalm,* measures 51–56.

accompanying commentary (supplied this time by the young Weber) elucidates errors in the former and virtues of the latter. But here, in contrast to the sanctimonious purity featured in the earlier treatise, these revisions bristle with chromatic inflections.

Why does Vogler, who previously had taken pains to simplify Bach, now attempt to overtake him in harmonic complexity? As clarified by Weber's preface, the question of sacred purity is not at issue. Bach, whom Vogler had taken to task in *Choral-System* for his shortcomings as a composer of sacred music, is now to be discredited as the preeminent master of harmony that his disciples take him to be. With this set of revised harmonizations, as radical in their extravagance as those of *Choral-System* were austere, the theorist sets out to prove that, within the realm of his harmonic system, the diversity and richness of Bach can be not only equaled but surpassed.

As witnessed in such diverse and even contradictory endeavors as *Choral-System, Davids Buss-Psalm,* and *Zwölf Choräle,* Vogler's contributions to the field of sacred music mirrored the conflicts that informed his age; and even as he worked to promote their resolution, his efforts caused the insolubility of basic problems to stand all the more sharply in relief. It was widely assumed that sacred music should maintain its own identity, and that its resources should be those that best served the exalted aims of spiritual sentiment and edification in an age of enlightenment. Vogler saw sacred music as pure, elevated, and timeless, yet it must also gain ready access to the contemporary listener's ear, heart, and mind. The *stile antico* evoked a sense of timelessness, and the simple, vernacular hymn was admirably comprehensible, but these customary materials of sacred expression proved bland by comparison with those of the forbidden secular realms where musical progress of the time seemed most vivid and astonishing: the virtuoso brilliance of the operatic stage and the pyrotechnics witnessed in the concert hall.

Vogler's recommendations and corroborating musical models were an attempt to retain some measure of purity and simplicity while in one way or another (apart from *Choral-System*) absorbing the tempting diversity of modern techniques and expressive means. Hybrids like the *Miserere* and *Deutsche Kirchenmusik* may be seen as efforts to place sacred music on a new footing, to combine restored sacred traditions with the benefits of musical progress and thereby achieve an acceptable and enduring compromise.

In Vogler's own sacred repertory, the practices he advocated bore fruit to some extent. Yet the fact that his own reformist goal of a purified, sacred ideal remained only partially fulfilled stands as the sign of a persisting dilemma. The ethic of restraint and simplicity suggested by *Andacht* proved insufficient, while the plundering of modern secular music seemed unacceptable. Vogler's work clearly reflects this quandary as he joined in the search for new inspiration through the revival of music from the past: whether that of antiquity, as applauded in *Choral-System;* of Palestrina or of Handel, whose musical legacies Vogler endorsed; or of J. S. Bach, whose impending revival he resisted. This quest was destined to bear immense consequences for subsequent generations of composers and their audiences, and its connection with Vogler's own experiences offers a glimpse of the conditions under which it arose and gathered momentum.

## CHAPTER 5

# Music and Drama

I N Vogler's 1808 essay on musical progress, written in connection with his revised German Mass of the previous year, the issue at hand was ostensibly that of stylistic change in sacred music. The original version of the Mass, written thirty years earlier for voices and organ, had weathered the passage of time only moderately well. The austerity of its harmony and texture was appropriate for the 1770s, but to modern ears the work sounded quaint. The point of the experiment was to breathe new life into an outdated composition by having the original material adorned with modern orchestral reinforcement. Transformed in this fashion, the revised Mass furnished an object lesson for composers and critics of music for the church.

But Vogler clearly had larger purposes in mind. Seeing change in musical styles, and perceiving a need on the part of his contemporaries for guidance and clarification, he found the notion of *Verbesserung* (revision) an agreeable medium of instruction, and the relative simplicity of a sacred piece made for a more efficient demonstration than a work of symphonic or operatic complexity. To be sure, the *Deutsche Kirchenmusik* project addressed the church-music composer no less directly than the earlier revision of Pergolesi's *Stabat Mater,* but it served to point up compositional problems relevant to secular as well as sacred practices. Indeed, both these lessons in modernization involved the transplanting of musical resources native to secular music, especially that of the theater, for it was in this field that Vogler saw the most important advances of his day taking place.

The special interest in theater music betrayed by the 1808 essay recalls that seen in the analyses and commentaries of the *Betrachtungen*. In those earlier writings, Vogler applauded the concision and restraint of Hasse's truly vocal idiom as well as the expressive intensity and eloquent feeling of Jommelli's music.[1] As witnessed in the operatic works of these composers, the musical language of the time was inherently dramatic, and its materials seemed naturally suited to the depiction of images and atmosphere or the portrayal of sentiment, action, tension, and conflict. In the discussions dealing with dramatic music, Vogler concerned himself mainly with traditions of *opera seria* and *buffa*. His displeasure with the empty virtuosity of the younger Italians notwithstanding, it was the model of Italian opera that he urged his countrymen to adopt for instruction in technique and taste. French opera received scant attention, and German achievements such as Hiller's *Singspiele* or the operas of Holzbauer and Schweitzer were largely ignored. Vogler mentioned Gluck, but the topic of Gluckian operatic reform was not one that he chose to treat in detail.

The narrow perspective of the *Betrachtungen* stands in contrast to the broadened scope of the late essay, where Vogler takes account of epoch-making achievements in the world of opera. He now sees that, while the Italians have languished, the Germans have produced two first-rank geniuses, Mozart and Gluck, whose works have set new standards of excellence in dramatic composition. Hiller's *Singspiele* are at least mentioned; and Grétry is praised for his contributions to the genre of *opéra comique,* in which he reveals an incomparable talent for declamation. But the Frenchman's gifts are limited, Vogler observes, and his style lacks the force necessary for anything more substantial than comedy.

The music of Mozart, by contrast, overflows with a surprisingly complex harmony and flashes of instrumental brilliance. Yet these qualities Vogler sees as a mixed blessing. Stunning in its richness and beauty, Mozart's music overshadows the text, and the drama suffers as a result. Gluck, though less inspired than Mozart as a musician, stands out as a more earnest, philosophically minded dramatist. His moments of epic grandeur—Orpheus's encounter with the Furies, the voice of the underworld spirits in *Alceste,* or the duet of Agamemnon and Achilles in *Iphigénie en Aulide*—demonstrate his mastery of lyric drama.[2]

Between these two depictions of a contemporary musical scene—the early *Betrachtungen* on one hand, the 1808 essay on the other—lie three decades of progress and change that have obliged Vogler to alter his point of view. New ideals of operatic reform have supplanted the now old-fashioned Metastasian aesthetic, and the naiveté of Galuppi and Hasse has been upstaged by the sophistication of Mozart.

Yet in certain respects, Vogler's later writings reveal the persistence of enduring attitudes despite the conspicuous adjustments he has made in reaction to a changing scene. His praise of Italian traditions in *Betrachtungen* rested on what he heard as a near-perfect balance of musical order and dramatic expression, and in the late essay he is still searching for such an ideal. Committed no less than before to his belief in musical progress, Vogler heartily endorses the innovations of his late eighteenth-century contemporaries; yet his enthusiasm is softened by a reluctance to fully endorse the reformist principles of Gluck or the richness of harmony and instrumental color in Mozart. Even though recent accomplishments have largely superseded those of Hasse and his generation, the goal of perfection in musical drama remains elusive.

The quest for an ideal union of music and drama, a central concern of Vogler's writings, is vividly reflected in his own stage works for Mannheim, Munich, Stockholm, Vienna, and Darmstadt. Many mysteries surround these compositions with regard to authenticity, dating, circumstances of performance, revivals, and revised versions, so that the extent of the repertory remains unclear. Among the major, extant works, the following may be included:[3]

*Der Kaufmann von Smyrna* (*Singspiel*), Mannheim 1771

*Lampedo* (melodrama), Darmstadt 1779

*Erwin und Elmire* (*Singspiel*), Darmstadt 1781

*Castore e Polluce* (*opera seria*), Munich c. 1786

*Gustav Adolf och Ebba Brahe* (serious opera), Stockholm 1787

*Samori* (heroic-comic opera), Vienna 1804

*Der Admiral (Der gewonnene Prozess)* (*Singspiel*), Darmstadt 1811

(Other dramatic endeavors include incidental music for Shakespeare's *Hamlet* [1778], Racine's *Athalia* [1786], and Skjöldebrand's *Hermann von Unna* [1795].)

Vogler was justifiably proud of his versatile ability to write no less capably for the theater than for the church. Though he did not pretend that his relatively small output of dramatic music qualified him as a leading master in the field, such major works as *Castore e Polluce, Gustav Adolf,* and *Samori* count among his most ambitious compositions, with some of his most felicitous inspirations.

### EARLY CRITICAL ANALYSIS

For an appraisal of Vogler's theater pieces and an understanding of their significance as reflections of his aims and ideals, the early critical writings provide a useful foundation. The most important of these are the extended essays in *Betrachtungen* on the *Singspiel, Der Kaufmann von Smyrna,* and the incidental music for Shakespeare's *Hamlet.* The lessons they offer are complemented by two studies of works by contemporaries: a critique of a Metastasian cantata by J. C. Bach, featured in the first volume of the *Betrachtungen,* and an essay on Anton Schweitzer's *Rosamunde,* published in 1780 in the periodical *Rheinische Beiträge zur Gelehrsamkeit.*[4] Since this last-mentioned study deals in general terms with issues of operatic style and technique, it provides a backdrop for examining other, more detailed analyses.

The subject of the *Rosamunde* critique was the second of Schweitzer's two experiments in serious opera for the Mannheim stage. Preceded by his famous *Alceste* of 1773, this work was a comparably ambitious mixture of French spectacle and Italian *opera seria.* It was originally intended for the Carnival of 1778, but owing to the political upheavals of that year (the death of the Elector of Bavaria and the subsequent removal of Carl Theodor's court to Munich) it remained unperformed until 1780, when Wolfgang Heribert von Dalberg's recently formed National Theater undertook its production.

Offered as a model of rational criticism, Vogler's account of the work aims for a balanced appraisal of its virtues and shortcomings. In the process, it sheds light on the theorist's opinions of what a large-scale musical drama should achieve, what the appropriate ingredients are, and how they should be organized to bring about a unified artistic creation. We learn that the composer should have a plan, an overview of the entire work, before he actually begins to set the first aria. For the benefit of the singers' voices as well as the audience's sensibilities, the effect of a gradual rise in emotional intensity (a large-scale rhetorical crescendo, in effect) should be sensed as the drama unfolds.

For the overture, both the outmoded pomposity of the traditional French style and the bustle of the Italian type are judged inappropriate. Instead, Vogler advocates an eloquent, dramatically significant prelude ("sprechender Eingang"). Unfortunately, he does not specify the kind of dramatic content he requires of such an overture. Should it be programmatic, or somehow thematically related to the substance of the opera? Addressing these matters only obliquely, he chooses to concentrate instead on the individual arias or ensembles and the issues of structure and expression to which they give rise.

On this level of structure—the individual, musically continuous number within a scene—the fragmentation and disorder Vogler sees in Schweitzer's work furnish an opportunity to hold forth on the need for structural and aesthetic coherence. In keeping with his rationalist views, he conceives musical drama in terms of static tableaux; and the analogy with painting, in which the composer designs a broad, artistically unified background against which foreground colors may be featured, plays a major part in his critique. While an aria may emphasize the portrayal of a single passion or a particular image, the possibilities of contrast and diversity need not be excluded: allusion is made to the idea of the subordinate image ("das subalterne Gemäld"). Tonal stability is essential, and far-reaching modulations should be applied only sparingly. The effectiveness of vocal and instrumental colors, like that of tonal resources, depends on their use with restraint and propriety. The singer's projection of his text must stand unchallenged by instrumental commentary, though instrumental obbligato parts are not to be disparaged if applied judiciously.

In tolerating virtuosity and insisting on the importance of lyrical continuity, Vogler's critique betrays a bias in favor of *opera seria* conventions. This preference is exemplified in his complaint about Schweitzer's fondness for recitative-like declamation, which contradicts the tone of noble lyricism that should prevail in a serious drama. Something of a reformist spirit nonetheless shines through as Vogler applauds particular instances of innovation and experiment. He admires the composer's effective use of accompanied recitative; and he endorses naturalistic delivery of text in an ensemble when required by dramatic circumstance, as in a duet between Rosamunde and the queen, where the contrast between a sustained syllable in one part and agitated declamation in the other emphasizes differences of emotion and personality in this confrontation of rivals.

Little mention is made of Wieland's text for the opera, nor is there any explicit discussion of aesthetic doctrine. The mixture of national elements— Italian aria, French grandeur, and German richness of harmony and orchestral fabric—evidently condoned, is not subjected to criticism; and despite the author's evident preference for Metastasian customs, he gives the impression that musical drama is an open-ended territory for exploration, a potentially eclectic, international genre in which German composers can succeed if properly guided by taste and reason.

It is not Vogler's purpose, however, to explore such weighty matters of style within the sixteen pages he allots to this critique, nor to offer more than an introduction to questions of operatic practice. For further illumination, he advises readers to turn to the pages of the *Betrachtungen,* where they would find detailed musical analyses devoted to aspects of the relationship between music and text.

An initial example is found in the opening fascicles of the Mannheim serial, where J. C. Bach's cantata *No, non turbarti o Nice* provides a basis for exploring the resources of dramatic expression. A "monodrama" for soprano, as this unpretentious setting of a pastoral Metastasian text is called, the work consists of two arias, each preceded by an obbligato recitative. The composition as a whole serves to demonstrate "how much [expressive] power resides in music, and how great is its capacity to depict even the most sharply contrasted opposites . . . with the most vivid colors."[5] Written, we learn, by a master whose incomparable musical gift extends to all styles and genres, Bach's cantata illustrates the normative framework, the figures, and the turns of phrase suitable to the setting of such a text. The rustling of leaves, the sounds of birds, wind, rain, and thunderstorm are deftly portrayed, and each of the song texts fills the conventional proportions of a *da capo* aria.

Vogler's commentary stresses the extent to which depictive and expressive details participate as essential elements in the musical design. In the first aria, the start of the middle section modulates from tonic (A major) to the relative minor, and the darkened tonal color suitably illustrates a raging storm. By measure 62 the music has come to a cadence in the relative minor, and the following phrase turns toward the subdominant of this key, B minor (see Example 1).[6] The process of change in key involves a fleeting reference to D, the relative major of B minor, and as the dominant seventh of D major is struck, the bright sound of this transitional harmony coincides with the poet's phrase "Quando il ciel si rassereni." The resulting effect is judiciously chosen, "with respect to the harmony in and of itself, and with respect to the contrast of the following harmony with the foregoing."[7] The momentary, expressively appropriate turn away from the orbit of the minor within the middle section, the ingratiating sonority of the transitional dominant, and its logical function as a pivot on the way to B minor—all contribute to a

Example 1
J. C. Bach, "Ma tu tremi," from the
cantata, *No, non turbarti o Nice,*
measures 60–65.

felicitous union of music and text within the hierarchic layers of a regular, unambiguous design.

As seen in the analysis of J. C. Bach's cantata, where standard aria forms offer a framework to which text-setting details may be attached, Vogler's endorsement of structural conventions seems largely a matter of convenience. The validity of these norms is assumed as part of the given materials of the age, and they furnish a universally understood basis for aesthetic unity and coherence. Once adopted, however, the mandatory constraints of a musical form pose a challenge to the musical dramatist. Essential ingredients, such as structural symmetry, modulatory scheme, and articulation of contrasting sections, must somehow be made to coincide with corresponding elements in the expressive message, whether this message is embodied in a program or a vocalist's text.

The nature of the challenge is merely suggested by the cantata essay, which invites the reader to draw connections between structural logic and the communication of expressive content. Further on in the *Betrachtungen,* this issue is treated more explicitly as Vogler presents a model of dramatic program music, his own recently composed overture and incidental music for Shakespeare's *Hamlet.*

Prepared in connection with productions of Shakespeare plays by Abel Seyler's theater troupe at Mannheim in the late 1770s, Vogler's music for *Hamlet* attempts to interpret images and actions in the drama. The composer's effort to explain this music—to elucidate its descriptive qualities and identify salient features of structure and style—leads to one of the most detailed critiques in the serial, and one in which the interaction of structure and extramusical content is featured as a principal topic of discussion.[8] Attention is directed mainly to the richly colored, programmatic overture. Designed as a dramatically significant prelude to the play, the piece features representations of four crucially important moments or images: Hamlet's sorrow over the loss of his father; the frightful appearance of the ghost; the prince's rage, ignited by knowledge of the assassination plot; and finally, Hamlet's feigned madness that serves to shield his plan of revenge. Having established this scheme for the theatrical content of the overture, Vogler proceeds to a description of his musical realization, explaining the rational compromise it achieves between dramatic requirements and the musical grammar of a symmetrical, sonata-like design.

His explanation of the tonal plan starts not with the beginning of the piece, but with the second of the four tone-pictures, the appearance of the ghost on the ramparts. As the decisive motivating force of the drama, this masculine image needs the authority of a major key; and since it must convey utterly somber darkness as well, the appropriate choice of tonal center is A-flat, a key that Vogler describes as suitable for evoking darkest night and underworld landscapes, in accordance with his concept of characteristic temperament.[9] This secondary key having been selected, Vogler now works backward to the musical depiction with which the overture begins, a representation of the prince in his state of sorrow. Here the key is C minor, a choice which is justified as follows: to express sadness, the minor quality is appropriate. The keys of F minor and B-flat minor, though related to A-flat major, are deemed inappropriate and thus rejected in favor of a third relative, C minor, whose natural strength derives from the open strings it allows the violins on two important scale degrees, D and G. Proceeding now to the musical connection that leads from his second image (the appearance of the ghost) to the third (Hamlet's anger), Vogler suggests that a causal relationship between the two can be represented by a simultaneous change from *largo* to *allegro* and from the key of A-flat major to its dominant, E-flat major. Finally, just as Hamlet's rage leads to his scheme of revenge, the progression to the last of these four depictions (Hamlet's pretended insanity) involves movement from the established center of E-flat major to its dominant, B-flat major.

The design this strategy yields may be described as an introduction and sonata-form exposition: Hamlet's sorrow and the appearance of the ghost form an extended introductory *largo;* the prince's rage becomes the dramatic basis for an impassioned *allegro* exposition of a symphonic-style primary theme group; and the depiction of feigned madness possesses the characteristics of a contrasting secondary theme.[10] After a vigorous closing passage, motivically related to primary-theme material, the requirements of musical logic demand that these contrasting segments be worked into a balanced overall design. Thus a "second part" is fashioned from the material of the first.[11] Primary and secondary themes are now treated to a brief symphonic development before the theme groups return in their entirety, transposed down a fifth (i.e., to A-flat and E-flat respectively). The approximately symmetrical design then concludes with an abbreviated recurrence of material from the *largo*. Incorporating a return to the key of A-flat major, this final passage lends structural balance, and it furnishes a transition to the opening scene of the play.

By designating the key of C minor as his overriding tonic (even though it fails to assert itself as a significant key center in the *allegro*), Vogler can claim that the whole is harmonically unified because none of the keys used lies further than one accidental away from this tonal starting-point. That the overture ends in A-flat major rather than in tonic is an anomaly that he readily acknowledges, and one that would admittedly be forbidden in an abstract, symphonic piece. But here, the raising of the curtain on the opening scene of the play demands the retrieval of material from the A-flat major section. In effect, the requirements of the larger dramatic context override the relatively local considerations of tonal logic within the overture itself.

In addition to his discussion of the overall design, Vogler provides the kind of phrase-by-phrase analysis that typifies the first volume of *Betrach-tungen*. But here, in addition to elucidating the purely musical logic of the harmony and phrasing, he takes pains to relate the unfolding of his design to the drama it represents: the details of expression within the four sections and the dramatic tensions involved in the movement from one to the next. In the *allegro* exposition, for example, he shows that the tonal struggle involved in the transition from primary key to dominant corresponds to the emotional tensions, vacillations, and inner conflict experienced by the protagonist.

The process begins with a suitably agitated string motive, introduced after a cadence in tonic. According to the musical-dramatic narrative that Vogler proceeds to recount, the dominant of B-flat major is introduced and the arrival in the new key seems imminent. But then the anticipated cadence in B-flat major is averted, a secondary-dominant inflection occurs in place of the expected cadence, and the music veers momentarily toward G minor. This potential tonic is contradicted in turn, so that the tensional span of transition is further prolonged before a cadence in the dominant key is accomplished. When it finally takes place, the firmness of a resolute close corresponds to Hamlet's decision on a plan of action. The stage is thereby set for the secondary theme and its contrasting dramatic message.

In the course of this critique, Vogler calls on the basic principles of his system as they apply to the understanding of dramatic music. Drama—conceived pictorially but also in terms of characterization, narrative, states of mind in flux, transition, and movement—forms an integral part of the musical design. Dramatic elements, such as the four episodes depicted in the *Hamlet* overture, suggest appropriate materials for a musical realization, including matters of key, tempo, texture, theme, and sectionalization. These elements are then molded into a coherent shape in accordance with purely musical considerations: the necessity of unity, the principles of musical rhetoric, and the matters of taste and convention by which musical forms are customarily organized.

As demonstrated by this overture, the coordinated unfolding of a musi-cal and dramatic plan involves a hierarchic order: the overture as a whole, framed by its mood-invoking *largo* sections, functions as a prelude to the play and as a dramatically appropriate preparation for its opening scene. Within its bounds, the four incidents represented yield the main articulations of the design; and within each of the sharply delineated portrayals, the succession of details contributes musical elaboration and dramatic substance.

For the reader of the *Betrachtungen,* the lessons furnished by the *Hamlet* overture pave the way for a more ambitious project found in the second and third volumes: a detailed examination of the author's Mannheim *Singspiel, Der Kaufmann von Smyrna.*[12] Consisting of a substantial one-movement overture, six arias, three duets, a trio, and a closing vaudeville, this is by far the largest work discussed in the serial, and it stands out as a demonstration of the composer's talent for theatrical expression. (According to his explanation, the version in *Betrachtungen,* which is presumed to differ from the 1771 version, includes two arias added after the libretto was printed.) As Vogler's remarks suggest, the lofty sentiments of the text call for relatively elaborate treatment; and the wealth of action, scene painting, and character portrayal encompassed by its numbers readily qualifies the work as an object lesson in dramatic composition.

A librettist's preface, which accompanies the printed text for the version from 1771, explains the circumstance of its creation: the one-act comedy by Chamfort on which it was based had been so warmly received by Mannheim audiences that the only fault of the play, its brevity, demanded rectification. This was to be happily accomplished by having it transformed into a *Singspiel* in which solo arias and ensembles suitably expanded the size of the piece.[13]

The plot of this naive and predictable drama features sharply etched stereotypes against the backdrop of a fashionably exotic, Turkish locale. A ship carrying a pair of European travelers, Amalie and Dornal, has been waylaid by corsairs. The pair have fallen into the hands of the greedy, villainous Kaled, a slavehandler in the port city of Smyrna; and as the play unfolds, Kaled celebrates the prosperity of his trade, while Dornal and Amalie lament their misfortune. The slavehandler's negotiations with his customers threaten to separate the unfortunate couple, but through the efforts of a good-hearted citizen, Hassan, and his wife Zayde, the two are liberated and reunited.

In Vogler's handling of the librettist's verses, the style of Italian comic opera prevails (as opposed to the dryness of the North German style or the rigid formality of the French); but in this instance the conventionally light-weight idiom is enriched with color, dynamism, and seriousness of expression. The gamut of vocal styles extends from a florid, Italianate manner in arias written for the two heroines, to the *buffo*-like patter of the comic dialogue between Kaled and his dissatisfied customer Nebi. Dornal expounds his predicament in a lyrical, romantic vein: Kaled exhibits his coarse personality (not unlike that of Osmin in Mozart's later *Singspiel, Die Ent-*

*führung aus dem Serail*) in a spirited comic aria; and Hassan and his wife engage in bantering domestic strife and reconciliation.

The orchestration is characteristically brilliant and varied in accordance with Mannheim tradition. Memorable features include an obbligato part for flute that adorns the flourishes of Zayde's aria; the pensive, woodwind-ensemble theme that opens the emotionally complex trio of Hassan, Dornal, and Kaled; and the trappings of Janissary music, including cymbals, drums, and triangle, that lend a barbarous accent to both of Kaled's arias. Most of the aria texts involve a pair of stanzas, and where this custom applies, the second stanza is normally set as a contrasting *B* section in a related key. Structural schemes range from straight *da capo* forms to binary and sonata-like designs with altered recapitulations. Virtually all the numbers feature text painting and musical imagery in which resources of harmony, texture, and orchestration bear the burden of characterization, mood, atmosphere, and dramatic action.

In discussing this assortment of arias and ensembles, Vogler makes almost no mention of the overall shape of the work as a musical entity, and no connection is drawn between the overture (which bears no evident thematic relationship to the vocal numbers) and the rest of the play. With the range of keys reaching from four sharps (Dornal's romantic *andante* aria) to three flats (the pathetic duet of Dornal and Amalie), there appears to be no overriding tonal order, and none is mentioned. Instead, attention is directed to individual numbers and the dramatic significance to be discerned in their musical substance.

The descriptive analyses provided are concerned in part with techniques for musical pantomime, characterization, and expressive nuance. In Hassan's opening aria, rhythmically animated figures in the orchestra underline reminiscences of storm and shipwreck, while the argument between a customer, Nebi, and Kaled is represented by a pattern of contrary motion in the violins. The instruction for strings to play on the fingerboard ("alla maniera di Gamba") serves to enhance a romantic aura in Dornal's song, and the entry of a solo oboe in the middle section of Amalie's aria shines through the texture like a ray of sunlight in the midst of thunderclouds. Kaled's first aria ("Ich hasse den Frieden und liebe den Krieg") calls for the imitation of military sonorities, but not for the sound of actual trumpets and timpani, which would sooner lead the hearer to expect the entry of an Alexander the Great than the appearance of the comical slave trader.[14]

In more complex ensembles, the calculated deployment of rhythm, line, and texture accommodates the juxtaposition of different personalities and states of mind. In the trio, Hassan's compassion and his altruistic pleasure in liberating his friend are contrasted to the representation of Dornal's intense, private anxiety over the impending separation from Amalie. Meanwhile, Kaled sings with savage delight over the profits he expects from the anticipated transaction. The various parts are subordinated to the overall design, but the listener can nevertheless perceive their individuality.

As implied in the *Rosamunde* essay and the critique of the *Hamlet* overture, colorful details and isolated nuances of text expression cannot stand on their own. They must be assimilated in an aesthetically unified whole in order to convey their message effectively. Pondering this issue toward the end of his *Kaufmann* discussion, Vogler emphasizes that the sense of the words must be expressed. He perceives the difficulty of portraying something that contradicts the main dramatic thrust: the repose, for example, of which a character in desperate circumstances speaks with longing. But he finds merit in situations where each word is endowed with significance, and "the union of several important words represents a complete picture."[15] Typically, the details of text expression cited in *Der Kaufmann von Smyrna* involve aspects of harmony, often in conjunction with other elements, and the harmonic functions involved can be specified in accordance with the theorist's system and his characteristic applications of its principles. In such instances, the harmonic detail bears some readily discernible relationship to particular words or ideas in the text. Each detail speaks for itself, yet each plays a logically appropriate role as part of a larger musical elaboration.

In Hassan's opening aria, prefaced by a long ritornello designed to form a dramatic introduction not only to the aria but to the work as a whole, the setting of the following lines comprises the first half of a binary form:

> Wie schön, wie hieter ist der Morgen!
> So heiter als mein Herz.
> Ich kenne weder Gram noch Sorgen;
> Mich quält kein innrer Schmerz.
>
> Nach überstandnem Sturm und Wetter,
> Geniess ich ganz der Ruh':
> Das ist dein Werk, grossmütiger Erretter!
> Dir weint mein Aug' dankbare Thränen zu.

The opening of the first stanza sets forth a main theme in F major, a key that Vogler associates with dead calm. The close of the second stanza gives occasion for an extended vocal flourish before a cadence falls to usher in the central ritornello in the dominant. In between, a contrasting image involves the line "Nach überstandnem Sturm und Wetter."[16] The setting of the first stanza has ended with a half cadence, and the move to the dominant now begins with the kind of rhythmic and harmonic unrest that generally accompanies a tonal transition. As crescendo–diminuendo patterns combine with oscillating sixteenth-note figures to animate the texture, the supertonic key (G minor) is temporarily tonicized with the aid of a diminished-seventh chord on F-sharp. Describing the result, a musical equivalent to the words being sung, Vogler observes that "the depiction of a storm was not necessary, since it is only a reminiscence." Nevertheless, he suggests, it lends commendable diversity to the text setting.[17] Occurring as a grammatically appropriate ingredient in a logical sequence of musical events, the image is properly subordinated as a detail within the design.

Vogler describes a more complex interaction of drama and musical structure in the duet of Dornal and Amalie. After the announcement of the opening C-minor theme in a short, agitated ritornello, Dornal sings the following lines:[18]

> So führt das Schiksal uns hieher,
> Um uns vielleicht noch grausamer zu trennen!

In purely musical terms, this portion of the duet requires a transition from tonic to relative major; and from the standpoint of text setting, the crucial words "vielleicht," "grausamer," and "trennen" demand special emphasis. Citing ingredients that contribute to the tonal design as well as text expression, Vogler calls attention to the chord of the lowered second scale degree, which enhances the expressive weight borne by the word "vielleicht" just prior to the half cadence in measure 20 (see Example 2). The syllables of the word "grausamer" are now appropriately emphasized by a succession of two diminished-seventh chords. Finally, as the cadence falls on "trennen," a contrary-motion figure in the first and second violins depicts the word both aurally and graphically, so that its meaning on paper is perceived no less vividly than in sound.[19]

Perhaps most intricate of all the connections between musical grammar and text expression are those seen in the trio of Hassan, Dornal, and Kaled.

Example 2
*Der Kaufmann von Smyrna,* duet
of Dornal and Amalie, measures
13–24.

This study in contrasting characters, images, and emotions (an effort to which the composer points with particular pride) begins with Hassan speaking of the brotherly affection he extends to Dornal as he offers to buy the Europeans' freedom. In the course of this outpouring of sentiment, which spans exposition, modulation from tonic B-flat major to the key of the dominant, and the first part of a modulatory middle section, he sings the following lines:

> Von deinem Vaterland entfernet,
> Kannst du auch hier im Schoss der Freundschaft ruhn:

As explained in the commentary, the harmonic plan to which these lines are joined depicts their meaning in musical terms.[20] First a gruff unison in measures 68–69 punctuates the close of the central ritornello and gives expression to Dornal's forced separation from his homeland by veering away from the established dominant key. An image of wandering is then evoked by a seemingly aimless, meandering transition of several measures (70–78); this passage leads, at precisely the right moment, to a resolute cadence in E-flat major. A tonal goal has been reached, yet it is not the true home territory of B-flat major, but rather a surrogate: the key of the fourth scale degree, which serves as a temporary tonic before Hassan's narrative proceeds to further modulations.

Implicit here is the mutual reinforcement of extramusical content and musical plan, for the symbolic wandering of the harmony has a specific tonal function in addition to its meaning as text illustration: it provides an elaborated transition from F major, the tonal goal of the first section, to the establishment of E-flat major in the second.

Like the analytical detail in his discussion of the *Hamlet* overture, descriptions of expressive devices in *Der Kaufmann von Smyrna* reflect Vogler's boundless enthusiasm for musical drama and scene painting.[21] But as both studies emphasize, the effectiveness of such devices depends on the composer's ability to integrate them into a coherent plan. Sharp contrasts may be juxtaposed, and the degree of available variety is unlimited. But the contrasts must be justified grammatically, and the diversity must be explainable in terms of a comprehensible structure. Expressive details, in other words, must be heard as plausible elaborations in a hierarchic design. By offering ample opportunity for such elaborations, the standard binary, sonata, and *da capo* forms involved in these analyses make ideal subjects for the theorist's lessons.

### THE MELODRAMA *LAMPEDO*

In light of the importance Vogler attaches to the unity of music and drama, it is not surprising that the attention enjoyed in the *Betrachtungen* by *Hamlet* and

*Kaufmann* is not shared in equal manner by his other major theatrical piece from this time—the melodrama *Lampedo* (1779), whose musical and dramatic premises virtually exclude close connection between structure and expression.[22]

According to the concept of melodrama then in vogue, the composer's task was to combine the naturalism and spontaneity of spoken declamation with the affective power of musical gesture, theme, harmonic color, and tone painting.[23] Like recitative, melodrama relied on the text for coherence. The possibilities for musical continuity, however, were even more restricted. Since the normal procedure involved silencing the orchestra altogether while a line was being spoken (or at most having a single tone or chord sustained), its role was reduced to that of providing isolated musical fragments. These could function as commentary on a line just spoken, as premonition of something about to occur, or as a vehicle of transition from one emotional state to another.

*Lampedo* was commissioned by the son of the Landgrave of Hesse-Darmstadt, who was eventually to become Vogler's employer, and the title role was performed by the young patron's wife.[24] The text, a *Sturm und Drang* prose creation by a functionary named Lichtenberg, centers on the Amazon queen and the storm of turbulent emotions by which she is seized after conquering King Argabyses and the Scythians. The first of the four scenes finds her entering on a chariot in a victory procession. She descends, exults over her triumph, and announces the impending sacrifice of the vanquished king on a sacred altar. Now that the Amazons have conquered their foe, she cries, the two domains will no longer be divided. As the scene changes, Argabyses and other prisoners of war are brought forth; and to Lampedo's shock and amazement, the king proclaims his love and his readiness to die for her. Plunged into reflection, she gives vent to the conflicting passions she suffers within her soul. At the crucial moment, her dagger falls from the disobedient hand that will not heed her resolve to proceed with the sacrifice.

In the third scene, Lampedo stands alone on stage, delivering an impassioned monologue that recounts her astonishment, frustration, and inability to comprehend or control her feelings. She searches for the agent of rebellion, addressing first the arm that held the dagger, then the true culprit, her heart. Resolving to turn the dagger on herself, she suddenly finds her attempted self-sacrifice interrupted by a storm. Stunned at first, then spiritually transfigured as the storm abates, she discards her weapon and announces that the prisoners shall be brought before the temple and liberated. The final scene begins with Lampedo declaring to the assembled crowd that she intends to join Argabyses in marriage. The king pledges his devotion to her and takes her hand, and the drama closes in general celebration.

In response to the demands of this heavily charged material, Vogler's setting uses a multitude of brief orchestral utterances inserted between words, phrases, and sentences. Set mainly for four-part string ensemble, these fragments derive their style from the conventions of obbligato recitative: triadic figures, dotted-rhythm punctuations, gestural motives that incorporate soaring and plunging scale lines, and mood-evoking sustained chords. Although alternation of music and text is the general rule, several of Lampedo's and Argabyses' lines at moments of great intensity are enhanced by sustained tones or chords; and in one instance (described below), the musical accompaniment actually develops a thematically significant motive.

The varied colors of brass and woodwinds come into play to reinforce the strings in extended orchestral spans. In the first scene, richly scored passages of undulating water figures (in C major, Vogler's water key) depict the broad, rolling expanse of the River Thermodon, whose banks will now embrace a united realm. More spectacular is the D-minor representation of a storm in the third scene. Here a dominant pedal point, sustained for no fewer than fifty-two measures, combines with tremolos, long crescendos, screeching piccolos, and soaring scalar lines to portray an overwhelming tempest. According to a contemporary account, the sound of the full orchestra (which included four horns in addition to pairs of piccolos, flutes, oboes, bassoons, trumpets, and timpani) was enhanced by a pair of wooden organ pipes, activated by bellows, whose rumble successfully imitated the sound of thunder.[25] The description of this passage in *Betrachtungen* (see note 22) emphasizes the carefully graduated participation of orchestral groups in depicting the storm's waxing and subsiding (the pair of organ pipes, in octaves on A, is mentioned, but the depiction of thunder is associated only with the timpani). The full ensemble is likewise engaged for two large-scale pieces that enclose the drama: a programmatic "Ouverture guerrière," which pits the orchestra against a separate wind band in symbolic combat, and a festive chaconne in rondo form attached to the end of the final scene.

Within the frame provided by overture and closing dance, the orchestral fragments serve to enhance the impact of the spoken lines, but they also manage to contribute structural unity and continuity, despite the continual interruptions endemic to the genre. In the opening scene a reiterated motive defines a tonic key, D minor, and helps to hold the musical and dramatic fabric together. Subjected to development as it punctuates the lines of Lampedo's triumphant monologue, it lends a sense of continuity to the process of movement away from the initial tonal center (see Example 3).[26] The later recurrence of this motive, where it effects a return to D minor in the manner of a recapitulation, leads to the sacrificial march with which the scene closes. By thus drawing on thematic repetition, development, and recurrence to establish a key and articulate a tonal design of departure and return, the scene acquires a musical cohesion more closely related to aria structure than recitative. The dramatic unity is reinforced, and the depiction of Lampedo's vacillating thoughts is set in relief.

Example 3
*Lampedo,* excerpt from beginning of
the opening scene.

The emphasis on tonal order and thematic unity is even more pronounced in the final scene, where Lampedo's declaration and Argabyses' reply form what may be described as a pair of self-contained musical forms. The scene begins with a ritornello in G major which returns after Lampedo's opening lines. Developed fragments of this material are then interspersed between subsequent phrases of text, before a recitative-like punctuation provides a decisive full stop.

The tonic now changes to the contrasting key of B-flat major and a new theme is announced. It introduces the king and proceeds to function as a ritornello in a manner comparable to that of Lampedo's theme. After the orchestral announcement concludes, thematic recurrence, development, and fragmentation punctuate Argabyses' utterances as the interrupted continuity of the music follows a path from tonic to dominant and back.

Other sources of coherence lend unity to longer spans. Especially striking is the dramatically motivated recurrence in scene 3 of motives first
presented in scenes 1 and 2. Musical ideas include Lampedo's motive of
triumph, heard at the outset, and the Amazons' victory march and vengeance
theme from the opening of scene 2. The device of recapitulation is also
applied to an *affettuoso* theme in E-flat major—melodically the most felicitous
idea in the work and dramatically the most important (see Example 4). The
second scene had begun with a ferociously brilliant *allegro* theme in A major
(a key Vogler describes as penetrating, bright, and luminous). As the prevailing mood changes, the key center changes correspondingly, softening first to
D major, then G minor, and finally to E-flat major (Vogler's key for night and
tenderness) as Argabyses and Lampedo gaze upon each other and the amo-
rously lyrical melody is announced. This theme, which furnishes a unifying
melodic thread, takes on the quality of a *Leitmotiv* when it returns in scene 3.
Identified with the unspoken emotion that arises and eventually unites the
antagonists, it becomes a musical symbol for the irresistible sentiments that

Example 4
*Lampedo*, excerpt from scene 2.

prevent the Amazon queen from obeying her own will and eventually cause her to embrace her former enemy.

As seen in the passages from *Lampedo* described above, Vogler's attempt to bestow musical order on the setting of this text leads to ingenious but also somewhat strained solutions. The critiques in *Betrachtungen* (where *Lampedo* and the melodrama fashion are largely ignored) showed that dramatic expression in a composition is inseparable from its structural logic. Aesthetic unity is deemed essential, and it involves some readily discernible relationship between the detail and the design as a whole. In the absence of such an order, confusion results and the rational premises of the system cannot apply.

By its very nature, a melodrama like *Lampedo* would seem ill-suited to Vogler's way of thinking as a theorist and composer. The virtue of such a form lies in the freedom it offers the resourceful musician to imitate nature and express passionate emotions. But its continuous alternation between speech and musical fragment leads to an unrelieved emphasis on detail: the expression of outbursts, moments of passion or reflection, pantomimic gestures, and fluctuating states of mind. In keeping with his theoretical and aesthetic ideals, Vogler has attempted to apply a logic of musical continuity to the fragmentary monologues, dialogues, and stage action of which the four scenes of the melodrama are composed. Elements of a larger musical order have been forcibly imposed, yielding a curious blend of *Sturm und Drang* theatrics and rational design.

Like Mozart, whose own melodrama experiments in *Thamos, König in Ägypten,* and *Zaide* date from about the same time as *Lampedo,* Vogler turned away from the medium after this early attempt, though he may have returned to it at a later time.[27] Whether or not he was disenchanted with the form, his response to its special challenges sheds light on his approach to the interaction of music and drama in later operatic works. In *Betrachtungen,* analyses of dramatic expression, whether in an aria, an ensemble, or a programmatic overture, have to do with musical traditions that assume the normal stability of thematically unified forms. These forms were simply part of a language whose natural authority the theorist's precepts were supposed to confirm and explain. Under the conditions imposed by *Lampedo,* the customary resources are excluded. But as Vogler demonstrates in this work, principles on which the standard forms are based—involving hierarchic structure, tonal center, and thematic unity—may nevertheless be applied, so that to some extent their potential organizing force may be realized in the unconventional medium.

By adhering to his principles, in other words, the theorist finds the guidance he needs to achieve dramatic expression in a medium foreign to the Italian tradition in which his style and outlook seemed so firmly planted. The result is a work that cannot be fully justified by the composer's criteria for musical and dramatic coherence as set forth in his early writings. Yet these are evidently the criteria that Vogler has applied in the attempt to create a unity of music and text in accordance with his teachings. The three large-scale operas that followed—*Castore e Polluce, Gustav Adolf,* and *Samori*—all posed similar problems involving some major departure from the older traditions of text setting. In each instance, it appears that Vogler's principles served him both as a liberating force, allowing him to abandon old conventions, and as a constraint whose application promoted musical coherence and aesthetic unity.

### MAJOR OPERATIC WORKS

The first of these later works, *Castore e Polluce,* originated with Vogler's stay in Munich as first kapellmeister (1784–86).[28] Like that of Mozart's *Idomeneo,* prepared several years previously for the same theater, the text of Vogler's opera (a shortened version of a libretto by C. I. Frugoni called *I Tintaridi*), was based on a French source from earlier in the century: Bernard Gentil's text for Rameau's opera *Castor et Pollux.*[29] In keeping with prevailing fashions at the Munich court, it represented a mixture of *opera seria* tradition, French spectacle, and Gluckian drama.

As described in the preface to the Italian libretto, much of the dialogue in the original play was condensed, and further changes were made to enable the singers to display their talents.[30] The prologue was excised, and a newly written Act 1, which begins with Phoebe's announcement of her scheme to win the hand of Pollux, harks back to events preceding the death of Castor. The start of the action in the French text—the scene of mourning at Castor's tomb—does not occur until the beginning of Act 2 in the adaptation. All five acts of the original, in other words, are compressed into the last two acts of this Italianized version.

Despite the abridgment and alteration, outstanding features of the original remain intact. Choruses of Spartan warriors, underworld Furies, and blessed spirits retain their prominent roles, providing a backdrop for the dialogues, conflicts, and expressions of passion that engage the principals. In each act, locale and action feature lavish scenes of dancing and choral singing: the demons invoked by Phoebe, the depiction of combat in Act 1; the second-act chorus of mourners, the subsequent spectacle of Spartan warriors and athletes, and the celestial Pleasures that tempt Pollux; and the evocations of the underworld in Act 3.

The text begs for vivid, grandiose effects, and Vogler responds with enthusiasm to its cues for action and scene depiction. The Act 1 battle features an animated contest of two male choruses (analogous to the divided-ensemble effects in the overture to *Lampedo*) against a background of military fanfares for full orchestra with trumpets and drums. In the second act, the spectacle of Mercury's shimmering, C-major descent contrasts with the celestial chorus and the dance of the Pleasures in E major. And the under-world scene in Act 3 incorporates a panoramic, F-minor tableau of monumental scope and proportions.

Embedded within the elaborately constructed scenes are the arias and occasional ensembles assigned to the principal and secondary characters in the drama. By and large, their texts belong to a traditional *opera seria* aesthetic, the characters giving relatively static expression to the sentiments with which they are associated: the brotherly affection and willing self-sacrifice of Castor and Pollux, Telaira's anxious yearning, and Phoebe's wrath. Accordingly, Vogler's settings of these verses conform to the dignity and formality he identifies with serious opera in his early criticism.

The formal, ritualistic aspect of the work can be seen in the juxtaposition of two contrasting arias that occupy the center of the third act. The spectacular struggle with the Furies has taken place, Phoebe's attempts to bar Pollux from the underworld have failed, and before departing in a rage, she delivers a turbulent, dark-hued F-minor aria. Then suddenly the sulphurous atmosphere dissipates, and in Gluckian fashion a group of blessed spirits presents a dance in F major.[31] Against this backdrop Castor delivers his complaint, which features the contrast between outer calm (the F major of the *A* section in his *da capo* aria) and inner unrest, depicted by a relatively agitated D minor in the *B* section.

The solo numbers, some self-contained, others attached to longer musical spans that incorporate chorus or ensemble, range in size from modest binary forms and cavatinas to extended, multi-section bravura arias. In addition to the mannered intensity of Phoebe's rage aria and the classical repose of Castor's meditation, the diversity of forms and styles includes a sprawling, lyrical rondo (Pollux's "Sì, rivedrai serena"), placed within the second act, and a large-scale, virtuosic scene and aria (Telaira's "Come parte animosa!"/"Non è la mia speranza") in the latter part of Act 1. This last-mentioned piece, a strategically designed highpoint of vocal and instrumental brilliance, takes place after the singer's voice has been prepared by relatively modest participation in a foregoing ensemble. Once she is left alone on stage, an extended section of arioso and recitative leads to an *allegro moderato* aria, complete with oboe obbligato, whose concerto-like proportions and phenomenal *passaggi* call to mind those of Constanze's "Martern aller Arten" from the second act of Mozart's *Die Entführung aus dem Serail*.

The ensembles, which include extended duets and trios, generally concern reflection and commentary rather than action or strife, and their formal designs tend to be logical and predictable. A first-act trio of Pollux, Castor, and Telaira begins with a stanza sung by Pollux, whose line moves from tonic (E-flat) to the dominant before dissolving into a string of *passaggi* that culminate with a decisive cadence in B-flat. Telaira and Castor respond. In the manner of a middle section, the music then veers toward the relative minor and its dominant, while Pollux alternates with the others. Finally, after the tonic has been reinstated, all three voices are united in an emphatic recapitulation and coda.

Providing musical and dramatic connection between arias, ensembles, and dances are the obbligato recitatives that carry dialogues adapted from the original French text, including the intense exchanges between Phoebe and Telaira, the dialogue of Jupiter and Pollux, and the crucial encounters of Pollux and Castor. Though most of these exchanges are delivered in rapid-fire, secco-like declamation with simple chordal support by the strings, depictions of action and emotional tension are occasionally heightened by rich orchestration, motivic gestures in the accompaniment, and in several instances by a kind of arioso that features thematic recurrence and development.

Evidently encouraged by the substance of his libretto to explore contrasts and fill his scenes with a variety of forms, colors, and textures, Vogler may also have felt compelled by his principles to weld the various parts of the drama together in an overriding, theoretically coherent design. His essay on the music of *Rosamunde* had taken Schweitzer to task for setting forth without a plan. Would he permit his own, comparably ambitious opera to be faulted on similar grounds? An overview of the work offers at least some evidence that a central tonality has been imposed and that this apparent element of large-scale order represents the highest level of a hierarchy by which the acts, individual scenes, and smaller details are controlled.

The stage is set for such a plan by a three-movement overture in D major, which borrows musical material from important scenes in the drama: the battle of the Spartans against the rival forces of Linceus, the D-minor funeral march that opens Act 2, and the apotheosis of Castor and Pollux. The prominence of D minor, in the close of the first movement as well as in the second-movement funeral march, foreshadows the incorporation of keys on the flat side (most notably the relative major, F) in addition to a primary orbit of keys built on the scale degrees of D major. Harmonic points of reference for the drama as a whole are thereby established: a principal tonic of D major and a secondary area featuring F major and its relatives.

Oriented toward one or the other of these poles, key centers and modulatory routes are chosen in ways that suggest at least some degree of coordination between tonal logic and dramatic circumstances. In the second act, a long-range progression may be traced in which the funereal D minor of the opening is followed by a gradually increasing emphasis on brighter keys—a plan that eventually leads to A major for Jupiter's aria at the end of his dialogue with Pollux, and to the ethereal realm of E major for the dance of the Pleasures. The underworld scenes of Act 3, by contrast, call for the gloom of F minor (whose relationship to the secondary tonic F major recalls the contrast between the primary tonic D major and the D minor of the funeral procession). Suggesting a progression from darkness to light, the flat keys (including F minor, A-flat major, B-flat major, and the prominent F major) are supplanted by the restored tonic D and its dominant in the closing numbers of the act.[32]

The sense of a large-scale tonal order, tenuous in Acts 2 and 3, is more clearly articulated in the first act. Here, after excursions to the flat side for the principal arias and ensembles (and also a brief return to D major that accompanies a call to arms), the opposing choruses of warriors take up the first-movement material of the overture in the manner of a recapitulation. Then, following the slaying of Castor and a frenzied call for vengeance in a restored D major, the act comes to a close with a prolonged half cadence which underscores the unresolved tension of the drama. The D-minor scene with which the second act begins thus functions as a delayed harmonic resolution. A link between the two acts, both tonal and dramatic, is thereby accomplished.

With regard to harmonic organization in individual numbers, Vogler is generally obliged by the static quality of his texts to apply tonal resources sparingly. Diminished seventh chords, augmented sixths, change of mode, and far-reaching tonal excursions are well-established ingredients of his vocabulary. But as he has observed, their use depends on the requirements of the text. In the *adagio* aria "Ombra cara" that Telaira sings after the opening scene of Act 2, the uniformity of sentiment calls initially for nothing more than a simply executed modulation to the dominant. Then, in the stately fashion appropriate to her words, the second section presents a change from major mode to minor, and the repeat of the first stanza of the text unfolds as a straightforward recapitulation.

Though most of the arias are comparably static, subordinate elements of greater complexity are occasionally involved. In Castor's first-act aria, "Parto . . . In quest' occhi," the word "morte" is dramatically enhanced by an augmented sixth chord which functions musically as a part of an extended process of modulation from tonic (F minor) toward the relative major (see Example 5a).[33] In the recapitulation of this verse, the rhetoric of Castor's lines is intensified as the mandatory tonal adjustment takes place (Example 5b). Here the reaffirmation of tonic is temporarily averted by an inflection on the word "bene," where the Neapolitan sixth is temporarily tonicized in a manner similar to that described by Vogler in his analysis of Prelude No. 8 from the *Zwei und dreisig Präludien* (see Chapter 2, pp. 73–74). The cadential augmented-sixth device now returns on the word "morte," this time leading from the tonicized G-flat major to the conclusive reestablishment of tonic. A subordinate element, the setting of the word "morte," is made to stand out with vivid color and dramatic significance, and at the same time the tonal unity is enhanced.

In other instances, especially those involving the alternation of soloists and chorus, self-contained structural units are enveloped within a tonally unified, composite design. In the chorus of shades from Act 3 ("Vivi felice"), the first section forms a miniature three-part design with modulation to the dominant and return (F–C–F). Then, in the manner of a middle section before a return to the material of this F-major chorus, a lone spirit steps out from the group to sing an affectingly simple melody:

Example 5
*Castore e Polluce,* Act 1, "Parto . . .
In quest' occhi," (a) measures 31–34;
(b) measures 59–68.

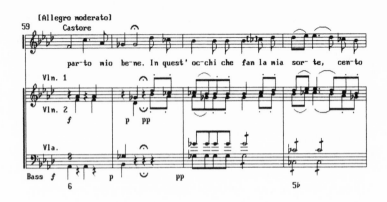

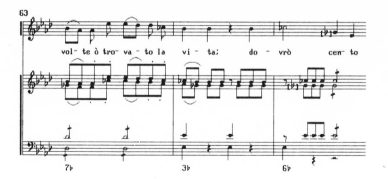

Veni o dolce obblio,
Fa che scordi le sue pene,
Vieni o nume lusinghier.
Sola lascia amabil dio,
Nel suo cor la nostra pace,
Bella madre del piacer.

The pathos of this text demands that a rhetorical norm be reversed: instead of a modulation to the dominant and the appearance of a theme whose animation reflects the tonal move, this song—whose tonic is the subdominant of the enveloping F—moves gracefully to its own subdominant (E-flat) where the singer's lines are presented in a serene yet wide-ranging melody suggestive of Mozart (see Example 6).

In contrast to the generally static quality of the arias, the relatively fast pace of the intervening dialogues (delivered in recitative or arioso) calls for

Example 6
*Castore e Polluce,* Act 3, excerpt
from "Veni o dolce obblio," measures
21–36.

harmonic color and diversity to enhance the action represented by the text. On occasion these passages are treated not merely as connective tissue between arias, or as interpolations between the ritornello and the commencement of an aria, but as virtually self-contained musical forms in a manner not unlike that of the monologues in *Lampedo.* In these spans of dialogue, the tonal grammar and thematic continuity of aria style have been implemented. Most outstanding in this respect is the setting of the Act 2 exchange between Jupiter and Pollux, an emotionally charged encounter whose pathetic content demands more musical substance than that of conventional recitative. A brief F-major ritornello for full orchestra lends weight to the scene from the start, and the principal musical idea—an authoritative wind motive in half and whole notes, accompanied by a contrasting sixteenth-note figure in the first violin—provides a tonal and thematic focus for the dialogue.

As Jupiter's address begins, with the development of his motive in the background, he explains to Pollux that the law of the underworld is strict and his plan to release Castor from Hades is futile. Pollux replies in protest, his anxiety mirrored by a faster tempo, rhythmically agitated accompaniment, and tonal instability. A modulatory fabric persists as Jupiter pleads and threatens to the accompaniment of his motive (see Example 7). The eventual reestablishment of the tonic F major coincides with a return to the affirmative character of Jupiter's opening lines. A tonal hierarchy and a sense of thematic continuity have been exerted on this main portion of the dialogue. As the music responds to expressive inflections in the text, this underlying order helps to highlight dramatic tensions and fluctuations of sentiment. In contrast to those passages of declamation enclosed within a thematically unified scene and aria, the recitative stands alone. While communicating essential dramatic action, the musical setting establishes its own tonal point of reference against which harmonic movement and thematic development take place.

In a scene such as the second-act encounter between Jupiter and Pollux, Vogler appears to be applying the lessons of his own writings while at the same time reaching beyond the conventional musical forms assumed by those lessons. The resources of French-inspired tableaux and Gluckian continuity are readily embraced in *Castore e Polluce* as means by which the Italian *opera seria* conventions may be modified; and though the composer pays little attention to French lyric tragedy or Gluckian reform in his early criticism, their influence in this work can be understood as something not inconsistent with his own musical doctrine.

Ingredients such as the choral tableaux and extended arioso passages conform to Vogler's demands for a dramatically "authentic" union of music and text, for the vivid representation of scene and atmosphere, and for shrewd economy in the use of orchestral resources. But even more important, they contribute to a palpable aesthetic unity in which the musical

Example 7
*Castore e Polluce,* Act 2, excerpt from
"Dolce o figlio," measures
40–44.

designs are molded to the composer's will and the demands of his harmonic system. The overture assumes significance as a programmatic introduction to the drama, the conventional aria forms are integrated within musically continuous scenes that involve dialogue and choral participation, and passages of orchestrally accompanied recitative are endowed with the structural cohesion necessary to insure an appropriate balance of musical logic and text expression. All these elements are then knit together, however loosely, as parts of a hierarchic order governed on its highest levels by a principle of tonal unity.

As Vogler has suggested in his writings and demonstrated in *Castore e Polluce,* the laws of harmony and musical order run deeper than the perishable fashions they serve. Stylistic norms of the day constitute given material with which the composer must work. Yet they are by no means immutable. They may be applied freely and mixed in original ways, all in the interest of an ideal synthesis of musical organization and dramatic expression. That the nature of such a synthesis may change in accordance with altered circumstances and requirements is amply demonstrated in Vogler's next major theatrical achievement, the Swedish opera *Gustav Adolf och Ebba Brahe.*

Among the most ambitious and original of Vogler's major works and certainly one of the most successful, *Gustav Adolf* was written in conformity with current tastes and attitudes of the Swedish court and the monarch Gustave III,[34] whose appetite for French culture had been whetted by visits to Versailles. Under his sponsorship, the traditions of French drama and the works of Lully, Rameau, and Gluck helped set the tone for the late eighteenth-century phenomenon of Gustavian opera. Traits of this idiom, as represented in works by Uttini, Naumann, and Joseph Martin Kraus, included historical and nationalistic plots, a fast dramatic pace with much emphasis on syllabic declamation, a corresponding suppression of large aria forms and virtuosic display, and the extensive use of choral singing and dance.

Vogler's sole contribution to the genre, *Gustav Adolf* features a libretto modeled on a historical drama written by the king himself. The play is an episodic piece whose interlocking strands of plot concern the events of a single day early in the reign of the young Gustav Adolf (1594–1632). As the drama opens, Gustav is betrothed to the noblewoman Ebba Brahe against the wishes of Gustav's widowed mother, Queen Christina. The queen, determined to thwart the young couple's marriage plans, intercepts communications from her son, who is expected to return shortly from military campaigns against Denmark and Poland. Shrewdly manipulating Ebba's sensibilities, the queen leads her to believe she has been betrayed and abandoned. Meanwhile, the military hero Delagardie, unaware of Ebba's love for Gustav and the king's intention to marry her, assumes that in reward for his valor he can win Ebba's hand himself. Ebba, convinced that she has been forsaken, declares herself ready for marriage to Delagardie.

Whereas the drama thus far takes place within the rooms of the coastal palace at Kalmar, with the island of Öland in the distance, the people of the island come to the fore in the second act as the mainland and palace recede into the background. The king (remaining incognito until near the end of the act) makes his first appearance among the common folk whose various occupations as nurse, messenger, or soldier have brought them into contact with the palace and its residents. For the final act, the scene of action returns within the palace to the inevitable confrontation of Ebba, Gustav, and Delagardie. The lovers are stunned and profoundly affected, but they choose to resign themselves to the dictates of fate and circumstance. Ebba pledges devotion to Delagardie, and Gustav, placing patriotic duty above personal sentiment, decides to retain the throne and dedicate himself to leading his people.

In the versified libretto, prepared by Johan Henrik Kellgren, the action is concentrated in scenes of dialogue that afford little room for large-scale arias. The drama hinges on emotionally intense encounters, and the text, demanding both continuity and rapid pace, requires that ongoing plot development take precedence over relatively static expressions of passion such as those in *Castore e Polluce*.

In his setting of this text, Vogler chooses an arioso-like obbligato recitative as the favored vehicle for conveying dialogue (in this respect the resemblance to Gluck is far more pronounced than in *Castore e Polluce*), and the arias and ensembles are kept relatively short. Text repetition is minimized, and large-scale sonata and *da capo* aria forms give way to simpler binary and ternary forms, rondos, and cavatinas. Ritornellos are avoided except where they serve a mood-defining purpose at the beginning of a scene or act; elsewhere the rapid pace of the action forbids their intrusion. As required by the text, choral participation plays a prominent part in composite scenes involving a flexible mixture of recitative, aria, and arioso styles.

The melodic idiom of these scenes reveals the composer's mature talent for writing clear, unadorned vocal lines, and the symmetrically designed phrases and rhythmic patterns faithfully reflect the cadence of the Swedish verse. Unity of music and text is especially apparent in the second act, where the Öland residents' passages of conversation and narrative require an ingenuous simplicity of expression, and where at least one authentic Swedish folksong is incorporated.[35] The orchestration, far less flamboyant than that of *Castore* and generally characterized by simpler textures than those of *Der Kaufmann von Smyrna,* places the main burden on a four-part string ensemble that usually accompanies the voices. Winds are used sparingly, though in several instances they are assigned important obbligato parts. Since the drama centers on relatively intimate, personal encounters rather than on scenic spectacle, the weight and brilliance of a full orchestra is only rarely summoned.

The tonal richness of *Gustav Adolf* stands in marked contrast to the austerity of its orchestration. The range of harmonic diversity, wider than that witnessed in *Castore e Polluce,* may be ascribed in part to certain tendencies found generally in Vogler's style and outlook—notably an eager assimilation of chromatic resources found in newer works by Mozart and other contemporaries, and a feeling that increased harmonic complexity was a natural manifestation of progress. But the greater harmonic richness of this later opera may also have to do with the special requirements of its text, whose complex interactions and nuances seem to demand corresponding complexities in the musical realization.

With the exception of incidental excursions to more remote territory, key centers fall within a limited spectrum to the sharp and flat side of C major, the key of the overture. The key of B-flat major, suggesting solitude according to Vogler's theory, is used repeatedly for soliloquies and expressions of lonely sentiment; and the tender key of E-flat major is assigned to Gustav in his third-act farewell. Whereas major keys beyond three flats are largely avoided, the gloom of F minor comes into play several times, most prominently in Ebba's despairing monologue at the beginning of Act 3. On the sharp side, the lively key of G major makes appearances mainly in connection with choruses of celebration. Occasional reference is made to the military brilliance of D major, and the further reaches of A major and E major (associated, like G major, with choral singing) are drawn upon as well, E major more sparingly than the other sharp keys.

In a manner evident to some extent in *Castore* and other earlier works,

Vogler extends his territory of harmonic relationships through modal alteration. The effect of juxtaposing major and minor is prominent in the overture, and it develops thereafter as a characteristic device: instances include the duet of Ebba and her confidante, Märta, with its opposition of an E-major tonic and a contrasting E minor; and Ebba's Act I monologue, in which a central passage in G major is framed by G minor in the opening and closing sections.

Such attempts to bring about a match between key and dramatic circumstance resemble those witnessed in *Castore e Polluce;* but the achievement of a larger, overriding unity is a more complicated matter. The fabric of the work, characterized by miniature song forms, choral fragments, and snippets of dialogue—each with its own key, theme, and texture—leads to a dissipated tonal focus. The sense of a higher-level tonic (governing the entire work, a whole act, or a succession of episodes) is tenuous at best, for the relatively fast pace of the drama and the sheer quantity of text to be set forbid the establishment of the broad, stable areas essential to such a large-scale tonal hierarchy.

Yet some evidence of a larger coherence is nonetheless discernible, notably in portions of the drama where recitative fragments are incorporated within the course of an otherwise continuous, aria-like design. Used with greater frequency and more flexibility in *Gustav Adolf* than in the earlier *Castore e Polluce,* the device similarly gathers a diversity of action within a musically unified scheme. In the latter work, however, there are numerous scenes whose texts oblige the composer to do without the predictable symmetries of a closed aria form altogether.

The challenge is met in various ways. In the first part of the opening scene of Act I, Christina's dialogue with her ladies-in-waiting conforms to the general outlines of a rondo. She sings her opening lines after an introductory ritornello in C minor. Motivic development and excursion to closely related keys (E-flat major and G minor) enhance the expression of her feelings. Then a reaffirming chorus enters, in tonic, with a reference to the theme of the queen's opening lines. A pattern of departure from tonic and return continues to evolve as she elaborates her treacherous plan. The chorus returns as tonic is reinstated. Christina's part then undertakes a further musical and expressive excursion—this time involving a modulatory recitative—before the chorus again reenters with a return to the opening theme and reaffirmation of tonic.

Elsewhere, the dramatic impulse prohibits even such a loosely unified

Example 8
*Gustav Adolf,* Act 2, no. 40,
measures 152–64.

framework. In the latter part of the second act, the music must articulate a series of events involving an interrupted conversation, an unexpected moment of peril, and a transformation of the relationships between characters on stage. The scene in question (no. 40) begins with the establishment of a tonic key (F major), which provides the foundation for an extended, musically continuous dialogue between the king (who has not yet revealed his identity) and the fisherman Johan. Johan asks the king for word of his son, and Gustav replies that the young soldier is a hero: he has actually saved the king's life.

A new development calls for a shift to tonic minor: a chorus of islanders enters, and their rapid exchange reveals that a boat has capsized offshore. The life of the bridegroom Erik is in danger, and Gustav now goes off to rescue him. The key changes to B-flat, with alternation of minor and parallel major; and as the scene reaches a point of crisis (see Example 8),[36] the progression from VI to IV in B-flat minor leads to the tensional harmony of the aug-mented-sixth chord (Gb–Bb–E). Gustav, returning to shore, announces that Erik has been saved. The music now slides chromatically into D major, which supplants the key of F major, and a chorus of celebration ensues in the newly established tonic.

A dramatically more complex transformation takes place in the third act, whose action centers on the climactic encounter of the three principals. The king, learning that he must relinquish his bride, expresses his sorrow in a brooding E-flat major cavatina. Then a bright, *allegro* ritornello in G major ushers in a distracting chain of events: a group of townsfolk from Öland arrives, intending to celebrate the king's marriage to Ebba, and Gustav is overcome by despair. The key changes to G minor as he explains the actual state of affairs. After the restoration of tonic major and the well-wishers' departure, he reflects upon his situation. A searching, modulatory recitative leads through the relatively dark regions of C minor and its flat relatives, gradually moving toward the brightened, more neutral atmosphere of C major. Here, underlining the tonal transformation and the king's change of heart, a lyrical, Mozartian melody (first heard in the overture) is woven into the fabric of the monologue (see Example 9).[37] As in the depiction of calamity and rescue in the second act, change of tonal center plays an essential role in portraying a dramatic transformation suggested by the text.

In the course of episodes such as these, the musical portrayal of dramatic crises, rapid exchanges, and fluctuating emotions involves a spontaneity quite foreign to the more formal, less flexible style of *Castore e Polluce*. Yet it is clear that the Gustavian idiom imposes constraints of its own. By dictating a fast dramatic pace, and by requiring continuity within its composite scenes, the text demands musical fragmentation and often prohibits structural clo-sure and symmetry. It is clearly assumed by Vogler—in the setting of *Gustav Adolf* no less than in the critiques of dramatic music in *Betrachtungen*—that

Example 9
*Gustav Adolf,* Act 3, no. 57,
measures 56–67.

closed, rationally conceived forms are necessary for the communication of
dramatic content. Such forms are imposed as a matter of course on the scenes
of his Swedish opera, but their proportions are small and the potential for
cumulative intensity is limited. The composer is instead generally restricted
to a language whose miniature designs, abrupt transitions, and thematically
neutral declamation stand in contrast to the broad–limbed, musically elaborate arias and ensembles found in his earlier operatic works.

In Vogler's next major stage work, *Samori,* the text called for a compromise between the dramatic continuity of the Swedish opera and the older
traditions of *opera seria* and *buffa* to which he was still at least partially
committed. Prepared for Schikaneder's Theater an der Wien contemporaneously with Beethoven's *Fidelio, Samori* follows the *Singspiel* custom in
which musical numbers are interspersed with spoken dialogue. The work is

thus comparable in format to the early *Kaufmann von Smyrna,* although the material employed in its self-contained arias, duets, and larger ensembles is far more complex.

Vogler's ideas on progress in theater music under the influence of Gluck and Mozart—enunciated in his 1808 *Deutsche Kirchenmusik* essay—are foreshadowed in this modern synthesis of operatic resources. The eclectic quality of the musical style mirrors that of the libretto. The text, supplied by Franz Xaver Huber, features an Eastern locale and references to Hindu mysticism that recall the exotic qualities of Mozart's *Zauberflöte* and its progeny. The ethos of Metastasian *opera seria,* suggested by the noble-tyrant figure of Tamburan, mingles with the buffoonery of German comedy and with such Gluckian apparatus as a chorus of spirits that engages in dialogue with the hero. These diverse elements are absorbed in a fashionably modern plot involving a good measure of political intrigue and suspense. As the drama begins, the young Indian prince, Pando (or Samori) is returning from exile with his sister, Naga, and a retinue of supporters. He intends to claim the throne, to which he is the rightful heir, but which has passed to Tamburan, the son of an evil usurper responsible for the assassination of Pando's father. Three sources of dramatic tension arise, to be played out in tandem: the political conspiracy of Pando and his supporters, the competition between Pando and Tamburan for the hand of the beautiful Maha, and the love that develops between Tamburan and Naga.

The complexity of the story offers a wealth of opportunities for depicting sentiment and dramatic tension. Of the eighteen musical numbers in Vogler's setting, no fewer than eight are ensembles (including two extended, composite finales) of animated exchange among three or more characters. Next in importance and emphasis are the solo arias (two with choral participation) for the main characters. Of less consequence are the comic aria of the servant Baradra, and three duets (a conspiratorial dialogue in the first act and two love duets in the second).

Within the variously shaped structures of these numbers, Vogler has occasion to indulge in a richer palette of harmony, melodic style, and orchestral color than in any of his previous stage works. The devices employed include what may be described as an early instance of *Sprechstimme:* as Vogler recounted in an 1810 paper that criticized a device for the simulation of the human voice, he applied a certain contemporary's notion of a "declamatory scale" that involved gradations of speech inflection. "In my opera *Samori,*"

Vogler writes, " . . . there occurs a trio [sung by] three men, in which the jovial courtier interjects the spoken words 'ich auch' several times. They are not notated and cannot by any means be rendered as specific pitches, yet the 'ich auch' must to some extent represent an ascending fourth in the declamatory scale."[38] The ensemble in question ("Ein Mann bin ich und ist mein Freund") features the courtier's "ich auch" (or "mir auch") as a cadential, rising-fourth punctuation at the end of each line sung by the others:

> Pando and Mahadowa: "Ein Mann bin ich und ist mein Freund."
> Baradra: "Ich auch."
> etc.

The *Sprechstimme* effect takes place when Pando and Mahadowa depart, leaving Baradra to sing through the text by himself, the repetitive affirmations now being rendered in this special kind of quasi-intoned speech.

In this later work, the varied harmonic language of *Gustav Adolf* is not only retained but explored with renewed enthusiasm. Change of mode is an important feature of the musical dramatist's strategy, and he takes full advantage of the widened spectrum of key relationships to which the device gives rise. Chromatic inflections highlight moments of crisis, and juxtapositions of remote key centers enhance the depiction of tension and conflict.

The orchestration is essentially economical, yet considerably more diverse than that of either *Castore* or *Gustav Adolf*. Wind instruments (in solo and ensemble) are used with greater frequency and prominence than in the earlier operas, and the now old-fashioned, concerto-like obbligato parts that distinguished *Castore* are supplanted by lyrical instrumental timbres—notably those of solo cello, clarinet, and bassoon—of a distinctly modern, romantic quality.

As in the earlier Munich work, the sound of a full orchestra amplifies the depiction of scenes, moods, and atmosphere, but the relatively massive and uniform sonorities of that work have been replaced by a variegated, quasi-symphonic texture resembling that of the revised *Deutsche Kirchenmusik*. Notable examples of this orchestral style include a Beethovenian fugato that crowns the third movement of the overture; the motivic dialogues among string, woodwind, and brass instruments that accompany Tamburan's first-act aria; and the coloristic effects of storm scene and battle suggested by the text.

In a manner virtually unavailable in *Gustav Adolf,* where the dramatic momentum had to be maintained at all costs, the *Singspiel* idiom of *Samori* enabled Vogler to expand his musical numbers with great amplitude. Resources such as ritornello, text repetition, and thematic development are used to extend transitions, delineate areas of contrast, or emphasize points of dramatic climax.

As in the earlier operas, connections may be drawn between the expressive content of the musical numbers and the composer's choice of key. Most prominently emphasized are D major (with which the opera begins and ends) and the relatively remote, contrasting key of B-flat major. The former is associated with both Pando and Tamburan and is used to depict military action as well as noble sentiments; while the latter, along with its sinister relatives B-flat minor and F minor, often appears in connection with expressions of anguish, foreboding, and revenge. (The sense of such a dichotomy of sentiment is suggested by the original title of the libretto, *Rache und Edelmuth*.) The fact that most other keys featured in the work are closely related to one or the other of these centers (G major, A major, and E minor on one hand; E-flat major and C minor on the other) reinforces the impression of a tonal duality of structural and dramatic significance.

The perceptibility of this duality is enhanced by certain aspects of design in the second, D-major overture that Vogler supplied for the work. As explained by the composer in a manuscript entitled "Über die neue Ouvertüre zur Oper Samori,"[39] the three main parts of the overture embody specific references to the drama and its musical setting. The opening *allegro* develops the processional march of the nabob, with its characteristic three-note timpani motive (heralded at the outset by sustained notes in the horns and trumpets);[40] the middle *andante* section alludes to the hymn to Siva from early in the second act; and the final *presto* employs an extended fugato in which the polyphonic combination of themes (including the three-note timpani motive) represents the double wedding (Naga to Tamburan, Maha to Pando) that follows the conclusion of the drama. With regard to key associations (not mentioned in Vogler's draft), the D major of the opening part, with its symbolic reference to the royal authority that Tamburan holds and that Pando seeks to regain, stands in contrast to the B-flat major of the *andante,* with its representation of prayerful supplication on the part of Rama and a terrified crowd. In the course of the final part, the incorporation of the tritone relationship (A-flat major) in an extended central passage helps depict both the confrontation and the reconciliation of opposing forces.

As in *Castore e Polluce,* correspondences between the overture and subsequent thematic elements suggest, at least tenuously, a hierarchy that extends to the largest dimensions of the opera. Yet just as in *Castore* and *Gustav Adolf,* it is clear that the dramatic complexity of such a large work prohibits any tightly unified plan on higher levels of structure. The expressive demands of individual arias or ensembles must override the musical logic of tonal unity or thematic recurrence.

Within the individual numbers, however, musical logic is of primary importance, and the flexible interactions of musical design and text expression demonstrate many ways in which the requirements of Vogler's system can accommodate dramatic action, rhetorical emphasis, and the expressive rendering of details (such as words, momentary images, or fleeting emotions) inside a larger dramatic framework. Especially notable in this respect are the large ensembles and the composite scene-and-aria designs. Enjoying broader proportions than those available in *Gustav Adolf,* they involve a comparable loosening of purely musical constraints while retaining elements of statement, contrast, development, culminating emphasis, and closure within a tonally unified plan.

Such a union of music and text is exemplified in the setting of Maha's great scene preceding the finale of Act 1. Conceived as a vehicle for expression as well as virtuosic brilliance, this number begins with a ritornello that exposes a wistful *larghetto* theme in E-flat, its color dominated by the plaintive sounds of solo clarinet and bassoon. Six lines of intensely emotional, musically varied recitative then follow, the changing passions reflected vividly in the music. For the line "Ach! Mein Himmel trübte sich sehr bald" (see Example 10),[41] the mode changes from major to minor. The mediant chord appears and instantly becomes an enharmonic pivot to the remote, dramatically contrasting area of B major (G-flat major as III of E-flat minor = F-sharp major as V of B major). The stunning brilliance of a B-major chord enhances the phrase "Der holde Sonnenschein" (measure 20), and with the addition of a seventh, A, this B-major chord becomes the enharmonic basis for an augmented sixth in E-flat minor (B–D♯–F♯–A = C♭–E♭–G♭–A). In the now restored tonic minor, Maha's recitative comes to its disconsolate close.

The aria now begins with a return to the *larghetto* theme of the ritornello, and after a placid rendition of the first two lines of text, the growing intensity of this opening stanza is reinforced by modulation to the dominant ("und von

Example 10
*Samori,* Act 1, "Wie traurig ist mein
Los!," measures 12–26.

meinem Glücke mahlte sich mein Geist ein reitzend Bild"). On this new tonal
level, the tempo changes to *allegro* and a new theme is announced. But since it
is motivically related to the *larghetto*, the contrasting passion represented in
the first line of this second stanza is integrated into a unified design.

Musical and dramatic logic is further pursued in Vogler's setting of the
remaining lines of the second stanza ("Doch ich Arme sah es kaum. So
verschwand es. Ich erwachte, und mein Glück war nur ein Traum."), where a
modified return to the theme and tempo of the *larghetto* coincides with
retrieval of the tonic key. In the manner of a contrasting *B* section, the
opening lines of the last stanza are treated to a new theme (*allegro*) in the
relative minor. "Kehrt zurück, ihr Wonnestunden," Maha then sings, *più
presto,* and the music recalls the material of the *allegro* theme from the start of
the second stanza, now in tonic. Structural balance and rhetorical climax are
now accomplished as Maha reiterates lines from each of the three stanzas,

developing both the second-stanza *allegro* theme and a *presto* transformation of the opening *larghetto*. And in an extended *presto* coda, brilliant *passaggi*—for solo wind instruments as well as the singer—adorn the continually reiterated phrase "Liebe, heile meinen Schmerz."

In the dramatically more complex situations that typify the ensembles, general similarities to Maha's scene may readily be discerned: multi-stage composite design, with elements of exposition, tonal transition, central contrast or development, and return to tonic; an overriding scheme of tempo acceleration and growth in textural complexity and brilliance; and a rationally devised scheme of correspondence between harmonic phenomena on different hierarchic levels and the text being expressed. In response to the requirements of dramatic action and plot development, the ensembles must sacrifice the thematic unity and structural symmetry of the arias; but with the exception of the loosely connected first-act finale, the principle of tonal unity is maintained.

Essential ingredients of Vogler's approach to the ensembles may be seen in the Act 1 quintet, where Pando and Maha find themselves confronting each other in the presence of Tamburan. At all costs, they must conceal the emotions that overwhelm them. Yet they are at a loss to answer coherently when addressed by the nabob, even when coaxed by their companions Mahadowa and Rama. The action begins as a hasty exchange between Pando and Maha defines the remote, sharp-edged tonic of E major. This is the only instance in which E major (lying one sharp beyond the orbit of D major and its close relatives) appears as a home key. Texture and mood are suddenly transformed as the two express their inner feelings. Observing their distraction, Mahadowa addresses Pando, Rama likewise pulls Maha aside, and Tamburan, seeing all, addresses his own aside to the audience (see Example 11). Here the scene proceeds in C major, approached as a tonicized VI in E minor. Abruptly established as a temporary center, the remote key conveys a feeling of suspense appropriate to the conspiratorial whisperings of the characters on stage.

The main tonic now returns as Tamburan addresses the two lovers. A nervous, continuously reiterated string motive depicts their agitation while at the same time lending thematic continuity to the musical fabric. Tamburan's questions correspond to movement from tonic to dominant, and the answers (supplied for the speechless pair by Rama and Mahadowa) involve reversion to tonic. A decisive modulation to the dominant is now articulated, and in the pungent key of B major, Rama and Mahadowa urge the pair to regain control of themselves.

The attempt is partially successful, and Pando and Maha are able to respond as Tamburan resumes his questioning. This event coincides with the return to tonic, and thematic material of the earlier interrogation is brought back in the manner of a recapitulation. Finally, an extended coda provides both reaffirmation of the tonic and a proper vehicle for unified expression of sentiment on the part of all five characters: "O, das Gefühl der mächt'gen Triebe bestürmet meine/ihre Brust zu sehr. Mich/Sie überwältigt ganz die Liebe. Mein/Ihr Herz verstellet sich nicht mehr."

The dramatic tension of this scene, which takes place shortly before the climactic first-act finale, corresponds logically to the tension of its key (the dominant of the dominant with respect to the presumed higher-level tonic of D major). Within its bounds, the dramatic framework of the ensemble—the exchange between Tamburan and the others—is linked to the local tonic, and various asides find their properly subordinate place within the harmonic unity and rhetorical coherence of the whole. A perceptible union of music and drama is thus accomplished in accordance with the theorist's precepts.

In the passages examined from *Samori,* the principles expounded in *Betrachtungen* remain in force, even though the predictable symmetries and limited vocabulary of an aria by say, Hasse, have been left far behind. As is evident in each of the later works, Vogler's operatic styles accommodate changes in fashion as he keeps himself attuned to manifestations of technical and artistic progress. Yet a similarity of approach persists, a common denominator that links the Mannheim works of the 1770s with later achievements at Munich, Stockholm, and Vienna. Despite contrasts in outward appearance, each of these compositions betrays an underlying consistency in the way theoretical ideals are honored and explored. And through their enduring similarities, they help clarify what Vogler understands as the essential elements of the language his theory attempts to explain.

The most basic message is that dramatic expression requires musical coherence. Traditional aria forms retain their usefulness, and the sonata principle enjoys virtually unchallenged authority. The standard designs of the 1770s, however, are by no means indispensable. The system merely requires that a hierarchic order be exerted on available materials, and that the drama—conceived as the appropriate rendering of diverse details within a larger framework—be made to coincide with scientific principles of musical order.

Example 11
*Samori,* Act 1, "Ihr Götter! Muss
mein Auge finden," measures 7–25.

Operatic conventions are thus subjected to modification in the name of dramatic authenticity as the composer accommodates his musical resources to the demands of his text. And since his music rests on a foundation not beholden to a particular idiom, it readily absorbs a mixture and synthesis of operatic styles typical of his later operas: the combination of French theater, Gluckian drama, and *opera seria* in *Castore e Polluce;* the harmonically enriched, natural declamation of *Gustav Adolf;* and the assimilation of *Singspiel,* symphonic, and Italian opera elements in *Samori.* Guided by adherence to rationalist principles, these works reveal the composer's effort to apply his resources wisely and economically in search of underlying truths of dramatic expression he felt to be inherent within the musical language itself.

CHAPTER 6

# The Performer and
# His Medium

VOGLER'S writings on church and theater music have enabled us to trace a connection between theoretical principles and the artist's practical experience. In both areas, his own compositions appeared prominently in explanations of musical organization and content. But what about the other field of activity for which he was famous, that of virtuoso performance on the organ and other keyboard instruments? In this realm, where improvisation played a major part, there are few surviving traces of notated music. Pertinent documents show that Vogler was dedicated to his role as a performer for most of his career; but because the subject is rarely addressed in his writings, and few known accounts supply more than general descriptions, we can gain only an approximate idea of what the content of his extemporized performances might have been. Examining the issue is nevertheless important to our understanding of Vogler's teachings and the links he intended to forge between theory and practice.

Vogler's reticence on the subject of extemporization may mean that in this kind of music he was not bound by the constraints of a rational system. Schubart's remark about his own preference for Vogler's improvisations over his rule-encrusted compositions lends weight to this supposition.[1] To the extent that Schubart's implication about the extemporizer's freedom from rules is valid, then the emphasis on improvisation in Vogler's life's work serves to remind us of the importance of license, even on the part of a musician avidly committed to his theoretical principles. License, after all, was an acknowledged element even in Vogler's model published compositions.

But there are other vantage points from which Vogler's work as a performer may be viewed. In light of his proud claims about the ease with which music could be written under the guidance of his harmonic system,[2] is it not possible that his improvisations were actually controlled by his concepts of harmonic reduction, elaboration, and rhetoric? If so, then the study of Vogler's teachings and their application may shed light on his approach to extemporized performance.

Moreover, even if his endeavors in performance were not directly guided by theoretical precepts, they did involve the formulation of a system, albeit one that dealt with the medium of performance rather than musical organization. Dedicated to the cause of progress and enlightenment in this field no less than in others, Vogler proposed an elaborate theory of organ design, the so-called Simplification System (to be discussed below), which stands alongside his theories of harmony and sacred music as a reflection of his ideals and their potential application to musical practice.

The intensity of Vogler's activity as a performer is remarkable, and suggests a need not only for self-expression, but for adulation as well. His extravagant concerts earned him fame throughout Europe, and his reputation was such that many organists misused his name, actually claiming to be either the master himself, or his pupil. The phrase "in the manner of Herr Abt Vogler" is found frequently on performers' programs.[3] From contemporary reports it appears that he commanded exceptional skills in execution and improvisation. Mozart's well-known disparagement notwithstanding,[4] he was revered as a performer of keyboard instruments. Schubart described him as "one of the foremost organ and harpsichord players in Europe,"[5] Junker ranked him among the most outstanding German clavier players,[6] and a report in the *Allgemeine musikalische Zeitung* called him "the greatest organist of our time."[7]

In hailing Vogler's powers of execution, contemporary writers give the impression of a truly remarkable technique. Schubart's praise of his skill in sightreading, transposition, and the facile execution of perilous leaps and difficult passages summarizes the thrust of many reviews.[8] In his *Chronik* of 1790, he equated certain technical aspects of Vogler's organ playing—wondrous pedal technique, endurance, penchant for full-bodied sonority—with those of J. S. Bach, Handel, and other prominent masters of the eighteenth century. But in the rendering of color through "rapid, magical registration," he thought Vogler unequaled in any age.[9]

Vogler's style of expression proved more controversial than his gifts as a technician. While some critics praised his sensitivity, others cited deficiencies, leading the reader to infer that on balance his powers were better suited to bold, dramatic effects than subtlety or nuance. In 1784, Junker's *Musikalischer Almanach* stated that wherever Vogler was heard it was said that "he plays with great dexterity, but not for the heart."[10] Elsewhere, referring specifically to his pianistic style, this same critic portrays him as an intensely energetic performer whose talents for evoking grandeur, heroism, or terror far exceed his ability to convey tender, tranquil sentiments—a Rubens but not a Caravaggio, capable of playing *allegro* far better than *adagio* and lacking the capacity for soft dynamic shadings.[11]

Critics favorably disposed toward Vogler reserved special praise for his skills in improvisation. Schubart, contending that he improvised better than he composed,[12] praised his magical variations and profound understanding of fugal technique. In the 1790 *Chronik,* he judged Vogler to be without equal in musical painting—especially in the depiction of natural phenomena.[13] A report in Knigge's *Dramaturgische Blätter* speaks of his inexhaustible invention, claims that he could devise a systematic plan on the spur of the moment, and reports that his fugues, though strict and correct, contained wholly unexpected harmonic developments.[14]

Though he concertized on piano as well as organ, the grandiose organ concerts attracted greater attention and notoriety. His performances included such traditional kinds of organ music as preludes and fugues, and also renditions of sacred vocal pieces: chorales and arrangements of favorite sacred works such as the "Halleluja" chorus from Handel's *Messiah,* an *Improperium* by Palestrina, and *Miserere* settings by Allegri and Baj. Featured most prominently were types of music not customarily associated with the church organ: variations on folk themes, abstract pieces modeled on orchestral or chamber music idioms, imitations of solo wind, string, and percussion instruments, and the much-discussed tone paintings. Typically, traditional and unconventional pieces appeared side by side in the same concert. The program for a performance of February 26, 1794, presented at St. Jacob's church in Stockholm, serves as an example.[15]

PART ONE

1. Ouverture: Marche, Allegro
2. Nocturno

3. Klockspel [Carillon]
4. Schweitzisk national-musik
5. Jerichos belägring
   [The Siege of Jericho]

PART TWO

1. Flöjt-concert. Allegro,
   Andante, Rondo
2. Kosackisk national-musik
3. Målning af ett sjöslag
   [Portrayal of a Naval Battle]
4. Stor phantasie och fuga
   [Grand Fantasia and Fugue]

The special preoccupation with folk music, doubtless fueled by his wide-ranging travels and the exposure to different national and regional traditions, reflects similar interests that can be seen contemporaneously in the writings of Johann Gottfried Herder and others.[16] Playing a prominent role in his teachings, the concern for secular oral traditions is likely to have been a stimulus for similar enthusiasms on the part of both Carl Maria von Weber and Meyerbeer, who was inspired to undertake transcriptions of folk music in Italy.

Folk songs used by Vogler in his concerts were derived from European and non-European cultures alike. Many in the former category were drawn from outside the central-European tradition, and included such items as a Venetian barcarolle, a Cossack song, a Scottish song, and settings of various Scandinavian melodies. More exotic specimens were supposedly transcribed in Africa, notably the *Romance africaine,* a Hottentot song, and the much discussed *Terrassenlied der Afrikaner* (Terrace Song of the Africans).

Insight into the nature of these materials can be gleaned from Vogler's chamber-music publications, notably the two *Polymelos* collections (c. 1791 and 1806) and *Pièces de clavecin* [1798], all of which include variations on pieces that have titles identical or similar to those found on his concert programs. In an introduction to the 1806 collection, he calls attention to the so-called "Polymelos" organ concerts given earlier that year in Munich, and explains that pieces he performed were extemporaneous fantasies and variations on fixed themes, some of which were represented in the published collection. Describing his national and folk melodies as "domestic and foreign plants, plucked in the open field of natural singers," he claims that it was his intention to transcribe faithfully, and then to set his borrowed tunes in an uncontrived fashion that retained something of their original character.[17]

As it pertained to pieces based on non-Western materials, such as those quoted from *Pièces de clavecin* in Example 1, the process of borrowing and adaptation resulted in few drastic departures from the norms of contemporary Western style. The *Romance africaine* melody (Example 1a) would scarcely sound out of place in a late eighteenth-century Italian opera, while the exotic element in the *Air barbaresque* is largely confined to unconventional

Example 1
Sample of Vogler's non-European
folk melodies in *Pièces de clavecin:* (a)
*Romance africaine,* measures 1–4; (b)
*Air barbaresque,* measures 1–8; (c)
*Cheu-Teu,* measures 1–6.

embellishment and articulation (Example 1b). Only moderately less Western-sounding are the modal and repeated-note effects in the *Cheu-Teu* melody, allegedly obtained by Vogler from a Chinese diplomat in London (Example 1c).[18]

The tendency for Vogler's titles to sound more exotic than the actual musical content (at least as represented in published form) is likewise evident in the *Terrassenlied der Afrikaner*, transcribed and excerpted in the *Allgemeine musikalische Zeitung*, but otherwise known only from programs and contemporary critiques.[19] The piece was reportedly an antiphonal work song for two alternating choirs, one singing in unison while the other pounded limestone. As shown in Example 2a, Vogler represented the original melody and rhythm in a bourrée-like tune with a repeated-note pedal to depict the work activity. According to the description offered in the journal, he subjected this material to various kinds of elaboration, including imitation and variation. Remarking skeptically that "the African terrace builders are even

Example 2
*Terrassenlied der Afrikaner,* (a) theme;
(b) imitative treatment of theme.

familiar with European musical imitation," the critic quoted the passage shown in Example 2b.

However questionable as a representation of non-European music, the piece was judged by the critic to be novel and attractive, and he believed the organ to be the sole instrument on which it might have been played with such consummate effect.

In the minds of contemporary critics, more problematical than Vogler's rendering of allegedly exotic folk music was his penchant for imitative sound effects and depictive tone painting.[20] The music in question included abstract improvisations designed to imitate certain instrumental ensembles or the timbres of particular solo instruments—for example, a double concerto for flute and bassoon, a carillon sonata, a flute concerto, a fanfare for trumpet and drums, and a harp sonata. Vogler traced his interest in such imitative possibilities to the year 1764, when he played organ as a university student and first began to elicit unusual effects from the organ by experimenting with registration.[21] In order to imitate a particular instrumental sound to his liking, such as a carillon, he resorted to unconventional combinations of registers, since no single register could yield the desired sound adequately.[22] He also selected organ registrations to feature contrasting instrumental sounds on different manuals. According to a description in the *Allgemeine musikalische Zeitung,* his double concerto for flute and bassoon employed four manuals, one reserved for flute, one for bassoon, one for the tutti, and one for a reduced accompanying ensemble.[23] Typically, these imitations would be enhanced by references to idiomatic passagework and such special effects as the double-tonguing represented in his "flute concerto."[24]

Far more sensational than the imitative concertos and sonatas were the tone paintings, which best exemplify what Junker described as Vogler's inclination toward the "bizarre."[25] Junker noted that this trait first surfaced after the abbé's departure from Mannheim; indeed, it may have been nurtured by his musical experiences there. Certainly the pages of the *Betrachtungen der Mannheimer Tonschule* reflect the deep impression made on him by the court's theatrical spectacles. It was on this ground that he felt confident in defending the musical superiority of the Germans over the Italians, and he drew a connection between his countrymen's experience with depictive ballet music and their special mastery of the art of tone painting.[26]

In exploring the possibilities of tone painting, Vogler did not concern himself exclusively with the coloristic diversity of the organ. A report in Forkel's *Musikalischer Almanach* describes a remarkable fortepiano concert at the Düsseldorf art gallery in the fall of 1785. Here, surrounded by art connoisseurs in an eighteenth-century version of Mussorgsky's idea, Vogler moved among the displayed art works, had his instrument placed before each of several paintings, and conveyed his musical impressions of their content.[27]

The organ was, however, Vogler's ideal vehicle for this type of music, and to judge from contemporary reports, his extemporized performances— supplied with such promising titles as *Das jüngste Gericht* (The Last Judgment), *Die Belagerung von Jericho* (The Battle of Jericho), *Eine Seeschlacht* (A Naval Battle), and *Die Spazierfahrt auf dem Rhein vom Donnerwetter unterbrochen* (The Excursion on the Rhine, Interrupted by a Thunderstorm)— more than satisfied his audiences' expectations through their ingenious and astonishing sound effects. A critic in the *Allgemeine musikalische Zeitung* claimed that Vogler's thunderstorm imitation stirred him profoundly and proved more realistic than any he had ever heard.[28] (According to one description, the imitation of thunder was accomplished by the organist's selecting several powerful bass registers, including trumpet, then depressing and sustaining three or four adjacent pedal keys simultaneously.)[29] Vogler himself reported that such imitations caused a deaf-mute to sense the thunder, children to scream and cry, and dogs to bark and howl.[30] Among other extant reports is that of Johanna Schopenhauer, mother of the philosopher. Present at Vogler's concert in Danzig in 1788, she heard his *Belagerung von Gibraltar* (Siege of Gibraltar) and averred that a true siege "could hardly have been filled with greater uproar and fury, and the bombs, guns, and cannons smoked, thundered, and boomed as genuinely as is possible."[31]

Literary programs for some of the improvised tone paintings have survived, including detailed notes for *Tod Leopolds* (Death of Leopold— Leopold of Brunswick, nephew of Frederick the Great, who died on April 25, 1785).[32] These notes, written in French, were prepared for the Amsterdam concert in November 1785. They provide descriptions for each of the five main sections of the work:

1. The tranquil flowing of the river; the winds, which drive it more rapidly; the gradual swelling of the water; total inundation.

2. The universal terror and cries of the unfortunate ones, who anticipate their misfortune; their shuddering, lamenting, crying and sobbing.

3. The arrival of the noble prince, who resolves to help them; the remonstrances and pleas of his officers, who wish to hold him back; his opposition, which in the end stifles all complaint.

4. Launching of the skiff; its pitching in the waves; the howling of the winds; the skiff capsizes; the prince drowns.

5. An emotion-filled piece, with sentiment appropriate to the event.

Whatever its musical substance may have been, an extemporization such as this could not have failed to draw fire from opponents of descriptive music. Forkel's *Musikalischer Almanach,* which persistently opposed Vogler's pictorial work in reports from the mid 1780s, roundly condemned it.[33] The reviewer not only dismissed the sound effects as "childish jangles," but challenged the very premise of such music by asserting that it could not possibly represent the explicit content that Vogler intended to convey. Certainly the programmatic titles lent themselves to parody—a risk that Vogler might have alleviated by heeding Junker's suggestion and suppressing the descriptive programs as well as the designation "musical painting."[34] One critic challenged Vogler to give a public concert with improvisations based on the following subjects:[35]

FIRST HALF

1. Sunrise
2. Sunset
3. Kant's philosophy
4. Tuberculosis

SECOND HALF

1. An unusually severe summer heatwave
2. The horribly biting cold weather that set in in St. Petersburg in the year 1748
3. Natural religion
4. A solar eclipse

Apart from the matter of aesthetic validity, the tone paintings raised another issue, one destined to remain unresolved: the appropriateness of the church and its organ for Vogler's performances, which were manifestly theatrical and often frankly secular in content. A witness to one of these spectacles acknowledged that the audience was enchanted by the *Jüngste Gericht, Kriegssymphonie* (Battle Symphony), *Hirtenleben, von einem Donnerwetter unterbrochen* (Pastoral Idyll, Interrupted by a Thunderstorm), and the like, but he nevertheless thought they sounded horrendous in their hallowed surroundings, "where dignity, gravity, and solemnity should prevail."[36] The author of a later critique in the *Allgemeine musikalische Zeitung,* looking back on Vogler's notorious concerts, concluded that such pieces as *Hirtenwonne,* African folk songs, and *Marsch des schwedischen Wasaordens* (March of the Swedish Order of the Wasa) were unworthy of the inherently noble instrument on which they were performed.[37]

Vogler himself asserted that to perform secular, dramatic music in a church posed no contradiction. He viewed the issue more as a question of genre and function than of the instrument itself or its location. In accordance with his professed ideal, true sacred music must indeed be pure, simple, and devoid of theatrics. Accordingly, he scoffs at the notion of an organist who would imitate thunder and lightning at a baptism, tumbling walls at a confirmation, or the sounds of a battle at a wedding.[38] Such depictions had their place in the secular arena, where music could create illusion in a language of heightened expression, and where, for the listener receptive to its pictorial powers, a performer could evoke raging floods, violent thunder, and howling winds.[39] The concert hall would certainly have been more appropriate than the church for such performances. But having chosen the organ as his medium, Vogler had little choice in the matter, church instruments outnumbering by far those in theaters and concert halls.

His distinction between sacred and secular functions allowed him to draw comparable distinctions between the different roles he assumed in playing the organ. He declared that only in the execution of preludes and fugues was it proper to judge him as an organist. For other kinds of music, including folk-song improvisations and tone paintings, his voice was that of the kapellmeister.[40] By distinguishing between "organist" and "kapellmeister" in this fashion, he meant to recognize that there were legitimate, time-honored styles, traditionally associated with the organ's churchly function, but that they need not exclude the possibility of a modern, innovative, and secular idiom—one which bestowed on the organ the properties of an orchestra by highlighting and blending a multitude of colors, and exploiting to the fullest the timbral potential of the instrument.

Eagerly playing the part of the "kapellmeister" in his quasi-orchestral manner of performance, Vogler chose not to limit himself to the capacities of existing instruments. As early as the Mannheim years there is evidence of his developing interest in possibilities of improvement through modification or redesign.[41] In the 1780s, the urge to accomplish change and reform was fueled by his dissatisfaction with organs he encountered as a traveling virtuoso. His subsequent involvement in this field became a major part of his mission to promote musical enlightenment and progress.

Vogler's complaints centered at first on characteristic deficiencies he noticed in organs' wind supply, but this was only the beginning. The search for solutions to the wind problem led to an elaborate, far-reaching, and in some respects radically unconventional set of proposals on organ design. Designated as his Simplification System, the method dealt with questions of sonority, mechanism, and appearance as well as size and wind power.

Early on he gave tangible shape to his developing principles of reform by designing an exemplary instrument called the *Orchestrion* (begun in the mid 1780s and completed in its original form by 1790). He also set forth his views on the subject in a treatise destined to remain unpublished.[42] Though the manuscript seemingly disappeared in the nineteenth century (attempts to locate it have proved fruitless), information surviving in contemporary manuscripts and publications furnishes a comprehensive picture of the system and its applications. Pertinent sources include the following:

a. Vogler's published essays and specifications for particular church organs: for example, those of the Church of St. Mary in Berlin, the Dreifaltigkeits Kirche in Schweidnitz, St. Peter's in Salzburg, the Evangelisches Hofbethaus and St. Peter's in Munich, and the Neumünster in Würzburg (this last essay being one of his most extended discussions of the topic).[43]

b. Two essays on acoustics: *Data zur Akustik* (Leipzig, 1801) and *Uiber die harmonische Akustik* [Munich, 1806].

c. A large set of manuscript organ specifications, the "Register-Dispositionen nach Abt Voglers Simplifications-System,"[44] probably intended for inclusion in his treatise on the system.

d. A description of the system in a short essay called "Système de simplification pour les orgues."[45]

The system is further clarified in eighteenth- and nineteenth-century journals, particularly the *Allgemeine musikalische Zeitung,* where readers were regaled with descriptions and critiques of the system, Vogler's organ reforms, and details of specific instruments. To these accounts may be added numerous references in treatises, letters, and miscellaneous documents by Vogler and others.

As outlined in the published essay on the simplified Neumünster organ (1812), the Simplification System embraced three broadly defined categories—acoustical, aesthetic, and mechanical. Each of these areas subsumed specific issues concerning economy of means, simplicity of design, and maximization of versatility and expressive capacity. The first category included harmonic acoustics (*Tonlehre:* the generation of sound and resultant tones), anatomical acoustics (the way in which sound waves impinge upon the ear), and physical acoustics (the transmission of sound). Within the area of aesthetics, the system addressed the selection and grouping of pipes, whereby all unnecessary duplication could be avoided. Mechanical considerations involved the simplification of an instrument's structure and the use of particular devices to produce dynamic shadings.

Further discussions in the Neumünster essay and other writings (notably an essay in vol. 1 of the *Allgemeine musikalische Zeitung,* which may have originated with Vogler)[46] show that the system also confronted other issues, including improvement of wind-supply mechanisms, removal of unnecessary pipes, compensation for pipes thus removed, design and structure of the pipes themselves, enclosure of the instrument in a case (to protect it from dust and dampness as well as to unify the sound), application of the theorist's so-called "characteristic" temperament, and the examination of architectural features that might enhance or detract from an instrument's acoustical potential.

Though its basic features were well in place by 1790 (enclosure, reduction in number of pipes, mechanical simplification, and use of swells), the system was subject to evolution and modification in accordance with particular circumstances. In the following discussion the emphasis falls not on tracing the chronological development of Vogler's principles of organ construction, but rather on the examination of essential, known elements of the system that pertained to new or redesigned instruments.

### THE SIMPLIFICATION SYSTEM

Vogler's chief stimulus and point of departure—rectifying weaknesses in wind supply—was scarcely a new issue. Eighteenth-century preferences for thick textures and full sonority had been taxing the capacities of northern- and central-European instruments well before Vogler's time. The issue of wind had been a chief concern of that earlier master, J. S. Bach, whose first step in testing and approving an organ was to pull all stops and play full-textured sonorities.[47] It was when such demands were placed on an instrument that weaknesses surfaced.

In his own confrontation with problems of wind supply, Vogler complained that most organs on which he performed were woefully deficient of breath: typically, if he pulled all stops and played sustained chords in the descant while executing a running *basso continuo* including a 32′ rank in the pedal register, the organ would make trembling sounds and gasp for air.[48]

To alleviate these symptoms, he began with construction of more durable bellows, placement of the bellows closer to the wind chests, and widening of the trunk and channels through which air was led under pressure.[49] Beyond such mechanical adjustments were his proposed changes in actual sound resources of an instrument, most notably the abolishing of very large pipes and the reduction in total number of pipes used.

Pursuing this line of attack, he advocated dispensing with the traditional facade pipes and their conductors, and the excising of those ranks of pipes that needlessly duplicated others.[50] Large facade pipes were seen as the chief offenders, mainly because they drew such great quantities of wind in order to sound. The drain on pressure caused by unstopped pipes more than twelve feet long seemed especially unjustified, since the streams of wind thus expended often proved inadequate to set the air columns properly in motion. An objectionable buzzing and rumbling was the typical result.[51] Vogler also complained that the conductors, through which the facade pipes drew air from the wind chest, caused the wind supply to be less concentrated and hence less efficiently used than when the whole mass of air under pressure was concentrated within a chest.[52]

The boldest of Vogler's solutions to wind-related problems involved the replacement of certain large pipes with something that proved to be a controversial substitute: simulation of the missing pitches through the phenomenon known as resultants, or difference tones. Identified by Tartini in his *Trattato di musica* as the *terzo suono,* the difference tone comes about when two pitches are sounded simultaneously, for example on two strings of a violin. The illusion of a third sound, corresponding in pitch to the difference in frequency between the two sounded tones, will be perceived.[53] This means that if the tones are adjacent members of a harmonic series, the difference tone produced will be equivalent to the fundamental of that series. In Example 3a, the difference between the given tones c' (256 cps) and g' (384 cps) produces the third tone c (128 cps). By the same token, each following pair of pitches (Examples 3b, c, and d, all involving adjacent members of the same series) produces the same third tone, c.

Example 3
(a–d). The *terzo suono.* In each
instance, the pitch c, represented by
a black notehead, is the difference
tone perceived when the two given
pitches are sounded.

Vogler's own introduction to difference tones dates from the time of his studies in Padua, where he allegedly read about the concept in a pamphlet by Tartini, *Del terzo suono nella natura.*[54] Using the term *trias harmonica* to designate the difference tone and the pitches sounded to produce it, he exploited the phenomenon as a way of expanding the sonorous capacities of the organ. While it served as a means of reinforcement in higher registers, it proved especially useful for obtaining low pitches—so useful that certain difference-tone relationships were adopted as the foundation of Vogler's economies in the Simplification System.[55] The special appeal of this idea was understandable, given his dedication to the cause of an economical wind system; and because it not only saved wind but also helped reduce the cost of materials and maintenance, it proved no less agreeable to the officials from whom he received contracts and commissions.

As a means of replacing low frequencies otherwise produced by single large pipes, the difference-tone relationships Vogler preferred were those involving the fifth, the major third, or both. Producing these resultants with traditionally available resources meant drawing on mutations, those registers that sound a third or fifth higher than played, or octave multiples thereof. With mutations, the effect of $C_2$ or 32' C, for example, could be produced on the key C by pulling the stops for 16' C and its Quint, 10 2/3' G, or the stops for 8' C and its Terz, 6 2/5' E, or both these combinations together. Although he may be credited with calling attention to the use of difference tones on the organ, the presence of low mutation registers (e.g., 10 2/3') on seventeenth-century instruments suggests a much earlier exploration of this acoustical possibility.[56]

To enhance the effect of his resultants, Vogler favored the use of stopped (closed) wood pipes for the low Quint and Terz registers: the tone of stopped pipes was duller, he claimed, and the overtones were less perceptible than with open pipes. Stopped wood pipes also had the advantage of being cheaper, a matter of no small importance in light of the emphasis placed on cost reduction as a selling point for his system.[57]

Further measures aimed at economizing on materials and resources involved the issue of duplication (i.e., duplicate ranks of pipes). This was found commonly in multi-rank mixtures, which Vogler proposed to ban altogether, and in unison doublings of individual ranks, installed by builders presumably to increase an instrument's power or to create special effects. Vogler determined that duplicates, especially of larger pipes, overtaxed the wind supply, interfered with the clarity of the sound, and escalated costs without contributing increased diversity—all in opposition to his aim of achieving maximum variety with limited means.[58]

Dwelling on this subject in the late *Neumünster-Orgel* essay, Vogler isolates three criteria for identifying an instance of duplication: quality, quantity, and harmonic relationship. Quality concerned timbral factors such as pipe design, scale (the relationship between width and length), and the materials of which a pipe was made, while quantity referred to parameters of pitch, such as the height of a pipe, circulation pattern of the wind, and whether or not a pipe was stopped. Harmonic relationship concerned the correspondence between a key struck on the manual and the actual pitch produced. To show how these determinants might apply, he explained that two Principal 4′ ranks represented duplication on all three counts: quality (both are Principal ranks), quantity (both are 4′), and harmonic relationship (both sound the pitch c when the note C is struck on the keyboard).[59]

Vogler's idea of duplication was misunderstood by various critics who seized upon apparent contradictions in its application. Did multiple ranks of differing timbre but comparable pipe length constitute duplication? What about two ranks of related timbre but different pitch (i.e., 8′ and 4′ Principals)? The theorist's writings state emphatically that the duplications to which he objected involved identical pitch, timbre, and harmonic relationship (or at least identical pitch and timbre).[60] In practice, however, he did remove or redefine ranks whose timbres were similar (but not identical) or whose pitch he judged to be over-represented.

Another means of limiting the number of organ pipes, in addition to removal of facade pipes and duplicates, involved the concept of declination control. Designed to promote both economy and clarity of sound, the procedure subsumed two complementary devices, the so-called reduction line and the reinforcement line. The former addressed the problematical "chirping, hissing, and buzzing" of extremely high-pitched pipes, notably those associated with the multi-rank mixtures that Vogler proposed to abolish.[61] Customarily, such mixtures (whose constituents might include numerous ranks reinforcing the harmonic series) are subject to the organ designer's procedure of "breaking": after a certain point on the manual, the highest ranks in the mixture cease to sound and are replaced by the entry of corresponding ranks in lower octaves. Objecting to the excessively high pipes found in traditional mixtures, Vogler also disparaged the lack of clarity he sensed in breaking, by which several ranks might be discontinued simultaneously. His remedy of a reduction line had to do with the individual overtone-reinforcing registers that he preferred to mixtures. It subjected each to termination at a specified sounding pitch not nearly as high as the pitch at which breaking was characteristically applied to mixtures. This chosen point of maximum height in pitch, which varied from one instrument to another, fell within the range c′′′′ to g′′′′′ according to known writings and specifications. An explanation furnished in the *St. Marien-Orgel* and *Neumünster-Orgel* essays involves an organ with keyboard and pipes terminating at c′′′′. On such an instrument, the cut-off of pipes at c'''' would affect neither the registers sounding as played (i.e., 8' registers) nor those sounding lower. However, registers higher than 8' would be subjected to arbitrary termination when c'''' was reached. These included all octave multiples, such as 4', 2', and 1' stops, and the various higher mutations. In a 4' rank, sounding an octave higher than played, the key c''' would activate the highest pipe, c''''. There would be no further pipes to sound for the keys beyond c'''. Likewise, for a Terz 3 1/5' register (sounding a tenth higher than played), the key a-flat'' would cause c'''' to sound; and in a Quint 2 2/3' register, the key f'' would activate c''''. In effect, the higher a rank sounded in relation to the manual, the lower the key required to activate c''''. The reduction line, then, referred to the descending pattern of keys on the keyboard (represented in Example 4), above which no pipes would sound for progressively higher-pitched registers.[62]

Example 4
Vogler's reduction line.

| Rank | | 4' | 3 1/5' | 2 2/3' | 2' | 1 3/5' | 1 1/3' |
|---|---|---|---|---|---|---|---|
| Pitch produced by depressing c' | | c'' | e'' | g'' | c''' | e''' | g''' |
| Key depressed on manual to produce c'''' | c''' | c''' | c''' | | | | | |
| | (keyboard) | | ab'' | | | | |
| | | | | f'' | | | |
| | c'' | | | | | c'' | |
| | | | | | | ab' | |
| | c' | | | | | | f' |

Balancing the reduction line, the reinforcement line designated certain points on the keyboard at which new ranks were automatically added as the organist moved from lower to higher octaves. (Often these entering ranks bore an altered relationship to the keyboard: for example, an 8' rank might be displaced upward by an octave, so that the key c would sound the pitch C rather than c.) A basic purpose served by the reinforcement line was to compensate for the higher registers terminated by the reduction line. Typically, a rank used for this purpose differed in timbre from the terminated rank it replaced. On the Neumünster organ, a Principal 4' rank provided continuation upon termination of a 1′ Flaccionet (see Example 5). As Vogler explains, the Flaccionet register (sounding three octaves above notated pitch) would have run out of pipes with the key c′, in accordance with the established cut-off of pipes at c″″. To compensate, he terminated the Flaccionet register with the key b (sounding b″″) and continued the line at c′ on the keyboard with the Principal 4′ rank, displaced upward by two octaves so that the key c′ sounded c.[63]

Example 5
Continuation of a terminated
register on the Neumünster organ,
Würzburg.

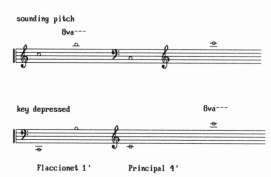

The reinforcement line could also reinforce a *trias harmonica* register as the difference-tone effect grew less audible in middle and higher octaves. For the St. Mary's organ in Berlin, this type of reinforcement also involved the displacement of ranks and had as its goal a continuous 32′ relationship (i.e., one in which the sounding pitch is two octaves lower than played) extending through the entire range of the keyboard. To accomplish this result, which assumes full organ, Vogler displaced several registers to coincide with successive points of reinforcement at c and c′ on the keyboard (see Example 6).[64] The steps were as follows:

—On the key C, a 32′ resultant of $C_2$ was produced by the Gross Nassat 10 2/3′ and 16′ registers.

—On the key c, the resultant pitch $C_1$ of the first *trias harmonica* was reinforced by a second resultant sounding two octaves lower than played: $C_1$ produced by 4′ c (in the 8′ register) and Terz 3 1/5′ from the Hauptmanual, displaced upward by an octave so that its lowest tone e sounded in response to the key c rather than C.[65]

—On the key c', the resultant C produced by all the above registers was strengthened by a sounding register in the Fernwerk rather than a resultant: an 8' Dulcian register, displaced upward by two octaves to form a 32' relationship in which the key c' sounded two octaves lower than played.[66]

Example 6
*Trias harmonica* reinforcement on the
St. Mary's organ, Berlin.

key depressed

pipes activated

8va---

registers:

| 10 2/3' | 3 1/5' * | 3 1/5' * |
|---------|----------|----------|
| 16'     | 8'       | 8'       |
|         | 10 2/3'  | 10 2/3'  |
|         | 16'      | 16'      |
|         |          | 8' Dulcian * |

resultant/sounding pitch

2 8va---      8va---

* Displaced registers

An important stipulation of the reinforcement line involved the design of the pipes involved: stopped wood pipes for the lowest pitches, progressing to open wood pipes, and finally to tin pipes in the highest octaves. In the *St. Marien-Orgel* essay and in *Data zur Akustik,* descriptions of this arrangement concentrated mainly on the Terz and Quint registers. But in a later essay concerned with oxidation in organ pipes, Vogler mentioned that his Simplification System required little if any use of tin pipes, and in any event only for pipes of 2' or smaller.[67]

In addition to his criteria for the elimination of pipes, Vogler introduced a certain pipe-sharing procedure that further affected the number and allocation of pipes in an instrument. Based on principles that originated well before his time, it required the use of coupling or transmission devices through which the pedal and manual shared registers. For one of Vogler's instruments, the newly built organ at Neu-Ruppin, C. F. G. Wilke, organist and later Royal Music Director there, gave a detailed account of the mechanism used.[68] According to his description, the pedal chest was eliminated altogether, and the pedal borrowed pipes from the bass half of the manual chests. The device that made this possible permitted a single pipe to be fed by either of two windways: one controlled by the pedal, the other by a manual. Such an arrangement could bring about substantial savings in pipes, but as Wilke's article pointed out, it was sensitive and not fully reliable.

Attempts such as this to wring the most out of minimal resources produced notable results, at least on paper. At Neu-Ruppin, Vogler was able to build a new instrument for the "remarkably low cost," as one report called it, of only 2,000 Prussian Thalers by applying his principles.[69] With redesigned organs, he substantially reduced the total number of pipes and claimed that, by comparison with the original instruments, these organs possessed more power and greater variety. Some idea of the extent to which he cut back on pipes may be seen in the following sampling of instruments before and after renovation:

|  | *Before* | *After* |
|---|---|---|
| St. Mary's, Berlin (1800) | 2,556 | 1,001 |
| Dreifaltigkeits Kirche, Schweidnitz (1802) | 3,661 | 1,734 |
| Evangelisches Hofbethaus, Munich (1805) | 1,217 | 1,010 |
| Neumünster, Würzburg (1812) | 1,539 | 975 |

By virtue of the economical selection and allocation of pipes—and especially the removal of facade pipes—an instrument designed according to Vogler's specifications could be enclosed in a case. According to the theorist's claims, this feature had notable advantages. It protected pipes from dust and dampness, concentrated the sound, and rendered the instrument more durable.[70] Moreover, in contrast to traditional organ designs with their ornate facades, it possessed the rare virtue of architectural simplicity. In place of the old-fashioned opulence and splendor, Vogler proposed a neo-Classical ideal of clarity and structural unity: "a great temple must represent a unified whole, and . . . the eye's attention must not be diverted from the whole by matters of secondary importance, such as pipes."[71]

Case enclosure bestowed further benefits by permitting a simplified internal design and mechanism. In contrast to the customarily symmetrical

array of pipes in a facade, which of course bore no relation to the order of keys
on a manual, enclosed pipes could readily be arranged chromatically on the
windchests. This approach (advocated by Vogler, though not his invention)
meant that no longer would "F-sharp growl from hither and F from yonder,
[or] c rumble from one corner and c-sharp from another" merely for the sake
of visual balance. Moreover, wind could be channeled more directly from
bellows to pipes (since conductors for facade pipes were no longer necessary),
and the builder could eliminate the traditional rollers and roller boards, which
took up space, created mechanical noise (especially when rapid passages were
played), and interfered with the responsiveness of the keys.[72]

Another measure aimed at enhancing both economy and efficiency
concerned the separation of bass and treble halves of a windchest. As Vogler
explained in his plan of 1806 for the St. Peter's organ in Munich, the windchests were to be divided so that bass and treble would each have separate
allocations of pressured air.[73] Since the sliders were also divided, this arrangement meant that the bass and treble halves of each full register—or of each
contrasting pair of partial registers—would have their own stop knobs. By
no means a new invention (they were relatively common on instruments of
the previous century, though rare in Vogler's day), divided registers made it
possible to link the bass of one register with the treble of another, thereby
producing new combinations that increased the variety of possible sonorities.

Compactly arranged and nestled within a case, Vogler's reformed organ
could accommodate devices for obtaining gradations of volume not normally available. In his quest for maximum variety, he saw such devices as a
means of breathing life into an instrument and endowing it with dynamically
flexible, quasi-orchestral qualities. Although the impetus was not new with
Vogler or his age, mechanisms for controlling dynamics were nonetheless
rare at this time in German-speaking countries.

The letter mentioned above from the first volume of the *Allgemeine
musikalische Zeitung* identified three mechanisms used by Vogler to produce
changes of volume: the door or roof swell, the wind swell, and the *Progressionsschweller.* The last of these, less frequently described than the others,
evidently involved automatic addition and subtraction of stops and allegedly
could produce a hitherto unimagined crescendo and diminuendo.[74] In a letter
published by Schubart in 1790, Vogler calls attention to this swell in connection with the *Orchestrion* and later mentions a related device for the Neumünster organ (1812).[75]

Evidently more common were the door and roof swell, both of which involved alteration of dynamic levels through a mechanism that opened and closed a swellbox. As used by Vogler, the swellbox could encompass an entire instrument (as with the *Orchestrion*) or else a single windchest and its pipes. The door (or *jalousie*) swell was common in eighteenth-century Britain, and Vogler may well have become familiar with it while concertizing there. Although not unknown in Germany, having been used earlier by Friedrich Marx and others, it seems for the most part to have been ignored until Vogler called attention to it.[76] It involved a case with louvers that could be opened and closed by means of a foot lever to produce crescendo and diminuendo effects. The roof swell was comparable in purpose and is described variously for Vogler's instruments as having a roof, a sectioned roof, or doors on the roof that opened and closed to produce the desired change in volume.

Unlike the swellbox, the wind swell yielded changes in dynamics by altering the pressure in the wind-supply system. Reportedly in use before Vogler's time, and therefore not truly his invention either, it involved the use of one or more cloth- or net-covered flaps, which when operated by a foot lever would partially obstruct the flow of air in the trunk. By permitting varying degrees of closure, the device could produce a diminuendo. The return to full volume could then be effected by restoring the wind supply to its original state.[77]

As suggested by one of Vogler's descriptions, the wind swell was related to yet another mechanical device called the Tremulant.[78] Encountered as early as the sixteenth century, the Tremulant was designed to produce fluctuations in wind pressure, which in turn caused the desired fluctuations in pitch. It may have been Vogler's model for the wind swell. In any event, the similarity between the two mechanisms—wind swell and Tremulant—points up a severe shortcoming of the former: when used with flue and standard reed pipes, it caused their pitch to drop as a result of diminution in wind supply. The effect was likened by Wilke to the moans of the dying.[79]

For another type of pipe, however—the free reed—the wind swell did prove effective, since its pitch was not affected by changes in wind pressure. With the free reed, pitch is determined by the vibration of a reed through an opening in an oblong plate. A resonator may be used to enhance the timbre, though it is not required in the production of pitch. In theory, the resonator might be of any length. Wilke reports that in the Neu-Ruppin organ, Vogler incorporated a metal resonator only five feet, two and one-half inches long for the lowest reed in a Posaune 32' register.[80] Free reeds, then, in addition to responding flexibly to changes in wind pressure, were also economical.

Vogler incorporated the free reed in his *Orchestrion,* and its use became widely associated with his name. Some writers attributed its invention to him, but as with other aspects of the system, his role was more that of borrower and creative adapter than inventor. The concept can be traced to an ancient Chinese instrument, the *sheng,* whose reeds furnished a model for Western experimenters, notably a Copenhagen professor named Kratzenstein, who applied the idea to a voice-simulating machine (it allegedly produced the sound of the words "Papa" and "Mama"), and an organ builder in St. Petersburg named Kirsnick, who adapted the Kratzenstein reeds for use in an organ. Vogler saw Kirsnick's pipes in 1788 during a visit to St. Petersburg and later engaged Kirsnick's assistant, named Rackwitz, to construct the free reeds used for his own *Orchestrion.*[81]

Vogler's extension of the Simplification System into the realm of sound generation and organ-pipe design led to the exploration of analogies with human vocal production (a natural connection in light of his experience as a voice teacher, and one that also involved a special interest in the question of voice simulation). In a paper of 1810, he draws comparisons between the glottis of the human throat and the flue of a flue pipe, as well as between the human tongue and the reed of a reed pipe.[82] Proposing the human vocal anatomy as a model for improvement in the construction of organ pipes, the paper expresses dissatisfaction with pipes having an ill-proportioned "glottis"—especially facade pipes—and with reeds in European organs, which he finds too thin (they yield a meager tone) and flexible (they cause an unpleasant fluttering).

Further extensions of the Simplification System reached beyond the confines of the instrument itself to the architectural environment and its effects on the quality of sounds produced. The larger issue, that of acoustical phenomena and the relationship between architecture and sound, whether in the theater, concert hall, lecture hall, or church, was a special preoccupation of Vogler, and his ideas on the subject are elaborated in a paper entitled "Harmonisch-akustische Bemerkungen über den Theaterbau" [c. 1807].[83] Concerned with the ideal design of a theater, the paper examines ways in which to improve the quality and projection of sound from the standpoint of the stage, the orchestra pit, and the auditorium. Proposals advanced, some of which are as relevant to the church as to the theater, include the installation of specially designed floors, repercussive curtains and screens, and various types of sound reflector.

With specific regard to the organ and its typical surroundings, Vogler's inquiries centered on the notion that the cupola of the church formed an acoustical focal point.[84] To take full advantage of this phenomenon, he recommended that the organ loft be placed as close as possible to a point under the cupola. This would allow maximum resonance and would promote a clear, powerful sound. (Presumably, the small, simplified organs that Vogler advocated would benefit especially from the maximization of sound to be derived from this strategic placement.) Concerning the elevation of the loft, Vogler cautioned that close proximity to the congregation might subject the listeners to excessively harsh and forceful sound from the performers. Excessive height would result in the opposite extreme, and moreover, the organ pipes would be prevented from speaking properly if they were too close to the ceiling. The loft itself, he advised, should have a floor of marble or stone for good reverberation, and its front should be straight, rather than convex or concave, to avoid interference with the placement of musicians and to ensure direct projection of sound. (As a less costly alternative to the marble floor, he suggested that placing beams side by side under the floorboards would help them reflect rather than absorb the sound. This procedure was allegedly followed at the Theater an der Wien, with excellent results, when Vogler oversaw the rebuilding of the floor in the orchestra pit).[85] As for the interior spaces of a church, he observed that a building with many vaults dissipated the focus and caused excessive echoing, while one with many corners blocked the transmission of sound by providing too much resistance.

## THE *ORCHESTRION*

A crucially important factor in Vogler's exploration of organ design and acoustics was the attention he lavished on his *Orchestrion,* the transportable, model instrument that he described as the "cradle of the Simplification System."[86] Concerning the origins of this instrument, Bernhard Anselm Weber reported in 1791 that Vogler, having traveled throughout Europe to perform on the large organs, thereafter intended to build an instrument that surpassed them all.[87] According to Vogler's own, more specific accounts, his aim was to banish the "usual incoherently hissing, trivial organ tone" that he associated with existing instruments, and in its place develop a sound that could so approximate the orchestra as to capture the essence of a popular orchestral concert on the organ.[88]

Initially completed at Rotterdam in 1790,[89] the *Orchestrion* was subject to major changes in subsequent years, chiefly in Stockholm, Copenhagen, and Prague. Writing in 1806, Vogler indicated that he had worked almost continually on the instrument for twenty years in order to simplify it more and more, and at the same time to enrich it with a variety of special effects.[90] In the process, he enlisted the services of Dutch, German, Swedish, and Danish organ builders,[91] prominent names among them including J. P. Kunckel of Rotterdam, G. C. Rackwitz (who completed the reed registers for the *Orchestrion* in Holland and remained in Vogler's employ for eight years),[92] Olaf Schwan of Stockholm, Pehr Schiörlin of Linköping, J. B. Scherr of Copenhagen, Leopold Sauer of Prague, and Georg Christian Knecht (son of Justin Heinrich Knecht), who made substantial changes on the instrument in Prague.

In a preliminary account published early in 1790[93] (almost a year before its completion), Vogler described the *Orchestrion* as having a square base measuring nine feet on each side,[94] and containing four manuals with sixty-three keys each ($F_1$ to $g''''$), thirty-nine pedal keys ($F_1$ to $g'$), twenty-four stop knobs, four bellows, and three swells (wind swell, door swell, and *Progressionsschweller*). Compact and unencumbered by facade pipes, it was designed to be readily dismantled for transport.

While certain features described in Vogler's original account remained constant in later descriptions (the number of manuals and bellows, overall manual and pedal range, size of the case), other aspects underwent modification and improvement, among them the swell mechanisms. Originally three in number, they had apparently been reduced to two by the time Sauer worked on the instrument in the early 1800s. The first, deemed ineffectual by the organ builder, involved door swells placed on either side of the case and on either half of the roof. Sensing that the thin walls of the case did not dampen the sound sufficiently, he replaced walls and doors with thicker wood, lined them with paper, and built channels to relieve excess air pressure. The second swell was a wind swell, to which Sauer added some refinements. It was used exclusively for the free reeds in the version of the instrument he knew, and according to his account it was highly effective.[95] The *Progressionsschweller* was evidently dropped. There is no mention of it either in Sauer's report or in that of an anonymous critic (believed to have been a monk from Salzburg), who heard the instrument at its introductory concert in Prague.[96]

As the *Orchestrion* evolved, the greatest alterations involved the number and selection of pipes. Changes in registration were made in Stockholm, and in Copenhagen the instrument was partially dismantled (a number of pipes and a bellows were removed for use in Vogler's renovation of the organ at the Reformed Church) then reassembled and likewise renovated.[97] In Prague, G. C. Knecht made extensive alterations, after which the number of pipes was reduced, by Vogler's account, to about 840.[98]

The number of pipes originally present in the Rotterdam version is still unknown. A list of registers was available c. 1790 from Varrentrapp and Wenner in Frankfurt as well as Bossler in Speyer,[99] but this crucial piece of evidence remains elusive. Fortunately, a specification that probably represents the early version survives in the "Register-Dispositionen." Depicted in Table 1, this information constitutes a valuable resource, whichever version it represents: it offers insight into Vogler's early ideals, and it reveals precedents for essential features incorporated in Vogler's most important church instrument, the organ at St. Peter's in Munich.

Especially striking in this specification are the departures from traditional approaches to the selection and grouping of registers. The Principals, which traditionally lent the organ its distinctive tone quality, are notably absent, and appropriately so in light of Vogler's intention to create a quasi-orchestral rather than organ-like sound. In keeping with this aim, the theorist chose to equate his manuals with orchestral choirs, reserving one manual for flutes (manual II), another for free reeds (manual III), and yet another for strings and string-like flutes (manual IV). To these he added a manual of mixtures and mutations which included the suitably named Tromba marina register, in which a pairing of 6' and 4' ranks produced a 12' resultant, and the Tromba trias harmonica, a coloristic treble mixture, which yielded a resultant an octave below its lowest-sounding rank and is likely to have reinforced the Tromba marina in the higher octaves.

As for the pedal, Vogler reported in 1802 that it shared pipes with bass portions of the manuals, though he described neither the extent of the sharing nor the coupling or transmission device used to bring it about.[100] To what degree this sharing applied to the specification at hand remains open to conjecture. Unfortunately, the use of differing names for pedal and manual

Table 1. Specification for the *Orchestrion*

| | ORCHESTRION |
|---|---|
| Pedals: Keys $F_1$ to g' | Manuals: Keys $F_1$ to g''' |
| | **IV** |
| *(Tremolo) | Violini 3', $F_1$ – Flauto traverso 1 7/9', d' |
| Viola di Gamba 6' | Viole d'amour 6', $F_1$ – Flauto d'amore 1 1/3', g' |
| | **III** |
| Cornetta 3' | Vox angelica 3', $F_1$ – Fluttuante 3 5/9', d' |
| Clairon 6' | Clarinett 6', $F_1$ – Vox humana 4', c' |
| Serpent 12' | Fagotto ed Oboe 12' |
| | **II** |
| Flauto rustico 1 1/2' | Flauto piccolo 1 1/2', $F_1$ – Ombra 4', c' |
| Flauto dolce 3' | Flûte à bec 3' |
| Sylvana 6' | Flûte à cheminée 6' |
| Basse de Flûte 12' | Flautone 12' |
| | **I** |
| | Rossignol-Cimbalino 1 1/2', 1 1/5', 1', 3/4' |
| | Campanella 2' |
| | Jeu d'acier 2 2/5' |
| Tromba marina 6', 4' | Tromba marina 6', 4' |
| | Tromba Trias harmonica 2', 1 1/3', 1', 4/5', c' |

*Accessory stop (Nebenzug)

registers of the same pitch offers no clue, since Vogler is known to have used two different names for one and the same shared register. Beyond the question of pipe-sharing, the pedal is of interest for its range of thirty-nine keys—wide even by North German standards, and a rarity in southern Germany in Vogler's time.

Also revealed by the specification is the use of divided registers on manuals II, III, and IV. Presumably their purpose was to provide added flexibility and increase the coloristic potential of the instrument. Only five registers were divided, as represented by the pairing of register names. For these pairs, the letter following each name indicates the manual key on which the register begins, and the beginning pitch is that of the pipe length given. Each half register represents an independent unit, and a substantial drop in sounding pitch separates the bass and treble registers. If the specification does indeed represent the Rotterdam version, then the pairs must have each been controlled by a single stop knob, since the instrument supposedly included only twenty-four such knobs.

When Leopold Sauer saw the instrument in Prague, after several meta-morphoses (including Knecht's work on the registers), it had a greater concentration of low registers and included at least one Principal stop. According to his report, there were nearly 900 pipes, distributed among three 12' registers, two 8', three 6', three 4', and several higher registers. Among the registers were a Principal and a Gamba, each 12', as well as six free reeds: Serpent 12', Vox humana 8', Clarinet 6', Basset horn 4', Vox angelica 3', and Oboe 2'. In *Handbuch zur Harmonielehre* (1802), where references made to the *Orchestrion* are likely to reflect changes undertaken in Prague, Vogler remarks on the presence of fourteen full registers, two descant registers, one double register, the use of thirty-five stop knobs, and the capacity to produce 24' pitch. [101]

Using his *Orchestrion* not only as a showcase for organ-building principles but also as a laboratory for acoustical inquiry, Vogler reported on two major experiments that involved the application of acoustical enhancements. The first took place in Stockholm, where he had set up the *Orchestrion* in the home of a man named Roos. Finding that the ceiling of the available room was not high enough to achieve the resonance he desired, Vogler chose to have the *Orchestrion* placed in an adjoining room. A large (apparently) circular opening was then cut in the wall between the two rooms, its purpose being to control the degree, quality, and direction of sound communicated from the instrument to the audience. Dynamics and tone quality were modified by a movable screen operated from the organ console by a pedal mechanism. In addition, a huge copper sound-reflector, shaped like an oversize kettledrum sliced in half, was attached to the lower perimeter of the opening so that it projected outward from the wall on the audience's side. By virtue of this device, vibrations passing from the *Orchestrion* through the opening in the wall would be deflected upward and would then resonate throughout the concert room. [102]

The site of Vogler's second experiment was his special *Orchestrion* room in Prague, at the Charles University. [103] The endeavor involved another attempt to improve the concentration and projection of sound—this time by means of a parabolic wall placed behind the instrument. The wall stood seventeen feet high, measured thirty-eight feet wide, and projected nine feet at the top and bottom. Unfortunately, the *Orchestrion* and its acoustical backdrop proved unsuccessful, and two years later the whole affair was dismantled, despite the theorist's ten-year contract from the government for use of the room.

After this fiasco with the acoustical wall the *Orchestrion* was placed in storage in Prague, and according to Sauer it suffered catastrophic damage there.[104] However, Vogler had plans to rescue it: in a letter of October 27, 1808, he informed Gänsbacher of his intention to visit Prague the following spring, accompanied by G. C. Knecht, the only one he deemed capable of saving this old and costly organ.[105] Eventually Vogler did reclaim or rebuild his instrument, for we encounter an *Orchestrion* again in connection with another, more grandiose project in which parts of the organ were to be incorporated.

In the course of its erratic career, the *Orchestrion* attracted much interest among critics and commentators. Some of Vogler's admirers praised it unconditionally: Schubart extolled the inventor's achievement before the instrument was completed, and Justin Heinrich Knecht wrote of its having twenty-four of the choicest registers, although he never actually heard the instrument.[106] Among those who did hear it and recorded their reactions, there was no consensus on its musical and acoustical merits, and the claim was made that some of the published encomiums originated with Vogler.[107] According to a report of the *Orchestrion*'s inauguration in Amsterdam (November 24–26, 1790), musical amateurs hailed the event as the *ne plus ultra* in the art of playing and building organs.[108] Listeners who heard the instrument in Prague were less enthusiastic. A critic in the *Allgemeine musikalische Zeitung* reported that it proved woefully deficient at the long-awaited concert in the *Orchestrion* hall (April, 1802).[109] In this writer's estimation, the "little organ" ("Orgelchen") lacked substance, its tone so weak that one had to hush his neighbors in order to hear a few tones. In response, the audience supposedly vacillated among laughter, anger, and embarrassment. A second account, found in the anonymous Salzburg manuscript mentioned earlier, was comparably negative, if less sarcastic. According to this author, the Prague concert aroused nothing but disappointment: no one had been able to perceive the promised sonorities of violins, winds, and other instruments, the trumpets and drums having been especially notable failures. Characterizing the instrument as nothing more than a compact organ, he concluded that it did little to bolster Vogler's theories about organ reform or his claims that it could replace an orchestra.

To some extent, discrepancies among accounts may reflect changes that the *Orchestrion* is known to have undergone, as well as differences in its acoustical surroundings. The monk from Salzburg acknowledged the theorist's claim that his instrument had not been completed in time for the notorious Prague concert; and in a letter of April 27, 1802 (in which this claim is made), Vogler reported that within three weeks he planned to give a second *Orchestrion* concert, at which time the organ would include eight additional, newly completed registers.[110]

Such references to improvement, simplification, and alteration lead us to conclude that the *Orchestrion* never did achieve a fixed, final form with which its restless designer might have been content. In this connection it is worth noting that the instrument was not alone among Vogler's keyboard experiments: the *Organochordion,* built by Rackwitz, c. 1791–92, supposedly to Vogler's specifications, consisted of a fortepiano, three and one-half organ registers, internal and external bellows, and devices to modify dynamics.[111] There was also a compact *Micropan,* described by Vogler as having been built between 1802 and 1808 by Knecht and Hagemann of Tübingen. According to a report by Schafhäutl, the *Micropan* made use of remarkably advanced features, including an improved type of spring chest.[112] As for the venerable *Orchestrion* itself, as late as 1806 Vogler was still reporting hopefully on its condition and prospects for the future. It was in storage, he wrote in *Uiber die harmonische Akustik,* awaiting a fourth, acoustically suitable home, where it would appear in vastly superior form.[113]

As reflected in the *Orchestrion,* Vogler's Simplification System challenged accepted standards of construction and sonority as well as technique and performance style. Such an approach was scarcely destined to enjoy a universally warm welcome among contemporary organists and critics. Vogler was nevertheless capable of shrewd salesmanship in promoting the novelty and flexibility of his method, its promise of reduced costs, and its appeal as a product of enlightened progress; thus he did manage to garner support among sovereigns and influential administrators. In 1798, Christian VII of Denmark entrusted him with overhauling the famous organ at Frederiksborg Castle, built by Esaias Compenius in 1610. As Vogler was pleased to report, this early application of his system took all of three hours to execute.[114] Two years later, in 1800, the Prussian monarch Frederick William III commissioned the new organ at Neu-Ruppin, and purportedly issued a decree recommending adoption of the system throughout Prussia, whether in the building of new organs or the redesigning of existing instruments.[115]

Vogler's patron, the Grand Duke of Hesse-Darmstadt, likewise endorsed the Simplification System. A printed circular of around 1808 announced that his court organ builder, Oberndörfer, would construct a model based on Vogler's design, according to which any congregation could have an organ built for the price of a mere 800 Gulden.[116] Compact in appearance and economically designed, this so-called *Normal-Orgel* embodied basic features of the system, including absence of facade pipes, case enclosure, and the capacity to produce low resultants. Containing one manual and a pedal, it made use of only 397 pipes, distributed among divided registers on the manual windchest. For the pedal, Vogler applied the procedure of drawing on registers from the treble half as well as the bass half of the manuals,[117] a device found principally in later projects such as the St. Peter's organ.

Other important commissions were sponsored by the Bavarian court at Munich. These included simplification of an existing organ at the Evangelisches Hofbethaus (1805), construction of a new organ at St. Peter's (1806–1809), and the design of two instruments for the court church of St. Michael: a provisional simplified organ and a new experimental instrument (to be described below) called the *Triorganon*.

Vogler's efforts in building and renovating church organs involved numerous projects in major cities as well as smaller towns, mainly in Germany and Scandinavia. Though the total number of instruments on which he worked cannot be specified with certainty, more than thirty can be documented. Most entailed the redesigning of existing instruments, including those of St. Peter's in Salzburg,[118] St. Mary's in Berlin,[119] St. Nicholas' in Prague, as well as churches in Copenhagen,[120] Würzburg, and Schweidnitz. Changes reportedly undertaken ranged from minor alteration, as in the Compenius organ, to extensive restructuring.

Features of the system that Vogler was able to apply to renovated instruments included partial or even full enclosure and the incorporation of couplers and swells. He also made crucial changes in registration, such as reduction in the number of pipes, replacement of mixtures with individual Terz and Quint registers, redefinition of selected ranks as Terz and Quint registers (chiefly for use in producing low resultants), displacement of ranks to other manuals, and displacement of pipes with respect to the keyboard.

As for the relatively small number of newly designed organs, some idea of Vogler's approach can be gleaned from surviving specification tables and other documents, including those that pertain to instruments in Sweden (Norrköping and Ramsberg),[121] North Germany (Neu-Ruppin), and Bavaria (most notably the Munich commissions mentioned above).

Among the known specifications, most fully representative of the system are those for the St. Peter's organ in Munich. Information on this project published by Vogler includes a description and diagram of its structural layout (*Erklärung der Buchstaben* and *Grundriss,* written 1806),[122] an annotated diagram of the available stops on the instrument (*Verzeichniss der Register* [c. 1808]), and an essay describing its general features (*Kurze Beschreibung,* [1809]). Built between 1806 and 1809 by Franz Frosch, it exemplified many of the theorist's cherished ideals. Since it lacked facade pipes and such attendant complexities as conductors and rollerboards, it could be fully enclosed in a case with the pipes chromatically arranged. To modify the volume, Vogler made use of two devices: a wind swell for three of the five manuals, and a roof swell, which not only altered dynamic levels but also projected the sound upward on a path toward the sound reflector (*Schallspiegel*) provided by the cupola.[123]

In keeping with the theorist's commitment to an orchestrally oriented sound, the disposition of pipes resembled the grouping found in the *Orchestrion.* While one manual was devoted to flutes and another to strings, a third featured a substantial chorus of free reeds (completed by Knecht). But as shown by the specification in Table 2, there was also a strong representation of Principals: two of the five manuals were devoted to Principal choirs.[124] They were designed to complement each other in terms of scale (one wide, the other narrow), and both incorporated complementary *trias harmonica* relationships: 32' and 8' in the first manual, 16' and 4' in the second. As in the Neu-Ruppin organ, wind chests were divided into bass and treble halves, and once again, the manual and pedal shared registers, but now the sharing process included treble pipes.[125]

With regard to the lowest pipes on the instrument, the *Verzeichniss* and *Kurze Beschreibung* both indicate that no pipes lower than 12' were placed on a manual chest: instead they were placed on a pedal chest with its own bellows. Vogler made much of this arrangement in *Kurze Beschreibung* and apparently devised it in response to complaints that placement of low pedal pipes on a

Table 2. Specification for the St. Peter's Organ, Munich[126]

ST. PETER'S ORGAN, MUNICH

| Full bass register | Man. | Pedal Bass: Keys C-g' | Manual Bass: Keys C-b | Manual Treble: Keys c'-c'''' | Pedal Treble: Keys C-g' |
|---|---|---|---|---|---|
| | V | Flute à bec 4', C=c; Flautone 8', C=C | Gemshorn 4', C=c; Basso del Flauto 8', C=C | Flauto piccolo 1', c'=c''; Flauto traverso 2', c'=c' | Spitzflöte 1', C=c''; Flauto dolce 2', C=c' |
| Violonbass 16' [5 pipes], C=$C_1$ | IV | Violoncello 8', C=C; † Contrabasso 12', F=$F_1$ | Viola di Gamba 8', C=C; Theorbe 12', F=$F_1$ | Flagiolet 2', c'=c'; Alto Viola 4', c'=c | Violini 2', C=c''; Gambetta 4', C=c |
| Serpent 16' [5 pipes], C=$C_1$; Bombarde 32' [17 pipes], C=$C_2$ | III | Clarinet 4', C=c; Bassethorn 8', C=C; † Contrafagotto 12', F=$F_1$; † Posaun 12', f=$F_1$ | Trompet 4', C=c; Crumhorn 8', C=C; Contrafagotto 12', F=$F_1$; Posaun 12', f=$F_1$ | Clarino u. Zink 1', c'=c''; Oboe 2', c'=c'; Vox humana 4', c'=c; Fagotto 8', c'=C | Cornetta 1', C=c''; Englisch Horn 2', C=c'; Dulcian 4', C=c; Fagotto 8', C=C |
| Grossnassat 10 2/3' [5 pipes], C=$G_1$; Principal 16' [5 pipes], C=$C_1$ | II | † Grossnassat 8', F=C; † Principal 12', F=$F_1$ | ★ Cimbalino, C=g'', e'''; Principal 1', C=c''; □ Grosscarillon, C=g, e'; Terz 3 1/5', c=e; Principal 4', C=c | ★ Cimbalino, c'=g'''', e''''; Principal 1/4', c'=c''''; □ Grosscarillon, c'=g'', e'''; Terz 1 3/5', c'=e'; Principal 1', c'=c''; Grossnassat 2 2/3', c'=g; Principal 4', c'=c | Quint 2 2/3', C=g; Principal 4', C=c |
| Fundamentalbass 32' [17 pipes] C=$C_2$ | I | Kleinnassat 5 1/3', C=G; Principal 8', C=C; † Principal 12', f=$F_1$ | § Kleincarillon, C=g', e''; Principal 2', C=c[']; Terz 3 1/5', c=e; Kleinnassat 5 1/3', C=G; Principal 8', C=C; Principal 12', f=$F_1$ | § Kleincarillon, c'=g''', e''''; Principal 1/2', c'=c'''; Terz 4/5', c'=e''; Quint 1 1/3', c'=g'; Principal 2', c'=c'; Principal 8', c'=C | Quint 1 1/3', C=g'; Principal 2', C=c'; Principal 8', C=C |

Windauslass, Tremulant

Couplers: manual II to I, III to II, IV to III, V to IV

† The "Register-Dispositionen" omits this register and lists the register to the left in its place as a full bass register.
★ Not cited in "Register-Dispositionen."
□ Carillon in "Register-Dispositionen."
§ Quint 1 1/3' (C=g') and Quint 1/3' (c'=g''') in "Register-Dispositionen."

manual windchest strained the supply of wind available to manual registers. As with the divided registers, each partial rank of low pipes—whether a mere five pipes for the 16′ registers or seventeen for the 32′ registers—had its own stop knob, bringing the total number of stops to seventy-four.

## THE *TRIORGANON*

Related in principle, though more ambitious and complex than any of the other projects, was the *Triorganon*. This "monument to the science of organ building," as Vogler described it,[127] was to have been a decisive, culminating achievement, perhaps a magnification of the Simplification System and its possibilities. According to his grandiose plan, there were to be three adjacent, connected consoles, to be played either simultaneously by three organists, or by a single performer controlling the entire instrument from one console.[128] In all, there were to be as many as thirteen manuals—five for the main, central console and four each for the smaller consoles to either side—and three pedalboards. In the disposition of register types, Vogler followed the orchestral arrangement of the St. Peter's organ: principal choirs in the first and second manuals (in one manual only for each of the flanking organs); and the reeds, strings, and flutes respectively in each of the remaining manuals.

As depicted in the "Register-Dispositionen," twenty-four registers are assigned to the central console. All are divided into bass and treble halves in accordance with Vogler's usual practice. The two side consoles are given twelve divided registers each, allocated in such a way that together they equal the full complement of registers of the main organ and are identical to them in name and pitch—an arrangement that clearly implies pipe sharing.

Within the pedalboard, a comparable duplication occurs between registers of the main console and those of the side consoles. To what extent, if any, a sharing of manual pipes with the pedal was intended remains uncertain. But it is worth noting that nearly half of the named pedal registers have no discernible manual counterparts. These include high as well as low registers, among them a true 48′ rank and registers capable of producing a 48′ resultant.

To assemble the *Triorganon,* Vogler planned to incorporate pipes from other instruments, including the *Orchestrion*. As revealed in a letter of December 10, 1812 to the Grand Duke, he had brought pipes from Darmstadt to Munich six months earlier to be used for the project along with pipes from the *Orchestrion* and two other instruments in his possession, presumably the *Micropan* and *Organochordion.*

Vogler's contract for construction of the *Triorganon,* awarded in 1809, specified that the job was to be finished by September 29 (Michaelmas), 1812. Meanwhile he was to complete a provisional organ (actually a renovation of an existing instrument) by 1810. But he did not come close to meeting these terms: becoming obsessively involved with the provisional instrument, not finished until October 1812, he evidently envisaged something far grander than what was originally intended. Communicating to the Grand Duke on August 16, 1812, he wrote of a plan to turn it into a more powerful organ than any in Bavaria, including that of St. Peter's. Upon its completion, he claimed that it was an instrument in which four-fifths of the *Triorganon* could be heard—perhaps not too wild an exaggeration, for even though it had only two manuals, it did contain a substantial number of registers.

As for the *Triorganon* itself, Vogler learned of plans to annul his contract, the provisional organ having been judged sufficient. In a letter to his patron on December 20, 1812, he described at length this "most oppressive catastrophe" of his life which, if it came to pass, would mean the loss of his *Orchestrion* and ensuing financial ruin.

Although he absolved himself of all blame, this was by no means the first time he had been in financial trouble with his instruments. Years earlier, for example, he had had difficulty reclaiming the *Orchestrion* after his return from Africa because of a sum of money he owed to J. P. Kunckel, the Dutch organ builder.[129] But the *Triorganon* debacle proved especially traumatic. Writing again to the Grand Duke on January 15, 1813, he declared that an "ill-fated hour has struck"—his contract has been annulled, and he has been plunged into bankruptcy.

The magnitude of the St. Michael's project and the theorist's intention to have it swallow up the *Orchestrion* cause one to reasonably suspect that he may have become disenchanted with his system's emphasis on minimal materials and compactness of design. Popular as its limitations had been with certain court and church authorities, the artist himself clearly retained a taste for projects that were more promising musically, if rather more challenging financially as well. In the draft of a letter to his patron, dated April 1810 (while he was still under contract to build the provisional organ and *Triorganon* at Munich), he writes of a plan to build for the cathedral at Frankfurt either another *Triorganon* "or perhaps an organ with five manuals of sixty-eight keys each and an acoustical . . . bass of 48′ pitch."[130]

Could it be that these later endeavors reflected not only Vogler's urge to extend the horizons of his experiments, but also his response to critics' disapproval of the system and its tendency to yield disappointing results? Optimistically (and perhaps naively), the theorist had promoted the Simplification System as something of a magical remedy, offering economy, correction of existing weaknesses, and the creation of a new sound ideal. Yet from surviving contemporary criticism it appears that the applications of his principles often delivered less than they promised.

### CRITICISM OF THE SYSTEM

Much of the controversy stirred by his instruments centered on the difference tones, to which Vogler was heavily committed on the strength of their cost-saving and wind-saving potential. But did they really work as a replacement for low-sounding pipes? The theorist himself cited experiments in which his resultants proved either superior to, or indistinguishable from, the corresponding pitches produced by conventional means;[131] even Wilke, who was severely critical of the system, conceded that the *trias harmonica* functioned like a true register in the Neu-Ruppin organ. Wilke did, however, judge the resultant registers to be less effective, and he expressed reservations about the quality and power of their sound.[132] Clearly there were problems with the difference tones. Critics complained that the pipes had to be exactly in tune in order for the *trias harmonica* to function properly.[133] G. C. F. Schlimbach, the cantor and organ theorist, pondered the results of Vogler's work on the organ at St. Mary's in Berlin and denounced his infatuation with the difference tone as a misguided whim that had sprung from Tartini's fantasy.[134] The famous physicist E. F. F. Chladni (1756–1827) called attention to a specific, basic flaw: the low resultants were comparatively weak, he observed, so that the higher tones producing them were more audible. He reported that at St. Mary's, Vogler's configuration of pipes had to be dismantled and the large pipes restored to the organ at great expense.[135]

Difficulties also surfaced with the principle of reinforcement, specifically with the use of displaced registers that entered in the second and third octaves of the keyboard to strengthen the *trias harmonica* in the bass or to compensate for pipe reduction in the treble. The procedure is reported to have caused an unevenness or discontinuity of sound, particularly with full organ,[136] and was disparaged by Wilke as an unsuccessful attempt to deceive the ear.[137]

Vogler's concept of duplication was likewise attacked. Schlimbach, for example, challenged him to identify one true duplicate among the ranks he had removed from the St. Mary's organ.[138] Other commentators questioned the very premises of Vogler's elimination of duplicate ranks, which were seen by at least one writer as a potentially effective means of projecting and clarifying an instrument's sound.[139]

To judge from some accounts of Vogler's simplification projects, his procedures could lead to unqualified disasters. Schlimbach, whose remarks on the overhauled St. Mary's organ sharply contradicted Vogler's own claims, declared that the instrument had been plundered, and he likened the new specification to the work of the most ignorant and capricious organ builder imaginable. Among the pieces of evidence he adduced were changes made in the Fernwerk manual, which now joined the weakest with the most blatant and screeching registers. Schlimbach could only conclude that Vogler's actions were irresponsible, the whole job a lamentable negation of cherished principles of organ construction.[140]

Wilke's judgment of the new organ at Neu-Ruppin was scarcely less devastating. He concluded that instead of the powerful, large, and energetic sounds a listener might have expected, the tones were weak, rumbling, and indistinct. The variety implicit in the seventy-two stop knobs was absent too: after subtraction of the six non-sounding stops and division of the remainder in two to adjust for the divided-register arrangement, Wilke determined that the instrument really possessed only twenty-three sounding registers; and that total could be even further reduced to about sixteen "low and grumbling" registers if all the Terz, Quint, and Octave stops were regarded collectively as mixtures.[141] Elaborating his complaint about the organ's tone quality, he observed that the stopped wood pipes Vogler used in lower registers, while less costly than metal, could not produce the full-bodied sound needed to accompany a congregation. (This was at least in part a reflection of differing tastes, the North Germans preferring metal pipes, while the softer tones produced by wood pipes were favored in the south.) Moreover, he felt that Vogler's virtual elimination of separate pedal ranks caused him to include an overabundance of lower registers in the manuals, with a resulting chaos of rumbling tones when all stops were pulled.[142]

Other complaints called attention to problems that affected the organist more directly. One critic wrote of difficulty in playing chords in the low registers, and in executing fugues and trios to which the organ was otherwise so eminently suited.[143] Wilke raised the basic issue that Vogler seemed out of touch with the practical needs of the church organist. Among other problems with the Neu-Ruppin organ, he cited the confusing arrangement of the stop knobs, so disorganized for the sake of mechanical efficiency as to hinder the task of registration; the unfortunate placement of the instrument, from which it was impossible to see the minister for proper and timely cues; and the lack of daylight reaching the organ.[144] Other, related criticisms focused on the difficulty experienced by congregations in attempting to follow a hymn, and on noisy mechanisms that distracted the worshipper.[145]

Complaints about the elimination of mixtures were especially emphatic. These were the "sharply cutting registers" that lent definition and clarity to an organ's sound, and were also widely regarded as indispensable for keeping a congregation in tune.[146] Even among those who shared Vogler's views on abuses with regard to mixtures (such as those with ten, twelve, and more ranks), there were critics who thought that smaller, well-constructed mixtures were indispensable.[147]

Reactions such as these were typical of organists and organ builders. Schlimbach denounced the Simplification System as the ruination of the organ, and the builder Friedrich Marx stated flatly that he would be ashamed to construct an organ according to the system.[148] In light of such resistance and disapproval, it is not surprising to find Vogler's innovations and simplifications being excised at the request of bewildered and disgruntled users obliged to cope with the instruments' idiosyncrasies. Not even the St. Peter's organ in Munich could escape change in the face of attacks by the church's organist, Johann Baptist Mossmayr, who relentlessly condemned Vogler's system as unworkable despite generally favorable critiques of the organ and a positive reaction from the court. On the advice of Caspar Ett, a Vogler supporter, changes were kept to a minimum. Still, the pedalboard was reduced from thirty-two to eighteen keys, a pipe facade was restored, and both the roof swell and the second of five manuals were removed altogether.[149]

It was in this form that the young Felix Mendelssohn came to know the St. Peter's organ in the autumn of 1831, during an extended stay in Munich. He described it at length to his sister, Fanny, in a remarkable passage:

I also play the organ daily for one hour, but cannot practice as I would like to, because the pedal is short by five high notes, so that passages of Seb. Bach cannot be played on it. But it contains exquisite registers, with which one can improvise on chorales; I am edified by the divine, flowing tone of the instrument; especially, Fanny, I have found registers here with which Seb. Bach's *Schmücke dich, o liebe Seele* must be played. It is as though they were made for it, and [the music] sounds so moving that it always fills me with awe when I begin it. For the moving parts, I have an 8' flute and a very gentle 4', which continually hovers over the chorale—you surely know it from Berlin. But for the chorale [melody], there is a manual that contains only reed registers, and from it I take a gentle Hoboe, a very soft Clairon 4', and a Viola. That draws out the chorale so quietly and so penetratingly, as though human voices from afar were singing it from the depths of their hearts.[150]

How different from the critiques of Wilke, Schlimbach, and the others! Mendelssohn's appreciation for the kind of sound Vogler envisaged is readily apparent, and his description helps shed light on much of the antipathy that Vogler suffered. Clearly, a central problem with the system was its distance from the mainstream of common practice and the consequent difficulty it posed for the modestly gifted, traditionally trained church organist. Schafhäutl, pondering the resistance with which the system was met, observed that when Vogler himself performed on the simplified organs, listeners were enchanted, but that their enthusiasm faded when the instruments were left to local organists.[151] In developing the system, Vogler had considered his own needs as a performing artist, and the organ on which he tested his theories was a concert instrument—a compact, transportable one at that. Inevitably, it seemed, an instrument designed or overhauled according to Vogler's methods was more likely to please the virtuoso tone painter than the accompanist of a congregation. After his renovation of the Evangelisches Hofbethaus organ, a report prepared by the court organist concluded that the instrument was not truly a church organ at all, but rather a "Galanterie Orgel" more suited to chamber or concert-hall performance.[152]

In the end, the system as an entity did not gain acceptance, other than in the work of several builders, especially G. C. Knecht, who was closely associated with the theorist, and who promoted the construction of organs built according to his specifications.[153] Yet Vogler's work in this realm was not without significant influence, even though the nature of his impact was largely indirect and intangible. As suggested by Wilke and other organ specialists of the time, the controversy surrounding the system helped call attention to certain concepts, resources, and structural possibilities hitherto ignored or forgotten, but now ripe for further exploration and development. In an essay published in 1836, Wilke detailed various areas in which elements of Vogler's method, while not new, served as a much-needed stimulus to contemporaries.[154] Those areas he specified were the exploitation of difference tones, the use of free reeds, the abolition of mixtures, and also distinctive structural aspects, notably the application of swell mechanisms.

But perhaps the most significant of Vogler's influences lies in his exploration of new sound ideals and functional possibilities for the organ—most notably his promotion of a secular, theatrical style that abandoned conventional assumptions in favor of the model provided by the modern orchestra and its wide palette of colors and dynamic contrasts. In this respect, his accomplishments mirror the distinctive qualities of his endeavors in other fields: a rational, enlightened premise (in this instance the goal of simplification and economy), pursued with an irrepressible energy and yen for progress, leading to fresh and innovative results through creative experimentation with existing customs and materials.

❦ ❧

# Epilogue

" **M**AY Madame Authority be banned forever from [the company of] scholars and artists. . . . Along with the eighteenth century, [she] must give up the ghost under convulsions. No longer, because a great theorist so believed, must it so be; no more, because a prominent composer so wrote, must it be good. Wake up, you blind adherents, you bourgeois Lilliputians, from your lethargic slumber! Listen! (To musical works.) See! (Musical scores.) Sense! (The resulting effects.) And think!"[1]

Greeting the new century, this exhortation from the close of *Choral-System* conveys Vogler's sense of his mission as artist and teacher. Art, he maintained, was governed by natural laws, and progress must be achieved by penetrating the secrets of musical organization. Challenging the stultifying forces of tradition and authority, he envisaged a harmonious universe whose potentials could be tapped through the guidance of reason, taste, and the knowledge of enduring truths.

Despite the ambitious scope of his rhetoric, Vogler's realm was by no means unbounded. It was restricted in part by certain creative, technical, and artistic limitations, and in part by his adherence to an eighteenth-century rationalist outlook. Evidently beyond his field of vision were such radical experiments as Anton Reicha's *Trente-six fugues* (listed in the catalogue of his library but ignored in the *System für den Fugenbau*), and the unprecedented individuality witnessed in Beethoven, whose imposing presence and monumental rhetoric overshadowed Vogler along with many other contemporaries. He nevertheless stands out as an open-minded and adventurous figure whose liberated spirit endowed him with a vantage point from which to criticize existing styles as well as contribute his own creative efforts.

According to the view that emerges from his writings, musical progress is continuous and open ended. He sees no dichotomy between the music of his predecessors and that of his day, nor between the music of the late eighteenth and the early nineteenth centuries. The art nevertheless advances, and as the critic glances over his shoulder at a given point in the past (as in his essay that accompanied the revised *Deutsche Kirchenmusik*), certain contrasts in style and technique become apparent. While recent music betrays greater diversity and a more specialized coordination of rhythm, harmony, dynamics, and texture, national differences have converged in an international style, and different idioms, previously distinct, now mingle and enrich one another. The modern orchestra inspires a new approach to the organ. Sacred music receives nourishment from the past while benefiting from recent progress in secular music. And music of the theater, by lending its harmonic and sonorous richness to instrumental genres, supplies them with an expressive language of unlimited eloquence. As the mixing of styles and genres spills over from European to exotic non-European traditions, the chromatic and modulatory capacity of the harmonic language expands, and the palette of available colors is extended through improved knowledge of acoustics and instrumental possibilities.

Given the multiplicity of choices the composer faced, the imposition of rational order proved essential. The related concepts of tonal hierarchy and harmonic reduction furnished a guide to compositional practice as well as a key to understanding the unity of a composition. Inviting extension along with the contemporary expansion of musical resources, they retained their usefulness as Vogler discovered new implications of his theory and sought to apply his teachings to the explanation of far-reaching tonal excursions.

However pertinent Vogler's lessons may have been to his day, they were destined to be largely ignored or misunderstood. His presentations of the harmonic system, such as those found in *Tonwissenschaft und Tonsezkunst* and *Handbuch zur Harmonielehre,* lacked an adequate explanation of how his ideas might apply in practice; and the published analyses, dissociated from any clear account of principles on which the concepts of hierarchy and reduction were based, proved difficult to comprehend in the absence of any conventional vocabulary or procedure.

Portions of Vogler's theories were nevertheless disseminated in central and northern Europe, largely by virtue of his pedagogical endeavors (at Mannheim, in Scandinavia, and also at Prague, where his *Harmonielehre* enjoyed numerous printings)[2] and through his sporadically successful efforts to gain official endorsement for his methods. As Leopold Mozart reported to his son in 1778, the *Kuhrpfälzische Tonschule* had been prescribed by the government of the Palatinate "for the use of all clavier teachers in the country, both for singing and composition";[3] and according to a notice in the *Allgemeine musikalische Zeitung* in 1800, the Danish government had 100 copies of Vogler's *Musik-skole* purchased and distributed for the benefit of organists and other musicians.[4]

In a number of German and Austrian harmony manuals from the early nineteenth century, signs of Vogler's influence, either direct or indirect, are apparent. Heinrich Christoph Koch's *Handbuch bei dem Studium der Harmonie* (1811), which constitutes a revision of the material on harmony in *Versuch einer Anleitung zur Composition* (1782–93), parallels Vogler's approach in numerous respects, including the extraction of a major chord from the acoustical properties of a single tone, derivation of a so-called natural scale from the eighth through sixteenth partials of the harmonic series, and construction of the artificial, diatonic major scale from tones of three adjacent, fifth-related triads. Other ideas that seem like possible echoes of Vogler (and are not found in the earlier *Versuch*) include Koch's identification of the raised-fourth scale degree as a leading tone to the dominant, the use of a triad on that degree to form a half cadence ($\sharp$IV–V), and the derivation of the augmented sixth chord from the diminished third to which the $\sharp$IV gives rise in minor.[5]

Further resemblances to Vogler may be seen in Koch's explanation of dissonance. Here, far more explicitly than in the *Versuch,* we encounter the procedure that Vogler had borrowed from Vallotti and adopted as a cornerstone of his own system: the derivation of suspension dissonances from outside the octave, so that consonant notes (which by inversion might be found situated a second, fourth, or sixth above the bass) could be distinguished from true dissonances above a triadic root, i.e., the ninth, eleventh, and thirteenth.[6]

A similar though less direct connection may be drawn between Vogler's principle of *Mehrdeutigkeit* and the early nineteenth-century theory of modulation proposed by Anton Reicha (1770–1836). Reicha's classification of modulations, which involves specifying the number of intermediate chords needed to connect two keys, includes examples of remote relationships (for example E-flat to E, or C to F-sharp) in which the modulatory path requires the same enharmonic spelling of diminished-seventh and augmented-sixth chords featured in Vogler's own tables of modulation.[7] Although Reicha, like Koch, could doubtless have arrived at his formulations independently of any direct Vogler influence, the correspondences are striking. If nothing else, they underscore the extent of common ground shared by these contemporary approaches.

A sharper reflection of Vogler's ideas can be seen in the work of several Viennese theorists whose manuals incorporated specific features of the system. Emanuel Aloys Förster, whose writings mention both Vogler and Knecht,[8] adopts the procedure of building triads on each scale degree and supplying each with a Roman numeral;[9] and Joseph Drechsler's *Harmonie und Generalbass-Lehre,* in which the abbé is praised as an organist,[10] likewise adopts the Roman numerals and describes a hierarchic concept of modulation recalling that found in Vogler's theory.

Such resemblances suggest that his system did to some extent address contemporary needs by offering systematic procedures for chord construction, identification of chord roots, dissonance treatment, and modulation. Yet the tone of his writings, speculative and often incoherent, was clearly out of step with the relatively pragmatic temperament of the times. A rationalist experimenter at heart, he suffered the practical musician's disdain for theoretical systems. And though he himself contributed impetus to the growing institutionalization of musical training, this was a trend that required methods more concrete and unproblematical than his. As a result, the influence of his teachings fell mainly on disciples and associates who enjoyed the advantage of first-hand acquaintance. Their warm enthusiasm, by comparison with the relative indifference of Vogler's contemporaries at large, indicates that such contact was essential to an appreciation of his principles and their application.

Pupils' testimony suggests that his instruction furnished a reliable guide from rudimentary knowledge of tonal organization to the creation of original compositions. Yet the actual nature and extent of his influence is difficult to assess. Those who gained rudimentary training from him received a schooling that in many respects resembled that experienced by students of other methods. And in the realm of more advanced studies, the degree of his impact remains indeterminate: there were too many sources of influence at work to permit ascribing a given pupil's accomplishment to a particular stimulus without more extensive study of the pupils in question—their training, the influences to which they were exposed, and the nature of their artistic development. Thus the question of how certain pupils' later development might represent an outgrowth—or perhaps a denial—of their studies with Vogler remains a topic for future investigation.

Be that as it may, the history of late eighteenth- and early nineteenth-century music embraces a generous scattering of musicians whose artistic personalities and contributions appear to have been shaped to some extent by Vogler and his teachings. Among the roster of early pupils, most illustrious of all was the opera composer Peter Winter (1754–1825), whose stage works for Munich, Prague, and Vienna earned him recognition as a leading theater composer of his generation.[11] To his name may be added those of Franz Danzi (1763–1826), the Mannheim cellist who served as deputy kapellmeister at Munich under Winter before eventually becoming kapellmeister at Karlsruhe; the cellist and composer Peter Ritter (1763–1846), associated for most of his career with the National Theater at Mannheim, where he was appointed kapellmeister in 1803; and the blind pianist and composer Maria Theresia von Paradis (1759–1824), who achieved international renown as a virtuoso performer, and who dedicated several compositions to her master.

Other pupils included Bernhard Anselm Weber (1764–1821), whose early encounter with Vogler at Mannheim was the first of several: they traveled together from the end of 1790 until the master's departure for the Mediterranean in 1792; and later still, he made contact with the abbé as Meyerbeer's teacher prior to the young Berliner's move to Darmstadt. Unrelated to Bernhard Anselm or the other Webers acquainted with Vogler was Friedrich Dionys Weber (1766–1842), whose manuals reflected both the spirit and substance of his mentor's writings. A student of Vogler at Mannheim who later attended his lectures at Prague (1801–2), Weber contributed to the founding of the Prague Conservatory and became director of the new institution in 1811.

Among the disciples who became theorists and teachers in their own right, none took it upon himself to transmit the system intact. Yet Vogler did have an articulate and widely respected champion, the Biberach kapellmeister, organist, and theorist Justin Heinrich Knecht. The author of several widely circulated texts, including *Gemeinnützliches Elementarwerk der Harmonie und des Generalbasses* (Augsburg, 1792–98)[12] and *Allgemeiner musikalischer*

*Katechismus* (Biberach, 1803), Knecht assumed the role of chief apologist. He defended the master's theories against critics' attacks,[13] and his own pedagogical works were largely devoted to clarifying and elaborating Vogler's ideas.

But as Vogler himself complained, Knecht's well-meaning efforts may have done the older theorist something of a disservice: his account of rudimentary principles tended to focus on details at the expense of the larger picture; and his comprehension of the system, stopping far short of the reduction theory expounded in *Zwei und dreisig Präludien* and *System für den Fugenbau,* was marked by an unfortunate tendency to emphasize the tabulation of chord types. Whereas Vogler's own litany of statistics (encompassing seven sevenths, eighteen intervals, and forty-four modulations from any given pitch) served to bolster his chain of deductions by furnishing a semblance of mathematical precision, Knecht's formidable tallies (for example his total of 6,336 modulations) seemed more like a caricature of the Vogler approach than a realization of its possibilities.[14]

Of greatest historical interest was Vogler's role as teacher of Carl Maria von Weber and Giacomo Meyerbeer, on whom he appears to have exerted decisive influence. According to the pupils' own accounts, his guidance contributed to the formation of their mature compositional styles, and by promoting the performance of their early works, he helped launch their theatrical careers.[15] A letter by Weber from Vienna in 1803 describes his total immersion in Vogler's theory, as well as an unflinching commitment to the thankless task of preparing a piano-vocal score of *Samori*.[16] The young Weber's compositions from that time included keyboard works based on Vogler themes (the sets of variations on themes from *Castore e Polluce* and *Samori*), and he specifically described the former as being composed according to the system.[17]

It is remarkable that Weber, having begun a promising career following his studies with Vogler in Vienna, returned to his master to resume the role of disciple at Darmstadt as late as 1810. He was joined there by others who were likewise scarcely beginners: Johann Gänsbacher, like Weber, was a professional musician who had also been a pupil of Vogler at Vienna; Meyerbeer had already undergone rigorous training in Berlin under Carl Friedrich Zelter and B. A. Weber; and Gottfried Weber was an experienced critic and practical musician.

Activities undertaken by this *harmonischer Verein,* as the group called themselves,[18] included analyses of compositions by Vogler and others, critiques of one another's work, sessions of listening to the master's improvisations, and exercises in the art of *Verbesserung* (the latter practice reflected in the *Zwölf Choräle* publication, a project in which Gottfried Weber apparently collaborated with Carl Maria von Weber). The disciples' involvement with Vogler's teachings is further reflected in the traces of Vogler terminology that crop up in their letters and budding journalistic endeavors.[19] Major compositions were undertaken with his supervision, and at one point, while Vogler was at work on his *Singspiel, Der Admiral,* he proposed that Meyerbeer compose a setting of the same text for comparison. Carl Maria von Weber's review of Meyerbeer's opera *Alimelik* emphasizes the importance of the young musician's study with Vogler to the development of his style; and the list of music and books he had shipped to Paris (1829) included numerous Vogler compositions in addition to the *System für den Fugenbau.*[20]

The devotion of Vogler's pupils presents a vivid contrast to the negative appraisals often encountered on the part of nineteenth-century scholars. Lacking any predisposition in his favor, and insufficiently familiar with the actual content of his writings, critics tended to belittle his contribution while perpetuating misinformation about his system. The judgment of François Joseph Fétis in his *Traité complet de la théorie et de la pratique de l'harmonie* was especially harsh, and also ill informed. Following a three-page summary that thoroughly misinterprets Vogler's derivation of dissonances and its relationship to his principle of reduction, he concludes that "such a theory [as Vogler's] constitutes the negation of any true theory, for it reduces art and science to a collection of absurd, disconnected facts, opposed to good harmonic sense."[21]

Following his predecessor's footsteps all too closely, Hugo Riemann chose to omit Vogler's name from either the index or the table of contents of his *Geschichte der Musiktheorie.* Possibly even less familiar with the substance of the abbé's writings than Fétis, he ignores the correspondences between Vogler's theory and Koch's *Handbuch,* and he credits Gottfried Weber with the notion of *Mehrdeutigkeit.* Vogler himself is dismissed with the claim "that between Rameau and Weber . . . chord construction by stacking of thirds declined to the most senseless results through Abt Vogler and especially his pupil Justin Heinrich Knecht," whose work ran counter to Rameau's efforts to simplify harmonic theory by nurturing an "impenetrable thicket" of possible chord types.[22]

Matthew Shirlaw was scarcely better informed than Riemann. His widely read *Theory of Harmony* (1917) allots two brief sentences to Vogler, one of which transmits an erroneous statement by Fétis about the alleged division of the string as far as the thirty-second term.[23] The status of Shirlaw's book as a standard reference source on which English-speaking readers have relied for several generations meant that his disdain was especially devastating. Surely it bears at least some of the blame for the persisting neglect of Vogler and his contribution.

Having foreseen both resistance and eventual acceptance of his ideas, Vogler was not inaccurate in his predictions.[24] But with the gradual adoption of that feature of his system which proved most fruitful—the reduction of vertical sonorities to scale-degree roots designated by Roman numerals—the man himself and his pioneering role were forgotten. Ironically, this product of Vogler's rationalism became associated instead with the adamant empiricist Gottfried Weber who, despite his association with Vogler, claimed to despise rational systems in general and asserted that his own theory was based solely on the observed practices of composers.[25]

Gottfried Weber's adoption of the Roman numerals in his *Versuch einer geordneten Theorie der Tonsetzkunst* (1817–21) was historically important in paving the way for their wide acceptance in the latter part of the nineteenth century. His presentation reveals insight into their usefulness in labeling chord functions, but it also betrays a limited perception of their more far-reaching potentials. For Weber, the Roman numerals furnished an identifying tag for each chord in terms of its quality and function in a specific, foreground sense. He used capital and lower-case numerals to distinguish between major and minor quality, added the arabic superscript "7" to identify seventh chords, and accompanied his Roman numerals with capital or lower-case letters to signify their relationship to a particular major or minor key. However precise, this approach imposed limitations to which Vogler himself was not constrained. As witnessed in the older theorist's own analyses (such as those of the *Davids Buss-Psalm, Zwei und dreisig Präludien,* and *System für den Fugenbau*), the functional designation of a given chord was relative and flexible: the succession ♯IV–V in major, for example, could be interpreted in a more local sense as VII–I. And the absence of symbols to specify keys meant that the structural significance assigned by the numerals remained open ended. The greater specificity of Weber's symbols, in other words, was achieved at the expense of the fluidity of Vogler's original concept.

It is for this reason that Vogler's approach seems closer than Weber's to the epoch-making theories of Heinrich Schenker as expounded in his *Harmonielehre* of 1906.[26] We have no evidence linking Schenker with Vogler's writings. Indeed, Schenker's comments on the divergence between his ideas and those of his predecessors suggest that he would have been astonished by the parallels between some of his own concepts and the analyses found in Vogler's *Präludien* and in the late fugue treatise. Like Vogler's writings, Schenker's *Harmonielehre* proposed a rationalistic notion of harmonic unity. Both theorists reasoned in comparable fashion from their initial premises to deductions that led from a tonic note and its natural triad to the construction of a hierarchic system that incorporated scales, chords on each scale degree, a vocabulary of dissonances (here Schenker followed a different path from Vogler), and a concept of nested functional relationships that served to explain tonal unity and elaboration on multiple levels of structure. For Vogler as well as for Schenker, the Roman numerals designated not only chord functions within a key, but also potential points of reference for tonal elaboration in which a designated degree could function temporarily as a tonic without losing its scale-step identity as part of a larger tonal picture.

In other respects, the two theorists' systems are scarcely comparable, and of course the cleavage between harmony and counterpoint found in Vogler's approach virtually excluded the possibility of exploring a linear dimension within the framework of his theory. But Vogler's glimmer of insight nonetheless established an important precedent by elevating the scale step to the position of a central point of reference. According to his system, it signified a functional relationship to a tonic, while at the same time laying potential claim to the status of a tonic in its own right. The scale step thus formed a link between the musical surface and the fundamental, triadic basis of all harmonic organization. In Vogler's writings, the idea led to experiments that mingled Roman numerals, thoroughbass numbers, and a spontaneously metaphorical vocabulary of tonal hegemony, strife, and reconciliation in the attempt to explain aspects of tonal unity, elaboration, movement, and tension.

Readily fashioned from traditional rationalist assumptions as well as from observations of contemporary practice, the concept of harmonic reduction would appear to have been scarcely foreign to other late eighteenth-century composers, performers, and theorists. Indeed, Vogler's teachings underscore the great extent to which such a concept was inherent in the customary musical language of the time. The true novelty of Vogler's teachings, and the historically important, pathbreaking effort with which he deserves to be credited, has to do less with his invention of new systems than with the application of his principles to projects in musical analysis and criticism. His procedures, which appear to have anticipated our modern need to examine, criticize, and impose order on processes of tonal organization, were still relatively new in his own time, only much later acquiring status as standard ingredients of musical training and learned discussion.[27]

In retrospect, it appears that Vogler was well suited both by temperament and experience to play such a historical role. A self-styled maverick, he was restrained neither by habitual adherence to pedagogical conventions (such as thoroughbass or Fuxian counterpoint) nor by the traditional pragmatism of the composer or performer. Bolstered by his rationalist convictions, which furnished the self-assurance he needed to pursue his ideals, he succeeded in articulating otherwise unspoken concepts of musical form and content.

As carried out in the abbé's writings and compositions, the effort yielded a fresh perspective on the nature of historical change and continuity in music of the late eighteenth and early nineteenth centuries. For in linking his vision of an enduring tonal order to his quest for progress, he demonstrated ways of comprehending this era not only in terms of the distinctions between one generation and another, but from the standpoint of stylistic continuities and dynamic, evolutionary processes. In light of this accomplishment, he surely merits respect as a worthy spokesman for his times.

◆§ ?◆

# Notes

## INTRODUCTION

1. Carl Maria von Weber, *Writings on Music,* trans. Martin Cooper, ed. John Warrack (Cambridge: Cambridge University Press, 1981), p. 253.

2. Weber, *Writings on Music,* "A Word on Vogler," pp. 43–45; "An Incident in Abt Vogler's Youth," pp. 187–89.

3. Donald J. Grout, *A History of Western Music,* 3d ed. (New York: W. W. Norton, 1980), p. 626.

4. Paul Henry Lang, *Music in Western Civilization* (New York: W. W. Norton, 1941), p. 589.

5. Principal early biographical sources include Ernst Ludwig Gerber, *Historisch-biographisches Lexicon der Tonkünstler,* 2 vols. (Leipzig, 1790–92), and *Neues historisch-biographisches Lexikon der Tonkünstler,* 4 vols. (1812–14), to which C. M. von Weber contributed material; Felix Joseph Lipowsky, *Baierisches Musik-Lexikon* (Munich, 1811); and Joseph Fröhlich, *Biographie des grossen Tonkünstlers Abt Georg Joseph Vogler* (Würzburg, 1845).

6. According to the diary of Cajetan Hagenauer, friend of the Mozart family who made Vogler's acquaintance in Salzburg in 1805, Vogler hoped to travel to Moscow and even Peking with his transportable organ, the *Orchestrion.* See excerpts from the diary in Hermann Spies, *Abbé Vogler und die von ihm 1805 simplifizierte Orgel von St. Peter in Salzburg* (Mainz: Paul Smets, 1932), p. 6.

7. In *Tonwissenschaft und Tonsezkunst* (Mannheim, 1776), p. 82, the symbol VII identifies the function of a diminished seventh chord built on the seventh degree of the scale. The *Gründe der kuhrpfälzischen Tonschule in Beispielen* (musical supplement to *Kuhrpfälzische Tonschule,* 2 vols. [Mannheim, 1778]) employs Roman

numerals for seventh chords and cadences. Found sporadically in *Betrachtungen der Mannheimer Tonschule,* Roman-numeral chord designations are further employed in articles written by Vogler for the *Deutsche Encyclopädie,* and in other writings that include the Swedish manual *Inledning til harmoniens kännedom* (1794), *Handbuch zur Harmonielehre* (1802), and several published essays. Cf. Arno Lemke, *Jacob Gottfried Weber: Leben und Werk* (Mainz: B. Schott's Söhne, 1968), pp. 33, 207, where the invention of the device is ascribed to Weber.

8. See Chapter 5, pp. 216–17.

9. *Allgemeine musikalische Zeitung* 2 (1799–1800): 494–95. The report also notes a prosperous trade on the part of ticket scalpers.

10. *Neue Zeitschrift für Musik* 8 (1838): 111.

11. See *Allgemeine musikalische Zeitung* 26 (1824): 585. The practice is reported earlier in a letter of 1811 from C. M. von Weber to Gottfried Weber, excerpted in Karl Emil von Schafhäutl, *Abt Georg Joseph Vogler* (Augsburg, 1888), p. 226. Cf. Carl Maria von Weber, *Writings on Music,* p. 166, n. 4.

12. According to a letter of January 15, 1813 by Vogler (Darmstadt, Hessisches Staatsarchiv, D 4, Nr. 695).

13. The promotion to second kapellmeister no later than this time is supported by a document of February 28, 1776, in which he is so described (Karlsruhe, Generallandesarchiv, Pfalz Generalia 77/1656). A document of March 15, 1773, also at Karlsruhe, makes reference to the court chaplain Vogler's threefold petition for financial support for his trip to Italy and, thereafter, appointment as vice kapellmeister and court organist.

14. This and other idiosyncratic spellings in Vogler's titles and terminology have been retained in the present study.

15. Emily Anderson, trans. and ed., *The Letters of Mozart and His Family,* 2d ed., 2 vols. (New York: St. Martin's Press, 1966).

16. The question of authorship of the essays and analyses in the *Betrachtungen* remains to be fully resolved. The notion of a collective effort engaging master and disciples is inherent in the title of the serial, and the intention of incorporating pupils' work is announced in the beginning of the first fascicle (pp. 3–4). Several pieces, including "Auflösung der Preisfrage" (1:243–75 [237–69]), "Was Tonwissenschaft, Tonsezkunst, und musikalische Aesthetik sei" (2:308–22 [344–48]), "Summe der Harmonik" (3:1–117), and "Harmonie zwischen den Grundsäzen ihrer Anwendung und der Wirkung der Musik" (3/10–12:2–57 [354–409]), are actually signed by Vogler, and three others, devoted to the defense of particular aspects of Vogler's theory, are signed by the pupils Pixis, Mezger, and Kornacher. The other material is unsigned. Throughout the serial (including the signed pieces cited above), the first-person plural is ubiquitous, and in the unsigned material there are references to Vogler as "our master" and "our music teacher."

The likelihood of pupils' participation notwithstanding, it is clear that the serial in its entirety was conceived and executed to elaborate Vogler's system. In the critiques, analyses, and explanations of theoretical doctrine, the tone is consistently authoritative, and the declarative pronouncements betray the rhetoric of Vogler's signed *Betrachtungen* essays and other writings. Portions of one of the anonymous essays, "Thätige Geschmaks-Bildung für die Beurtheiler der Tonstücken" (1:277–312 [271–306]), are incorporated wholesale in the theorist's later French publication, *Essai propre à diriger le goût de ceux qui ne sont pas musiciens* [Paris, 1782]; and the analyses of Vogler's own compositions are strewn with explanations of compositional choices and procedures that could only have originated with the composer himself. In the absence of any indication of independent critical thought on the part of anyone but Vogler, ideas contained in the anonymous critiques and analyses are generally ascribed to the theorist in the present study.

17. Michel Brenet, "L'Abbé Vogler à Paris en 1781–83," *Archives historiques, artistiques et littéraires* 2 (1891): 150–56. See also *Musikalischer Almanach für Deutschland auf das Jahr 1789,* pp. 140–41, and Vogler, *Handbuch,* pp. iii, xv. In *Betrachtungen* 3/10–12:58 [410], Vogler makes reference to plans to perform *Eglé* and a tragedy *Ariadne en Naxe.*

18. Vogler, *Handbuch,* p. xiii. See also *Allgemeine musikalische Zeitung* 1 (1798–99): 575–76.

19. According to some accounts, the work was not actually premiered until 1787. See Chapter 5, note 28.

20. For information on Vogler's contracts at Stockholm, see Patrik Vretblad, "Abbé Georg Joseph Vogler i Stockholm" (typescript, 1949, Stockholm, Musikaliska Akademiens Bibliotek, Handskr. 306), p. 6.

21. *Allgemeine musikalische Zeitung* 6 (1803–4): 250–51.

22. A report of this soirée, recounted by Johann Gänsbacher, was published in Fröhlich's *Biographie,* p. 55; it is retold in Elliot Forbes, rev. and ed., *Thayer's Life of Beethoven* (Princeton: Princeton University Press, 1967), p. 338. See also Franz Grillparzer, *Beethoven: Erinnerungen, Reden, Gedichte,* ed. Hans Schumacher (Herrliberg-Zurich: Bühl-Verlag-Blätter, 1946), pp. 3–4, where a soirée attended by Vogler, Beethoven, and Cherubini is described.

23. See Hertha Schweiger, "Abbé Voglers Simplifikationssystem und seine akustischen Studien," *Kirchenmusikalisches Jahrbuch* 29 (1934): 79. See also a document at Munich, Bayerisches Hauptstaatsarchiv, MInn 24059: 151–52. At Darmstadt he made comparable proposals (Darmstadt, Hessisches Staatsarchiv, D 4, Nr. 695.)

24. Mentioned in a letter from C. M. von Weber to Gänsbacher (October 9, 1810), printed in Carl Maria von Weber, *Carl Maria von Weber: Briefe,* ed. Hans Christoph Worbs (Frankfurt am Main: Fischer, 1982), p. 29.

25. *Allgemeine musikalische Zeitung* 16 (1814): 350–51.

26. "A Word on Vogler," p. 44.

27. *Allgemeine musikalische Zeitung* 16 (1814): 351.

28. C. F. D. Schubart, *Ideen zu einer Ästhetik der Tonkunst* (Vienna, 1806), p. 133.

29. *Letters* 1:370.

30. *Baierisches Musik-Lexikon,* p. 360.

31. François-Joseph Fétis, *Traité complet de la théorie et de la pratique de l'harmonie,* 7th ed. (Paris, 1861), pp. 224–27.

32. Otto Jahn, *Life of Mozart,* trans. Pauline D. Townsend, 3 vols. (London, 1891), 1:389.

33. Ernst Pasqué, *Abt Vogler als Tonkünstler, Lehrer und Priester* (Darmstadt, 1884).

34. The listing in Robert Eitner's *Biographisch-bibliographisches Quellen-Lexikon,* 10 vols. (Leipzig: Breitkopf & Härtel, 1900–1904), 10:124–32, also leaves many questions unanswered and demonstrates the need for a revised, thematic index.

35. Emile Rupp, *Abbé Vogler als Mensch, Musiker und Orgelbautheoretiker unter besonderer Berücksichtigung des sog. "Simplificationssystems"* (Augsburg: Bärenreiter, [1922]).

36. James Simon, *Abt Voglers kompositorisches Wirken mit besonderer Berücksichtigung der romantischen Momente* (Berlin: Gustav Schade, 1904).

37. Hertha Schweiger, "Abt Vogler," *Musical Quarterly* 25 (1939): 156–66. The various chapters of Schweiger's dissertation were published in the form of a monograph, *Abbé G. J. Vogler's Orgellehre* (Vienna: Johannes Kmoch, 1938), and an extended article, "Abbé Voglers Simplifikationssystem und seine akustischen Studien," *Kirchenmusikalisches Jahrbuch* 29 (1934): 72–123.

38. Helmut Kreitz, "Abbé Georg Joseph Vogler als Musiktheoretiker" (Ph.D. diss., University of the Saarland, 1957).

39. David Britton, "Abbé Georg Joseph Vogler: His Life and His Theories on Organ Design" (D.M.A. thesis, University of Rochester, 1973).

CHAPTER I

1. Translated and edited by Alfred Mann in *Steps to Parnassus: The Study of Counterpoint* (New York: W. W. Norton, 1943; reprinted as *The Study of Counterpoint,* 1965) and in Mann's *The Study of Fugue* (New York: W. W. Norton, 1965), Part 2, pp. 78–138.

2. Translated and edited by Philip Gossett as *Treatise on Harmony* (New York: Dover, 1971).

3. See Helmut Kreitz, "Abbé Georg Joseph Vogler als Musiktheoretiker" (Ph.D. diss., University of the Saarland, 1957), pp. 74–80, where resemblances in form and substance between Vogler's early writings and the teachings of Marpurg are discussed.

4. Vogler, *Choral-System,* (Copenhagen, 1800), pp. 1–2, 6–7.

5. Published as *Trattato della moderna musica* (Padua: Il messaggero di S. Antonio, 1950). This edition includes the previously published Book 1.

6. See Alejandro Planchart, "A Study of the Theories of Giuseppe Tartini," *Journal of Music Theory* 4 (1960): 32–61. Of Tartini's explorations of combination tones (mentioned in the preface to Vallotti's *Della scienza teorica, e pratica della moderna musica,* vol. 1 [Padua, 1779], p. xi), there is little trace in the harmonic systems of either Vallotti or Vogler, though the latter did put the concept to practical use in his theory of organ design (see Chapter 6, pp. 240–41).

7. Vallotti, *Trattato,* pp. 285–88. See Walter W. Schurr, "Francesco Antonio Calegari (d. 1742): Music Theorist and Composer," 2 vols. (Ph.D. diss., Catholic University of America, 1969), which includes an edition of Calegari's unpublished treatise, "Ampla dimostrazione degli armoniali musicali tuoni" (1732).

8. While the origin of this approach to the derivation of dissonances remains unclear, the idea of exceeding the octave to distinguish specifically between suspension dissonances and consonant members of a triad is a distinctive feature of the Paduans' theories. The intervals of eleventh and thirteenth, in addition to the ninth, are invoked by Rameau and his followers, but when they appear, it is usually with respect to the concept of *supposition* (whereby the seventh persists as the true, functional dissonance) or else in connection with the stacking of thirds to build chords of the ninth, eleventh, or thirteenth. Cf. David A. Sheldon, "The Ninth Chord in German Theory," *Journal of Music Theory* 26 (1982): 61–100. See also Tartini, *De' principi dell'armonia musicale* (Padua, 1767), pp. 88–90.

9. *Della scienza teorica,* vol. 1, pp. 62–63, 162–67.

10. See Vallotti, *Della scienza teorica,* vol. 1, pp. 96–100. See also William J. Mitchell, "Chord and Context in 18th-Century Theory," *Journal of the American Musicological Society* 16 (1963): 221–39; Joyce Mekeel, "The Harmonic Theories of Kirnberger and Marpurg," *Journal of Music Theory* 4 (1960): 169–93; and Cecil Powell Grant, "The Real Relationship between Kirnberger's and Rameau's Concept of the Fundamental Bass," *Journal of Music Theory* 21 (1977): 324–38.

11. Vogler acknowledges his debt to Vallotti in *Choral-System,* p. 6.

12. See Karl Emil von Schafhäutl, *Abt Georg Joseph Vogler* (Augsburg, 1888), pp. 201–10, where the dimensions and construction of the *Tonmaass* are discussed in detail.

13. See *Betrachtungen der Mannheimer Tonschule* 2:87–93 [95–101].

14. See Vogler, *Handbuch zur Harmonielehre* (Prague, 1802), p. 16; *Notenbeispiele,* p. 1. While both Tartini and Vallotti call attention to the phenomenon of this natural scale, neither actually employs it as a theoretical resource: see Tartini, *De' principi dell'armonia musicale,* p. 91; Vallotti, *Della scienza teorica,* p. 93.

15. See Tartini, *Trattato di musica secondo la vera scienza dell'armonia* (Padua, 1754), pp. 98–99; see also Matthew Shirlaw, *The Theory of Harmony* (London, 1917), pp. 137–43; Vallotti, *Della scienza teorica,* pp. 163–64.

16. See Shirlaw, *The Theory of Harmony,* p. 146.

17. See Shirlaw, *The Theory of Harmony*, pp. 187–90, where Rameau's construction of a scale on G in *Génération harmonique* (Paris, 1737) is discussed.

18. Vogler, *Tonwissenschaft und Tonsezkunst* (Mannheim, 1776), pp. 9–10.

19. Vogler, *Handbuch*, pp. 38–39. See also *Choral-System*, pp. 11–12.

20. A precedent for this procedure is suggested in Calegari, "Ampla dimostrazione," fol. 96r: see Schurr, "Francesco Antonio Calegari," 1:21–22.

21. See Introduction, note 7.

22. Vogler, *Handbuch*, pp. 45–46.

23. In *Tonwissenschaft und Tonsezkunst*, Vogler has discussed all the intervals, including the sevenths, by the time he introduces cadences. In the *Handbuch*, where cadences precede intervals in the altered chain of deductions, he is obliged to leap ahead of himself by invoking the dominant seventh at this point.

24. Here and in subsequent discussions of harmonic function, superscript arabic 7s are used when necessary for clarification. Vogler himself did not adorn his Roman numerals with superscripts in theoretical writings where these symbols are employed.

25. Cf. the tally of intervals in *Handbuch*, pp. 70–72, where the frame of reference is not the different chord types, but rather the major and minor scales.

26. Rameau, *Treatise on Harmony*, pp. 4–7; see Shirlaw, *The Theory of Harmony*, pp. 69–74.

27. Vallotti, *Della scienza teorica*, vol. 1, pp. 92–93.

28. See *Tonwissenschaft und Tonsezkunst*, p. 14. While Vogler's term for this interval may be translated literally (though not very helpfully) as "entertaining seventh," his description of its function emphasizes its distinctively tensional properties: "Sie dienet zur Unterhaltung, und vergnügt das Gehör, sie stellet es aber nicht zufrieden; denn es erwartet noch ganz unruhig die Bewegung, und Auflösung in einer Wohlklang."

29. *Tonwissenschaft und Tonsezkunst*, p. 10; *Handbuch*, p. 17. Cf. Vallotti, *Trattato*, p. 222.

30. For an instance of the freely sounded seventh, see Chapter 2, Example 10a, measure 33. The example of the upward-resolving seventh is from *Handbuch*, *Notenbeispiele*, p. 11. See also *Notenbeispiele*, p. 5, figs. 4 and 5, and *Gründe ker kuhrpfälzischen Tonschule in Beispielen* (musical supplement to *Kuhrpfälzische Tonschule*, 2 vols. [Mannheim, 1778]), p. 17, fig. 2.

31. As Vogler acknowledges (*Tonwissenschaft und Tonsezkunst*, pp. 54–55), the comparable succession in minor:

|   |   |   |   |   |   |   | 7 |    |   | 7 |
|---|---|---|---|---|---|---|---|----|---|---|
| 7 | 7 | 7 | 7 | 7 | 7 | 7 | 5 | 3♯ | 7 | 3 |
| A | D | G | C | F | B | E | A | D  | E | G♯ | A |

lacks decisiveness except for the eventual progression of the dominant and seventh (with raised seventh degree) to tonic.

32. Vallotti, *Della scienza teorica*, vol. 1, p. 96. For a discussion of Calegari's precedent for this procedure, see Schurr, "Francesco Antonio Calegari," 1:48–84.

33. *Handbuch, Notenbeispiele*, p. 5.

34. *Della scienza teorica*, vol. 1, pp. 96–97.

35. *Tonwissenschaft und Tonsezkunst*, p. 25.

36. *Handbuch*, p. 6.

37. Cf. David W. Beach, "The Functions of the Six-Four Chord in Tonal Music," *Journal of Music Theory* 11 (1967): 2–31.

38. *Betrachtungen* 3:1–108; music in *Betrachtungen* 4 *(Gegenstände der Betrachtungen):* [318–32].

39. *Handbuch*, pp. 56–59; *Notenbeispiele*, p. 3.

40. Adapted from *Handbuch, Notenbeispiele*, p. 7.

41. Adapted from *Handbuch, Notenbeispiele*, p. 8.

42. Cf. *Betrachtungen* 3:39–40.

43. Examples 14a–c discussed in *Betrachtungen* 3:41–48; music adapted from *Betrachtungen* 4 *(Gegenstände):* [321]. Here and in subsequent examples, thoroughbass numbers represent those found in the sources.

44. Examples 15a–d discussed in *Betrachtungen* 3:28–40; music in *Betrachtungen* 4 *(Gegenstände):* [320]. See also *Handbuch*, pp. 113–14 and *Notenbeispiele*, p. 9.

45. See J. Murray Barbour, *Tuning and Temperament* (East Lansing: Michigan State College, 1951), pp. 156–77.

46. *Handbuch*, pp. 116–24.

47. *Deutsche Encyclopädie*, 23 vols. (Frankfurt am Main, 1778–1804), 2:386; cf. article "Farbe," 9:509. See also *Betrachtungen* 1:284, 288 [278, 282]; 3/10–12:41 [393] for further characterizations, some of which are different but related. See also Rita Steblin, *A History of Key Characteristics in the Eighteenth and Early Nineteenth Centuries* (Ann Arbor: UMI Research Press, 1983), pp. 126–38.

48. Vogler, *Vergleichungs-Plan der, nach dem Vogler'schen Simplifikazions-System umgeschaffenen, Neumünster-Orgel in Würzburg* (Würzburg, 1812), pp. 14–15.

49. *Handbuch*, pp. 129–30. See the discussion of this work in Chapter 4, pp. 135–38, 145–48.

50. *Handbuch, Notenbeispiele*, p. 12.

51. See Robert W. Wason, *Viennese Harmonic Theory from Albrechtsberger to Schenker and Schoenberg* (Ann Arbor: UMI Research Press, 1985), pp. 15–19, where Vogler's harmonized chromatic scale is linked to the phenomenon of the "omnibus" progression. A notable instance of a partial "omnibus" is found in Prelude No. 12 of the *Zwei und dreisig Präludien*, measures 17–19 (modern edition in *"Pièces de clavecin" [1798] and "Zwei und dreisig Präludien" [1806]*, ed. Floyd K. Grave [Madison: A–R Editions, 1986]). Vogler supplies a Roman-numeral analysis of the passage on p. 34 of the analytical commentary that accompanied the publication.

52. *Betrachtungen* 2:86 [94]; 3/10–12:60–61 [412–13].
53. *Choral-System*, pp. 8–9.
54. Ibid., p. 9.
55. See Mitchell, "Chord and Context in 18th-Century Theory," pp. 234–36.
56. *Betrachtungen* 3:26.
57. Ibid., p. 22.
58. *Betrachtungen* 2:245 [271].

CHAPTER 2

1. Rameau analyzed his motet, *Laboravi clamans,* in Book 3 of *Traité de l'harmonie* (1722); an analysis of Armide's monologue from Lully's *Armide* appeared in the *Nouveau systême de musique théorique* (1726), and was reprinted in d'Alembert's *Elémens de musique, théorique et pratique, suivant les principes de M. Rameau* (1752).

2. Translated by David W. Beach and Jurgen Thym as *The True Principles for the Practice of Harmony* in *Journal of Music Theory* 23 (1979): 163–225. See David W. Beach, "The Origins of Harmonic Analysis," *Journal of Music Theory* 18 (1974): 274–307, where Kirnberger's and Schulz's analyses are discussed.

3. Emily Anderson, trans. and ed., *The Letters of Mozart and His Family,* 2d ed., 2 vols. (New York: St. Martin's Press, 1966), 1:370.

4. Vogler, *Trichordium und Trias Harmonica, oder Lob der Harmonie* (Offenbach, [c. 1815]); orchestral score and piano reduction appear to have been published at the same time (plate numbers 3468, 3469, respectively). In *Allgemeine musikalische Zeitung* 1 (1798–99): 592, reference is made to a performance of a version of the work in April 1799; see also *Allgemeine musikalische Zeitung* 14 (1812): 313, where it is reviewed favorably.

5. See Gottfried Weber, review of Vogler, *Trichordium und Trias Harmonica, oder Lob der Harmonie,* in *Allgemeine musikalische Zeitung* 17 (1815): 513–18, where Rousseau's aim of writing the song as a model of vocal simplicity is discussed. See also Johann Friedrich Rochlitz's comments on the song (*Allgemeine musikalische Zeitung* 1 [1798–99]: 437–38, as well as p. 592, where reference is made to Supplement 14 [p. xliii], in which a five-voice setting by Vogler is quoted with the original French text and a German translation).

6. See Jean-Jacques Rousseau, *Dictionnaire de musique* (Paris, 1768), article "Harmonie" (pp. 236–42), referred to in the *Trichordium* preface. In his essay, *Uiber die harmonische Akustik* [Munich, 1806], p. 4, Vogler challenges the condemnation of harmony voiced in the *Dictionnaire*, p. 242.

7. See *Betrachtungen der Mannheimer Tonschule* 3:214–15 [228–29].

8. See Introduction, note 16, where the question of authorship in *Betrachtungen* is addressed.

9. *Betrachtungen* 1:41–48; music in *Betrachtungen* 4 (*Gegenstände der Betrachtungen*): [20–21].

10. *Betrachtungen* 2:364 [390]; music in *Betrachtungen* 4 (*Gegenstände*): [308]. Here, as in subsequent examples, slurs, other articulation markings, and dynamics reflect those in the source from which the excerpt is quoted.

11. *Betrachtungen* 1:342–44 [336–38]; music in *Betrachtungen* 4 *(Gegenstände):* [100].

12. See *Betrachtungen* 3:22; see also 1:324 [318], 2:239 [265], 3:145.

13. See *Betrachtungen* 3/7–9:88–91 [344–47].

14. *Betrachtungen* 1:342–43 [336–37].

15. See also *Betrachtungen* 2:53, for example.

16. Cf. *Tonwissenschaft und Tonsezkunst* (Mannheim, 1776), p. 59; *Betrachtungen* 3/10–12:11 [363]; *Handbuch zur Harmonielehre* (Prague, 1802), pp. 60–61. Cf. Tartini, *Trattato di musica secondo la vera scienza dell'armonia* (Padua, 1754), pp. 103–7, where the IV–V succession is justified on somewhat comparable grounds as part of the *cadenza mista*.

17. See *Betrachtungen* 3/7–9:90 [346]. See also Vogler's article "Ausführen" in *Deutsche Encyclopädie*, 23 vols. (Frankfurt am Main, 1778–1804), 2:409, where he distinguishes between monotony (the exclusive adherence to a single key center) and unity (the allegiance of all harmony in a piece to a single tonic).

18. *Betrachtungen* 3/7–9:90–91 [346–47].

19. In the article "Ausweichen," *Deutsche Encyclopädie* 2:574, where Vogler applies the term to processes of modulation within a tonally unified composition, a hierarchy of importance among closely related scale degrees is proposed for major and minor keys.

20. *Betrachtungen* 3:238–39 [252–53].

21. *Betrachtungen* 1:102–3; music in *Betrachtungen* 4 *(Gegenstände):* [50–51].

22. *Betrachtungen* 1:103.

23. Ibid., p. 152; music in *Betrachtungen* 4 *(Gegenstände):* [68].

24. *Betrachtungen* 2:50; music in *Betrachtungen* 4 *(Gegenstände):* [130].

25. *Präludien*, p. 8. For a more detailed discussion of this publication, see Vogler, *"Pièces de clavecin" (1798) and "Zwei und dreisig Präludien" (1806)*, ed. Floyd K. Grave (Madison: A–R Editions, 1986); see also Grave, "Abbé Vogler's Theory of Reduction," *Current Musicology* 29 (1980): 41–69.

26. *Präludien*, pp. 36–37.

27. Ibid., pp. 22, 25.

28. Ibid., pp. 35–36.

29. *Zergliederung der musikalischen Bearbeitung des Busspsalmen im Choral-Styl*, Utile dulci (Munich, 1807), p. 8.

30. See the discussion of *Davids Buss-Psalm* in Chapter 4, pp. 174–75.

31. *Präludien*, pp. 22–23.

32. Ibid., p. 21.

33. Ibid., p. 10n.

34. Ibid., pp. 38–40. (The analysis given in Example 12 follows that which accompanies the actual music on p. 15 of the preludes. It differs slightly from, and is more explicit than, the analysis given in the commentary.)

35. Ibid., pp. 9–10.

36. Ibid., p. 27.

37. See *Betrachtungen* 3/7–9:38–74 [294–330]; see also *Betrachtungen* 3:131–34, 138–44.

38. See Floyd K. Grave, "Abbé Vogler and the Study of Fugue," *Music Theory Spectrum* 1 (1979): 43–66.

39. Vogler, *System für den Fugenbau* (Offenbach, [c. 1817]), pp. 8–10, 29–30.

40. Ibid., p. 53.

41. See, for example, Giuseppe Tartini, *Trattato di musica secondo la vera scienza dell'armonia* (Padua, 1754), p. 109; Francesco Antonio Vallotti, *Della scienza teorica, e pratica della moderna musica,* vol. 1 (Padua, 1779), pp. 21–22, 31, 34–35.

42. *Fugenbau,* pp. 13–15, 19–21.

CHAPTER 3

1. *Betrachtungen der Mannheimer Tonschule* 1:5–8; music in *Betrachtungen* 4 *(Gegenstände der Betrachtungen):* [2–4].

2. *Betrachtungen* 1:14–15.

3. See *Betrachtungen* 1:277–312 [271–306].

4. *Betrachtungen* 3/10–12:1–57 [353–409].

5. Ibid., p. 13 [365]; music in *Betrachtungen* 4 *(Gegenstände):* [516]. Vogler's concept of sacred style is treated in detail in Chapter 4.

6. *Betrachtungen* 3/10–12:23–24 [375–76]; music in *Betrachtungen* 4 *(Gegenstände):* [517].

7. *Betrachtungen* 3/10–12:47–48 [399–400].

8. *Betrachtungen* 2:30.

9. *Betrachtungen* 1:287–95 [281–89].

10. See ibid., pp. 290–91 [284–85].

11. Ibid., pp. 286–87 [280–81]. See the detailed discussion of rhetoric and music in George J. Buelow, "The *Loci Topici* and Affect in Late Baroque Music: Heinichen's Practical Demonstration," *Music Review* 27 (1966): 161–76; see also Leonard Ratner, *Classic Music: Expression, Form, and Style* (New York: Schirmer Books, 1980).

12. See, for example, *Betrachtungen* 3:238–39 [252–53]; also 1:87, 103, 311–12 [305–6].

13. See *Betrachtungen* 2:365–67 [391–93]; see also 1:18, 40, 174, 379 [373].

14. *Betrachtungen* 3/10–12:5 [357]; music in *Betrachtungen* 4 *(Gegenstände)*: [515].

15. *Betrachtungen* 2:352–67 [378–93]; music in *Betrachtungen* 4 *(Gegenstände)*: [306–10].

16. *Betrachtungen* 2:29–61; keyboard score in *Betrachtungen* 4 *(Gegenstände)*: [124–50]; orchestral parts in *Betrachtungen* 4 *(Gegenstände)*: [239–90].

17. See Edwin J. Simon, "Sonata into Concerto: A Study of Mozart's First Seven Concertos," *Acta musicologica* 31 (1959): 170–85.

18. See *Betrachtungen* 1:52.

19. Ibid., p. 58; music in *Betrachtungen* 4 *(Gegenstände)*: [30–31].

20. See, for example, *Betrachtungen* 1:303–4 [297–98]; 2:86 [94]; 3/10–12:60 [412].

21. *Betrachtungen* 1:116–20. See Mozart's letter to his father, October 31, 1777, where a rehearsal for this performance is mentioned in Emily Anderson, trans. and ed., *The Letters of Mozart and His Family*, 2d ed., 2 vols. [New York: St. Martin's Press, 1966], 1:350.)

22. *Betrachtungen* 3/7–9:1–32 [257–88].

23. For further discussion of Vogler's attitude toward the music of Bach, see Floyd K. Grave, "Abbé Vogler and the Bach Legacy," *Eighteenth-Century Studies* 13 (1979–80): 119–41.

24. See Johann Philipp Kirnberger, *Die Kunst des reinen Satzes in der Musik*, 2 vols. [Berlin, 1771–79], 2/1:63–65.

25. *Betrachtungen* 3/7–9:25–32 [281–88]; music in *Betrachtungen* 4 *(Gegenstände)*: [441–42].

26. *Betrachtungen* 2:330–46 [356–72]; music in *Betrachtungen* 4 *(Gegenstände)*: [299].

27. *Betrachtungen* 1:129–39; music in *Betrachtungen* 4 *(Gegenstände)*: [62–66].

28. *Betrachtungen* 1:139–44; music in *Betrachtungen* 4 *(Gegenstände)*: [75–87].

29. See Floyd K. Grave, "Abbé Vogler's Revision of Pergolesi's *Stabat Mater*," *Journal of the American Musicological Society* 30 (1977): 43–71.

30. *Betrachtungen* 1:369 [363]; music in *Betrachtungen* 4 *(Gegenstände)*: [110–13].

31. *Betrachtungen* 1:159–64.

32. Vogler, *Deutsche Kirchenmusik, mit einer Zergliederung die vorläufig die Inaugural-Frage beantwortet: Hat die Musik seit 30 Jahren gewonnen oder verlohren?*, Utile dulci (Munich, 1808), pp. 3–35.

33. See Vogler, *Erste musikalische Preisaustheilung für das Jahr 1791* (Frankfurt am Main, 1794), p. 12. See also the "Fuga" article in *Deutsche Encyclopädie*, 23 vols. (Frankfurt am Main, 1778–1804), 10:630, written after Vogler's first sojourn in London.

34. See Robert Manson Myers, *Handel's Messiah: A Touchstone of Taste* (New York: Macmillan, 1948).

35. Vogler, *Erste musikalische Preisaustheilung*, p. 12.

36. Vogler, *Verbesserung der Forkel'schen Veränderungen* (Frankfurt am Main, 1793), pp. 8–9.

37. See Vogler, *Deutsche Kirchenmusik, mit einer Zergliederung*, pp. 19–22.

38. Ibid., pp. 4–5.
39. Ibid., pp. 54–56.
40. See Floyd K. Grave, "Abbé Vogler and the Study of Fugue," *Music Theory Spectrum* 1 (1979): 43–66.
41. See the discussion of Vogler's harmonic analysis of the fugal subject and answer in Chapter 2, pp. 79–83.
42. *System für den Fugenbau* (Offenbach, [c. 1817]), pp. 66–69.
43. Ibid., pp. 8–9.
44. Ibid., p. 23.
45. Ibid., pp. 73–74.
46. Vogler's notion of coordinated action among different musical elements may be compared with the concept of a late eighteenth-century "concinnity" identified by Jan LaRue in *Guidelines for Style Analysis* (New York: W. W. Norton, 1970), p. 16.
47. See Vogler, *Zwei und dreisig Präludien . . . nebst einer Zergliederung in ästhetischer, rhetorischer und harmonischer Rücksicht* (Munich, 1806), pp. 18–29.
48. Ibid., pp. 21, 27–28.
49. Ibid., p. 47.
50. Ibid., p. 11.

## CHAPTER 4

1. See Friedrich Walter, *Geschichte des Theaters und der Musik am kurpfälzischen Hofe* (Leipzig, 1898), p. 181.
2. In his *Critischer Musikus,* Johann Adolf Scheibe decried a certain priest's penchant for transforming Italian operatic arias into church music by substituting sacred German texts (see *Critischer Musikus,* 2d ed. [Leipzig, 1745], pp. 175–76). Comparable accounts appear elsewhere, including the anonymous "Etwas über Kirchenmusik," *Musikalische Real-Zeitung für das Jahr 1788,* p. 177.
3. A translation of *Annus qui* is published in Robert F. Hayburn, *Papal Legislation on Sacred Music 95 A.D. to 1977 A.D.* (Collegeville, MN: Liturgical Press, 1979), pp. 92–107; quotation on p. 103.
4. See Reinhard G. Pauly, "The Reforms of Church Music under Joseph II," *Musical Quarterly* 43 (1957): 372–82. For detailed surveys of musical reforms in the Protestant and Catholic churches, see Georg Feder, "Decline and Restoration," in Friedrich Blume et al., *Protestant Church Music: A History* (New York: W. W. Norton, 1974), pp. 319–404, and collected essays in Karl Gustav Fellerer, ed., *Geschichte der katholischen Kirchenmusik,* 2 vols. (Kassel: Bärenreiter, 1972–76), 2:149–213.
5. *Betrachtungen der Mannheimer Tonschule* 1:291–92 [285–86].

6. Ibid., 1:131.

7. *Betrachtungen* 3:121–22. Cf. Rousseau's *Dictionnaire de musique* (Paris, 1768), article "Musique," p. 309. Vogler was familiar with the *Dictionnaire*.

8. *Betrachtungen* 3:121–22. Cf. Martin Gerbert's orientation in *De cantu et musica sacra a prima ecclesiae aetate usque ad praesens tempus*, 2 vols. (St. Blasien, 1774). Vogler owned a copy of this work.

9. Vogler cites these three works repeatedly in his writings, and may not only have heard them in Italy but also have been familiar with them from Burney's edition: *La musica che si canta annualmente nelle funzioni della settimana santa, nella cappella pontificia, composta dal Palestrina, Allegri e Bai* (London, 1771).

10. *Betrachtungen* 1:301–3 [295–97].

11. See Joseph Müller-Blattau, "Zur Musikübung und Musikauffassung der Goethezeit," *Euphorion* 31 (1930): 445–53.

12. Vogler, *Essai propre à diriger le goût de ceux qui ne sont pas musiciens* [Paris, 1782], p. 7.

13. *Betrachtungen* 1:77.

14. *Betrachtungen* 2:194 [218].

15. See, for example, Vogler, *System für den Fugenbau*, (Offenbach, [c. 1817]), p. 29, and *Erste musikalische Preisaustheilung für das Jahr 1791* (Frankfurt am Main, 1794), p. 24.

16. *Betrachtungen* 3/7–9: 42–43 [298–99].

17. *Erste musikalische Preisaustheilung*, p. 12.

18. *Fugenbau*, pp. 26–27.

19. *Erste musikalische Preisaustheilung*, p. 30.

20. Ibid.

21. *Betrachtungen* 1:297–98 [291–92].

22. Vogler, *Deutsche Kirchenmusik, mit einer Zergliederung die vorläufig die Inaugural-Frage beantwortet: Hat die Musik seit 30 Jahren gewonnen oder verlohren?*, Utile dulci (Munich, 1808), pp. 16–17, 24–25.

23. *Betrachtungen* 1:89–94; music in *Betrachtungen* 4 *(Gegenstände)*: [47].

24. *Betrachtungen* 1:93–94.

25. Ibid., p. 94.

26. *Betrachtungen* 3:121–44; music in *Betrachtungen* 4 *(Gegenstände)*: [353–368].

27. Darmstadt, Hessische Landes- und Hochschulbibliothek, Mus. ms. 1103. Cf. Karl Emil von Schafhäutl, *Abt Georg Joseph Vogler* (Augsburg, 1888), pp. 217, 249.

28. But Forkel, a noted adversary of Vogler, published an article which heaped contempt upon both the *Miserere* and the analysis. See *Musikalischer Almanach für Deutschland auf das Jahr 1789*, pp. 141–42.

29. *Betrachtungen* 3:124.

30. See *Betrachtungen* 1:288 [282].

31. See *Deutsche Encyclopädie*, 23 vols. (Frankfurt am Main, 1778–1804), 3:173, article "a Capella."

32. *Betrachtungen* 3:135–36.

33. Ibid., p. 123. Although Vogler did not publish the *Miserere* with orchestral parts, he announced in *Betrachtungen* that an optional, hand-written instrumental accompaniment was available for the price of one Gulden. The added parts (specific instrumentation was not enumerated) may have consisted of no more than strings: in addition to the dated autograph score and published edition, a second and undated autograph score (Darmstadt, Hessische Landes- und Hochschulbibliothek, Mus. ms. 1103a) includes additional parts for two violins and two violas.

34. See *Betrachtungen* 1:293 [287].

35. *Deutsche Encyclopädie* 2:384. See also *Essai propre*, pp. 8–9.

36. *Betrachtungen* 3:130–31.

37. Ibid., p. 136.

38. *Deutsche Kirchenmusik, mit einer Zergliederung*, pp. 3–4.

39. Wilhelm Kurthen, "Zur Geschichte der deutschen Singmesse," *Kirchenmusikalisches Jahrbuch* 26 (1931): 76, 79–82. Kurthen discusses at length settings of the *Singmesse* by Vogler and Holzbauer. For additional discussion of the *Singmesse* and other vernacular genres, see Josef Gotzen, "Das katholische Kirchenlied im 18. Jahrhundert insbesondere in der Aufklärungszeit," *Kirchenmusikalisches Jahrbuch* 40 (1956): 63–86.

40. *Betrachtungen* 2:170–73 [194–97].

41. Ibid., p. 219 [243].

42. *Musikalische Korrespondenz der teutschen Filarmonischen Gesellschaft für das Jahr 1790*, p. 186.

43. *Betrachtungen* 2:174 [198], 181 [205].

44. Ibid., p. [245].

45. A manuscript score of c. 1780 (Darmstadt, Hessische Landes- und Hochschulbibliothek, Mus. ms. 1091b) offers the likely instrumentation of two flutes, two oboes, two bassoons, two horns, two trumpets, timpani, strings, and *continuo*.

46. *Betrachtungen* 2:181–82 [205–6].

47. Ibid., p. 210 [234].

48. From the edition *Deutsche Kirchenmusik* [Mannheim, 1779].

49. *Deutsche Kirchenmusik, mit einer Zergliederung*, pp. 45–48.

50. See W. A. Mozart, *Neue Ausgabe sämtlicher Werke*, Ser. VII/1, "Vorwort," p. x, n. 20.

51. *Betrachtungen* 2:214 [238].

52. Datings may be found in an auction catalogue from 1814 of Vogler's musical *Nachlass* (*Verzeichniss der von dem als Theoretiker und Compositeur in der Tonkunst*

*berühmten . . . Abt G. J. Vogler nachgelassenen . . . im Manuscript vorhandenen Werke, so wie seiner im Druck erschienen und mehrerer fremden Musikalien* [Darmstadt, 1814] and in manuscript sources, especially at Munich, Bayerische Staatsbibliothek.

53. Munich, n.d.; the autograph is included in a set of collected manuscripts, *Voglers XXI lateinische Hymnen,* at Munich, Bayerische Staatsbibliothek, Mus. Mss. 4298. This and the remaining musical examples in this section on unaccompanied vocal works appear in both collections and follow the reading in the printed edition.

54. "a Capella," *Deutsche Encyclopädie* 3:173.

55. Documentation on these works is provided in the 1814 auction catalogue and in manuscript sources, chiefly in the major collections of Vogler's music at Munich, Darmstadt, and Stockholm.

56. *Deutsche Kirchenmusik, mit einer Zergliederung,* pp. 35, 46.

57. Ibid., pp. 4–5.

58. Ibid., pp. 35–36; cf. pp. 6–7.

59. Ibid., pp. 51–52.

60. Ibid., pp. 46–47, 51.

61. Ibid., p. 44.

62. Manuscript score, Darmstadt, Hessische Landes- und Hochschulbibliothek, Mus. ms. 1104.

63. *Fugenbau,* p. 29.

64. From the edition by Johann André (Offenbach, [1822]).

65. Autograph score, 1804, Darmstadt, Hessische Landes- und Hochschulbibliothek, Mus. ms. 1127.

66. Autograph score, 1809, Darmstadt, Hessische Landes- und Hochschulbibliothek, Mus. ms. 1126.

67. Manuscript score, Darmstadt, Hessische Landes- und Hochschulbibliothek, Mus. ms. 1101. The title page of the *Gegenstände der Betrachtungen* for vol. 3/10–12, 1781 (see *Betrachtungen* 4:[483]), mentions a "Versett: Suscepit Israel," but it is not included in the Olms reprint. This "Versett" is likely to be a version for soprano and orchestra of the movement from the *Magnificat.* According to the *Verzeichniss,* a "Suscepit Israel" for soprano and orchestra was published in 1781 (the same year as the *Gegenstände* fascicles), with the same instrumentation as the *Magnificat.* Manuscript sources for an independent "Suscepit Israel" survive at Stockholm, Musikaliska Akademiens Bibliotek and Munich, Bayerische Staatsbibliothek, Mus. Mss. 4230, the latter source mentioning a performance of the movement at a *concert spirituel* in Paris on April 17, 1781.

68. Autograph score, 1805, Darmstadt, Hessische Landes- und Hochschulbibliothek, Mus. ms. 1153.

69. Gottfried Weber, "Über das Wesen des Kirchenstyls," *Cäcilia* 3 (1825): 173–204.

70. Ibid., p. 187.

71. Ibid., pp. 194–95.

72. Shortly after Vogler's death, a critic in the *Allgemeine musikalische Zeitung,* inspired by the "ingeniously wrought" *Missa pastoritia,* asked that those who had acquired works from Vogler's musical *Nachlass* share these treasures with the public, since Vogler had withheld them from publication (*Allgemeine musikalische Zeitung* 17 [1815]: 61). But a decade later, the body of known works remained small (see *Allgemeine musikalische Zeitung* 27 [1825]: 92–93).

73. *Allgemeine musikalische Zeitung* 32 (1830): 114; 4 (1801–2): 590–91.

74. *Allgemeine musikalische Zeitung* 8 (1805–6): 318, 318n.; 27 (1825): 92–93.

75. *Allgemeine musikalische Zeitung* 15 (1813): 257.

76. Carl Maria von Weber, *Writings on Music,* trans. Martin Cooper, ed. John Warrack (Cambridge: Cambridge University Press, 1981), p. 44.

77. *Allgemeine musikalische Zeitung* 25 (1823): 682.

78. See *Cäcilia* 1 (1824): 113–17.

79. Jacob Adlung, *Anleitung zu der musikalischen Gelahrtheit* (Erfurt, 1758), pp. 659, 681–82. For detailed surveys of other approaches to chorale or plainsong harmonization, see Karl Gustav Fellerer, *Beiträge zur Choralbegleitung und Choralverarbeitung in der Orgelmusik des ausgehenden 18. und beginnenden 19. Jahrhunderts* (Strassburg: Heitz & Cie, [1932]), Martin Blindow, *Die Choralbegleitung des 18. Jahrhunderts in der evangelischen Kirche Deutschlands* (Regensburg: Gustav Bosse, 1957), and Leo Söhner, *Die Geschichte der Begleitung des gregorianischen Chorals in Deutschland* (Augsburg: Benno Filser, 1931).

80. J. G. Walther, *Musikalisches Lexikon, oder Musikalische Bibliothek* (Leipzig, 1732), article "Modus Musicus," pp. 409–15.

81. Johann Philipp Kirnberger, *Die Kunst des reinen Satzes in der Musik,* 2 vols. [Berlin, 1771–79], 2/1:41–67.

82. J. H. Knecht, *Vollständige Orgelschule für Anfänger und Geübtere,* 3 vols. (Leipzig, 1795–98), 3:8–17, 19, 44–55.

83. Vogler, *Kuhrpfälzische Tonschule,* 2 vols. (Mannheim, [1778]), 1:66–67.

84. Among earlier writings of Vogler's that address the subject are several entries in the *Deutsche Encyclopädie,* and an article on plainsong reported in *Musikalische Real-Zeitung für das Jahr 1789,* p. 391.

85. Material from *Organist-schola* contained in the text included the descriptions of church modes and guidelines for correct harmonization from volume one (1798), and the critiques, from volume two (1799), of Vogler's ninety chorale harmonizations.

86. Gottfried Weber, "Chor und Choral: Zwei Artikel aus Gfr. Webers musikalischem Lexikon," *Cäcilia* 4 (1826): 150.

87. Vogler, *Choral-System* (Copenhagen, 1800), p. 102.

88. *Ueber Choral- und Kirchen-Gesänge* (published anonymously in Munich, 1813), p. 34.

89. See Floyd K. Grave, "Abbé Vogler and the Bach Legacy," *Eighteenth-Century Studies* 13 (1979–80): 119–41.

90. *Choral-System*, pp. 21–24, 46–47.

91. In letters of February 22 and November 25, 1791, Bernhard Anselm Weber mentions Vogler's plans for a journey to Spain and Portugal (these letters are published in Max Unger, "Aus Bernhard Anselm Webers Jugendjahren: Briefe von Weber und anderen," *Allgemeine Musik-Zeitung* 38 [1911]: 882 and 904–5).

92. Two books of Vogler's sermons from the time of his sojourn at Gibraltar are extant in autograph at Munich, Bayerische Staatsbibliothek, Cod. ital. 256/1–2 (Cim. 387).

93. Letter of April 8, 1793, published in Unger, "Aus Bernhard Anselm Webers Jugendjahren," p. 928.

94. Vogler, *Uiber die harmonische Akustik* [Munich, 1806], p. 24.

95. *Polymelos, ein nazional-karakteristisches Orgel-Konzert* (Munich, 1806); *Pièces de clavecin faciles, doigtées, avec les variations d'une difficulté graduelle* (Stockholm, [1798]).

96. According to Vogler's unpublished travel diary (current whereabouts unknown), quoted in C. A. von Mastiaux, *Ueber Choral- und Kirchen-Gesänge*, p. 52n. Information concerning other destinations and experiences is inconclusive at best: see *Uiber die harmonische Akustik*, p. 24, where Carthage is mentioned; *Organist-schola*, introduction to vol. 1, and *Data zur Akustik*, p. 10n., where ambiguous references are made to Greece; *Choral-System*, p. 24, where Vogler refers to his visit to "Gross Griechenland" (Magna Graecia); *Choral-System*, p. 45, where "Gross Griechenland" and "ancient towns" on the Adriatic are mentioned; and *Choral-System*, p. 26, where he mentions being on the "Armenian Islands."

97. *Choral-System*, p. 24. See the detailed condemnation of this aspect of *Choral-System* in the anonymous "Ueber die sogennanten alten Kirchentonarten und deren gegenwärtigen Werth," *Eutonia* 5 (1831): 8–21.

98. Both the location of the church and the time of Vogler's visit there remain unclear. Leo Söhner speculates that his "Armenian Islands" may refer to the island of San Lazzaro in Venice, which houses a Mechitarist monastery (*Die Geschichte der Begleitung des gregorianischen Chorals in Deutschland*, p. 120, n. 104).

99. See *Choral-System*, pp. 28–35.

100. Ibid., pp. 35–36.

101. Ibid., p. 42; see also p. 33.

102. See *Choral-System*, pp. 26–27, 36.

103. As recorded in Vogler's unpublished travel diary (see Mastiaux, *Ueber Choral- und*

*Kirchen-Gesänge,* pp. 52–56n.), his views on preserved ancient traditions were later reinforced by an encounter in Berlin with a Turkish diplomat who recognized several melodies that Vogler had collected in Morocco. Vogler reasoned that, in light of the relatively great distance between Morocco and Constantinople and the absence of close ties between Africa and Asia, these melodies must have migrated in ancient times and been preserved intact. Here the theorist also discusses in more detail why he believes oral tradition to be more reliable than notation.

104. *Choral-System,* pp. 37–38.

105. Ibid., pp. 42–46.

106. Ibid., pp. 47–53.

107. See *Choral-System,* pp. 79–80, 83.

108. Ibid., pp. 58–68; music, Tab. II.

109. Ibid., p. 62.

110. Ibid., p. 59.

111. Ibid., pp. 65–67.

112. Music, Tab. III; See Grave, "Abbé Vogler and the Bach Legacy," pp. 131–33.

113. *Organist-schola,* vol. 1, p. 17.

114. See Ernst Ludwig Gerber, *Neues historisches-biographisches Lexikon der Tonkünstler,* 4 vols. (Leipzig, 1812–14) 4:478.

115. See Gerber, "Noch etwas über den Choralgesang und dessen Begleitung mit der Orgel," *Allgemeine musikalische Zeitung* 12 (1809–10): 435.

116. *Allgemeine musikalische Zeitung* 3 (Leipzig, 1800–1801): 264–65.

117. Justin Heinrich Knect, *Vollständige Orgelschule für Anfänger und Geübtere,* vol. 3 (Leipzig, 1798).

118. See "Chor und Choral: Zwei Artikel aus Gfr. Webers musikalischem Lexikon," pp. 150–53.

119. Cf. *Allgemeine musikalische Zeitung* 3 (1800–1801): 133, where an anonymous critic commented that Vogler's system would not make much of an impact.

120. Copy, with autograph modal table, at Darmstadt, Hessische Landes- und Hochschulbibliothek, Mus. ms. 1064, dated 1813.

121. Autograph, with additional pieces in a copyist's hand, at Vienna, Österreichische Nationalbibliothek, Cod. 19263, dated 1813.

122. Autograph, Munich, Bayerische Staatsbibliothek, Mus. Mss. 4226/1, dated 1812.

123. *Pater noster* (Munich, Bayerische Staatsbibliothek, Mus. Ms. 4335); *Praefatio di S. S. Trinitate* (Munich, Bayerische Staatsbibliothek, Mus. Ms. 4334); *Praefatio de Beata Maria Virgine* (Munich, Bayerische Staatsbibliothek, Mus. Ms. 4334). For a discussion of evidence in the sources that suggests, but does not prove, a late dating, see Söhner, *Die Geschichte der Begleitung des Gregorianischen Chorals in Deutschland,* pp. 117, 122–23.

124. Vogler, *Zergliederung der musikalischen Bearbeitung des Busspsalmen im Choral-Styl* (with accompanying volume of music), Utile dulci (Munich, 1807). Reviewed in *Allgemeine musikalische Zeitung* 10 (1807–8): 121–27, with favorable comments on the music but negative reactions to the analysis and its purpose.

125. Vogler states that the first harmonization of each segment can be used to harmonize every recurrence of the segment when the piece is sung without organ, but that when the organ accompanies it may be preferable to perform the harmonically diverse version. For the execution of this optional accompaniment, he supplies thoroughbass figures under the vocal bass line, noting that these figures may also be used for purposes of analysis.

126. From the edition of *Davids Buss-Psalm,* Utile dulci (Munich, [1807]).

CHAPTER 5

1. *Betrachtungen der Mannheimer Tonschule* 1:159–64.

2. Vogler includes a substantial discussion of the operatic accomplishments of Gluck, Grétry, and other contemporaries in the article "Genie" in volume 11 of the *Deutsche Encyclopädie* (published in 1786).

3. Datings given represent the earliest known, which may be either dates of composition or of first performance. In addition to miscellaneous pieces of incidental music (including overtures, marches, and choruses), other works not mentioned in the text include the *Singspiel, Albert der Dritte von Bayern,* the music for which is lost (if indeed it ever existed); another *Singspiel, Epimenides,* of doubtful authenticity; two additional German works which are evidently lost: *Der Koppengeist auf Reisen, oder Rübezahl* (Breslau, 1802) and the melodrama *Zoroastre* (1796); and several works written for Paris or Versailles in the early 1780s (*Eglé, Le Patriotisme, La Karmesse,* and *Ariadne en Naxe*), all of which seem to have disappeared. See Michel Brenet, "L'Abbé Vogler à Paris en 1781–83," *Archives historiques, artistiques et littéraires* 2 (1891): 150–56, and *Betrachtungen* 3/10–12:58 [410].

4. "Über die Musik der Oper *Rosamunde,*" offprint from *Rheinische Beiträge zur Gelehrsamkeit,* no. 6, 1780.

5. *Betrachtungen* 1:64.

6. Music in *Betrachtungen* 4 *(Gegenstände der Betrachtungen):* [28].

7. *Betrachtungen* 1:72.

8. Ibid., pp. 313–59 [307–53]; music in *Betrachtungen* 4 *(Gegenstände):* [98–107]. Schafhäutl proposes that the essay is not by Vogler, although he offers no evidence to substantiate this claim other than his impression of the writing style. (See *Abt Georg Joseph Vogler* [Augsburg, 1888], p. 215.)

9. See Chapter 1, pp. 40–43.

10. On the question of thematic contrast in sonata form, see Leonard G. Ratner, *Classic Music: Expression, Form, and Style* (New York: Schirmer Books, 1980),

pp. 218–20; see also Bathia Churgin, "Francesco Galeazzi's Description of Sonata Form," *Journal of the American Musicological Society* 21 (1968): 181–99.

11. *Betrachtungen* 1:354 [348].

12. *Betrachtungen* 2:62–76, 161–66 [185–90]; 3:162–87 [176–201]; music in *Betrachtungen* 4 *(Gegenstände):* [152–69, 210–20, 414–37, 443–59]. Facsimile of a manuscript score (Darmstadt, Hessische Landes- und Hochschulbibliothek, Mus. ms. 1090) published in *German Opera, 1770–1800,* vol. 8, ed. Thomas Bauman (New York: Garland Publishing, 1986).

13. See *Der Kaufmann von Smyrna, eine Operette in einem Aufzuge,* adapted by C. F. Schwan (Mannheim, 1771). Facsimile of libretto published in *German Opera, 1770–1800,* vol. 21, ed. Thomas Bauman (New York: Garland Publishing, 1986).

14. *Betrachtungen* 2:165 [189].

15. *Betrachtungen* 3:177–78 [191–92].

16. *Betrachtungen* 2:74; music in *Betrachtungen* 4 *(Gegenstände):* [164–65].

17. *Betrachtungen* 2:74.

18. *Betrachtungen* 3:165–67 [179–81]; music in *Betrachtungen* 4 *(Gegenstände):* [418].

19. *Betrachtungen* 3:166 [180].

20. Ibid., p. 178 [192]; music in *Betrachtungen* 4 *(Gegenstände):* [434].

21. See the article "Ausdruck" in *Deutsche Encyclopädie,* 23 vols. (Frankfurt am Main, 1778–1804), 2:387, where Vogler describes specific orchestral devices for depicting images of nature, including brilliant sunlight, moving clouds, rain, thunder, howling wind, and turbulent seas.

22. In *Betrachtungen* 2:255–57 [281–83], there is a description of one striking portion of *Lampedo,* a violent storm featuring an extended crescendo and diminuendo.

23. See Ratner, *Classic Music: Expression, Form, and Style,* pp. 167–68.

24. See "Ueber das musikalische Drama," *Allgemeine musikalische Zeitung* 1 (1798–99): 356–59.

25. Ibid., pp. 358–59. As described here, the thunder imitation was produced by two pipes tuned to the pitch F an octave apart. The pitch named was apparently a misrecollection on the part of the anonymous author, who quotes a passage for piccolo in a music example in which the pitch level is wrong. According to a discussion in the *Betrachtungen* (see note 22), the pipes were tuned to A.

26. Manuscript score, Darmstadt, Hessische Landes- und Hochschulbibliothek, Mus. ms. 1097. Facsimile of this score, and of the libretto, published in *German Opera, 1770–1800,* vols. 9 and 21, ed. Thomas Bauman (New York: Garland Publishing, 1986).

27. According to the *Verzeichniss der von dem als Theoretiker und Compositeur in der Tonkunst berühmten . . . Abt G. J. Vogler nachgelassenen . . . im Manuscript vorhandenen Werke, so wie seiner im Druck erschienenen und mehrerer fremden Musikalien* (Darmstadt, 1814), Vogler left in his collection an autograph for a melodrama *Zoroastre,* dated 1796.

28. The date of the work's first performance cannot be determined with certainty on the basis of available information. A critique in the *Allgemeine musikalische Zeitung* 8 (1805–6): 318–19, gives 1784, while Felix Joseph Lipowsky's *Baierisches Musik-Lexikon* (Munich, 1811), p. 362, gives both 1786 and 1787. Schafhäutl's catalogue lists the work under the year 1785, a date (apparently taken from the *Verzeichniss*) which conflicts with two references in his text to 1786; and while the biographical essay in Eitner gives 1786, Eitner's catalogue gives 1785, and it also refers to libretti from 1787 and 1788. A manuscript copy in the Bayerische Staats-bibliothek, Munich, bears the date 1787. Although this would place the premiere subsequent to Vogler's departure from Munich, it is nevertheless the date given in Franz Michael Rudhart, *Geschichte der Oper am Hofe zu München* (Freising, 1865), p. 173, and Franz Stieger, *Opernlexikon*, 4 pts. in 11 vols., (Tutzing: Hans Schneider, 1975–83), 3/3:1145, where the specific date of January 12 is listed.

29. See Alfred Loewenberg, *Annals of Opera, 1597–1940*, 3d ed. (Totowa, NJ: Rowman and Littlefield, 1978), pp. 439–40.

30. According to an excerpt cited in Rudhart, *Geschichte der Oper am Hofe zu München*, p. 173.

31. It was this setting to which Vogler appears to allude in his essay *Vergleichungs-Plan der, nach dem Vogler'schen Simplifikazions-System umgeschaffenen, Neumünster-Orgel in Würzburg* (Würzburg, 1812), p. 14. See Chapter 1, p. 43.

32. Concerning Vogler's concept of gradations in color among the sharp and flat keys, see Chapter 1, p. 42.

33. Manuscript score, Darmstadt, Hessische Landes- und Hochschulbibliothek, Mus. ms. 1063.

34. Bernhard Anselm Weber wrote that the work would have made no impact at all in Germany, but the Swedes were moved by it. According to his account of a performance in Stockholm, the entrance of the victorious (Swedish) general Delagardie, with his prisoners and banners, brought the house down—a remarkable reaction to what reportedly was perhaps the forty-eighth performance. (Letter of February 20, 1791, published in Max Unger, "Aus Bernhard Anselm Webers Jugendjahren: Briefe von Weber und anderen," *Allgemeine Musik-Zeitung* 38 [1911]: 881–82.)

35. *Höns gummans visa*, on which a set of variations is based, in *Pièces de clavecin*.

36. *Gustaf Adolf och Ebba Brahe*, piano-vocal score by P. C. Boman, facsimile edition, ed. Martin Tegen (Stockholm: Wilhelm Hansen, 1973), pp. 134–35.

37. Facsimile edition, p. 185.

38. Vogler, "Vergleich der Kempeln'schen Sprach-Maschine mit dem, der Men-schenstimme täuschend nachahmenden, singbaren Orgel-Register, von dieser Ähnlichkeit *Vox humana* genannt," [1810], Darmstadt, Hessisches Staatsarchiv, D 4, Nr. 695, [p. 2], n. 2.

39. Darmstadt, Hessisches Staatsarchiv, D 4, Nr. 695.

40. The composer's procedures in creating a theme from this motive recall the development to which a three-note kernel is subjected in *Trichordium und Trias Harmonica, oder Lob der Harmonie.* See Chapter 2, pp. 52–54.

41. Manuscript score, Darmstadt, Hessische Landes- und Hochschulbibliothek, Mus. ms. 1130.

CHAPTER 6

1. C. F. D. Schubart, *Ideen zu einer Ästhetik der Tonkunst* (Vienna, 1806), p. 133.

2. See for example "Zergliederung der Ouverture zur Tragödie: Hamlet," *Betrachtungen* 1:318 [312].

3. *Musikalische Korrespondenz der teutschen Filarmonischen Gesellschaft für das Jahr 1790,* pp. 197–200.

4. See Emily Anderson, trans. and ed., *The Letters of Mozart and His Family,* 2d ed., 2 vols. (New York: St. Martin's Press, 1966), 1:428, 448–49.

5. *Ideen zu einer Ästhetik der Tonkunst,* p. 133.

6. "Brief an einen musikalischen Freund," *Musikalische Real-Zeitung für das Jahr 1788,* p. 60. The critique, signed "Jk," is attributable to Junker. See Roye E. Wates, "Karl Ludwig Junker (1748–1797): Sentimental Music Critic," Ph.D. diss., Yale University, 1965, pp. 32–34.

7. *Allgemeine musikalische Zeitung* 8 (1805–6): 317.

8. *Ideen zu einer Ästhetik der Tonkunst,* pp. 133, 135.

9. *Chronik, 1790,* p. 662. On p. 670, Schubart celebrates Vogler's artistry on the organ in his poem "An Vogler, bei seinem Abschiede von mir."

10. *Musikalischer Almanach auf das Jahr 1784,* p. 125.

11. "Brief an einen musikalischen Freund," p. 61.

12. *Ideen zu einer Ästhetik der Tonkunst,* p. 133.

13. *Chronik, 1790,* p. 662.

14. Adolph von Knigge (?), "Ueber des Herrn Abt Voglers Anwesenheit in Hannover," cited in *Musikalische Real-Zeitung für das Jahr 1789,* pp. 342–43.

15. From Patrik Vretblad, "Abbé Georg Joseph Vogler i Stockholm" (typescript, 1949, Stockholm, Musikaliska Akademiens Bibliotek, Handskr. 306), p. 20.

16. See Joseph Müller-Blattau, "Zur Musikübung und Musikauffassung der Goethezeit," *Euphorion* 31 (1930): 427–54, especially 433–42.

17. Introduction to *Polymelos* (1806). For further information on the concert and the edition, see the anonymous discussions in *Allgemeine musikalische Zeitung* 8 (1805–6): 553–54; 9 (1806–7): 382–87.

18. As reported in *Polymelos* (1806) and *Musikalische Korrespondenz . . . 1790,* p. 184n.

19. "[Briefe an einen Freund über die Musik in Berlin:] Vierter Brief, vom 29sten November," *Allgemeine musikalische Zeitung* 3 (1800–1801): 192–94.

20. Vogler, *Choral-System* (Copenhagen, 1800), p. 102.

21. Ibid.

22. To produce his famed carillon imitation, for example, he combined the Quint 2 2/3′ and Terz 4/5′ stops, or else Gemshorn 2′ and Terz 1 3/5′, to which the addition of Quintatön 8′ added the illusion of bass bells. See his *Vergleichungs-Plan der, nach dem Vogler'schen Simplifikazions-System umgeschaffenen, Neumünster-Orgel in Würzburg* (Würzburg, 1812), p. 10, and *Uebersicht der Orgel-Umschaffung in der Dreifaltigkeits Kirche zu Schweidnitz* (Schweidnitz, 1802), [p. 4].

23. "[Briefe an einen Freund über die Musik in Berlin:] Vierter Brief, vom 29sten November," p. 194.

24. See description in "Ueber des Herrn Abt Voglers Anwesenheit in Hannover," pp. 347–48. Justin Heinrich Knecht, in his popular and influential organ treatise, likewise advocated the use of idiomatic style for playing on instrument-name stops (*Vollständige Orgelschule für Anfänger und Geübtere*, 3 vols. [Leipzig, 1795–98], 2:36–38). Apparently influenced by Vogler here, as in most areas of his work, he also included a short flute concerto (pp. 56–61), with appropriate registration, for solo flute and orchestra-like ritornellos "à la Vogler," as evidence that "the organ is capable of each and every style of playing."

25. "Brief an einen musikalischen Freund," pp. 76–77.

26. *Betrachtungen* 1:295 [289].

27. *Musikalischer Almanach für Deutschland auf das Jahr 1789*, pp. 136–37.

28. "[Briefe an einen Freund über die Musik in Berlin:] Vierter Brief, vom 29sten November," p. 195.

29. *Allgemeine musikalische Zeitung* 8 (1805–6): 317.

30. *Choral-System*, p. 103, n. 1.

31. Johanna Schopenhauer, *Jugendleben und Wanderbilder* (Brunswick, 1839), cited in Herbert Kelletat, *Zur Geschichte der deutschen Orgelmusik in der Frühklassik* (Kassel: Bärenreiter, 1933), p. 67.

32. J. H. Knecht, Vogler's disciple, reportedly wrote a symphony in 1785 also inspired by this subject. Other programmatic works of his include an organ piece *Die durch ein Donnerwetter unterbrochene Hirtenwonne* (1794), apparently inspired only by the idea of Vogler's thunderstorm improvisations, since Knecht claimed in the introduction to the edition not to have heard them.

33. *Musikalischer Almanach für Deutschland auf das Jahr 1789*, pp. 133–34, which also supplies the program included above.

34. "Brief an einen musikalischen Freund," pp. 76–77.

35. *Stockholms posten*, May 22, 1799, allegedly published first in *Kopenhagen im Jahr 1798, eine Wochenschrift*, vol. 1, no. 5. Cited in Patrik Vretblad, "Abbé Vogler som programmusiker," *Svensk tidskrift för musikforskning* 9 (1927): 93 (also in "Abbé Georg Joseph Vogler i Stockholm," p. 56).

36. *Musikalischer Almanach für Deutschland auf das Jahr 1789*, p. 138.

37. *Allgemeine musikalische Zeitung* 28 (1826): 467–68.

38. *Choral-System*, p. 104.

39. See Vogler's discussion of expressive pictorialism in *Betrachtungen* 1:293–96 [287–90].

40. *Lübeckische Anzeigen,* June 10, 1786, according to Hertha Schweiger, *Abbé G. J. Vogler's Orgellehre* (Vienna: Johannes Kmoch, 1938), p. 32.

41. For discussion of an early project at the Jesuit Church in Mannheim, see Bernd Sulzmann, "Eine Planung Abbé G. J. Voglers aus dem Jahre 1806," *Acta organologica* 11 (1977): 67–68.

42. The treatise was entitled "Orgel-Simplifications-System," according to the auction catalogue of Vogler's *Nachlass.* In *System für den Fugenbau* (1811), Vogler indicated that his "Simplifikazions-System für den Orgelbau" was, as it were, completed and he expressed the hope that it would be published that same year. Earlier references to this treatise antedate *Fugenbau* by several years.

43. *Ueber die Umschaffung der St. Marien-Orgel in Berlin* [Berlin, 1800]; *Uebersicht der Orgel-Umschaffung in der Dreifaltigkeits Kirche zu Schweidnitz* (Schweidnitz, 1802); *Prüfungs-Plan der nach dem Voglerschen Simplifikations-System unternommenen Umschaffung der grossen Orgel im Benediktiner-Stifte zu St. Peter in Salzburg* [Salzburg, 1805]; *Vergleichungsplan der nach dem Vogler'schen Simplifikazionssystem umgeschaffenen Orgel in dem evangelischen Hofbethause zu München* [Munich, 1805]; *Erklärung der Buchstaben, die im Grundriss, der nach dem Vogler'schen Simplifikazions-System neu zu erbauenden St. Petersorgel in München, vorkommen,* with accompanying *Grundriss* [Munich, 1806]; *Verzeichniss der Register der nach dem Vogler'schen Simplifikazions-System vom Orgelbauer Frosch neu erbauten St. Peters Orgel in München* [Munich, c. 1808]; *Kurze Beschreibung der, in der Stadt Pfarrkirche zu St. Peter in München nach dem Voglerschen Simplifikations-System vom Orgelbauer Herrn Franz Frosch neu erbauten, Orgel erster Grösse* [Munich, 1809]; *Vergleichungs-Plan der, nach dem Vogler'schen Simplifikazions-System umgeschaffenen, Neumünster-Orgel in Würzburg* (Würzburg, 1812). Others were published in Vogler's lifetime.

44. Munich, Bayerische Staatsbibliothek, Mus. Mss. 503.

45. Autograph, Stockholm, Dec. 23, 1798; now at Regensburg, Bischöfliche Zentralbibliothek.

46. "Korrespondenz: Stockholm im Februar 1799," *Allgemeine musikalische Zeitung* 1 (1798–99): 413–15.

47. Letter from C. P. E. Bach to Forkel [1774], in *The Bach Reader,* ed. Hans T. David and Arthur Mendel, rev. ed. (New York: W. W. Norton, 1966), p. 276.

48. Vogler, *Data zur Akustik* (Leipzig, 1801), p. 12.

49. Ibid., pp. 6–9.

50. Vogler described how during his concert tours he compensated for wind deficiency through the use of economical registration that took account of these principles. See *Kurze Beschreibung* [p. 4n].

51. *Data zur Akustik,* pp. 11–12.

52. *Kurze Beschriebung,* [pp. 3–4].

53. Giuseppe Tartini, *Trattato di musica secondo la vera scienza dell'armonia* (Padua, 1754), pp. 13–19. See also Alejandro Planchart, "A Study of the Theories of Giuseppe Tartini," *Journal of Music Theory* 4 (1960): 36–39. Hertha Schweiger, in "Abbé Voglers Simplifikationssystem und seine akustischen Studien," *Kirchenmusikalisches Jahrbuch* 29 (1934): 84, n. 54, makes reference to letters of Tartini and Vallotti concerning the question of difference tones.

54. A revised extract from the *Trattato di musica,* Chapter 1, according to Mastiaux in *Ueber Choral- und Kirchen-Gesänge* (Munich, 1813), pp. 90–91n.

55. *Data zur Akustik,* pp. 15–16.

56. See Peter Williams, *The European Organ, 1450–1850* (London: B. T. Batsford, 1966), p. 90.

57. See *Data zur Akustik* pp. 19, 20n.

58. See "Korrespondenz: Stockholm im Februar 1799," p. 414; *Data zur Akustik,* p. 7n.; *Vergleichungs-Plan der . . . Neumunster-Orgel,* p. 5.

59. *Vergleichungs-Plan der . . . Neumünster-Orgel,* pp. 5–6.

60. *Uebersicht der Orgel-Umschaffung in der Dreifaltigkeits Kirche zu Schweidnitz,* [p. 3], n. 2; *Data zur Akustik,* p. 7n.; and *Vergleichungs-Plan der . . . Neumünster-Orgel,* p. 5.

61. Representative discussions of his objections appear in *Ueber die Umschaffung der St. Marien-Orgel in Berlin,* [pp. 2–3], and *Vergleichungs-Plan der . . . Neumünster-Orgel,* pp. 6–7.

62. According to Hans Martin Balz, *Orgeln und Orgelbauer im Gebiet der ehemaligen hessischen Provinz Starkenburg* (Marburg: Gärich & Weiershäuser, 1969), p. 427, there were Italian precedents for this procedure.

63. *Vergleichungs-Plan der . . . Neumünster-Orgel,* p. 7.

64. The stops Vogler used with full organ are enumerated in "Nachtrag zur Recension des Orgel Konzerts in der St. Marienkirche in Berlin," *Allgemeine musikalische Zeitung* 3 (1800–1801), *Intelligenz-Blatt* 5, p. 19.

65. In *Data zur Akustik,* p. 18n., Vogler indicated that he eliminated the Terz 6 2/5′ because the third was too prominent in the lowest octave. Indeed, he began the register with its second octave, as a displaced Terz 3 1/5′.

66. *Ueber die Umschaffung der St. Marien-Orgel in Berlin,* [pp. 1–2].

67. See Vogler, "Über die Oxydazion der schwingenden Metallkörper," [1809, p. 4n.], Darmstadt, Hessisches Staatsarchiv, D 4, Nr. 695 (ostensibly published in *Allgemeine Anzeiger der Deutschen* in 1810).

68. In "Ueber das Wirken des Abts und Geh. Raths Vogler im Orgelbaufache," *Allgemeine musikalische Zeitung* 26 (1824): 673–77, 689–94.

69. *Allgemeine musikalische Zeitung* 3 (1800–1801): 336.

70. See Vogler (?), "Korrespondenz: Stockholm im Februar 1799," p. 414.

71. *Data zur Akustik*, p. 10n.

72. "Korrespondenz: Stockholm im Februar 1799," pp. 413–14; *Kurze Beschreibung*, [pp. 2–4].

73. "Erklärung der Buchstaben," published in Sulzmann, "Eine Planung Abbé G. J. Voglers aus dem Jahre 1806," pp. 56–61 (see p. 60).

74. This may have been related to the swell on J. Moreau's organ at St. Jan in Gouda, with which Vogler was familiar.

75. *Chronik, 1790*, p. 64, and *Vergleichungs-Plan der . . . Neumünster-Orgel*, p. 5, n. 3.

76. See Friedrich Marx, *Ueber die misslungene Umschaffung der St. Marien-Orgel in Berlin, nach Vogler's Angabe* (Berlin, 1801), reprinted in *Ökonomisch-technologische Encyklopädie, oder Allgemeines System der Staats-, Stadt-, Haus- und Landwirthschaft, und der Kunstgeschichte*, ed. Johann Georg Krünitz, vol. 105 (Berlin, 1807), p. 417.

77. The door, roof, and wind swells are described in more detail by Leopold Sauer, "Ueber das Crescendo in des Abt Voglers Orchestrion," *Allgemeine musikalische Zeitung* 26 (1824): 370–73, and Wilke, "Ueber die Crescendo- und Diminuendo-Züge an Orgeln," *Allgemeine musikalische Zeitung* 25 (1823): 113–17. See also Vogler, *Kurze Beschreibung*, [p. 5].

78. Vogler, *Vergleichungsplan der . . . Orgel in dem evangelischen Hofbethause*, specification table.

79. "Ueber die Crescendo- und Diminuendo-Züge an Orgeln," pp. 116–17.

80. In "Die Orgel in Neu-Ruppin, erbauet unter dem Hrn. geh. Rath, Abt Vogler in Darmstadt," *Allgemeine musikalische Zeitung* 13 (1811): 236, Wilke stated that this was comparable to stringing a cello with strings intended for a double bass—and equally ineffectual.

81. Recounted in Wilke, "Ueber die Erfindung der Rohrwerke mit durchschlagenden Zungen," *Allgemeine musikalische Zeitung* 25 (1823): 151–53, and based on information supplied in a letter from Rackwitz to the author.

82. Vogler, "Vergleich der Kempeln'schen Sprach-Maschine mit dem, der Menschenstimme täuschend nachahmenden, singbaren Orgel-Register, von dieser Ähnlichkeit *Vox humana* genannt," [1810, pp. 10–11], Darmstadt, Hessisches Staatsarchiv, D 4, Nr. 695.

83. Darmstadt, Hessisches Staatsarchiv, D 4, Nr. 695. See also Vogler's discussions of early acoustical experiments in "Bemerkungen über die der Musik vortheilhafteste Bauart eines Musikchors," *Journal von und für Deutschland* 9 (1792): 181, and *Data zur Akustik*, pp. 25–26, 26–27n.

84. *Data zur Akustik*, pp. 24–30.

85. Vogler, "Harmonisch-akustische Bemerkungen über den Theater-Bau," [c. 1807; p. 8n.].

86. *Uiber die harmonische Akustik*, p. 5, and in other writings.

87. Letter of February 22, published in Max Unger, "Aus Bernhard Anselm Webers

Jugendjahren: Briefe von Weber und anderen," *Allgemeine Musik-Zeitung* 38 (1911): 881–82.

88. *Uiber die harmonische Akustik,* p. 5, and *Data zur Akustik,* p. 1.

89. For a discussion of the Rotterdam project, see J. W. Enschedé, "De orgelconcerten van den Abt Vogler in de Nederlanden 1785–1790," *Oud-Holland* 38 (1920): 54–57.

90. *Uiber die harmonische Akustik,* p. 6n.

91. As reported in *Data zur Akustik,* p. 3n.

92. According to Vogler's "Vergleich der Kempeln'schen Sprach-Maschine," [p. 9].

93. *Chronik, 1790,* p. 64.

94. Other reports—also of later versions—describe the size in comparable terms, the shape typically called cubic. But Leopold Sauer, in "Ueber das Crescendo in des Abt Voglers Orchestrion," p. 370, described the instrument as resembling a small house with a square base (nine feet on each side), its height tapering off from nine feet in the center to three feet on either side.

95. For further details on the swell devices and Sauer's improvements, see "Ueber das Crescendo," pp. 370–73.

96. The critique appears in Heinz Wolfgang Hamann, "Abt Vogler in Salzburger Sicht," *Österreichische Musikzeitschrift* 17 (1962): 367–70.

97. Concerning the registers that were removed, see Sven Wistedt, "Ett bidrag till en Vogler-biografi," *Svensk tidskrift för musikforskning* 15 (1933): 21–22. A letter by Vogler (at Berlin, Staatsbibliothek Preussischer Kulturbesitz, Mus. Slg. Härtel [7 Briefe von G. J. Vogler]), confirms that a renovation of the *Orchestrion* also took place.

98. According to a letter from Prague, dated April 27, 1802 (also at Berlin, Staatsbibliothek Preussischer Kulturbesitz). The anonymous critic from Salzburg claimed that the total was reduced from 1,500 to 900 (before changes in Prague, the total claimed by Vogler in his *St. Marien-Orgel* essay [1800] had been 1,137).

99. According to the *Journal des Luxus und der Moden* 6 (1791), *Intelligenz-Blatt* 6, p. lxxii.

100. Vogler, *Uebersicht der Orgel-Umschaffung in der Dreifaltigkeits Kirche zu Schweidnitz,* [p. 4].

101. *Handbuch zur Harmonielehre,* p. vii n.

102. Described by Vogler in *Data zur Akustik,* pp. 31–34.

103. See Vogler's description in *Uiber die harmonische Akustik,* pp. 11–12n.

104. "Ueber das Crescendo in des Abt Voglers Orchestrion," p. 372.

105. Letter at Vienna, Gesellschaft der Musikfreunde (Gänsbacher *Nachlass*). Knecht is not named but is readily identified by association with both the *Orchestrion* and the *Micropan,* a portable organ he built for Vogler.

106. Schubart, *Chronik, 1790,* p. 64; Knecht, *Vollständige Orgelschule* 1:5.

107. Felix Joseph Lipowsky, *Baierisches Musik-Lexikon* (Munich, 1811), p. 361.

108. From a description of the *Orchestrion* published in *Musikalische Korrespondenz* . . . *1790*, p. 192. The description (with minor differences) also appeared in *Journal des Luxus und der Moden* 6 (1791), *Intelligenz-Blatt* 6, p. lxxii, and was identified as an excerpt from an Amsterdam paper of November 27, 1790; it appears to have been the basis for other reports as well. Schubart (in *Chronik, 1790,* p. 773) wrote of Vogler's plans to introduce his *Orchestrion* on St. Cecilia's Day (November 22), but the concert had to be postponed, as reported by the *Amsterdamsche Courant.*

109. *Allgemeine musikalische Zeitung* 4 (1801–2): 509–10.

110. Letter at Berlin, Staatsbibliothek Preussischer Kulturbesitz, Mus. Slg. Härtel (7 Briefe von G. J. Vogler).

111. See *Allgemeine musikalische Zeitung* 1 (1798–99): 428–29 and Wilke, "Ueber die Erfindung der Rohrwerke mit durchschlagenden Zungen," p. 153.

112. Darmstadt, Hessisches Staatsarchiv, D 4, Nr. 695. Schafhäutl gives the dates 1810–14 for the instrument he examined; if correct, they probably apply to a renovation rather than a second instrument.

113. *Uiber die harmonische Akustik,* p. 5.

114. See references to this simplification in Vogler's *Ueber die Umschaffung der St. Marien-Orgel in Berlin,* [p. 3], and in "Korrespondenz: Stockholm im Februar 1799," p. 415; see also Joseph Sonnleithner's remarks in "Etwas über die Vogler'sche Simplification des Orgelbaues," *Allgemeine musikalische Zeitung* 2 (1799–1800): 565.

115. Vogler, *Uebersicht der Orgel-Umschaffung in der Dreifaltigkeits Kirche zu Schweidnitz,* [p. 2].

116. A copy of the circular resides at Darmstadt, Hessisches Staatsarchiv, D 4, Nr. 695.

117. This may be deduced from a specification found in "Register-Dispositionen," fol. 12, which corresponds to details cited in the published circular. The "Register-Dispositionen" included four additional specifications for *Normal-Orgeln,* two for one-manual instruments, and each of the remaining two for two- and three-manual instruments. An 1812 advertisement by Oberndörfer (quoted in Balz, *Orgeln und Orgelbauer im Gebiet der ehemaligen hessischen Provinz Starkenburg,* p. 430) suggests that instruments of this type were actually constructed.

118. Discussed at length in Hermann Spies, *Abbé Vogler und die von ihm 1805 simplifizierte Orgel von St. Peter in Salzburg* (Mainz: Paul Smets, 1932).

119. See Schweiger, "Abbé Voglers Simplifikationssystem und seine akustischen Studien," pp. 98–108.

120. See Wistedt, "Ett bidrag till en Vogler-biografi," pp. 11–24.

121. For further information on the Norrköping instrument, including a specification, see Wistedt, "Abbé Vogler och svensk orgelbyggnadskonst jämte några nyupptäckta Voglerdokument," *Svensk tidskrift för musikforskning* 14 (1932): 39–57.

Regarding the Ramsberg instrument, Vogler is named in the contract as having supplied a plan and suggestions, although the contract was awarded to Pehr Schiörlin. See Josef Sjögren, *Orgelverken i Västerås Stift* (Stockholm: Nordiska Museet, 1952), pp. 153–54, which also provides a specification.

122. The text of this description (from a manuscript copy) and the accompanying diagram are published in Sulzmann, "Eine Planung Abbé G. J. Voglers aus dem Jahre 1806," pp. 55–61.

123. Vogler described the roof swell in *Kurze Beschreibung* as being divided into three frames, covered with coarse linen that was painted to give it more substance. This version of the roof apparently differed from the contrivance described in the earlier *Erklärung der Buchstaben*.

124. This specification has been distilled mainly from information in the *Verzeichniss der Register,* which depicts only the arrangement of stop knobs on the console. The *Verzeichniss* was chosen in preference to the much-cited specification in "Register-Dispositionen" because its enumeration of pedal registers represents more closely than the "Register-Dispositionen" Vogler's description of the manner in which he distributed the lowest pipes and because registers correspond in number (21 treble, 21 bass, 32 pedal) to those listed in *Kurze Beschreibung,* presumably the pamphlet sold at the entrance to St. Peter's for Vogler's demonstrations on the new organ (see *Allgemeine musikalische Zeitung* 12 [1809–10]: 155).

125. The extent of sharing intended between manual bass and pedal may have changed for the different versions Vogler describes, as suggested by the initially large (but progressively smaller) numbers of pipes in question and comments made in *Erklärung der Buchstaben* and the *Verzeichniss.*

126. The essence of Vogler's unconventional approach to designating registers has been retained here, but requires explanation. For all treble registers and any displaced bass registers, both the pipe length and the pitch name must be taken into account. In the treble of manual 5, for example, Vogler's designation *Flauto piccolo* 1′, *c″ zu c′* signifies a register in which 1′ C (i.e., c″) sounds when the key c′ is struck. This is represented in Table 2 as Flauto piccolo 1′, c′ = c″.

127. According to a letter to the Grand Duke [1809], at Darmstadt, Hessisches Staatsarchiv, D 4, Nr. 695. All letters named in connection with the *Triorganon* project reside within this collection, unless otherwise specified.

128. See *Allgemeine musikalische Zeitung* 12 (1810): 510–11.

129. Letter from Gothenburg, July 26, 1794, located at Stockholm, Musikaliska Akademiens Bibliotek, B III: 2.

130. Berlin, Deutsche Staatsbibliothek, Mus. Ms. Autogr. Vogler, Georg Jos. (Abt).

131. *Data zur Akustik,* pp. 18–22.

132. "Die Orgel in Neu-Ruppin," pp. 235–36.

133. "Gedanken über des Hrn. Abt Voglers Orgel-Simplifications-System," *Allge-*

*meine musikalische Zeitung* 4 (1801–2): 51, and "Fortgesetzte Unterhaltungen über einige im 50. Stücke des vorigen Jahrgangs dieser Zeitung zur Sprache gekommene Gegenstände," *Allgemeine musikalische Zeitung* 6 (1803–4): 140.

134. G. C. F. Schlimbach, "Ueber des Abts Vogler Umschaffung der Orgel zu St. Marien in Berlin," *Berlinische musikalische Zeitung* 2 (1806): 13, 16.

135. E. F. F. Chladni, "Über Kostenersparniss durch Hervorbringung mehr als eines Tones auf derselben Orgelpfeife," *Cäcilia* 5 (1826): 43.

136. See, for example, "Gedanken über des Hrn. Abt Voglers Orgel-Simplifications-System," pp. 50–51, 57, and Schlimbach, "Ueber des Abts Vogler Umschaffung," *Berlinische musikalische Zeitung* 2 (1806): 13–14.

137. "Die Orgel in Neu-Ruppin," p. 236.

138. Schlimbach, "Ueber des Abts Vogler Umschaffung," *Berlinische musikalische Zeitung* 1 (1805): 394.

139. "Gedanken über des Hrn. Abt Voglers Orgel-Simplifications-System," p. 53.

140. "Ueber des Abts Vogler Umschaffung," *Berlinische musikalische Zeitung* 1 (1805): 391, 393–94; 2 (1806): 13–14.

141. "Die Orgel in Neu-Ruppin," p. 233.

142. "Die Orgel in Neu-Ruppin," p. 236; "Ueber das Wirken des Abts und Geh. Raths Vogler im Orgelbaufache," pp. 689–90.

143. "Gedanken über des Hrn. Abt Voglers Orgel-Simplifications-System," pp. 55–56, 57.

144. "Die Orgel in Neu-Ruppin," pp. 220–24, 235.

145. See ibid., pp. 236–39.

146. See, for example, Schlimbach, "Ueber des Abts Vogler Umschaffung," p. 394.

147. See "Fortgesetzte Unterhaltungen," pp. 140–41, and "Gedanken über des Hrn. Abt Voglers Orgel-Simplifications-System," pp. 51–52.

148. Schlimbach, "Ueber des Abts Vogler Umschaffung," p. 384; Marx, *Allgemeine musikalische Zeitung* 4 (1801–2), *Intelligenz-Blatt* 6, p. 22.

149. Hermann Fischer and Theodor Wohnhaas, "Zur Geschichte der Orgel von St. Peter in München," *Kirchenmusikalisches Jahrbuch* 57 (1973): 97–98; Karl Emil von Schafhäutl, *Abt Georg Joseph Vogler* (Augsburg, 1888), pp. 156–57. Through Schafhäutl's efforts, a restoration project in 1865 brought the instrument closer to its original version.

150. Felix Mendelssohn-Bartholdy, *Briefe aus den Jahren 1830 bis 1847,* ed. Paul and Carl Mendelssohn-Bartholdy, 4th ed., 2 vols. (Leipzig, 1878) 1:217. Cited in Schafhäutl, *Abt Georg Joseph Vogler,* pp. 157–58, with minor differences.

151. *Abt Georg Joseph Vogler,* p. 190.

152. Munich, Bayerisches Hauptstaatsarchiv, MInn 24059: 80–83.

153. See "Vorläufige Nachricht von einem Mikropan," *Allgemeine musikalische Zeitung*

5 (1802–3): 533–35 and Sulzmann, "Eine Planung Abbé G. J. Voglers aus dem Jahre 1806," pp. 63–64.

154. "Geschichtlicher Ueberblick der Verbesserungen und neuen Erfindungen im Orgelbau seit fünfzig Jahren," *Allgemeine musikalische Zeitung* 38 (1836): 697–99.

EPILOGUE

1. Vogler, *Choral-System* (Copenhagen, 1800), pp. 104–5.

2. See Jitka Ludvová, "Abbé Vogler a Praha," *Hudebni Veda* 19 (1982): 122.

3. See Emily Anderson, trans. and ed., *The Letters of Mozart and His Family,* 2d ed., 2 vols. (New York: St. Martin's Press, 1966), 2:548–49. See also Leopold's letter of August 3, 1778, in which he writes "you need not send me Vogler's book, as we can get it here" (p. 592). Cf. Vogler, *Kuhrpfälzische Tonschule,* 2 vols. (Mannheim, [1778]), 1:vi, where the official endorsement of his system is mentioned.

4. *Allgemeine musikalische Zeitung* 2 (1799–1800), *Intelligenz-Blatt* 18, p. 75. The *Musik-skole* comprised Danish translations of three of Vogler's Swedish manuals: *Inledning til harmoniens kännedom, Clavér-schola,* and *Organist-schola,* vol. 1.

5. Heinrich Christoph Koch, *Handbuch bei dem Studium der Harmonie* (Leipzig, 1811), pp. 77–78.

6. See Koch, *Handbuch,* pp. 91–129. It should be noted that the device of finding dissonances outside the octave was by no means unique to Vogler and his Italian mentor, and that a particular aspect of Koch's procedure, involving the building of *chords* of the ninth, eleventh, and thirteenth (rather than interval relationships) is perhaps more directly related to Vogler's disciple Knecht than to Vogler himself.

7. See Anton Reicha, *Course of Musical Composition* [London, 1854], p. 58, trans. by Arnold Merrick of *Cours de composition musicale* (Paris, 1818).

8. Emanuel Aloys Förster, *Practische Beyspiele als Fortsetzung zu seiner Anleitung des Generalbasses* (Vienna, [1819]), pp. 12, 88.

9. Emanuel Aloys Förster, *Anleitung zum General-Bass* (Vienna, 1805). See Robert W. Wason, *Viennese Harmonic Theory from Albrechtsberger to Schenker and Schoenberg* (Ann Arbor: UMI Research Press, 1985), pp. 21–25, where aspects of Förster's approach, including his objections to Vogler's theory, are elaborated. For a discussion of Beethoven's special respect for Förster as a teacher of counterpoint and composition, see Elliot Forbes, rev. and ed., *Thayer's Life of Beethoven* (Princeton: Princeton University Press, 1967), pp. 261–62.

10. Joseph Drechsler, *Harmonie und Generalbass-Lehre* (Vienna, [1816]), pp. 5–6.

11. See the obituary in *Allgemeine musikalische Zeitung* 28 (1826): 354, which discusses Vogler's relationship with Winter, who wished not to be known as the abbé's pupil.

12. The 2d ed., Munich, 1814, was entitled *Elementarwerk der Harmonie, als Einleitung in die Begleitungs- und Tonsetzkunst, wie auch in die Tonwissenschaft.*

13. Justin Heinrich Knecht, *Erklärung einiger von einem der R. G. B. in Erlangen angetasteten, aber missverstandenen Grundsätze aus der Voglerschen Theorie* (Ulm, 1785); "Kritische Briefe an einen jungen Tonsezer über wichtige Materien aus der Tonwissenschaft und Tonsezkunst," *Musikalische Real-Zeitung für das Jahr 1788,* pp. 10–14, 42–47; "Erster [ . . . Sechster] belehrender Brief," *Musikalische Korrespondenz der teutschen Filarmonischen Gesellschaft für das Jahr 1790,* pp. 125–28, 140–43; *1791,* 134–36, 140–42, 257–60, 265–68; "Kurze Beantwortung der Frage: Was für Vortheile hat sich die praktische Musik vor der Anwendung des Voglerschen Systems zu versprechen?" *Allgemeine musikalische Zeitung* 3 (1800–1801): 725–32, 741–50.

14. See Vogler, "Aeusserung über Hrn. Knechts Harmonik," *Allgemeine musikalische Zeitung* 2 (1799–1800): 689–96; see also the Knecht obituary in *Allgemeine musikalische Zeitung* 20 (1818): 208.

15. See Giacomo Meyerbeer, *Briefwechsel und Tagebücher,* ed. Heinz and Gudrun Becker, 4 vols. (Berlin: Walter de Gruyter, 1960–85), vol. 1; Carl Maria von Weber, *Writings on Music,* trans. Martin Cooper, ed. John Warrack (Cambridge: Cambridge University Press, 1981), pp. 253–54.

16. Excerpted in Karl Emil von Schafhäutl, *Abt Georg Joseph Vogler* (Augsburg, 1888), p. 52; cf. reading in Carl Maria von Weber, *Carl Maria von Weber: Briefe,* ed. Hans Christoph Worbs (Frankfurt am Main: Fischer, 1982), pp. 16–17.

17. Both pieces are quite simple harmonically, revealing an unfaltering command of basic compositional techniques. Though specific traces of Vogler's influence are subtle at best, at least one instance of a genuine Vogler trademark merits mention: the simultaneous chromatic passing tones in Variation 2 of the *Variations on a Theme from 'Samori',* which yield passing chords of the diminished seventh and augmented sixth, and which temporarily tonicize all scale degrees but VII.

18. See Weber, *Writings on Music,* pp. 59–63.

19. See for example Meyerbeer, *Briefwechsel und Tagebücher* 1:75, 104–5, 149–51.

20. *Briefwechsel und Tagebücher* 2:591.

21. François-Joseph Fétis, *Traité complet de la théorie et de la pratique de l'harmonie,* 7th ed. (Paris, 1861), pp. 224–27; originally published in 1844.

22. Hugo Riemann, *Geschichte der Musiktheorie im IX.–XIX. Jahrhundert,* 2d ed. (Berlin, 1921), p. 511.

23. "Vogler makes use of the harmonic as well as the arithmetical division of a string, which he extends to the thirty-second term. From the sounds obtained by this process he then constructs all the chords he requires." Shirlaw, *The Theory of Harmony* (London: Novello, 1917), pp. 329–30.

24. Vogler, *Handbuch* (Prague, 1802), pp. x–xii.

25. The circumstances under which Gottfried Weber acquired the device are unclear. Closely associated with the Darmstadt circle, he experienced personal contact with Vogler, wrote enthusiastically of his music, dedicated compositions to him, and participated in the *Zwölf Choräle* project; and though Weber's use of the term *Tonsetzkunst* echoes Vogler, and various correspondences may be discerned between Weber's pedagogy and Vogler's, it is nevertheless possible that he acquired the idea through Knecht's writings (mentioned in Weber's preface), or from one of the early nineteenth-century Viennese thoroughbass manuals such as those of Förster or Drechsler mentioned above.

26. Cf. Robert P. Morgan, "Schenker and the Theoretical Tradition: The Concept of Musical Reduction," *College Music Symposium* 18 (1978): 87–92. See also Robert W. Wason, "Schenker's Notion of Scale-Step in Historical Perspective: Non-Essential Harmonies in Viennese Fundamental Bass Theory," *Journal of Music Theory* 29 (1985): 49–73.

27. See David W. Beach, "The Origins of Harmonic Analysis," *Journal of Music Theory* 18 (1974): 274–307.

# Bibliography

Abert, Hermann. "Wort und Ton in der Musik des 18. Jahrhunderts." *Archiv für Musikwissenschaft* 5 (1923): 31–70. Reprinted in *Gesammelte Schriften und Vorträge*, edited by Friedrich Blume, pp. 173–231. Tutzing: Hans Schneider, 1968.

Adlung, Jacob. *Anleitung zu der musikalischen Gelahrtheit.* Erfurt, 1758. Reprint. Kassel: Bärenreiter, 1953.

———. *Musica mechanica organoedi.* 2 vols. Berlin, 1768. Reprint. Kassel: Bärenreiter, 1961.

d'Alembert, Jean le Rond. *Elémens de musique, théorique et pratique, suivant les principes de M. Rameau.* Paris, 1752. Reprint. New York: Broude Brothers, 1966.

Allen, Warren D. *Philosophies of Music History: A Study of General Histories of Music, 1600–1960.* New York, 1939. Corrected republication. New York: Dover, 1962.

*Allgemeine musikalische Zeitung.* Edited by Johann Friedrich Rochlitz et al. 50 vols. Leipzig, 1798–1848. Reprint. Amsterdam: Frits Knuf, 1964.

Andersen, Poul-Gerhard. *Organ Building and Design.* Translated by Joanne Curnutt. New York: Oxford University Press, 1969.

Anderson, Emily, trans. and ed. *The Letters of Mozart and His Family.* 2d ed. 2 vols. New York: St. Martin's Press, 1966.

Bach, Carl Philipp Emanuel. *Essay on the True Art of Playing Keyboard Instruments.* Translated and edited by William J. Mitchell. New York: W. W. Norton, 1949.

Balz, Hans Martin. *Orgeln und Orgelbauer im Gebiet der ehemaligen hessischen Provinz Starkenburg: Ein Beitrag zur Geschichte des Orgelbaues.* Marburg: Gärich & Weiershäuser, 1969.

Barbour, J. Murray. "Irregular Systems of Temperament." *Journal of the American Musicological Society* 1/3 (1948): 20–26.

———. *Tuning and Temperament: A Historical Survey.* East Lansing: Michigan State College Press, 1951.

Beach, David W. "The Functions of the Six-Four Chord in Tonal Music." *Journal of Music Theory* 11 (1967): 2–31.

———. "The Origins of Harmonic Analysis." *Journal of Music Theory* 18 (1974): 274–307.

Benary, Peter. *Die deutsche Kompositionslehre des 18. Jahrhunderts.* Leipzig: Breitkopf & Härtel, 1961.

*Berlinische musikalische Zeitung.* Edited by Johann Friedrich Reichardt. 2 vols. Berlin, 1805–6. Reprint. Hildesheim: Georg Olms, 1969.

Birke, Joachim. *Christian Wolffs Metaphysik und die zeitgenössische Literatur- und Musiktheorie: Gottsched, Scheibe, Mizler.* Berlin: Walter de Gruyter, 1966.

Blindow, Martin. *Die Choralbegleitung des 18. Jahrhunderts in der evangelischen Kirche Deutschlands.* Regensburg: Gustav Bosse, 1957.

Blume, Friedrich. "Bach in the Romantic Era." *Musical Quarterly* 50 (1964): 290–306.

———. *Two Centuries of Bach: An Account of Changing Taste.* Translated by Stanley Godman. London, 1950. Reprint. New York: Da Capo Press, 1978.

———, with Ludwig Finscher and others. *Protestant Church Music: A History.* Translated from the German. New York: W. W. Norton, 1974.

Bopp, August. *Das Musikleben in der Freien Reichsstadt Biberach, unter besonderer Berücksichtigung der Tätigkeit Justin Heinrich Knechts.* Kassel: Bärenreiter, 1930.

Brenet, Michel [Marie Bobillier]. "L'Abbé Vogler à Paris en 1781–83." *Archives historiques, artistiques et littéraires* 2 (1891): 150–56.

"[Briefe an einen Freund über die Musik in Berlin:] Vierter Brief, vom 29sten November." *Allgemeine musikalische Zeitung* 3 (1800–1801): 191–96.

Britton, David James. "Abbé Georg Joseph Vogler: His Life and His Theories on Organ Design." D.M.A. thesis, University of Rochester, 1973.

Buelow, George J. "The *Loci Topici* and Affect in Late Baroque Music: Heinichen's Practical Demonstration." *Music Review* 27 (1966): 161–76.

———. *Thorough-Bass Accompaniment According to Johann David Heinichen.* Berkeley: University of California Press, 1966.

Burney, Charles. *A General History of Music from the Earliest Ages to the Present Period.* 4 vols. London, 1776–89. Modern edition by Frank Mercer. London, 1935. Reprint. New York: Dover, 1957.

Bury, J. B. *The Idea of Progress: An Inquiry into its Origin and Growth.* London: Macmillan, 1921. Reprint. Westport, Conn.: Greenwood Press, 1982.

Busch, Hermann Richard. *Leonhard Eulers Beitrag zur Musiktheorie.* Regensburg: Gustav Bosse, 1970.

*Cäcilia: Eine Zeitschrift für die musikalische Welt.* Edited by Gottfried Weber and Siegfried Wilhelm Dehn. 27 vols. Mainz, 1824–48. Reprint. Hildesheim: Georg Olms, 1979.

Cassirer, Ernst. *The Philosophy of the Enlightenment.* Translated by Fritz C. A. Koelin and James P. Pettegrove. Princeton: Princeton University Press, 1951.

Cattin, Giulio, ed. *Francescantonio Vallotti nel II centenario dalla morte (1780–1980): Biografia, catalogo tematico delle opere e contributi critici.* Padua: Edizioni Messaggero, 1981.

Chladni, Ernst Florens Friedrich. "Über Kostenersparniss durch Hervorbringung mehr als eines Tones auf derselben Orgelpfeife." *Cäcilia* 5 (1826): 41–43.

Christmann, Johann Friedrich. "Ueber Voglern, aus einem Schreiben des Herrn Pfr. Christmanns an J***." *Musikalische Korrespondenz der teutschen Filarmonischen Gesellschaft für das Jahr 1790,* pp. 113–20, 121–22.

*Chronik, 1790 [–91].* Edited by Christian Friedrich Daniel Schubart. Stuttgart. (Continuation of *Vaterländische Chronik* (1787) and *Vaterlandschronik* [1788–89].)

Churgin, Bathia. "Francesco Galeazzi's Description of Sonata Form." *Journal of the American Musicological Society* 21 (1968): 181–99.

Cowart, Georgia. *The Origins of Modern Musical Criticism.* Ann Arbor: UMI Research Press, 1981.

Daube, Johann Friedrich. *General-Bass in drey Accorden, gegründet in den Regeln der alt- und neuen Autoren.* Leipzig, 1756.

David, Hans T. and Arthur Mendel, eds. *The Bach Reader: A Life of Johann Sebastian Bach in Letters and Documents.* Rev. ed. New York: W. W. Norton, 1966.

David, Werner. *Die Orgel von St. Marien zu Berlin und andere berühmte Berliner Orgeln.* Mainz: Paul Smets, 1949.

Descartes, René. *Compendium of Music.* Translated by Walter Robert. Introduction and notes by Charles Kent. Rome: AMI Studies & Documents, 1961.

*Deutsche Chronik, auf das Jahr 1774 [–77].* Edited by Christian Friedrich Daniel Schubart. 4 vols. Stuttgart. Reprint. Heidelberg: Lambert Schneider, 1975.

*Deutsche Encyclopädie oder Allgemeines Real-Wörterbuch aller Künste und Wissenschaften.* Edited by Kasten and Roos. 23 vols., A–K. Frankfurt am Main, 1778–1804.

Drechsler, Joseph. *Harmonie und Generalbass-Lehre.* Vienna, [1816].

Ehmann, Wilhelm. "Der Thibaut-Behagel-Kreis: Ein Beitrag zur Geschichte der musikalischen Restauration im 19. Jahrhundert." *Archiv für Musikforschung* 3 (1938): 428–83; 4 (1939): 21–67.

Eitner, Robert. *Biographisch-bibliographisches Quellen-Lexikon der Musiker und Musikgelehrten der Christlichen Zeitrechnung bis zur Mitte des neunzehnten Jahrhunderts.* 10 vols. Leipzig, 1900–1904. Reprint. Graz: Akademische Druck- u. Verlagsanstalt, 1959–60.

Engel, Johann Jakob. *Ueber die musikalische Malerey.* Berlin, 1780. Also published in *Magazin der Musik* 1 (1783): 1139–98.

Engländer, Richard. "Joseph Martin Kraus und der schwedische Dichterkreis." In *Festschrift für Ernst Hermann Meyer zum sechzigsten Geburtstag,* edited by Georg Knepler, pp. 257–64. Leipzig: Deutscher Verlag für Musik, 1973.

Enschedé, J. W. "De orgelconcerten van den Abt Vogler in de Nederlanden 1785–1790." *Oud-Holland* 38 (1920): 37–59.

Ettelson, Trudy Gottlieb. "Jean-Jacques Rousseau's Writings on Music: A Quest for Melody." Ph.D. dissertation, Yale University, 1974.

"Etwas über Kirchenmusik." *Musikalische Real-Zeitung für das Jahr 1788,* pp. 177–82, 185–88.

Feder, Georg. "Decline and Restoration." In Friedrich Blume et al., *Protestant Church Music: A History,* trans. from the German, pp. 319–404. New York: W. W. Norton, 1974.

Fellerer, Karl Gustav. "Die Aufgaben des Organisten beim Hochamt im 18. Jahrhundert." *Musica sacra* 57 (1927): 303–9.

———. *Beiträge zur Choralbegleitung und Choralverarbeitung in der Orgelmusik des ausgehenden 18. und beginnenden 19. Jahrhunderts.* Strassburg: Heitz & Cie, [1932]. Reprint. Baden-Baden: Valentin Koerner, 1980.

———. "Ferdinand D'Anthoins Ästhetik der Kirchenmusik 1784." In *Colloquium amicorum: Joseph Schmidt-Görg zum 70. Geburtstag,* edited by Siegfried Kross and Hans Schmidt, pp. 82–92. Bonn: Beethovenhaus, 1967.

———. *Der Gregorianische Choral im Wandel der Jahrhunderte.* Regensburg: Friedrich Pustet, 1936.

———. *Der Palestrinastil und seine Bedeutung in der vokalen Kirchenmusik des achtzehnten Jahrhunderts: Ein Beitrag zur Geschichte der Kirchenmusik in Italien und Deutschland.* Augsburg: Benno Filser, 1929. Reprint. Walluf bei Wiesbaden: Sändig, 1972.

———. "Zum Bild der altklassischen Polyphonie im 18. Jahrhundert." In *Festschrift für Ernst Hermann Meyer zum sechzigsten Geburtstag,* edited by Georg Knepler, pp. 243–52. Leipzig: Deutscher Verlag für Musik, 1973.

———. "Zur Choralbewegung im 19. Jahrhundert." *Kirchenmusikalisches Jahrbuch* 41 (1957): 136–46.

———. "Zur Neukomposition und Vortrag des gregorianischen Chorals im 18. Jahrhundert." *Acta musicologica* 6 (1934): 145–52.

———, ed. *Geschichte der katholischen Kirchenmusik.* 2 vols. Kassel: Bärenreiter, 1972–76.

Fétis, François-Joseph. *Biographie universelle des musiciens et Bibliographie générale de la musique.* 2d ed. 8 vols. & supplement (2 vols.). Paris, 1873–80. Reprint. Brussels: Culture et Civilisation, 1963.

———. *Traité complet de la théorie et de la pratique de l'harmonie.* 7th ed. Paris, 1861.

Finkel, Klaus. *Musik in Unterricht und Erziehung an den gelehrten Schulen im pfälzischen Teil der Kurpfalz, in Leiningen und in der Reichsstadt Landau.* Tutzing: Hans Schneider, 1978.

Fischer, Hermann and Theodor Wohnhaas. "Zur Geschichte der Orgel von St. Peter in München: Beispiele für die Beziehungen zwischen dem mainfränkischen und Münchner Orgelbau." *Kirchenmusikalisches Jahrbuch* 57 (1973): 79–98.

Fischnaler, C. *Johann Gänsbacher.* Innsbruck, 1878.

Flaherty, Gloria. *Opera in the Development of German Critical Thought.* Princeton: Princeton University Press, 1978.

Forbes, Elliot, rev. and ed. *Thayer's Life of Beethoven.* Princeton: Princeton University Press, 1967.

Forkel, Johann Nicolaus. *Allgemeine Geschichte der Musik.* 2 vols. Leipzig, 1788–1801. Reprint. Graz: Akademische Druck- u. Verlagsanstalt, 1967.

———. *Allgemeine Litteratur der Musik.* Leipzig, 1792. Reprint. Hildesheim: Georg Olms, 1962.

———. *Über die Theorie der Musik.* Göttingen, 1777. Also published in *Magazin der Musik* 1 (1783): 855–912.

Förster, Emanuel Aloys. *Anleitung zum General-Bass.* Vienna, 1805.

———. *Practische Beyspiele als Fortsetzung zu seiner Anleitung des Generalbasses.* Vienna, [1819].

"Fortgesetzte Unterhaltungen über einige im 50. Stücke des vorigen Jahrgangs dieser Zeitung zur Sprache gekommene Gegenstände." *Allgemeine musikalische Zeitung* 6 (1803–4): 138–42.

Fröhlich, Joseph. *Biographie des grossen Tonkünstlers Abt Georg Joseph Vogler.* Würzburg, 1845.

———. "Georg Joseph Vogler." *Euphemia: Beiblatt zur Religions- u. Kirchenfreund. Neue Folge* 6 (1846): 137–52.

———. Review of Vogler's *Grande Sinfonie. Allgemeine musikalische Zeitung* 19 (1817): 93–105.

———. Review of Vogler's *Requiem* in E-Flat. *Cäcilia* 1 (1824): 105–12, 113–28.

———. "Ueber die musikalische Feyer des katholischen Gottesdienstes überhaupt, und die Art einer dem Zeitbedürfnisse gemässen Einrichtung und Verbesserung derselben." *Allgemeine musikalische Zeitung* 22 (1820): 369–80, 389–96, 405–13, 421–30.

Frotscher, Gotthold. *Geschichte des Orgelspiels und der Orgelkomposition.* 2 vols. Berlin-Schöneberg, 1935. Reprint. Berlin: Merseburger, 1959.

Fux, Johann Joseph. *Steps to Parnassus: The Study of Counterpoint.* Translated and edited by Alfred Mann. New York: W. W. Norton, 1943. Reprinted as *The Study of Counterpoint from Johann Joseph Fux's "Gradus ad Parnassum."* New York: W. W. Norton, 1965.

"Gedanken über des Hrn. Abt Voglers Orgel-Simplifications-System, besonders über die laut einer öffentlichen Bekanntmachung bewürkte Umschaffung der St. Marien-Orgel in Berlin." *Allgemeine musikalische Zeitung* 4 (1801–2): 49–58.

Gerber, Ernst Ludwig. *Historisch-biographisches Lexicon der Tonkünstler.* 2 vols. Leipzig, 1790–92. Reprint. Graz: Akademische Druck- u. Verlagsanstalt, 1977.

———. *Neues historisch-biographisches Lexikon der Tonkünstler.* 4 vols. Leipzig, 1812–14. Reprint. Graz: Akademische Druck- und Verlagsanstalt, 1966.

————. "Noch etwas über den Choralgesang und dessen Begleitung mit der Orgel." *Allgemeine musikalische Zeitung* 12 (1809–10): 433–40.

Gerbert, Martin. *De cantu et musica sacra a prima ecclesiae aetate usque ad praesens tempus.* 2 vols. St. Blasien, 1774. Reprint. Graz: Akademische Druck- u. Verlagsanstalt, 1968.

Ginsberg, Morris. *The Idea of Progress: A Revaluation.* London, 1953. Reprint. Westport, Conn.: Greenwood Press, 1972.

Goldschmidt, Hugo. *Die Musikästhetik des 18. Jahrhunderts und ihre Beziehungen zu seinem Kunstschaffen.* Zurich: Rascher, 1915. Reprint. Hildesheim: Georg Olms, 1968.

Gotzen, Josef. "Das katholische Kirchenlied im 18. Jahrhundert insbesondere in der Aufklärungszeit." *Kirchenmusikalisches Jahrbuch* 40 (1956): 63–86.

Grandaur, Franz. *Chronik des königlichen Hof- und National-Theaters in München.* Munich, 1878.

Grant, Cecil Powell. "The Real Relationship between Kirnberger's and Rameau's Concept of the Fundamental Bass." *Journal of Music Theory* 21 (1977): 324–38.

Grave, Floyd K. "Abbé Vogler and the Bach Legacy." *Eighteenth-Century Studies* 13 (1979–80): 119–41.

————. "Abbé Vogler and the Study of Fugue." *Music Theory Spectrum* 1 (1979): 43–66.

————. "Abbé Vogler's Revision of Pergolesi's *Stabat Mater.*" *Journal of the American Musicological Society* 30 (1977): 43–71.

————. "Abbé Vogler's Theory of Reduction." *Current Musicology* 29 (1980): 41–69.

Grillparzer, Franz. *Beethoven: Erinnerungen, Reden, Gedichte.* Edited by Hans Schumacher. Herrliberg-Zurich: Bühl-Verlag-Blätter, 1946.

Grout, Donald J. *A History of Western Music.* 3d ed. New York: W. W. Norton, 1980.

Haase, Rudolf. *Geschichte des harmonikalen Pythagoreismus.* Vienna: Elisabeth Lafite, 1969.

Hamann, Heinz Wolfgang. "Abbé Voglers Simplifikations-System im Urteil der Zeitgenossen." *Musik und Kirche* 33 (1963): 28–31.

————. "Abt Vogler in Salzburger Sicht." *Österreichische Musikzeitschrift* 17 (1962): 367–70.

Hasse, Johann Adolf and Johann Adam Hiller. *Beyträge zu wahrer Kirchenmusik.* 2d ed. Leipzig, 1791.

Hayburn, Robert F. *Papal Legislation on Sacred Music 95 A.D. to 1977 A.D.* Collegeville, MN: Liturgical Press, 1979.

Hegar, Elisabeth. *Die Anfänge der neueren Musikgeschichtsschreibung um 1770 bei Gerbert, Burney und Hawkins.* Baden-Baden: Valentin Koerner, 1974.

Hennerberg, Carl Fredrik. "Einige Dokumente, den Abt Georg Joseph Vogler betreffend." In *Report of the Fourth Congress of the International Musical Society: London,*

*29th May-3rd June 1911,* edited by Charles Maclean, pp. 134–38. London: Novello, 1912.

Herder, Johann Gottfried von. *Vom Geist der Ebräischen Poesie: Eine Anleitung für die Liebhaber derselben, und der ältesten Geschichte des menschlichen Geistes.* Vol. 2. Dessau, 1783.

Hiller, Johann Adam. *Lebensbeschreibungen berühmter Musikgelehrten und Tonkünstler neuerer Zeit.* Leipzig, 1784. Reprint. Leipzig: Edition Peters, 1979.

———. "Ueber Kirchenmusik." *Berlinische musikalische Zeitung* 2 (1806) 190–92.

———. "Vorrede." *Allgemeines Choral-Melodienbuch,* pp. ix–xviii. Leipzig, [1793]. Reprint. Hildesheim: Georg Olms, 1978.

[Hoffmann, Ernst Theodor Amadeus.] "Alte und neue Kirchenmusik." *Allgemeine musikalische Zeitung* 16 (1814): 577–84, 593–603, 611–19.

Hoffmann, Kurt. "Herder und die evangelische Kirchenmusik." *Music und Kirche* 7 (1935): 121–27.

Horstig, [Karl Gottlob]. "Ein Wort für die Veredlung der Kirchenmelodien." *Allgemeine musikalische Zeitung* 9 (1806–7): 439–44.

———. "Ueber das Voglerische Simplifications-System." *Allgemeine musikalische Zeitung* 5 (1802–3): 821–24.

Horton, John. *Scandinavian Music: A Short History.* London: Faber and Faber, 1963.

Hosler, Bellamy. *Changing Aesthetic Views of Instrumental Music in 18th-Century Germany.* Ann Arbor: UMI Research Press, 1981.

Jahn, Otto. *Life of Mozart.* Translated by Pauline D. Townsend. 3 vols. London, 1891. Reprint. New York: Kalmus, n.d.

[Junker, Carl Ludwig.] "Brief an einen musikalischen Freund." *Musikalische Real-Zeitung für das Jahr 1788,* pp. 60–63, 68–71, 75–78.

*Journal des Luxus und der Moden.* Edited by Friedrich Justin Bertuch, Georg Melchior Kraus, et al. Weimar, 1786–1822. (Begun as *Journal der Moden* [1786]; title later changed to *Journal für Literatur, Kunst, Luxus und Mode.*)

Kauffmann, Ernst Friedrich. *Justinus Heinrich Knecht, ein schwäbischer Tonsetzer des 18. Jahrhunderts.* Tübingen, 1892.

Kaul, Oskar. *Geschichte der Würzburger Hofmusik im 18. Jahrhundert.* Würzburg: C. J. Becker, 1924.

Kelletat, Herbert. *Zur Geschichte der deutschen Orgelmusik in der Frühklassik.* Kassel: Bärenreiter, 1933.

Kirnberger, Johann Philipp. *Grundsätze des Generalbasses als erste Linien zur Composition.* Berlin, [c. 1781]. Reprint. Hildesheim: Georg Olms, 1974.

———. *Die Kunst des reinen Satzes in der Musik.* 2 vols. [Berlin, 1771–79]. Reprint. Hildesheim: Georg Olms, 1968.

———. *The True Principles for the Practice of Harmony.* Translated by David W. Beach and Jurgen Thym. *Journal of Music Theory* 23 (1979): 163–225. (Treatise written by J. A. P. Schulz and published under Kirnberger's name with the latter's approval.)

Kleemann, Gotthilf. *Die Orgelmacher und ihr Schaffen im ehemaligen Herzogtum Württemberg unter Hervorhebung des Lebensgangs und der Arbeit des Orgelmachers Johann Eberhard Walcker, Canstatt (1756–1843)*. Stuttgart: Musikwissenschaftliche Verlags-Gesellschaft, 1969.

Knecht, Justin Heinrich. "Abgenöthigte Selbstvertheidigung gegen den Hrn. Abt Vogler." *Musikalische Korrespondenz der teutschen Filarmonischen Gesellschaft für das Jahr 1791*, pp. 97–101.

———. *Erklärung einiger von einem der R. G. B. in Erlangen angetasteten, aber missverstandenen Grundsätze aus der Voglerschen Theorie*. Ulm, 1785.

———. "Erster [ . . . Sechster] belehrender Brief." *Musikalische Korrespondenz der teutschen Filarmonischen Gesellschaft für das Jahr 1790*, pp. 125–28, 140–43; *1791*, 134–36, 140–42, 257–60, 265–68.

———. *Gemeinnützliches Elementarwerk der Harmonie und des Generalbasses*. 3 vols. Augsburg, 1792–98. 2d ed. published as *Elementarwerk der Harmonie, als Einleitung in die Begleitungs- und Tonsetzkunst, wie auch in die Tonwissenschaft*. Munich, 1814.

———. "Kritische Briefe an einen jungen Tonsezer über wichtige Materien aus der Tonwissenschaft und Tonsezkunst." *Musikalische Real-Zeitung für das Jahr 1788*, pp. 10–14, 42–47.

———. "Kurze Beantwortung der Frage: Was für Vortheile hat sich die praktische Musik vor der Anwendung des Voglerschen Systems zu versprechen?" *Allgemeine musikalische Zeitung* 3 (1800–1801): 725–32, 741–50.

———. Review of Vogler's *Choral-System*. *Allgemeine musikalische Zeitung* 3 (1800–1801): 264–69, 286–89, 315–18.

———. "Ueber die Harmonie." *Allgemeine musikalische Zeitung* 1 (1798–99): 129–34, 161–66, 321–27, 527–36, 561–65, 593–99.

———. "Versuch einer Theorie der Wohl- und Uebelklänge." *Allgemeine musikalische Zeitung* 2 (1799–1800): 348–67, 385–93, 433–38, 448–55, 465–70.

———. *Vollständige Orgelschule für Anfänger und Geübtere*. 3 vols. Leipzig: 1795–98.

[Knigge, Adolph von?] "Ueber des Herrn Abt Voglers Anwesenheit in Hannover." *Dramaturgische Blätter*. Cited in *Musikalische Real-Zeitung für das Jahr 1789*, pp. 342–43, 347–49.

Koch, Heinrich Christoph. *Handbuch bei dem Studium der Harmonie*. Leipzig, 1811.

———. *Musikalisches Lexikon*. Frankfurt, 1802. Reprint. Hildesheim: Georg Olms, 1964.

———. *Versuch einer Anleitung zur Composition*. 3 vols. Rudolstadt and Leipzig, 1782–93. Reprint. Hildesheim: Georg Olms, 1969.

[Kraus, Joseph Martin]. *Etwas von und über Musik fürs Jahr 1777*. Frankfurt am Main, 1778. Reprint. Munich: Emil Katzbichler, 1977.

Kreitz, Helmut. "Abbé Georg Joseph Vogler als Musiktheoretiker: Ein Beitrag zur Geschichte der Musiktheorie im 18. Jahrhundert." Ph.D. dissertation, University of the Saarland, 1957.

Kümmerle, Salomon. *Encyklopädie der evangelischen Kirchenmusik*. 4 vols. Gütersloh, 1888–95. Reprint. Hildesheim: Georg Olms, 1974.

Kurthen, Wilhelm. "Zur Geschichte der deutschen Singmesse." *Kirchenmusikalisches Jahrbuch* 26 (1931): 76–110.

Lang, Paul Henry. *Music in Western Civilization*. New York: W. W. Norton, 1941.

LaRue, Jan. *Guidelines for Style Analysis*. New York: W. W. Norton, 1970.

"Lebensbeschreibung Herrn Justin Heinrich Knecht, evangelischen Schullehrers und Musikdirektors der freien Reichsstadt Biberach." *Musikalische Real-Zeitung für das Jahr 1790,* pp. 41–45, 49–52, 58–62.

Lemke, Arno. *Jacob Gottfried Weber: Leben und Werk*. Mainz: B. Schott's Söhne, 1968.

Lindley, Mark. "La 'Pratica ben regolata' di Francescantonio Vallotti." *Rivista italiana di musicologia* 16 (1981): 45–95.

Lipowsky, Felix Joseph. *Baierisches Musik-Lexikon*. Munich, 1811. Reprint. Hildesheim: Georg Olms, 1982.

Loewenberg, Alfred. *Annals of Opera, 1597–1940*. 3d ed. Totowa, N.J.: Rowman and Littlefield, 1978.

Lottermoser, Werner. "Akustische Untersuchungen an der Compenius-Orgel im Schlosse Frederiksborg bei Kopenhagen." *Archiv für Musikwissenschaft* 15 (1958): 113–19.

Ludvová, Jitka. "Abbé Vogler a Praha." *Hudebni Veda* 19 (1982): 99–122.

Lyall, Harry Robert. "A French Music Aesthetic of the Eighteenth Century: A Translation and Commentary on Michel Paul Gui de Chabanon's *Musique considérée en elle-même* . . . (1785)." Ph.D. dissertation, North Texas State University, 1975.

*Magazin der Musik*. Edited by Carl Friedrich Cramer. 2 vols. Hamburg 1783–86. Reprint. Hildesheim: Georg Olms, 1971–74.

Mann, Alfred. "Padre Martini and Fux." In *Festschrift für Ernst Hermann Meyer zum sechzigsten Geburtstag,* edited by Georg Knepler, pp. 253–55. Leipzig: Deutscher Verlag für Musik, 1973.

———. *The Study of Fugue*. New York: W. W. Norton, 1965.

Marpurg, Friedrich Wilhelm. *Abhandlung von der Fuge, nach den Grundsätzen und Exempeln der besten deutschen und ausländischen Meister*. Berlin, 1753–54. Reprint. Hildesheim: Georg Olms, 1970.

————. *Handbuch bey dem Generalbasse und der Composition.* 3 vols. and suppl. Berlin, 1755–60. Reprint. Hildesheim: Georg Olms, 1974.

————. *Historisch-kritische Beyträge zur Aufnahme der Musik.* 5 vols. Berlin, 1754–78. Reprint. Hildesheim: Georg Olms, 1970.

————. *Kritische Briefe über die Tonkunst.* 3 vols. Berlin, 1759–64. Reprint. Hildesheim: Georg Olms, 1974.

————. *Kritische Einleitung in die Geschichte und Lehrsätze der alten und neuen Musik.* Berlin, 1759.

————. *Versuch über die musikalische Temperatur, nebst einem Anhang über den Rameau- und Kirnbergerschen Grundbass.* Breslau, 1776.

Martini, Giambattista. *Esemplare, o sia Saggio fondamentale pratico di contrappunto sopra il canto fermo.* 2 vols. Bologna, 1774–75. Reprint. Ridgewood, N.J.: Gregg Press, 1965.

Martini, Ulrich. *Die Orgeldispositionssammlungen bis zur Mitte des 19. Jhs.* Kassel: Bärenreiter, 1975.

Marx, Friedrich. Critique of Vogler's Simplification System. *Allgemeine musikalische Zeitung* 4 (1801–2), *Intelligenz-Blatt* 6, pp. 21–23.

————. *Ueber die misslungene Umschaffung der St. Marien-Orgel in Berlin, nach Vogler's Angabe.* Berlin, 1801. Reprinted in *Ökonomisch-technologische Encyklopädie, oder Allgemeines System der Staats-, Stadt, Haus- und Landwirthschaft, und der Kunstgeschichte,* edited by Johann Georg Krünitz, vol. 105, pp. 413–17. Berlin, 1807.

[Mastiaux, Caspar Anton von]. *Ueber Choral- und Kirchen-Gesänge: Ein Beitrag zur Geschichte der Tonkunst im neunzehnten Jahrhundert.* Munich, 1813.

Mattheson, Johann. *Der vollkommene Capellmeister.* Hamburg, 1739. Reprint. Kassel: Bärenreiter, 1954.

Mekeel, Joyce. "The Harmonic Theories of Kirnberger and Marpurg." *Journal of Music Theory* 4 (1960): 169–93.

Mendelssohn-Bartholdy, Felix. *Briefe aus den Jahren 1830 bis 1847.* Edited by Paul and Carl Mendelssohn-Bartholdy. 4th ed. 2 vols. Leipzig, 1878.

Metzler, Wolfgang. *Romantischer Orgelbau in Deutschland.* Ludwigsburg: E. F. Walcker & Cie, [1965].

Meyerbeer, Giacomo. *Briefwechsel und Tagebücher.* Edited by Heinz and Gudrun Becker. 4 vols. Berlin: Walter de Gruyter, 1960–85.

Michaelis, [Christian Friedrich]. "Ueber den Charakter der Kirchenmusik." *Berlinische musikalische Zeitung* 2 (1806): 137–40.

Mintz, Donald. "Some Aspects of the Revival of Bach." *Musical Quarterly* 40 (1954): 201–21.

Mitchell, William J. "Chord and Context in 18th-Century Theory." *Journal of the American Musicological Society* 16 (1963): 221–39.

Mizler, Lorenz Christoph. *Die Anfangs-Gründe des General Basses, nach mathematischer Lehr-Art abgehandelt.* Leipzig, 1739. Reprint. Hildesheim: George Olms, 1972.

Morgan, Robert P. "Schenker and the Theoretical Tradition: The Concept of Musical Reduction." *College Music Symposium* 18 (1978): 72–96.

Müller-Blattau, Joseph. *Geschichte der Fuge.* 3d ed. Kassel: Bärenreiter, 1963.

————. *Hamann und Herder in ihren Beziehungen zur Musik. Mit einem Anhang ungedruckter Kantatendichtungen und Liedmelodien aus Herders Nachlass.* Königsberg: Gräfe und Unzer, 1931.

————. "Zur Musikübung und Musikauffassung der Goethezeit." *Euphorion* 31 (1930): 427–54.

Münster, Robert and Hans Schmid. *Musik in Bayern.* Vol. I: *Bayerische Musikgeschichte.* Tutzing: Hans Schneider, 1972.

*Musikalische Korrespondenz der teutschen Filarmonischen Gesellschaft für das Jahr 1790 [–92].* Edited by Heinrich Philipp Carl Bossler. 3 vols. Speyer, 1790–92.

*Musikalische Real-Zeitung für das Jahr 1788 [–90].* Edited by Heinrich Philipp Carl Bossler. 3 vols. Speyer. Reprint. Hildesheim: Georg Olms, 1971.

*Musikalischer Almanach auf das Jahr 1782 [–84].* (*Musikalischer und Künstler-Almanach* in 1783.) [Edited by Carl Ludwig Junker.] 3 vols. Alethinopel [Berlin], Kosmopolis [Leipzig], Freiburg.

*Musikalischer Almanach für Deutschland auf das Jahr 1782 [–84,–89].* Edited by Johann Nicolaus Forkel. 4 vols. Leipzig. Reprint. Hildesheim: Georg Olms, 1974.

*Musikalisches Kunstmagazin.* Edited by Johann Friedrich Reichardt. 2 vols. Berlin, 1782–91. Reprint. Hildesheim: Georg Olms, 1969.

Myers, Robert Manson. *Handel's Messiah: A Touchstone of Taste.* New York: Macmillan, 1948.

"Nachtrag zur Recension des Orgel Konzerts in der St. Marienkirche in Berlin." *Allgemeine musikalische Zeitung* 3 (1800–1801), *Intelligenz-Blatt* 5, p. 19.

Nauenburg, Gustav. "Ueber das Wesen der christlichen Kirchenmusik." *Cäcilia* 15 (1833): 81–96.

Niecks, Frederick. "Bach, Vogler and Weber." *Monthly Musical Record* 40 (1910): 146–48.

————. "Vogler and Weber on Twelve Chorales of J. S. Bach." *Monthly Musical Record* 40 (1910): 170–71.

Nohl, Ludwig. *Musiker-Briefe.* Leipzig, 1873.

*Ökonomisch-technologische Encyklopädie, oder Allgemeines System der Staats-, Stadt-, Haus- und Landwirthschaft, und der Kunstgeschichte.* Edited by Johann Georg Krünitz. Vol. 105. Berlin, 1807.

Ottenberg, Hans-Günter. *Die Entwicklung des theoretisch-ästhetischen Denkens innerhalb der Berliner Musikkultur von den Anfängen der Aufklärung bis Reichardt.* Leipzig: Deutscher Verlag für Musik, 1978.

Pasqué, Ernst. *Abt Vogler als Tonkünstler, Lehrer und Priester.* Darmstadt, 1884.

Pauly, Reinhard G. "The Reforms of Church Music under Joseph II." *Musical Quarterly* 43 (1957): 372–82.

Petrobelli, Pierluigi. "Tartini, le sue idee e il suo tempo." *Nuova revista musicale italiana* 1 (1967): 651–75.

Planchart, Alejandro. "A Study of the Theories of Giuseppe Tartini." *Journal of Music Theory* 4 (1960): 32–61.

Rameau, Jean-Philippe. *Nouveau systême de musique théorique.* Paris, 1726. Reprint. New York: Broude Brothers, 1965.

———. *Treatise on Harmony.* Translated and edited by Philip Gossett. New York: Dover, 1971.

Ratner, Leonard G. *Classic Music: Expression, Form, and Style.* New York: Schirmer Books, 1980.

———. "Harmonic Aspects of Classic Form." *Journal of the American Musicological Society* 2 (1949): 159–68.

Reckziegel, Walter. "Georg Joseph Vogler." *Die Musik in Geschichte und Gegenwart* 13:1894–1905.

Reicha, Anton. *Course of Musical Composition.* Translated by Arnold Merrick. Edited by John Bishop. London, [1854].

Review of *Utile dulci! Voglers belehrende musikalische Ausgaben: Davids Buss-Psalm. Allgemeine musikalische Zeitung* 10 (1807–8): 121–27.

Riedel, Friedrich Wilhelm. "Johann Joseph Fux und die römische Palestrina-Tradition." *Die Musikforschung* 14 (1961):14–22.

Riemann, Hugo. *Geschichte der Musiktheorie im IX-XIX. Jahrhundert.* 2d ed. Berlin, 1921. Reprint. Hildesheim: Georg Olms, 1961.

Rochlitz, Johann Friedrich. Review of Vogler's *Requiem* in E-flat. *Allgemeine musikalische Zeitung* 25 (1823): 681–96.

Rousseau, Jean-Jacques. *Dictionnaire de musique.* Paris, 1768. Reprint. Hildesheim: Georg Olms, 1969.

———. *Ecrits sur la musique.* Paris, 1838. Reprint. Paris: Editions Stock, 1979.

Rudhart, Franz Michael. *Geschichte der Oper am Hofe zu München.* Freising, 1865.

Rupp, Emile. *Abbé Vogler als Mensch, Musiker und Orgelbautheoretiker unter besonderer Berücksichtigung des sog. "Simplificationssystems".* Augsburg: Bärenreiter, [1922].

Sabbatini, Luigi Antonio. *Elementi teorici della musica.* 3 vols. Rome, 1789–90.

———. *Trattato sopra le fughe musicali.* 2 vols. Venice, 1802. Reprint. Bologna: Forni Editore, n. d.

———. *La vera idea delle musicali numeriche segnature diretta al giovane studioso dell'armonia.* Venice, 1799.

Sadowsky, Rosalie D. Landres. "Jean-Baptiste *Abbé* Dubos: The Influence of Cartesian and Neo-Aristotelian Ideas on Music Theory and Practice." Ph.D. dissertation, Yale University, 1960.

Sanner, Lars Erik. "Abbé Georg Joseph Vogler som musikteoretiker." *Svensk tidskrift för musikforskning* 30 (1950): 73–102.

Sauer, Leopold. "Ueber das Crescendo in des Abt Voglers Orchestrion." *Allgemeine musikalische Zeitung* 26 (1824): 370–75.

Schafhäutl, Karl Emil von. *Abt Georg Joseph Vogler: Sein Leben, Charakter und musikalisches System; seine Werke, seine Schule, Bildnisse etc.* Augsburg, 1888. Reprint. Hildesheim: Georg Olms, 1979.

————. *Der aechte gregorianische Choral in seiner Entwicklung bis zur Kirchenmusik unserer Zeit: Ein Versuch zur Vermittlung in der Streitfrage, Welche ist die wahre katholische Kirchenmusik.* Munich, 1869.

————. "Erinnerungen an Ett." *Kirchenmusikalisches Jahrbuch* 9 (1891): 58–69.

Scheibe, Johann Adolph. *Critischer Musikus.* 2d ed. Leipzig, 1745. Reprint. Hildesheim: Georg Olms, 1970.

Schenker, Heinrich. *Harmony.* Edited and annotated by Oswald Jonas. Translated by Elisabeth Mann Borgese. Chicago: University of Chicago Press, 1954.

Schering, Arnold. "Joh. Phil. Kirnberger als Herausgeber Bachscher Choräle." *Bach-Jahrbuch* 15 (1918): 141–50.

————. "Die Musikästhetik der deutschen Aufklärung," *Zeitschrift der internationalen musikwissenschaftlichen Gesellschaft* 8 (1906–7): 263–71, 316–22.

Schlimbach, Georg Christian Friedrich. "Ideen und Vorschläge zur Verbesserung des Kirchenmusikwesens." *Berlinische musikalische Zeitung* 1 (1805): 231–34, 235–38, 243–45, 260–61, 271–73, 277–78, 283–84, 355–58, 368–70, 387–90, 408–10.

————. "Nachtrag zu der Abhandlung: über die Kirchenmusik im vorigen Jahrgange der musikal. Zeit." *Berlinische musikalische Zeitung* 2 (1806): 145–48, 150–52.

————. "Ueber des Abts Vogler Umschaffung der Orgel zu St. Marien in Berlin, nach seinem Simplifications-System, nebst leicht ausführbaren Vorschlägen zu einigen bedeutenden Verbesserungen der Orgel." *Berlinische musikalische Zeitung* 1 (1805): 383–86, 391–94, 404–6; 2 (1806): 13–16.

————. *Ueber die Struktur, Erhaltung, Stimmung, Prüfung etc. der Orgel, nebst 5 Kupfertafeln und 1 Blatt Noten.* Leipzig, 1801. Reprint. Hilversum: Frits Knuf, 1966.

Schneider, Michael. *Die Orgelspieltechnik des frühen 19. Jahrhunderts in Deutschland dargestellt an den Orgelschulen der Zeit.* Regensburg: Gustav Bosse, 1941.

Schnoebelen, Anne. *Padre Martini's Collection of Letters in the Civico Museo Bibliografico Musicale in Bologna: An Annotated Index.* New York: Pendragon Press, 1979.

Schubart, Christian Friedrich Daniel. *Ideen zu einer Ästhetik der Tonkunst.* Vienna, 1806. Reprint. Hildesheim: Georg Olms, 1969.

————. *Leben und Gesinnungen, von ihm selbst im Kerker aufgesezt.* 2 vols. Vol. 2 edited by Ludwig Schubart. Stuttgart, 1791–93.

Schurr, Walter W. "Francesco Antonio Calegari (d. 1742): Music Theorist and Composer." 2 vols. Ph.D. dissertation, Catholic University of America, 1969.

Schweiger, Hertha. *Abbé G. J. Vogler's Orgellehre.* Vienna: Johannes Kmoch, 1938.

————. "Abbé Voglers Simplifikationssystem und seine akustischen Studien." *Kirchenmusikalisches Jahrbuch* 29 (1934): 72–123.

————. "Abt Vogler." *Musical Quarterly* 25 (1939): 156–66.

Seiffert, Max. "Die Mannheimer 'Messias'-Aufführung 1777." *Jahrbuch der Musik-bibliothek Peters* 23 (1916): 61–71.

Serauky, Walter. *Die musikalische Nachahmungsästhetik im Zeitraum von 1700 bis 1850.* Münster (Westphalia): Helios-Verlag, 1929.

Sheldon, David A. "The Ninth Chord in German Theory." *Journal of Music Theory* 26 (1982): 61–100.

Shirlaw, Matthew. *The Theory of Harmony: An Inquiry into the Natural Principles of Harmony, with an Examination of the Chief Systems of Harmony from Rameau to the Present Day.* London: Novello, 1917. Reprint. New York: Da Capo Press, 1969.

Simon, Edwin J. "Sonata into Concerto: A Study of Mozart's First Seven Concertos." *Acta musicologica* 31 (1959): 170–85.

Simon, James. *Abt Voglers kompositorisches Wirken mit besonderer Berücksichtigung der romantischen Momente.* Berlin: Gustav Schade, 1904.

Sjögren, Josef. *Orgelverken i Västerås Stift: En historisk översikt 1952.* Stockholm: Nordiska Museet, 1952.

Söhner, Leo. *Die Geschichte der Begleitung des gregorianischen Chorals in Deutschland vornehmlich im 18. Jahrhundert.* Augsburg: Benno Filser, 1931.

————. *Die Orgelbegleitung zum gregorianischen Gesang.* Regensburg: Friedrich Pustet, 1936.

Sonnleithner, Joseph. "Etwas über die Vogler'sche Simplification des Orgelbaues." *Allgemeine musikalische Zeitung* 2 (1799–1800): 565–68.

Sorge, Georg Andreas. *The Secretly Kept Art of the Scaling of Organ Pipes.* Reprint with translation by Carl O. Bleyle. Buren: Frits Knuf, 1978.

————. *Vorgemach der musicalischen Composition.* 3 vols. Lobenstein, 1745–47.

Spies, Hermann. *Abbé Vogler und die von ihm 1805 simplifizierte Orgel von St. Peter in Salzburg.* Mainz: Paul Smets, 1932.

Stahl, Ernst Leopold. *Das Mannheimer Nationaltheater.* Mannheim: J. Bensheimer, 1929.

Steblin, Rita. *A History of Key Characteristics in the Eighteenth and Early Nineteenth Centuries.* Ann Arbor: UMI Research Press, 1983.

Stieger, Franz. *Opernlexikon.* 4 pts. in 11 vols. Tutzing: Hans Schneider, 1975–83.

Stölzle, Remigius. *Erziehungs- und Unterrichtsanstalten im Juliusspital zu Würzburg.* Munich, 1914.

*Studien für Tonkünstler und Musikfreunde: Eine historisch-kritische Zeitschrift mit neun und dreissig Musikstücken von verschiedenen Meistern fürs Jahr 1792.* Edited by F. A. Kunzen and Johann Friedrich Reichardt. Berlin.

Sulzer, Johann Georg. *Allgemeine Theorie der schönen Künste.* 2d ed. 4 vols. Leipzig, 1792–94. Reprint. Hildesheim: Georg Olms, 1967–70.

Sulzmann, Bernd. "Eine Planung Abbé G. J. Voglers aus dem Jahre 1806." *Acta organologica* 11 (1977): 54–69.

Sumner, William Leslie. *The Organ: Its Evolution, Principles of Construction and Use.* New York: Philosophical Library, 1952.

Tartini, Giuseppe. *De' principi dell'armonia musicale contenuta nel diatonico genere.* Padua, 1767. Reprint. Hildesheim: Georg Olms, 1970.

————. *Trattato di musica secondo la vera scienza dell'armonia.* Padua, 1754. Reprint. New York: Broude Brothers, 1966.

Taylor, Eric. "Rousseau's Conception of Music," *Music and Letters* 30 (1949): 231–42.

Thomson, Ulf. *Voraussetzungen und Artungen der österreichischen Generalbasslehre zwischen Albrechtsberger und Sechter.* Tutzing: Hans Schneider, 1978.

Tittel, Ernst. "Die Wiener Pastoralmesse." *Musica Divina* 23 (1935): 192–96.

Türk, Daniel Gottlob. *Von den wichtigsten Pflichten eines Organisten: Ein Beytrag zur Verbesserung der musikalischen Liturgie.* Halle, 1787. Reprint. Hilversum: Frits Knuf, 1966.

"Ueber das musikalische Drama." *Allgemeine musikalische Zeitung* 1 (1798–99): 353–59, 369–72.

"Ueber die sogenannten alten Kirchentonarten und deren gegenwärtigen Werth." *Eutonia* 5 (1831): 1–25, 105–40; 6 (1831): 1–12, 193–207.

Unger, Hans-Heinrich. *Die Beziehungen zwischen Musik und Rhetorik im 16.–18. Jahrhundert.* Würzburg, 1941. Reprint. Hildesheim: Georg Olms, 1969.

Unger, Max. "Aus Bernhard Anselm Webers Jugendjahren: Briefe von Weber und anderen." *Allgemeine Musik-Zeitung* 38 (1911): 835–36, 859–61, 881–83, 903–5, 927–29.

Ursprung, Otto. *Restauration und Palestrina-Renaissance in der katholischen Kirchenmusik der letzten zwei Jahrhunderte.* Augsburg: Benno Filser, 1924.

Vallotti, Francesco Antonio. *Della scienza teorica, e pratica della moderna musica.* Vol. 1. Padua, 1779.

————. *Trattato della moderna musica.* (A modern edition of *Della scienza teorica, e pratica della moderna musica,* Books 1–4.) Padua: Il messagero di S. Antonio, 1950.

*Verzeichniss der von dem als Theoretiker und Compositeur in der Tonkunst berühmten . . . Abt G. J. Vogler nachgelassenen, grösstentheils noch nicht bekannten praktischen und theoretischen, im Manuscript vorhandenen Werke, so wie seiner im Druck erschienenen und mehrerer fremden Musikalien.* Darmstadt, 1814.

*Verzeichniss der von Dr. Gottfried Weber . . . nachgelassenen musikalischen Bibliothek.* Darmstadt, 1842.

Vogler, Georg Joseph. "Ästhetisch-kritische Zergliederung des wesentlich vierstimmigen Singsatzes des vom H. Musikdirektor Knecht in Musik gesetzten ersten Psalms." *Musikalische Korrespondenz der teutschen Filarmonischen Gesellschaft für das Jahr 1792.*

————. *"Aeusserung über Hrn. Knechts Harmonik."* Allgemeine musikalische Zeitung 2 (1799–1800): 689–96.

————. "Bemerkungen über die der Musik vortheilhafteste Bauart eines Musikchors: Ein Auszug aus einem Brief des Abt Voglers von Bergen in Norwegen 1792." *Journal von und für Deutschland* 9 (1792): 178–81.

————. *Betrachtungen der Mannheimer Tonschule.* 3 vols. with musical supplements (*Gegenstände der Betrachtungen*). Mannheim, 1778–81. Reprint. 4 vols. (Vol. 4: *Gegenstände.*) Hildesheim: Georg Olms, 1974.

————. *Choral-System.* (With accompanying volume of music.) Copenhagen, 1800.

————. *Clavér-schola, med 44 graverade tabeller.* (With accompanying volume of music: *Pièces de clavecin faciles, doigtées, avec des variations d'une difficulté graduelle.*) Stockholm, 1798.

————. *Data zur Akustik: Eine Abhandlung vorgelesen bey der Sitzung der naturforschenden Freunde in Berlin, den 15ten Dezember 1800.* Leipzig, 1801. Also published in *Allgemeine musikalische Zeitung* 3 (1800–1801): 517–25, 533–40, 549–54, 565–71.

————. *Deutsche Kirchenmusik, mit einer Zergliederung die vorläufig die Inaugural-Frage beantwortet: Hat die Musik seit 30 Jahren gewonnen oder verlohren?*, Utile dulci. (With accompanying volume of music.) Munich, 1808.

————. *Entwurf eines neuen Wörterbuchs für die Tonschule, gewidmet einem musikalischen Deutschland, um Beiträge und Stimmen zu sammeln.* Frankfurt, 1780.

[————.] *Erklärung der Buchstaben, die im Grundriss, der nach dem Vogler'schen Simplifikazions-System neu zu erbauenden St. Petersorgel in München, vorkommen,* with accompanying *Grundriss der nach dem Voglerschen Simplifikazions System in der St. Peters Pfarrkirche in München neü zu erbauenten Orgel.* [Munich, 1806].

[————.] *Erste musikalische Preisaustheilung für das Jahr 1791. Nebst vierzig Kupfertafeln die aus dem Magnificat beider Preisträger ein Stück und die Umarbeitung beider Stücke vom Preisrichter liefern.* Frankfurt am Main, 1794.

————. *Essai propre à diriger le goût de ceux qui ne sont pas musiciens, & à les mettre en état d'analyser & de juger un morceau de musique.* [Paris: 1782].

————. *Gründliche Anleitung zum Clavierstimmen, für die, welche gutes Gehör haben, nebst einer neuen Anzeige, jedes Saiteninstrument vortheilhaft und richtig zu beziehen.* Stuttgart, 1807.

————. *Handbuch zur Harmonielehre und für den Generalbass, nach den Grundsätzen der Mannheimer Tonschule, zum Behuf der öffentlichen Vorlesungen im Orchestrions-Saale auf der k. k. Karl-Ferdinandeischen Universität zu Prag.* (With accompanying set of music examples.) Prague, 1802.

————. "Harmonisch-akustische Bemerkungen über den Theater-Bau." [c. 1807]. Darmstadt. Hessisches Staatsarchiv. D 4, Nr. 695.

————. *Inledning til harmoniens kännedom, med åtta dertil hörande graverade tabeller.* Stockholm, 1794.

[————?] "Korrespondenz: Stockholm im Februar 1799." *Allgemeine musikalische Zeitung* 1 (1798–99): 413–15.

————. *Kuhrpfälzische Tonschule*. 2 vols. with musical supplement (*Gründe der kuhrpfälzischen Tonschule in Beispielen als Vorbereitung zur Mannheimer Monatschrift und zu den Herausgaben des öffentlichen Tonlehrers*). Mannheim, [1778].

[————.] *Kurze Beschreibung der, in der Stadt Pfarrkirche zu St. Peter in München nach dem Voglerschen Simplifikations-System vom Orgelbauer Herrn Franz Frosch neu erbauten, Orgel erster Grösse*. [Munich, 1809].

————. *Lection til choral-eleven M. H.; Andra lection til choral-eleven M. H.* 2 vols. Stockholm, 1799–1800.

————. *Musik-skole i trende dele, med 60 kobberstukne tabeller*. 3 vols. (With accompanying volume of music examples.) Copenhagen, 1800. (Translation of *Inledning til harmoniens kännedom, Clavér-schola,* and *Organist-schola,* vol. 1.)

————. *Organist-schola, med 8 graverade tabeller; Organist-scholans andra del: Förklaring öfver Choral-boken*. 2 vols. (Vol. 2 accompanied by a volume of music.) Stockholm, 1798–99.

————. *Pièces de clavecin* and *Zwei und dreisig Präludien*. Edited by Floyd K. Grave. Madison: A-R Editions, 1986.

[————.] *Prüfungs-Plan der nach dem Voglerschen Simplifikations-System unternommenen Umschaffung der grossen Orgel im Benediktiner-Stifte zu St. Peter in Salzburg*. [Salzburg, 1805].

————. "Register-Dispositionen nach Abt Voglers Simplifications-System." Munich. Bayerische Staatsbibliothek. Mus. Mss. 503.

————. "Sermones, in Hispania Italice habiti." Autograph, 1792–93. Munich. Bayerische Staatsbibliothek. Cod. ital. 256/1–2 (Cim. 387).

————. *Stimmbildungskunst*. Mannheim, 1776.

————. "Systême de simplification pour les orgues." Autograph, 1798. Regensburg. Bischöfliche Zentralbibliothek.

————. *System für den Fugenbau, als Einleitung zur harmonischen Gesang-Verbindungs-Lehre*. (With accompanying volume of music.) Offenbach, [c. 1817].

————. *Tonwissenschaft und Tonsezkunst*. Mannheim, 1776. Reprint. Hildesheim: Georg Olms, 1970.

————. "Über die Musik der Oper *Rosamunde*." Offprint from *Rheinische Beiträge zur Gelehrsamkeit,* no. 6, 1780.

————. "Über die Oxydazion der schwingenden Metallkörper." [1809]. Darmstadt. Hessisches Staatsarchiv Darmstadt. D 4, Nr. 695.

[————.] *Ueber die Umschaffung der St. Marien-Orgel in Berlin, nach dem Vogler'schen Simplifikazions-System, eine Nachahmung des Orchestrion in Rücksicht auf Stärke, Würde, Mannichfaltigkeit, Feinheit, Deutlichkeit, Reinheit und Dauer*. [Berlin, 1800].

[————.] *Uebersicht der Orgel-Umschaffung in der Dreifaltigkeits Kirche zu Schweidnitz*. Schweidnitz, 1802.

————. *Uiber die harmonische Akustik (Tonlehre) und über ihren Einfluss auf alle musikalische Bildungs-Anstalten.* [Munich, 1806].

————. *Verbesserung der Forkel'schen Veränderungen über das Englische Volkslied "God Save the King," nebst acht Kupfertafeln.* (With accompanying volume of music.) Frankfurt am Main, 1793.

————. "Vergleich der Kempeln'schen Sprach-Maschine mit dem, der Menschenstimme täuschend nachahmenden, singbaren Orgel-Register, von dieser Ähnlichkeit *Vox humana* genannt." [1810]. Darmstadt. Hessisches Staatsarchiv. D 4, Nr. 695.

[————.] *Vergleichungs-Plan der, nach dem Vogler'schen Simplifikazions-System umgeschaffenen, Neumünster-Orgel in Würzburg.* Würzburg, 1812.

[————.] *Vergleichungsplan der nach dem Vogler'schen Simplifikazionssystem umgeschaffenen Orgel in dem evangelischen Hofbethause zu München.* [Munich, 1805].

[————.] *Verzeichniss der Register der nach dem Vogler'schen Simplifikazions-System vom Orgelbauer Frosch neu erbauten St. Peters Orgel in München* [Munich, c. 1808].

————. *Zergliederung der musikalischen Bearbeitung des Busspsalmen im Choral-Styl, zu vier wesentlichen und selbstständigen Singstimmen, doch willkührlichem Tenor. Utile dulci.* (With accompanying volume of music.) Munich, 1807.

————. *Zwei und dreisig Präludien für die Orgel und für das Fortepiano, nebst einer Zergliederung in ästhetischer, rhetorischer und harmonischer Rücksicht, mit praktischem Bezug auf das Handbuch der Tonlehre vom Abt Vogler.* (Text with accompanying volume of music.) Munich, 1806.

————. *Zwölf Choräle von Sebastian Bach, umgearbeitet von Vogler, zergliedert von Carl Maria von Weber.* Leipzig, [1810].

"Vorläufige Nachricht von einem Mikropan." *Allgemeine musikalische Zeitung* 5 (1802–3): 533–35.

Vretblad, Patrik. "Abbé Georg Joseph Vogler i Stockholm." Typescript. Stockholm, 1949. Stockholm. Musikaliska Akademiens Bibliotek. Handskr. 306.

————. "Abbé Vogler som programmusiker." *Svensk tidskrift för musikforskning* 9 (1927): 79–98.

Wagener, Heinz. *Die Begleitung des gregorianischen Chorals im neunzehnten Jahrhundert.* Regensburg: Gustav Bosse, 1964.

Wagner, Manfred. *Die Harmonielehren der ersten Hälfte des 19. Jahrhunderts.* Regensburg: Gustav Bosse, 1974.

Walter, Friedrich. *Geschichte des Theaters und der Musik am kurpfälzischen Hofe.* Leipzig, 1898. Reprint. Hildesheim: Georg Olms, 1968.

Walther, Johann Gottfried. *Musikalisches Lexikon, oder Musikalische Bibliothek.* Leipzig, 1732. Reprint. Kassel. Bärenreiter, 1953.

Wason, Robert W. "Schenker's Notion of Scale-Step in Historical Perspective: Non-Essential Harmonies in Viennese Fundamental Bass Theory." *Journal of Music Theory* 29 (1985): 49–73.

———. *Viennese Harmonic Theory from Albrechtsberger to Schenker and Schoenberg.* Ann Arbor: UMI Research Press, 1985.

Wates, Roye E. "Karl Ludwig Junker (1748–1797): Sentimental Music Critic." Ph.D. dissertation, Yale University, 1965.

Weber, Carl Maria von. "Briefe von C. Mar. v. Weber an Gfr. Weber. Mitgetheilt von Letzterem. Jahr 1810." *Cäcilia* 15 (1833): 30–58.

———. *Carl Maria von Weber: Briefe.* Edited by Hans Christoph Worbs. Frankfurt am Main: Fischer, 1982.

———. *Writings on Music.* Translated by Martin Cooper. Edited and introduced by John Warrack. Cambridge: Cambridge University Press, 1981.

Weber, Friedrich Dionys. *Allgemeine theoretisch-praktische Vorschule der Musik, oder Inbegriff alles dessen, was dem angehenden Musiker zum Verstehen der Tonschrift und zum Vortrage eines Tonstückes zu wissen unentbehrlich ist.* Prague, 1828.

———. *Theoretisch-praktisches Lehrbuch der Harmonie und des Generalbasses, für den Unterricht am Prager Conservatorium der Musik.* 4 vols. Prague, 1830–41.

Weber, Gottfried. *Allgemeine Musiklehre zum Selbstunterricht für Lehrer und Lernende.* Darmstadt, 1822.

———. "Chor und Choral: Zwei Artikel aus Gfr. Webers musikalischem Lexikon." *Cäcilia* 4 (1826): 141–54.

———. Eulogy for Vogler. *Allgemeine musikalische Zeitung* 16 (1814): 350–51.

———. *Die Generalbasslehre zum Selbstunterricht.* Mainz, 1833.

———. Review of *Trichordium und Trias Harmonica, oder Lob der Harmonie. Allgemeine musikalische Zeitung* 17 (1815): 513–18.

———. "Über das Wesen des Kirchenstyls." *Cäcilia* 3 (1825): 173–204.

———. "Über Tonmalerei." *Cäcilia* 3 (1825): 125–72.

———. *Versuch einer geordneten Theorie der Tonsetzkunst.* 3 vols. Mainz, 1817–21.

Weber, Wilhelm. "Compensation der Orgelpfeifen." *Cäcilia* 11 (1829): 181–202.

Weissbeck, Johann Michael. *Protestationsschrift, oder Exemplarische Widerlegung einiger Stellen und Perioden der Kapellmeister Voglerischen Tonwissenschaft und Tonsetzkunst.* Erlangen, 1783.

———. *Seltsame Geschichte der bisherigen Lebensaltersumme der Orgelvirtuosen Hässler, Rössler und Vogler.* Nuremberg, 1800.

Werckmeister, Andreas. *Erweiterte und verbesserte Orgel-Probe.* Quedlinburg, 1698. Reprint. Hildesheim: Georg Olms, 1970.

Wiechens, Bernwald. *Die Kompositionstheorie und das kirchenmusikalische Schaffen Padre Martinis.* Regensburg: Gustav Bosse, 1968.

Wilke, Christian Friedrich Gottlieb. "Geschichtlicher Ueberblick der Verbesserungen und neuen Erfindungen im Orgelbau seit fünfzig Jahren." *Allgemeine musikalische Zeitung* 38 (1836): 697–703.

———. "Die Orgel in Neu-Ruppin, erbauet unter dem Hrn. geh. Rath, Abt Vogler in Darmstadt." *Allgemeine musikalische Zeitung* 13 (1811): 217–24, 233–39.

———. "Ueber das Wirken des Abts und Geh. Raths Vogler im Orgelbaufache." *Allgemeine musikalische Zeitung* 26 (1824): 673–77, 689–94.

———. "Ueber den jetzigen Verfall des Kirchengesanges, und über seine Verbesserung." *Allgemeine musikalische Zeitung* 18 (1816): 99–103, 113–17.

———. "Ueber den Nutzen und Unentbehrlichkeit der Orgelmixturen," *Cäcilia* 12 (1830): 190–206.

———. "Ueber die Crescendo- und Diminuendo-Züge an Orgeln." *Allgemeine musikalische Zeitung* 25 (1823): 113–19.

———. "Ueber die Erfindung der Rohrwerke mit durchschlagenden Zungen." *Allgemeine musikalische Zeitung* 25 (1823): 149–55.

Williams, Peter. *The European Organ, 1450–1850.* London: B. T. Batsford, 1966.

———. *A New History of the Organ: From the Greeks to the Present Day.* Bloomington: Indiana University Press, 1980.

Wiora, Walter. "Herders Ideen zur Geschichte der Musik." In *Im Geiste Herders,* edited by Erich Keyser, pp. 73–128. Kitzingen am Main: Holzner-Verlag, 1953.

Wistedt, Sven. "Abbé Vogler och svensk orgelbyggnadskonst jämte några nyupptäckta Voglerdokument." *Svensk tidskrift för musikforskning* 14 (1932): 28–58.

———. "Ett bidrag till en Vogler-biografi." *Svensk tidskrift för musikforskning* 15 (1933): 5–28.

Wolf, Eugene K. and Jean K. Wolf. "A Newly Identified Complex of Manuscripts from Mannheim." *Journal of the American Musicological Society* 27 (1974): 379–437.

Wolff, Christoph. *Der Stile Antico in der Musik Johann Sebastian Bachs: Studien zu Bachs Spätwerk.* Wiesbaden: Franz Steiner, 1968.

Würtz, Roland. *Ignaz Fränzl: Ein Beitrag zur Musikgeschichte der Stadt Mannheim.* Mainz: B. Schott's Söhne, 1970.

Zenger, Max. *Geschichte der Münchener Oper.* Ed. Theodor Kroyer. Munich: Verlag für praktische Kunstwissenschaft, Dr. F. X. Weizinger, 1923.

# Index

*Page references to music examples are given in boldface type.*

*A cappella,* 141–42

Adlung, Jacob, 159

Analysis, schematic, 55–57

Anfossi, Pasquale, "Se cerca, se dice" (aria), 105

Annus qui (papal bull), 125

Augmented sixth chord, 24. *See also* Enharmonic notation

Augmented triad, 36. *See also* Enharmonic notation

*Ausführung. See* Thematic development

*Ausweichung. See* Modulation

Bach, Johann Christian: *No, non turbarti o Nice* (cantata), 183–84, **184**; overture to *La calamità de cuori,* 138

Bach, Johann Sebastian: chorale harmonizations of, 160, 175–76; *Das alte Jahr vergangen ist* (chorale), 105, **106**; discredited by Vogler as a pedagogical model, 105; *O Haupt voll Blut und Wunden* (chorale), 167–68, **169**; testing of organs by, 239; Vogler's antipathy toward, 111, 160; Vogler's objection to fugues by, 127

Banks, Joseph, 4

Baroque style, Vogler's emulation of, 115

*Basso continuo,* 131, 133–34, 136

Batteux, Charles, 93

Beethoven, Ludwig van, 6, 215

Benedict XIV (pope), 125

Bernasconi, Andrea, 5

Britton, David, 10

Burney, Charles, 289n

Cadences, 23–24; and fugal procedure, 79–82; in harmonization of modal melodies, 164–66, 168–71; hierarchy of, 57

Cadential six-four chord, as dissonance, 58–61, 66, 67–68

Calegari, Francesco Antonio, 282n, 283n; "Ampla dimostrazione degli armoniali musicali tuoni," 281n; theories of, 15–16

Carl Theodor (Elector Palatine), 3–4, 136, 181

Chamfort, Sébastien Roch Nicholas, 188

Cherubini, Luigi, 6

Chladni, Ernst Florens Friedrich, 262

Chorale harmonization: contemporary discussion of, 158–59; correction of Bach's errors in, 102–3, 167–68, 175–76; and modal purity, 158–59; practices of, condoned by Vogler, 166–67; Vogler's identification of errors in, 166; Vogler's principles of, 164–67

Chord succession, 23–24, 62, 88

Christian VII (king of Denmark), 256

Chromatic alteration, and musical expression, 91–92

Church modes: Vogler's cadences for, 165–66, 169–71; Vogler's theories on origins of, 162–64

Combination tones, 281n

Compenius, Esaias, 256

Concerto: structure of, 97–98; Vogler's speculation on origins of, 97

Concinnity, 288n

Counterpoint, pedagogy of, 13

Criticism, Vogler's methodology of, 90

Dalberg, Wolfgang Heribert von, 181

D'Alembert, Jean le Rond, *Elémens de musique,* 14

Danzi, Franz, 271

Daube, Johann Friedrich, 14

Deceptive cadence, 88

Depiction, musical, 98; in instrumental music, 185; of nature, 234–35, 296n. *See also* Tone paintings

Diminished seventh, 26

Diminished seventh chord. *See* Enharmonic notation

Dissonance: compound-interval, 29–30, 58–61, 281n; preparation and resolution of, 28–32; theory of, 16, 269, 281n

Dominant seventh, 25

Drechsler, Joseph, and Roman-numeral analysis, 270

Durchfuhrung. *See* Thematic development

Eitner, Robert, *Biographisch-bibliographisches Quellen-Lexikon,* 280n

Enharmonic notation: of augmented sixth chord, 36; of augmented triad, 37; of diminished seventh chord, 36, 40

Enlightenment, and musical progress, 100–101

Ett, Caspar, 264

Euler, Leonhard, 14

Fétis, François-Joseph, 9, 273

Folk music, Vogler's interest in, 230–33

Forkel, Johann Nikolaus, 289n; *Musikalischer Almanach,* 235

Förster, Emanuel Aloys, and Roman-numeral analysis, 270

*Fortführung. See* Thematic development

Frederick William III (king of Prussia), 256

Fröhlich, Joseph, 8, 157–58

Frosch, Franz, 258

Frugoni, C. I., 199

Fugue: *enucleatio fugae* in, 79; in sacred music, 127; Vogler's concept of, 78–79, 116–17

Fundamental bass, 14, 50

Fux, Johann Joseph, 13, 15

*Galant* style, in sacred music, 152

Galuppi, Baldassare, "Se cerca, se dice" (aria), 104–5, **105**

Gänsbacher, Johann, 6–7, 272

Gentil, Bernard, 199

Gerber, Ernst Ludwig, 171

Gerbert, Martin, *De cantu et musica sacra,* 289n

German Mass. *See* Vogler, Georg Joseph, works by (music), *Deutsche Kirchenmusik*

*Gesangverbindung,* 79

Gluck, Christoph Willibald, 179, 180

Grétry, André Ernest Modeste, 179

Grillparzer, Franz, 279n
Grout, Donald J., 1
Gustave III (king of Sweden), 5, 161;
and Gustavian opera, 209

Hagemann (organ builder), 256
Handel, George Frideric: choral music
of, 111, 127; *Messiah,* 101, 229
Harmonic analysis: and context, 68–69;
Vogler's early technique of, 54–55;
Vogler's late experiments in, 66–67;
in writings of Vogler's predecessors,
51
Harmonic elaboration, 47–48, 53–54,
58, 59–61
Harmonic function: borrowed, 74; and
context, 45–46
Harmonic generation, principle of, 16.
*See also* Sounding string, division of
Harmony: and metrical emphasis, 57–
58; relationship to melody, 52–53
Hasse, Johann Adolph, 3; comparison
with Jommelli, 109, 179
Hauner, Norbert, 136
Haydn, Franz Joseph, 156; as represen-
tative of musical progress, 111
Herder, Johann Gottfried, 230
Hiller, Johann Adam, 85, 127, 179
Holzbauer, Ignaz, *Günther, von
Schwarzburg,* 101
Huber, Franz Xaver, 216

Imitation, aesthetics of, 93, 94
Instrumental music: aesthetics of, 114–
15, 121–22; expression in, 93–95
Intervals, 25; augmented fifth, 25; chromatically inflected, 24; diminished
third, 92; fifth, 47–48; fourth, 19;
sevenths, 25–28
Inversion, law of interval, 29–30
Italian music, Vogler's endorsement of,
103–4, 126

Jahn, Otto, 9
Jommelli, Niccolò, 109, 179
Joseph II (Holy Roman Emperor), 125
Junker, Carl Ludwig, 228, 229, 233,
235

Kellgren, Johan Henrik, 5, 210
Kerpen, Wilhelm von, 64
Key characteristics, 42–43, 195, 197,
202, 211–12; and musical expression,
131, 185–86
Kirnberger, Johann Philipp, 17, 41, 51;
on chorale harmonization, 101–2,
159; *Lied nach dem Frieden,* 102–3,
**104**; theories of, criticized by Vogler,
45–46; and theory of dissonance, 28
Kirsnick (organ builder), 249
Knecht, Georg Christian, 251, 252,
255, 256, 258, 265
Knecht, Justin Heinrich, 159, 171–72,
255, 271–72, 273, 299n
Knigge, Adolph von, 229
Koch, Heinrich Christoph, 119, 307n;
*Handbuch bei dem Studium der Harmo-
nie,* 269, 273
Kohlbrenner, Johann Franz Seraph von,
135–36
Kratzenstein (inventor of a voice sim-
ulator), 249
Kraus, Joseph Martin, 5
Kreitz, Helmut, 10
Kunckel, J. P., 251, 261

Lang, Paul Henry, 1
Leading tones, 34–35
Leibniz, Gottfried Wilhelm, 14
Lipowsky, Felix Joseph, 9

Mannheim, 138; musical accomplishments of, 99, 101; sacred music in,
124; theatrical music in, 233
Mannheim music school (*Mannheimer
Tonschule*), 13, 17

Marpurg, Friedrich Wilhelm, 14, 17, 41, 280n

Martini, Giambattista (Padre), 3, 14–15, 124

Marx, Friedrich, 248, 264

Mastiaux, Caspar Anton von, 160

*Mehrdeutigkeit. See* Modulation, multiple function chords in

Meissner, August Gottlieb, 52

Melodrama, 194

Mendelssohn, Felix, 264–65

Mendelssohn, Moses, 174

Mettenleiter, Johann Georg, 173–74

Meyerbeer, Giacomo: and folk music, 230; *Gott, des Weltalls Herr* (fugal chorus), 115–18; as pupil of Vogler, 1, 7, 272, 273

*Micropan,* 256, 261

Minor harmony, in contrast to major, 91

Mizler, Lorenz, 14

Modal melodies, oral transmission of, 162–63, 294n

Modulation, 33–34; and enharmonic equivalents, 33–34, 35–37, 38–39, 39–40; multiple function chords in, 34–40; process of, 37–38, 270; and tonal digression, 63–64; and tonicization, 63

Monochord, Vogler's rejection of, 18–20

Mossmayr, Johann Baptist, 264

Mozart, Leopold, 269

Mozart, Wolfgang Amadeus, 179, 180, 205, 214, 287n; and concerto form, 97; criticism of Vogler, 8, 9, 52, 228–29; *Don Giovanni,* 3; and melodrama, 198; Piano Concerto in A major, K. 414, 138–39; Piano Concerto in D major, K. 537, 113; as representative of musical progress, 111; as rival of Vogler's in Mannheim, 4; Vogler's

homage to, 112–13; *Die Zauberflöte,* 216

Munich, 199; Vogler's organ-design projects in, 257

Mutations (on the organ), 240–41

Natural Seventh, 25–26

Neapolitan sixth, 74–75, 77

Normal-Orgel, 257, 304n

North Germans, Vogler's criticism of, 101–3

Oberndörfer (organ builder), 257, 304n

Omnibus progression, 283n

*Opera seria,* 200; Vogler's attitude toward, 182

Operatic overture, appropriate style for, 181

Operatic style, 91

Orchestrion, 237, 304n; criticism of, 255–56; features of, 247–48, 249, 250–56, 303n

Organ: Vogler's concert programs for, 229–30; Vogler's imitation of instruments on, 233, 299n; Vogler's performance of folk music on, 230–33; Vogler's tone paintings on, 233–35

Organ concerts, criticism of Vogler's, 235–36

Organ design, Vogler's writings on, 237–38, 300n. *See also* Simplification System

*Organochordion,* 256, 261

Organs: Evangelisches Hofbethaus (Munich), 265; Neu-Ruppin, 246, 248–49, 262–63; Neumünster organ (Würzburg), 243–44; Ramsberg, 304–5n; St. Mary's (Berlin), 244–45, 262–63; St. Peter's (Munich), 247, 258–60, 264–65, 305nn.123, 124, 125, 306n; Vogler's register designation for, 305n.126; *See also* Micropan,

Normal-Orgel, Orchestrion, *Organochordion, Triorganon*

Palestrina, Giovanni Pierluigi da, 124, 126, 229
Paradis, Maria Theresia von, 271
Pasqué, Ernst, 9
Pergolesi, Giovanni Battista, *Stabat Mater,* 106–9, **108**
Periodization, 119, 120–21
Pius VI (pope), 4
Plagal cadence, in fugue, 82
Plainsong, accompanied, 174
Progress, Vogler's concept of, 105–6; in musical performance, 110; in operatic music, 109; in the theory of music, 110
Proportion: arithmetic, 18–19, 82–83; harmonic, 16, 19, 82–83

Rackwitz, G. C., 249, 251, 256
Rameau, Jean-Philippe, 16, 17, 20, 22, 51, 282n; and dissonance, 28; and fundamental-bass theory, 14; and the *note sensible,* 34; and the principle of harmonic generation, 44, 46; and the *sixte ajoutée,* 45; and *supposition,* 281n; theories of, criticized by Vogler, 45
Rationalism, 15, 52; and musical expression, 90, 92–93
Reduction: applied to fugue, 79–83; principle of, 58–59, 67, 69–70, 78–83; system of, 30–32, 47, 58, 67
Reichardt, Johann Friedrich, 126
Reicha, Anton, 269–70; *Trente-six fugues,* 267
Revision (*Verbesserung*): of Bach chorales, 102–3, 167–68, 175–76; of Meyerbeer's fugue, 115–18; of Pergolesi's *Stabat Mater,* 106–9; Vogler's methodology of, 106; of Vogler's *Schuster Ballet,*, 112–13

Rhetoric, and music, 94–95, 116, 117–18, 119–22
Riemann, Hugo, 273
Ritter, Peter, 271
Rochlitz, Johann Friedrich, 157, 284n
Roman-numeral analysis, 2, 23, 274–75, 277–78n; and fugue, 79–82; Vogler's application of, 70, 119, 164, 169–70
Rondo, nature of, 87
Rousseau, Jean-Jacques, 52–53, 105; *Dictionnaire de musique,* 289n; and primeval music, 126
Rupp, Emile, 9

Sacred music: *a cappella* ideal in, 125; comprehensibility in, 125, 136; criticism of Vogler's, 156–58; ideal of simplicity in, 140; *Lied* style in, 137, 140; reform movements in, 124, 125; theatrical elements in, 125, 127–28, 155–56, 164–65; use of instruments in, 127, 132–33, 150–56; vernacular texts in, 125, 136; vocal ideal in, 126–27, 137, 140; Vogler's models of, 128; Vogler's non-orchestral, 138–45; Vogler's orchestrally accompanied, 145, 148–56
Sacred style, 91
Sauer, Leopold, 251, 252, 253
Scale: artificial, 20–21, 25–26; chromatic, 21–22; minor, 21; natural, 20–21; and tonal hierarchy, 47
Schafhäutl, Karl Emil von, 9–10, 265, 306n
Scheibe, Johann Adolf, 288n
Schenker, Heinrich, 275
Scherr, J. B. (organ builder), 251
Schikaneder, Emanuel, 6, 215
Schiörlin, Pehr, 251
Schlimbach, G. C. F., 262–63, 264

Schopenhauer, Johanna, 234

Schubart, Christian Friedrich Daniel, 8, 255, 298n; on Vogler as performer, 227, 228, 229

Schulz, J.A.P., 51

Schumann, Robert, 3

Schwan, Olaf, 251

Schweiger, Hertha, 9–10

Schweitzer, Anton, *Rosamunde,* 181–83

Seyler, Abel, 185

*Sheng,* 249

Shirlaw, Matthew, 274

Simon, James, 9–10

Simplification System, 239–50; applications of, 256–57, 257–61; background for, 237–39; criticism of, 262–66

Six-four chord, as dissonance, 29–30. *See* Cadential six-four chord

Skjöldebrand, A. F., 5

Sonnleithner, Joseph, 6

Sorge, Georg Andreas, 14

Sounding string: division of, 16, 25, 29, 44, 48, 54, 78; relationships embodied in, 82–83

*Sprechstimme,* 218–19

*Stile antico. See* Strict style

Strict style, 127, 131, 138, 140–41

Suspension. *See* Dissonance, compound-interval

Symphony, nature and purpose of, 98–99

Syntonic comma, 27

Tartini, Giuseppe, 15, 20, 281n; and *cadenza mista,* 285n; and proportions, 82; and *terzo suono,* 240

Telemann, Georg Philipp, 86, 101

Temperament: characteristic, 41–43; Vogler's disparagement of other approaches to, 41

Text expression: and depiction, 183, 189–90; and harmony, 88, 183, 202–

3, 219; and musical structure, 190–93; in sacred music, 129–31, 133–34

Theater an der Wien, Vogler's acoustical floor for, 250

Theater music: sonata form in, 186; structure in, 181–82; 184–85, 186–87; tonal unity in, 186; Vogler's criticism of, 178–80

Theatrical style, in sacred music, 125, 127–28, 155–56, 164–65

Thematic development, 95–97, 116

Thematic process, 116–18, 119

Thoroughbass, 13, 43–44, 46–47

Tonal hierarchy, 22–23, 51, 57–58, 78

Tonal unity, 47–48, 50–51, 58, 63, 70, 75, 84, 131; and fugue, 79–82; and remote excursions, 177

Tonal unity and diversity, 54

Tone paintings: Vogler's, on the fortepiano, 234; Vogler's, on the organ, 234–36

Tonicization of scale degrees, 63

*Tonmaass,* 18–20, 21, 30, 32

*Tonsetzkunst:* concept of, 32; and *Tonwissenschaft,* 66

*Trias harmonica* (on the organ), 240

*Triorganon,* 260–62

*Übergang. See* Modulation

*Unterhaltungssiebente,* 282n. *See also* Dominant seventh

Uttini, Francesco Antonio Baltassare, 5

Vallotti, Francesco Antonio, 4, 15–16, 25, 124, 281n; *Della scienza teorica,* 15; and proportions, 82; theories of, 16; and theory of dissonance, 28, 29–30

Vogler, Georg Joseph: authorship of *Betrachtungen* articles, 278–79n; biography, 3–8; critics' judgments of, 8–9; in Darmstadt, 7, 272; dissemination of theories, 268–69; dramatic works of, 180, 295n; influence of harmonic theory, 269–70; in Italy, 3–4, 14–15, 16; and judgment of posterity, 8; in Mannheim, 3–4, 124, 278n; Mannheim writings of, 4; in Munich, 5, 6–7; negative appraisals of, 273–74; as organ designer, 5; as performer, 3, 227–37; in Prague, 6, 17; pupils of, 6–7, 270–71, 272–73; and rationalism, 14; in Stockholm, 5, 279n; studies of, 9–10, 277n; Swedish writings of, 5; travels, 2, 4–7, 161–62, 277n; in Würzburg, 3

—works by (music): *Air barbaresque*, 162, 231–32, **231**; *Alma Redemptoris Mater* in E-flat major, 142, **144**; *Aus tiefer Not* (chorale), 169; *Ave maris stella* in C major, 140–41, **141**; *Ave Regina coelorum* in F major, 144; *Belagerung von Gibraltar*, 234; *Castore e Polluce*, 3, 6, 199–209, **204–5, 206, 208**, 297n; *Cheu-Teu*, **231**, 232; Concerto in B-flat major for keyboard, 64, **65**; *Davids Buss-Psalm*, 70–71, **72**, 174–75, **175**; *Der Kaufmann von Smyrna*, 188–93, **192**; *Deutsche Kirchenmusik*, 110, 112, 136–38, **139**, 145–48; *Ecce panis angelorum*, 129–31, **130**; *Gustav Adolf och Ebba Brahe*, 209–15, **213, 215**; *Hamlet*, overture to, 59–61, 62, 185–87; *Hermann von Unna*, 2; *Lampedo*, 193–99, **196, 197**, 296n; *Magnificat* in C major, 151–52, **153**; *Miserere* in C major, 131–34, **132, 133, 134, 135, 136**, 140–41, 289n; *Missa pastoritia* in E major (1804 revision), 148–49, **149**, 157; *Missa solennis* in D minor, 149–50, **150**, 155–56, **155**, 156–57; *Pater noster* (plainsong harmonization), 174; *Pièces de clavecin*, 162, 230–32, **231**; *Polymelos*, 230–31; *Praefatio di Beata Maria Virgine* (plainsong harmonization), 174;

*Praefatio di S. S. Trinitate* (plainsong harmonization), 174; Prelude No. 3 in C minor, 76, **121**; Prelude No. 8 in D minor, 68–69, **68**, 73–74, 77, 119; Prelude No. 14 in E minor, 69; Prelude No. 15 in F major, 67–68; Prelude No. 22 in G major, 120–21, **120**; *Requiem* in E-flat major, 145, 151, **153**, 157–58; *Romance africaine*, 162, 231, **231**; *Salve Regina* in G major, 142, **143**; *Samori*, 6, 215–23, **220–21**, 272; *Schuster Ballet*, 112–13, **114**; *Serenissimae puerperae sacrum*, 150–51, **152**, 174; *Sì mio ben* (rondo), 87–88, **89**; Six Easy Keyboard Concertos, 97–98; Sonata in G for violin and keyboard, 55–58, **56**; *Terrassenlied der Afrikaner*, 162, 230, 232, **232**; *Tod Leopolds*, 234–35; *Trichordium und Trias Harmonica*, 52–54, **53**; "Versett: Suscepit Israel," 291n; *Versperae de Paschate* 155, **154**; *14 Choräle*, 173; *Zwei und dreisig Präludien*, see Preludes; *Zwölf Choräle von Sebastian Bach*, 176

—works by (theory and criticism): *Betrachtungen der Mannheimer Tonschule*, 54–55, 86, 88–90, 278–79n; *Choral-System*, 6, 161–68, 171–72, 267; *Data zur Akustik*, 6; *Gegenstände der Betrachtungen*, 55; *Handbuch zur Harmonielehre*, 6, 17–18, 66, 269; *Kuhrpfälzische Tonschule*, 269; *Musikskole*, 269; *Organist-schola*, 160; *System für den Fugenbau*, 78–84, 114–15; *Tonwissenschaft und Tonsezkunst*, 13, 17, 52; *Uiber die harmonische Akustik*, 284n; *Utile dulci*, 71; *Verbesserung der Forkel'schen Veränderungen*, 111; *Zwei und dreisig Präludien*, 115, 118–19

Voice leading, rules of, 33

Walther, Johann Gottfried, 159
Wason, Robert W., 283n

Weber, Bernhard Anselm: on *Gustav Adolf och Ebba Brahe,* 297n; on the *Orchestrion,* 250; as pupil of Vogler, 271; on Vogler's travels, 161

Weber, Carl Maria von, 7–8; biography of Vogler, 8; and folk music, 230; as pupil of Vogler, 1, 6, 7, 272–73; on Vogler's *Requiem* in E-flat, 157; *Zwölf Choräle von Sebastian Bach,* 176

Weber, Friedrich Dionys, 271

Weber, Gottfried, 273; on *Choral-System,* 160, 172; collaboration in *Zwölf Choräle,* 273; discusses sacred style, 156–57; eulogy for Vogler, 7–8; review of *Trichordium und Trias Harmonica,* 284n; and Roman-numeral analysis, 2, 7, 274; Vogler's influence on, 309n

Wieland, Christoph Martin, 182

Wilke, C.F.G., 246, 248, 262, 263, 264, 266

Winter, Peter: as pupil of Vogler, 271; Symphony in D minor, 58–59, **59**, 63–64, 96, 98–99

Wolff, Christian, 14